**Kandy Shepherd** swa[...] editor for a life writin[...] small farm in the Blue[...] Australia, with her hu[...] pets. She believes in love at first sight and real-life romance—they worked for her! Kandy loves to hear from her readers. Visit her at kandyshepherd.com.

**Justine Lewis** writes uplifting, heart-warming contemporary romances. She lives in Australia with her hero husband, two teenagers and an outgoing puppy. When she isn't writing she loves to walk her dog in the bush near her house, attempt to keep her garden alive, and search for the perfect frock. She loves hearing from readers and you can visit her at justinelewis.com.

# THE TYCOON'S CHRISTMAS DATING DEAL

KANDY SHEPHERD

# SWIPE RIGHT FOR MR PERFECT

JUSTINE LEWIS

MILLS & BOON

First published in Great Britain 2024
by Mills & Boon, an imprint of HarperCollins*Publishers* Ltd,
1 London Bridge Street, London, SE1 9GF

www.harpercollins.co.uk

HarperCollins*Publishers*, Macken House, 39/40 Mayor Street Upper, Dublin 1, D01 C9W8, Ireland

The Tycoon's Christmas Dating Deal © 2024 Kandy Shepherd

Swipe Right for Mr Perfect © 2024 Justine Lewis

ISBN: 978-0-263-32141-8

10/24

This book contains FSC™ certified paper
and other controlled sources to ensure responsible forest management.

For more information visit www.harpercollins.co.uk/green.

Printed and Bound in the UK using 100% Renewable Electricity
at CPI Group (UK) Ltd, Croydon, CR0 4YY

# THE TYCOON'S CHRISTMAS DATING DEAL

KANDY SHEPHERD

MILLS & BOON

To my long-time friend and fellow author
Cathleen Ross, for being my first reader.

Thank you!

# CHAPTER ONE

MARISSA GRACEY HATED CHRISTMAS. As she strode along Kensington High Street in London, two weeks before December the twenty-fifth, she felt assaulted by Christmas cheer. Everything that could possibly be festooned with lights twinkled garishly in the evening gloom—trees, lampposts, storefronts, even a bus stop shelter, which should surely be illegal. Alcoves and shop windows were stuffed with overdecorated Christmas trees. Clashing Christmas carols, loud and shmaltzy, blared out from doorways.

*Fa-la-la-la-la, la-la-la-la*, indeed, she thought with a deep scowl.

Every step she took she was exhorted to feel merry, happy and jolly. But she didn't feel any of that. Not even a glimmering of merriment. Not anymore.

Marissa knew that behind her back she was called a Scrooge and a Grinch. That hurt. But she couldn't share the details of why she no longer celebrated the season. Because she couldn't bear to be reminded of the heartbreak and pain. Bad things had happened to her at Christmas. The car crash five years ago that had killed her parents. Her brother's departure to the other side of the world. The out-of-the-blue firing from her dream job on

Christmas Eve. And the most recent—the betrayal of her boyfriend, whom she'd last year caught kissing another woman under the mistletoe. Disasters that had rocked her world at Christmastime. She'd begun to believe she was jinxed. If she allowed herself to enjoy Christmas, who knew what other horrible thing might happen?

There was excited chatter among her fellow pedestrians when a scattering of fat snowflakes drifted down from the sky. She looked up but resisted the temptation to try to catch a snowflake on her tongue, like she'd done when she was a child. Back then, Christmas had seemed magical.

A man started to sing, very off-key, that he was dreaming of a white Christmas.

*Huh*, Marissa thought, *a sleety, slippery Christmas more likely.*

London rarely had decent snow in December. Thankfully, she would be out of here in five days, flying to a small island off the east coast of Bali, where Christmas wasn't part of the culture. By the time she got back, the decorations and all the painful reminders they brought with them would be taken down.

She detoured into the supermarket—more detestable carols were piped through the store—in search of a ready meal for her dinner. She lived alone in her flat in West Kensington and often couldn't be bothered to cook for herself. She studiously avoided the displays of mince pies. Her father had loved the small, sweet, spiced fruit pastries, traditionally only available at Christmastime. His Christmas Eve ritual had been to eat an entire packet of six mince pies—with lashings of custard and ice cream—in one sitting, egged on by a laughing Marissa and her brother while her mother pretended to be shocked. Until that Christmas Eve five years ago when the mince pies had remained uneaten in the kitchen while her dad lay still on a hospital bed, attached to tubes and monitors that hadn't saved his life. It still hurt to see mince pies and remember his joy in them.

When her friend Caity Johnston called on her mobile phone, Marissa had to swallow hard against the lump of remembered grief that threatened to choke her.

'Everything okay?' she asked, when she was in control of her voice. Caity was expecting twins, due in the middle of January.

'Actually, no,' Caity said. Her friend's voice sounded anxious, frayed at the edges.

Terror for her friend shot through Marissa. 'The babies?'

'Okay.'

Marissa breathed a sigh of relief.

'But I have to go to hospital and stay in bed until the due date. Or whenever the consultant decides it's time for the babies to be born.' Caity's voice rose.

'Oh, Caity. What can I do to help?'

'Could you... Could you get over here now?'

'On my way,' Marissa said as she hailed a black cab.

Mentally, she urged the driver to hurry. It seemed the longest trip ever to the west London suburb of Ealing. She'd normally go by the Underground, it was nearly as fast and a tenth of the cab fare, but there was an edge of fear to Caity's voice that had truly scared Marissa. Two years ago, her friend had miscarried at twenty weeks. Marissa would do anything she could to help her carry her twins to term.

When she arrived at Caity's house twenty minutes later, a terrace in a street of terraces that she and her husband, Tom, had painstakingly remodelled, her friend was waiting for her. Her face was pale, and she was anxiously wringing her hands. Caity was tiny and slight except for her enormous bump. Marissa noticed a bulging overnight bag in the hallway.

She hugged her friend gently. 'What's happened?'

'I'm sure I mentioned before that the twins share the same placenta. That can be dangerous so the doctors want me under observation. My bump and I will be hooked up to monitors for the next few weeks.'

'Oh, no!' Marissa exclaimed, and then immediately backpedalled. She didn't want her alarmed reaction to add further to Caity's obvious fears. 'I mean, that's good they're being vigilant.'

'It's unlikely I'll leave hospital until the babies are born.'

'You'll be in good hands. Do you want me to go with you to the hospital, to get you settled?'

Caity shook her head. 'No. Tom's taken time off work. He's out getting the car from where it's parked. But there is something you could do to help me.'

'Anything,' Marissa said.

She and Caity had started work as interns in a public relations firm back when they'd been fresh out of uni. They'd both specialised in event planning until there was a big downturn in business and they were both let go from the jobs they'd loved—just before Christmas. Caity had bounced back quickly and started her own company, while Marissa freelanced for her and other marketing companies in the city, trying to find the place where she best fit. Now, at age thirty, Marissa wasn't sure about what direction she wanted her career to take. She only knew that she didn't want to tie herself down to the one employer. Not yet. Experience had taught her that it was too dangerous to put her fate in someone else's hands.

'I hate to ask you this, as I know you're not a fan of Christmas...' Caity began, tentatively, not meeting Marissa's eyes.

Marissa's heart sank. Caity was one of the few people who understood her aversion to the festive season. So why was she bringing it up now?

She narrowed her eyes. 'Er, yes?' she said.

Caity's words spilled out. 'There's this Christmas event I've been working on. Longfield Manor is a beautiful country house hotel in Dorset. Family run. Christmas is a huge deal for them. People come from around the country—even the world—year after year to celebrate the holiday season there, and this year is the first time the family has brought in an event planner to organise the festivities. And now, two weeks out from the most important commission of my career, I have to go into hospital.'

*To save her babies' lives.*

The words were unspoken but Marissa heard them.

'And you want me to step in?' she said, trying to keep the dismay from her voice. 'Caity, you know how I feel—'

'About Christmas? I know. And I wouldn't ask you if I had any choice. The grandson of the hotel owners, Oliver Pierce, is the CEO of The Pierce Group of hotels.'

'The most exclusive, fashionable hotels in London. I know of them.' Although as she'd need to take out a mortgage to buy a cocktail there, Marissa had never been to one.

'I've done some work for him in the past and it went really well, and I *need* to keep The Pierce Group as a client. Oliver Pierce himself asked me to help with the Longfield Manor Christmas. Marissa, this job could change the entire trajectory for my company. It's my big break. I can't risk losing his business.'

'Couldn't someone else—?'

'He's a very discerning man,' Caity said, cutting her off. 'I couldn't trust anyone else but you to take over this particular job.'

'Surely there must be another planner who—?'

'You're the only person who is good enough and I know you would never let me down,' Caity said. 'Or try to steal my client.'

That was Caity all right. A shrewd businesswoman whose boutique event planning business was very successful, yet not established enough to be able to risk losing an important client. Marissa knew how vital the personal relationship between client and planner could be. And satisfied clients led to recommendations and further business. If Caity couldn't trust anyone else but her—her best friend—to run this job, Marissa could put up no further resistance.

'Please,' Caity pleaded. 'I… I'm begging you. You know how much I want these babies.' Her voice caught. 'And I can't do the job from a hospital bed.'

Marissa took a deep breath. 'Of course not. Nor should you. All your energies should be going to keeping your babies safe and getting ready to welcome them.' She had read up about the risks for identical twins who shared a placenta and knew how dangerous it would be for her best friend not to follow her doctors' advice to the letter.

She had a momentary vision of warm aquamarine waters, golden sands, palm trees—her tropical holiday far, far away from the commercial frenzy of Christmas in London. It had been booked and paid for months ago and she had been eagerly anticipating the escape. But as she focussed on her friend's wan face, the vision faded away. She needed to be here, and she needed to do this for Caity. She only hoped she'd be able to get at least a partial refund.

'Of course I'm happy to do the job for you,' she said. She injected as much enthusiasm as she could into her voice. And was rewarded by the relief in her friend's eyes.

'I knew you wouldn't let me down,' Caity said. She took a deep breath. 'I'll quickly brief you. Longfield Manor is in Dorset, near the coast. Very traditional. Nothing like the ultra-contemporary Pierce Group hotels. It was owned by my client's grandparents. But the grandfather died this year, so Oliver Pierce stepped in to help his grandmother run it. There's a story there but I didn't get a chance to dig into it. You might have more luck. Christmas has always been a big deal, and they want it even bigger and better this year.'

Marissa was determined not to let her friend see how she dreaded the thought of working on Christmas for an entire week. 'Understood,' she said.

'Everything that can be ordered has been ordered. Local staff have been briefed. You'll find all the files waiting in your inbox so you can hit the ground running. I sent them as soon as I knew you were on your way over.'

Marissa smiled. 'You were very sure I'd say yes.'

'I trusted you'd help me,' Caity said simply.

Marissa gently hugged her friend. 'You know you won't have to worry about a thing.'

'I know. I trust you implicitly. But you can get in touch with me any time.'

'I promise I'll try not to bother you.'

It had been heartbreaking when Caity had lost her first baby, and Marissa feared what state her friend might sink into if something were to go wrong with the twins. She had to step up for her. Even though immersing herself in Christmas at some staid country house hotel was the last thing she wanted to do.

At the sound of a key turning in the door, Caity stepped back. 'Here's Tom to take me to hospital.'

Marissa greeted her friend's husband, then picked up her handbag and the shopping bag containing her solitary dinner. 'Go. The sooner you're in that hospital bed, the better.'

'Just one thing before you go. Oliver Pierce is expecting you to stay on site at Longfield Manor for the seven days before Christmas.'

'On site? For a week?'

'It's a hotel. Why would you stay elsewhere?'

Marissa would prefer to keep a distance from a client. But this was Caity's client so she really had no choice. 'Done. Can't say I like it. But done.'

'And…there's one more thing.'

A sneaky smile played around her friend's lips. Marissa knew that smile could spell trouble. 'Yes?' she said warily.

'Oliver Pierce is hot. Really hot. Movie-star hot.' She put up her hand to stop Marissa from protesting. 'I know you're on a break from dating. An overly long break in my opinion. But I respect that. I just thought you should know how gorgeous your new client is. And I believe he's single. Single, sexy and solvent.'

Marissa rolled her eyes. 'No, thank you. I won't ever get mixed up with a client again. Totally not interested. Besides, you know I'm immune to gorgeous men. Next time—if there is ever a next time—I'll be going for ordinary, average and safe.'

Caity laughed. 'I wouldn't call Oliver Pierce safe. Not in a million years would I call him safe.'

Could this be his last Christmas at Longfield Manor? The thought troubled Oliver. If there was one thing he didn't care for, it was uncertainty. And the future of the beautiful old manor house, which had been in his family for five generations, was shrouded in uncertainty.

He stamped his feet against the cold and rubbed his gloved hands together as he observed the familiar front elevation of the house. It was lit by the soft, early-morning sun that shone from a cloudless winter sky. He never tired of admiring the building that dated back to the sixteen hundreds, its ancient walls made of the local limestone, the peaked roofs and mullioned windows, the perfection of its proportions. The surrounding gardens were stark in their winter beauty, the only splashes of colour coming from large urns overflowing with lush purple pansies, the pride and joy of his grandmother.

Oliver hadn't lived there for years, but he considered Longfield Manor his home; his grandparents, Charles and Edith, were more his parents than his parents ever had been. He had spent so much of his childhood here, an only child caught in the to-and-fro that had been his parents' disastrous marriage. And it was the refuge to which he'd fled after his mother had abandoned him when he was fifteen years old. If he honoured his late grandfather's dying wish, he would have to put Longfield Manor on the market. And there lay the uncertainty.

Just days before he took his last laboured breath at the age of eighty-seven, his grandfather had taken Oliver aside for a private, heartbreaking conversation. His grandpa had known he was dying and he'd told Oliver he feared for his beloved wife, five years his junior at eighty-two. He had shared his concern that Edith could be displaying signs of dementia. It seemed she'd had memory lapses, misplaced things, sometimes seemed confused about long-standing everyday routines, and her devoted husband was worried how she would cope after he'd gone.

It had been gut wrenching for Oliver to listen to that, but he'd owed it to the grandfather he'd adored not to show his own anguish. Grandpa had also worried that with the pending retirement of a longtime trusted manager, overseeing the running of the hotel would be too much for Edith. He'd believed the best option would be to sell, then find Edith a home, perhaps in London so she could be closer to Oliver, somewhere she could easily access the round-the-clock care she might soon need.

Oliver had been shocked, not just by the news about Granny, but also because he had never imagined Longfield Manor would be sold. He had long expected that it would pass down to him—his mother had been disinherited—and in due course to his children. Not that so far, at the age of thirty-two, he had ever met a woman who inspired thoughts of marriage and parenthood. He made very sure his girlfriends knew the score—he wasn't ready to commit.

He had immediately reassured his grandfather he would take over the hotel alongside his grandmother. Hotels were his business. He had got his love of hospitality from growing up here, absorbing what worked and what didn't from the way his grandparents ran the place. Longfield Manor was a successful and profitable business, as well as a cherished private home.

But his grandfather had asked him to think long and hard before declaring an intention to add Longfield Manor to his portfolio. Not to make that offer out of sentimentality or obligation. Charles hadn't wanted the hotel to become a burden on his grandson. Oliver's life was in the city with his ultra-contemporary boutique hotels. And didn't he want to expand into New York? Where did a traditional hotel in the country fit into that plan? A hotel that needed hands-on management with buildings that required ongoing repair.

Oliver had acknowledged all that, and yet he fought against the idea of losing Longfield Manor. His grandfather had repeatedly asked him to agree to selling the hotel after he died. Oliver prided himself on being a hardheaded negotiator yet finally, to put Grandpa's mind at ease, he had acquiesced and said he would 'look into' selling. Now Oliver felt duty bound to honour that deathbed promise. Even if he'd had his fingers crossed behind his back at the time.

Since Grandpa's passing in August, Oliver had observed some out-of-character behaviour from his grandmother but nothing overly untoward. Many of those quirks could be, he thought, attributed to her intense grief at losing her husband of so many years. Granny was grieving, as was he, although he knew he had to keep it together for her sake. The only thing that sparked her back into her old self was discussing plans for Christmas.

His grandparents had put their hearts and souls into Christmas every year. Guests came from around the country—even the world—to share in the hotel's fabled Christmas celebrations. And Oliver was determined their first Christmas without Charles would be extra special so that his absence hopefully wouldn't be felt quite so keenly.

To that end, he had engaged an event planner with whom he had worked very successfully at his London hotels. Caity Johnston was a small, blonde dynamo who was totally on his wavelength. She had reacted to the brief on the Longfield Manor Christmas with enthusiasm, and he had been pleased she had accepted the job. However, complications with her pregnancy meant Caity had had to be hospitalised. 'Never fear,' Caity had rushed to reassure him. She had secured someone wonderful to take over from her. Marissa Gracey was the absolute best, she'd assured him.

There had been no opportunity to interview Marissa Gracey. He'd had to accept her sight unseen—and that didn't sit well with Oliver. Marissa Gracey had become yet another uncertainty. He hoped Caity hadn't overdone the enthusiasm for her substitute. This Christmas was important. A successful celebration would not only lift his granny's spirits, it would also reassure the guests that the hotel could go on successfully without Charles. In his experience, fans of a hotel liked things to stay the same. He needed to prove to both himself and others that the

future of Longfield Manor would be safe in his hands—
one way or another.

But planning a traditional Christmas celebration on a
grand scale was outside his area of expertise. He needed
help. There were seven days to Christmas and as the
celebrations went into full swing on Christmas Eve, the
countdown was on. He glanced at his watch. Marissa
Gracey was due to arrive in half an hour for a midmorning start. He hoped her work would be up to scratch.

Marissa swung her vintage Citroen van through the
ornate iron gates that were set between high stone walls
and led up to a sweeping gravel driveway lined with
well-kept gardens. Even in winter the grounds of the
hotel showed a certain stark grandeur. If she was here
for anything other than Christmas, she'd be feeling stirrings of excitement.

Marissa had looked up the hotel's impressive website
and read with interest the high-rating reviews on impar-
tial travel sites. The reviews from guests had raved about
the beauty of the buildings, the comfort of the rooms,
the excellence of the food. It was clear that the hotel's
guests came back again and again and one regular had
described it as a 'home away from home—a very posh
home, that is.'

If only she were coming here to work in summer. Or
autumn. Really anytime but Christmas. The thought of
the extravaganza to come made her feel queasy, but for
Caity's sake she had to overcome her aversion to the job.
She could do this. The back of her van was filled with
bespoke Christmas ornaments from a famous London
designer and all other manner of expensive and stylish
decorations that would give an 'old with a new twist' feel

to the festive decorations here. Apparently, the grandson of the family, Oliver Pierce, wanted to put his own stamp on the family traditions. She wondered why he would mess with a formula that clearly worked.

As the house came into view, Marissa caught her breath. It was stately and magnificent, yet not so large as to dominate the landscape. Framed by two enormous winter-bare oak trees, the hotel sat nestled into the landscape like it belonged—as it had been standing in that very spot for hundreds of years.

She thought of Oliver Pierce with a stab of...not envy—not exactly—more like curiosity, at how it must feel to be born to a place like this. To take the immense wealth that this house and the grounds that surrounded it stood for, as his due. She had grown up in a middle-class family, comfortable but not wealthy. This was a different realm altogether. And that, she had realised from reading the reviews of the hotel, was its charm. A place like this gave the guests the chance to imagine for the length of their stay that they were taking part in an exclusive house party. That was the key to Christmas at Longfield Manor, to create welcoming, intimate but extravagant festivities. A posh home away from home, where the Christmas holiday was utterly splendid and utterly without worry or stress or hours in the kitchen.

She confidently swung the van—its quirky exterior finished in a rich brown and chrome as befit its former life as a coffee van—into the circular drive that led up to the house. The discreet signage at the entrance of the hotel maintained the illusion of arriving at your own house in the country. Marissa knew there was parking around the back, but she'd been asked to check in with reception when she arrived, so she pulled the van into the closest space out front.

Once inside, she caught her breath at the splendour of the entrance hall. Ornate high ceilings, wood-panelled walls, a magnificent staircase, wooden floors laid in a centuries-old herringbone pattern, paintings in heavy gilded frames. A large arrangement of artistically styled winter-bare stems and brightly coloured berries sat in a marble urn on a tall plinth. It was all perfect, but not too perfect, which befit a house of such venerable years. She'd read that the house had been sympathetically re-modelled to become a hotel, but on first glance it still retained both the grandeur and the intimacy of a private home to the privileged.

Inside, she was greeted by a charming young woman behind the reception desk. Marissa put down her small suitcase and wondered when she'd meet with the client, Oliver Pierce. She didn't have to wonder for long.

Almost immediately, the grandson of the house strode into the foyer. Suddenly, the room seemed smaller, as if he took up more space than one man should. He was taller than she'd thought he'd be, and broad shouldered in an immaculately cut dark suit. Black hair framed a handsome—a very handsome—face. Caity was right. He was hot. So hot Marissa could not help but stare. And then, when he got closer, stare some more.

'Marissa Gracey?' he said in a deep, well-spoken voice that managed to be just as attractive as his looks. 'Oliver Pierce.'

All Marissa could do was nod before he continued.

'You're right on time. That's good.'

It was as well he hadn't expected a reply because she

was suddenly without a voice. She felt the colour flush hot on her cheeks then rush back to pale as a realisation struck her.

*She knew this man.*

Only he'd called himself Oliver Hughes back then. Back when they'd both been teenagers and she'd thought him the most insufferable, arrogant, rude person she had ever met. When he offered his hand for her to shake, she didn't know what to do.

# CHAPTER TWO

MARISSA'S THOUGHTS FLASHED back to when she'd been fourteen years old and deeply, desperately and very secretly in love with a sixteen-year-old boy she'd known as Oliver Hughes.

This couldn't be the same guy.

*It just couldn't be.*

Yet, he looked like him, spoke like him. Did he have a twin? If so, wouldn't they have the same surname? And why the same first name?

Oliver Hughes had been the friend of her schoolfriend Samantha's brother, Toby. Toby had been at boarding school with Oliver and brought him home to stay for a midterm break. Marissa had immediately crushed on tall, quietly spoken Oliver like only a totally inexperienced girl could. She'd jumped at any chance she could to be at Samantha's house.

But that crush had come crashing down the day she'd overheard Toby and Oliver discussing her and Samantha. Toby had asked Oliver what he thought of Sam's friend Marissa. Oliver had made a rude comment about Marissa's appearance, then both boys had sniggered in a mean, hurtful and entitled way. Marissa had been shocked, horrified and deeply hurt. It had been a first lesson painfully learned—men weren't always what they appeared to be.

Now she realised she couldn't hesitate any longer before taking Oliver Pierce's hand in a short, businesslike grasp. She'd never got even handshake-close to Oliver Hughes. It had been purely a crush from a distance. She looked up at Oliver Pierce and caught her breath. The black hair. The green eyes. His height. It had to be the same guy. Super-attractive as a teenager, devastatingly handsome as an adult. Why hadn't she researched him when she'd agreed to take on this job? She'd only looked up Longfield Manor and had trusted Caity's notes for the details of the Christmas plans.

*I'm immune to gorgeous men*, she'd boasted to her best friend.

She'd had no interest whatsoever in the hotness levels of her client.

'Welcome,' he said. 'Thank you for taking Caity's place.'

His voice was deep and resonant. More mature than at age sixteen, but somehow it sounded the same to her. Oliver Hughes had had the beginnings of a man's voice even then. *The fantasies she had had over him.* She almost gasped at the memory of the feelings he had aroused in her.

'I'm…er…glad I was able to help out, Mr Pierce,' she said.

*Not.*

As if having to fake a love of Christmas was bad enough, now she would be trapped for a week with a man she'd never forgotten. She remembered him not because of his extraordinary good looks that back then had set her teenage heart thumping, but because of how deeply he had wounded her. It had taken a long time to restore the confidence his mocking words had caused to her fragile teenage ego.

'Oliver, please,' he said.

'Sure,' she said. 'Oliver.' She felt like she was choking on his name.

He smiled. Yep, same toothpaste-commercial white teeth. Almost too perfect to be true. 'There's a lot to do,' he said. 'I'm sure Caity briefed you about how I want this year's Christmas to be better than ever?'

As he spoke, Marissa realised there was not even the merest spark of recognition in his eyes. He had no idea that they'd met before.

*If indeed they had.*

Perhaps it was an insane coincidence that this Oliver was so like teenage crush Oliver. But she didn't think so. It had to be him. But she couldn't really be sure until she investigated his surname. In the meantime, as he had not recognised her—which added further insult to his insults of sixteen years ago—she wouldn't say a thing. That would only revive the humiliation.

'Caity briefed me very thoroughly,' Marissa said, in a cool, businesslike tone, totally at odds with her inner turmoil. 'I'm looking forward to going through the time-table of events with you and meeting the local staff and suppliers Caity engaged. There are, however, questions I need to ask you, to fill in the gaps.'

'Of course. How about we set up a meeting in half an hour at my grandfather's study.' He paused and she was surprised at the flash of pain across his face. 'I mean *my* study.' He sighed. 'Grandpa died in August. I forget sometimes that he isn't here.'

'I understand,' she said, fighting the sudden empathy she felt towards this man. She knew only too well about loss in various heartbreaking ways. 'It does get better with time. Although I don't believe you ever completely get over losing someone you love.'

He looked down into her eyes—she was tall but he was taller—and she saw the pain in his eyes. 'You...?' he said.

Marissa met his gaze as she swallowed against the lump in her throat. 'My parents. Five years ago. A car accident.'

*On Christmas Eve.*

'I'm sorry.'

'I'm sorry about your grandfather.'

An awkward silence fell between them. How did that business conversation suddenly swerve to something so personal?

Oliver Pierce cleared his throat. 'Did you drive directly from London?' he said, very obviously changing the subject.

Marissa jumped at the opportunity to do so. 'Yes,' she said. 'The traffic wasn't too bad.'

Traffic was always a safe topic of conversation between strangers. It had taken three hours in her van, which wasn't as fast on the road as more modern vehicles. But she loved her van; it was different and quirky but very practical.

'I'll show you to your room.' Oliver Pierce picked up the small suitcase she had brought in with her. She had another with more clothes in the van.

'Where should I park my van?'

'If you leave the keys at the desk, someone will take your van to the garage at the back of the hotel.'

'Is it secure? There are boxes of valuable things in there.'

The moment she uttered the query she chastised herself. They were in the middle of nowhere, up a long driveway behind secure gates on a private property. Who was going to break into her van and steal Christmas decorations? She was too used to living in central London.

'Very secure,' he said. 'But I'll arrange for someone to transfer them to a storeroom, if that would make you feel better?'

'Thank you,' she said, nodding.

She followed Oliver Pierce up the magnificent carved wooden staircase. As she trailed her hand over the top of the balustrade, she thought about how many other hands must have trailed along it over hundreds of years, what stories these wood-panelled walls could tell. She also couldn't stop wondering about Oliver Pierce, possibly Hughes. How would she deal with him?

'There are ten bedrooms on this floor, all en suite, and a further ten on the next floor,' he said when they reached the first floor. 'A further twelve bedrooms are located in a converted barn. Our family lives in a separate wing.'

'It's such an amazing building,' she said, still disconcerted by the thought that this Oliver must be *that* Oliver. She felt she had to weigh up every word she said to him.

'Longfield Manor has been in my family for a long time,' he said. 'My grandparents turned it into a hotel thirty years ago.'

Oliver strode ahead of her with athletic grace. Marissa couldn't help but admire the view as she followed him.

Broad shoulders, long, strong legs. He was one of those men who looked really good in a business suit.

He stopped at a door at the farther end of the corridor. 'This is your room,' he said, opening the door. 'It makes sense for you to stay here as a guest rather than stay in the village, where the rest of the staff lives or stays, and have to drive in every day.'

'Of course. I appreciate it,' she said. He would have had to pay for her to stay elsewhere so why not have her on site? It made good business sense.

But it was immediately evident that he hadn't stinted on her accommodation. Her room was spacious and elegant, with antique-style furnishing, curtains and upholstery. It had been brought into this century with a light hand that allowed its historical charm to shine through. There was nothing stuffy about the decor, no heavy dark colours or cumbersome furniture. Rather, muted colours and lush, pale carpets gave it a feel of contemporary luxury that was not at odds with the building's history. A top interior designer had obviously been employed to find the perfect balance. 'What a beautiful room,' she said, looking around her. 'Timeless and elegant.'

'My grandmother always likes to hear that kind of feedback,' he said. 'She was an interior designer when she was younger and has put her heart and soul into this place.'

'She's done a wonderful job.' Marissa paused. 'About your grandmother. It's my understanding she and your grandfather organised the Christmas festivities themselves. Will I be treading on her toes?'

'Good question,' he said.

Marissa didn't like it when people said, *good ques-*

*tion.* It usually served to stall an answer or was a condescending response to a question they didn't think was good at all.

But Oliver Pierce spoke the words as if he meant them. 'I asked her about that before I got Caity on board. Granny said she was relieved that she didn't have to do all the work by herself. That even with my grandfather organising it with her, the Christmas festivities were beginning to become too much.'

'That's good to hear. I know you want to make changes and I wondered how she felt about that.'

'Granny is eighty-two years young, as she likes to say. She's not resistant to change, but she'll certainly let you know what she thinks if she disagrees with anything.'

Marissa smiled, in spite of her resolve to stay distant. His words were underscored with affection and she liked that. She respected people who were close to their families—she who had been left without family and ached for their loss.

'Granny and Grandpa were partners in every sense of the word. She's struggling without him, but grateful that I can take over some of what he did. She will be sure to want to meet you as soon as possible. I'll ask her to attend our meeting.'

'I'll look forward to meeting her.' Caity had told her she'd liked Edith Pierce very much and had enjoyed working with her.

'I'll leave you to unpack. See you in half an hour.'

The second he shut the door behind him, Marissa threw her coat on the bed and reached for her phone. An internet search might help clear up the mystery of the two Olivers.

Thankfully, it was a mystery quickly solved. Oliver Pierce, according to the gossip columnists, was notoriously private. But that didn't stop stories about the handsome hotelier finding their way into the news. Oliver had changed his name from his father's name, Hughes, to his mother's name, Pierce, when he'd been about twenty-four. A bold move to make. His mother, an only child, had been a famous model and, according to well-documented gossip, it seemed her marriage to Oliver's father had been tumultuous. But to change his name? As Caity had said, there was a story there. Perhaps it was a sad one. But it was none of Marissa's business. What she'd discovered didn't make her change her mind about Oliver.

*Odious Oliver*, she'd called him in her secret thoughts for so long.

Today's Oliver seemed very personable. Charming even. She'd found herself warming to him when there was still a doubt he might not be the Oliver from her past. But now she knew the truth. She shuddered. His mean words were indelibly carved into her memory. However, that would not stop her from treating a client—Caity's client—with professional courtesy. Aside from that, she intended to avoid him as much as possible.

Marissa Gracey was gorgeous. Oliver didn't know why the fact that Caity's replacement was so attractive should come as such a shock. Perhaps because Caity had gone overboard on stressing how smart and efficient and capable her friend Marissa was. He hadn't given a thought to what the paragon might look like.

Not that the appearance of his new event planner mattered in the slightest. Of course it didn't. He never dated staff—even those on a short-term contract. An early disaster dating an assistant manager had made sure he steered clear of such ill-advised liaisons. He just wanted the event planner to have all the attributes Caity had promised that would ensure Christmas at Longfield Manor this year was outstanding.

Still, he found it disconcerting that Marissa was such a classic beauty, tall and willowy with dark hair that tumbled over her shoulders, deep blue eyes, a generous mouth, cheeks flushed pink from the cold outside. Oliver had found it hard not to stare earlier when he'd seen her waiting for him at the reception desk, elegant in narrow black trousers, high-heeled black boots and a striking purple wool coat. He'd also found himself taking surreptitious side glances at her as he showed her to her room, where she'd slipped off her coat to reveal a long-sleeved silk shirt in an abstract black-and-white pattern. While discreetly professional, the snug-fitting shirt made no secret of her curves. She really was a stunner.

She was punctual, too. He was pleased to see that Marissa arrived at his office for their meeting five minutes early. Punctuality and order were important to him, among the tools with which he'd tried to ward off the craziness of his early years. His mother had fallen pregnant with him 'accidentally' when she was at the peak of her modelling career and married his father because it was the done thing at the time. He didn't know if it had ever been a happy marriage. His earliest memories were of them arguing—noisy and angry, and worse when they'd been drinking. Every time he'd been dumped off with Granny and Grandpa, their house had been a haven of peace and unconditional love.

Had his mother loved him? She'd told him she loved him, but it was difficult for him to believe her when she'd left him so often. Every time, he'd felt abandoned. 'Mummy's working, models have to travel,' Granny used to explain as she'd wiped away his tears. His father had been in a never-quite-made-it rock band and was also away on tour a lot of the time. However, the truth was obvious to him now—a child got in the way of their complicated lives, and they took the easy route of foisting him onto others so that they didn't have to worry themselves with his care. He sometimes wondered if they had ever considered what it was like for a child to be constantly referred to—to their face—as *an accident*.

They'd shunted him into boarding school at the age of eight. His parents had then separated and reconciled several times before divorcing when he'd been thirteen. When he was fifteen, his mother had met a man who lived in New Zealand. She'd gone to visit him and hadn't come back since, except for occasional fleeting visits to England. Oliver had expected to go with her but his mother hadn't thought it appropriate for him to change schools at that stage of his studies. So she'd left him behind. Like a piece of unwanted baggage. Again.

Marissa sat down in the visitor's chair opposite from him. She put a large folder and a tablet on the desk in front of her and outlined an agenda. Professional. He liked that, too.

'Caity's already done all the hard work,' she said. 'She's organised suppliers, discussed the menus with your chefs, engaged musicians, briefed the florist, hired decorating staff and so on. As per your instruction, she's used local people wherever possible. Now it's up to me to make it happen flawlessly so your guests have the best Christmas ever.'

'Sounds like everything is on track to me,' he said.

She paused and a frown pleated her forehead. 'One thing I'm not quite sure of is the gift-giving ceremony after lunch on Christmas Day presided over by Santa Claus and Mrs Claus. I understand all the guests receive a gift from the jolly couple?'

'Oh, yes,' he said, unable to stop himself from smiling. The mention of the tradition had sparked so many happy memories from over the years. 'It's a family tradition that morphed into a hotel tradition.'

'How so?' she said, her head tilted to one side.

'When I was a child, Grandpa and Granny dressed up as Santa and his wife on Christmas morning. Apparently, they'd done that for my mother when she was a child. I loved it. When they started the hotel, it turned out the guests loved Santa and Mrs Claus, too. The hotel ceremony takes place after the long Christmas lunch.'

'I see,' she said.

Oliver wondered why a shadow passed over Marissa's face as he explained the tradition. That could mean she had happy memories of Christmas or, on the other hand, memories that were less than happy. People who spent Christmas at a hotel often included those who were escaping unhappy family situations, those with no families, people who were far away from home at Christmas, as well as the people who wanted a traditional Christmas with all the trimmings without all the work. Marissa had agreed to work Christmas Day at Longfield Manor without hesitation or demands for extra remuneration.

Where would she be on Christmas Day otherwise? Or with whom?

'That sounds fun,' she said at last. 'I find it endearing that the owners of a hotel would celebrate like that with their guests. I'm wondering, though…how will it happen this year?' she said, as though carefully choosing her words.

'Without Grandpa, you mean?' he said, with a painful wrench to his gut.

She nodded.

Oliver felt overwhelmed by sadness that Grandpa wouldn't be here to play Santa. It was just another reminder that Christmas wouldn't be the same ever again. Marissa's sympathy for his loss was there in her expressive blue eyes. He looked away, unable to bear it. 'It will be me stepping into Santa's big black boots. I can do a *ho-ho-ho* with the best of them,' he said, forcing positivity into his voice.

'And your grandmother?'

'She'll be Mrs Claus as usual.' He put up his hand to stop any possible objection. 'I know I should be Grandson Claus. But the white curly hair and beard of the Santa outfit will disguise the age difference. It's all in the Christmas spirit.'

'Of course it is,' she said.

*Damn*. He suspected she could tell how upsetting he found this conversation. Oliver knew he was good at masking his feelings—he'd learned that from a very early age—so how could this woman he barely knew see through his mask?

There was a loud knock on the door, accompanied by

the door opening. Granny. She never waited for a *come in* invitation before she entered the room.

He was pleased she'd chosen to join them. It must come as a shock to her every time she saw her grandson seated behind her husband's big antique desk. It was still a shock to him, too. He'd known his grandfather wouldn't live forever, but he'd wanted more years with him than what he'd been given.

He rose and came around his desk to greet her. 'Talking of my grandmother. Here she is,' he said to Marissa. She got up from her chair, too, so they stood side by side.

His grandmother swept into the room with her usual aplomb. She paused as she took in Marissa, then smiled. He hadn't seen her smile like that since Grandpa's death.

'Granny, this is Marissa Gracey. Marissa, my grandmother, Edith Pierce. Marissa is here to help us with Christmas.'

His grandmother positively beamed as she turned to Marissa. 'I know why Marissa is here. It's very good of you, my dear, to come down to us from London to help.'

'I'm glad I was able to make it,' Marissa said politely.

Granny turned back to him with a puzzled frown. 'But Oliver darling, why did you put Marissa in Room eight?'

'It's a lovely room,' he said. 'I want her to be comfortable while she's here working with us.' Did Granny think it more appropriate for Marissa to be in the staff quarters?

'It's a very nice room,' Marissa said.

'But surely she should be in your room with you, Oliver?'

Marissa gasped. Oliver stared at his grandmother in disbelief.

'I might be old but I'm broad minded, you know.

There's no need for you and your girlfriend to scurry around behind my back playing musical beds. I suggest you move her into your room right now.'

# CHAPTER THREE

MARISSA STARED AT Edith Pierce, speechless with shock. Why would the older woman say such a thing? She glanced at Oliver, but he seemed equally shocked.

Mrs Pierce looked from her grandson to Marissa and back to Oliver again. She was an elegant older woman, beautifully groomed with silver hair cut in a short bob and discreet jewellery of the very expensive kind. A smile danced around her perfectly lipsticked mouth.

'Do I shock you? Your generation didn't invent sex, you know.'

Oliver looked mortified. He glanced at Marissa, as if beseeching her for help. But what could she do? This was his grandmother, a stranger to her.

The thought of having sex with Oliver Pierce in his bedroom sent a flush to Marissa's cheeks, those fervent teenage fantasies she'd had about him rushing back.

'I know that, Granny, but—' Oliver finally said.

Marissa found her voice. 'I'm not his—'

'Marissa is our new event planner, Granny. Remember Caity, who you liked so much, had to go into hospital to have her pregnancy monitored?'

'Of course I remember that,' Mrs Pierce said, sounding annoyed. 'My memory might fail me a little these days, but not about important things like our Christmas celebrations.'

'Marissa is her replacement. She's a very experienced event planner and comes with glowing references.'

Mrs Pierce smiled. 'You don't have to hide from me the fact she's also your girlfriend. She's lovely and—'

'She is that,' said Oliver. 'Very lovely, I mean.'

*That's not what he said about me when he was sixteen.*

'But she's not my—'

Mrs Pierce spoke over him. 'I know you like to keep your private life private, Oliver. But I'm delighted Marissa is able to spend Christmas with you, and that I get the chance to get to know her. It makes me so very happy to see you with such a beautiful girl. Smart, too, as you say.' Her words were gushing, but to Marissa they seemed sincere—if completely misguided.

The older lady paused. To gather her emotions or for dramatic effect? Marissa couldn't be sure. This was so awkward she could scarcely breathe. Oliver had to say something. It was up to him to stop this nonsense. She, Marissa, was a stranger and a contracted employee to boot. She couldn't get into an argument with the owner of Longfield Manor.

But before either of them could say anything, his grandmother continued. 'You know, Oliver, how sad I've been since my beloved Charles's death. So miserable I... I've sometimes wondered if it's worth living.' Her voice wavered as she bowed her head. Oliver looked alarmed. He stepped towards her, put a hand on her arm. Mrs Pierce looked up at her grandson. 'There seemed... nothing to look forward to.'

'Granny. You can't say that.' There was an edge of anguish to his voice.

'I just did, though, didn't I? I'm sorry. I know you're grieving him, too. But the loss of a husband is something else. Soulmates. That's a term we didn't use when we were young. But that's what we were—soulmates.'

'I know,' Oliver said. 'You were so happy with Grandpa.' It was his turn to sound bereft.

Marissa shifted from foot to foot, uncomfortable at being witness to his family's pain and loss. She was an outsider who shouldn't really be there. If she could back out of the room without them noticing her, she would.

However, the older woman seemed intent on involving her. 'But this. Marissa. I'm not jumping the gun or anything, but perhaps… Well, the prospect of seeing my grandson settled, that makes me happier than I'd imagined I'd ever be again. You know, new life and all that.'

'Granny,' said Oliver, obviously through gritted teeth. 'It's not like that. It really isn't.' He didn't look at Marissa. *Couldn't* look at her, more likely.

This was awkward. To see this tall, powerful man at a loss of what to say to this petite older woman, whom he obviously loved and respected. Did Edith Pierce really believe her to be Oliver's girlfriend? Or was it…old age speaking? She didn't know her so couldn't make a judgement. Her own grandmother had become decidedly odd in her final years.

Mrs Pierce sighed, a sound Marissa found heart wrenching. With that sigh, the older lady seemed somehow to diminish, and even her beautiful, smooth skin and expertly applied make-up couldn't hide the fact that she was frail. Marissa noticed that her cashmere cardigan hung loosely on her and that her tailored tweed skirt seemed loose at the waist.

'My first Christmas without my beloved Charles in more than sixty years. I… I don't know how I'll manage.'

Oliver put his arm around her. She was tiny, and only came up to his elbow. 'Granny, I'm here. You're not on your own.' His voice was kind and gentle.

'I know. And neither are you. You have Marissa.'

He spoke through gritted teeth. 'Granny, you really have got the wrong idea about—'

Edith Pierce aimed a sweet smile at Marissa. 'You've made an old lady very happy, my dear,' she said. 'Thank you for coming here with Oliver. He's never had a girl-friend visit Longfield Manor before, so you must be very special. I'm looking forward to getting to know you.'

Marissa had to say something in response. She cast a quick glance at Oliver but got no help from him. He seemed as stunned as she was. 'Er, me, too,' she managed to choke out. 'Getting to know you, I mean.'

Oliver Pierce had never brought a girlfriend home before? What did that say about him? Marissa was so disconcerted she couldn't utter another word.

'Now, shall we go through our plans for Christmas?' said Mrs Pierce in a matter-of-fact tone.

Oliver shot Marissa a glance and gave the slightest shrug of his shoulders. Marissa nodded in reply.

He indicated for her and his grandmother to take seats at a round conference table in the corner of the spacious study. Feeling more ill at ease than she could ever remember, Marissa picked up her folder and tablet and followed him. Initially, she found it an effort to act normal and businesslike with the owner of Longfield Manor.

Especially after Mrs Pierce had expressed so firmly her belief that she was her grandson's girlfriend. Why hadn't Oliver denied it more vehemently?

But once seated at the table, Oliver's grandmother became pure businesswoman, alert and savvy when it came to finalising the plans for the hotel's Christmas. She was totally on top of things, including the financials. She referred to her meetings with Caity and expressed her pleasure at the way the traditional Christmas celebrations were to be enlivened with some more contemporary twists. She also liked the idea of the new designer ornaments and decorations. And was in full agreement with the innovative vegetarian and vegan additions to the menu, as more guests were requesting those alternatives to the traditional fare.

'Well done, Marissa,' she said, as she viewed the final presentation on Marissa's tablet. She seemed very much the competent, well-established owner of the hotel. Perhaps the girlfriend confusion had been an aberration.

'I'm glad you approve,' Marissa said, feeling as though she'd passed an exam.

Edith—she'd asked Marissa to call her by her first name—turned to Oliver. 'Where did you say you first met Marissa?' she asked.

'I didn't say,' he said. He looked to Marissa and back again to his grandmother. 'But...it was through a mutual friend.'

Caity. That was what he believed and it was true. Their mutual friend Caity had indeed organised their meeting for Marissa to take over from her while she was in hospital. But it was also true in another context, given he'd actually first met her through his friend Toby, brother to her friend Samantha, when they were teenagers. Oliver appeared to have no memory of that first meeting all those years ago, but she wasn't about to remind him of it. Did he still see Toby? She and Toby's sister had lost touch after Samantha had moved to a different school.

'The best way to meet your life partner,' his grandmother said approvingly. 'I don't like the idea of these dating apps.'

Oliver spluttered an indecipherable reply.

*Life partner?*

Marissa was so astounded she had to stop her mouth from gaping open. Yet, secretly, she found it amusing to see this hot, super-successful tycoon, who had been so vile to her years ago, shocked speechless by his grandmother. How the tables had turned.

Despite that, she was beyond relieved when the meeting concluded and Edith left the room. She waited with Oliver, near the door, until she could be sure the older woman had definitely gone and wouldn't overhear her. She swung around to face Oliver. 'What was that about? Why did you allow your grandmother to believe I was your girlfriend?' She wasn't speaking as contractor to client; his grandmother's absurd assumptions had swung them beyond that.

'I did not. I explained who you were.' He appeared very sure of himself, yet she could tell he was shaken by the encounter with his grandmother.

'You didn't outright deny it. And I didn't know her well enough to contradict her. Although I did try. You noticed I did try. It was so awkward for me.'

He gestured with his hands. 'I'm sorry, Marissa. Granny took me by surprise. You are here to do a job, we have no personal connection and it was…unprofessional of me not to try harder to stop her. I can only say in my defence that I was stunned almost speechless.'

Marissa had been just about to accuse him of being unprofessional, so that somehow took the wind out of her sails. What family drama had she found herself caught up in here?

'I was so embarrassed. Where on earth did your grandmother get the idea I was your girlfriend? What did you tell her about me that would have made her think that?'

Oliver shrugged broad shoulders. He had discarded his suit jacket during the course of their meeting and his tailored linen shirt did nothing to hide the ripple of muscle beneath. Gone was the gangly teenager she remembered. Oliver Pierce was built.

*But she was immune to gorgeous guys.*

Wasn't she?

'Nothing. I told her you were replacing Caity to work with us on Christmas.'

'That's all?'

'That's all,' he said emphatically. 'She's very old and has recently had some memory issues, but nothing like this level of confusion.'

Marissa took a moment to answer. 'I see.' She took another moment. 'I can tell you care very much for your grandmother,' she said carefully.

'I do. She was more a mother to me than my own mother, her daughter.'

Really? She would love to ask for more details. But the way his face closed up and his green eyes shadowed, stopped her from asking. It was none of her business.

But his grandmother mistaking her for her grandson's

*life partner*-status girlfriend was very much her business. She realised he felt uncomfortable about the situation. But not as uncomfortable as she did. She had to work here for the next week.

'Can you please clear up the misunderstanding with her as soon as you can?' she said. 'I'll feel awkward dealing with her until you do.'

'I understand that. Thank you for your patience and kindness towards her,' he said. He took a deep breath and paced the space in front of his desk before coming to a halt to face her. 'But here's the thing. I haven't seen Granny smile like that since before Grandpa got ill.'

'What do you mean?'

'The way she smiled at you. The look on her face when she said how happy the thought of us—' he cleared his throat '—uh, of us being together, how happy that made her feel.'

'But she got it wrong, didn't she?'

'Very wrong.' He looked down at her, his eyes narrowed, his expression intent. 'But what if she got it right?'

Marissa took a step back from him. 'What are you saying?'

'Would it be asking too much for you to pretend to be my girlfriend for the week you are here?'

*'What?'* She was too stupefied to say anything more.

'I want you to pretend to be my girlfriend to make my grandmother happy and give her a wonderful Christmas—her first since she lost my grandfather.'

She shook her head in disbelief. 'You can't be serious.' She realised she had crossed her arms over her chest, and she had to force herself to uncross them.

'I know it's out there, but you can see how frail she is,

and how unhappy. She really took to you, although I have no idea why she thinks you're my girlfriend.'

'My own grandmother got a bit, well, eccentric is the kind way to put it, when she got older. Is Edith...?' This conversation was getting surreal.

'Before he died, my grandfather told me he was worried Granny might be displaying signs of dementia. You know, memory loss, forgetting things. I haven't seen serious signs of it myself, apart from some minor lapses that I could put down to the loss of her husband, and possible fears about her future. But this. This has shocked me and, to tell the truth, the extent of her delusion frightened me.'

Marissa frowned. 'She seemed very *compos mentis* to me when we were going over the Christmas plans.'

'She did. As sharp as she's always been. Which makes this girlfriend thing hard to understand. Unless it is a sign of...of mental deterioration.'

'Or wishful thinking, perhaps?'

'What do you mean?' he said.

'Your granny seemed so happy about the idea of us being a couple. Perhaps she's become aware of her own mortality and wants her grandson to be settled. You know, ready to produce the next generation of your family. The walls of the downstairs corridor are lined with portraits of your ancestors. There are more in here.' She indicated the panelled walls, the bronze bust of some revered past Pierce on the bookshelf. 'She might be clutching at straws. Are you the oldest son?'

She couldn't meet him in the eye, especially as the fantasies she'd had about them being a couple when they were teenagers flashed again through her mind. Although her brain might dismiss those feelings, her body knew only too well that the attraction still simmered, no matter how deeply she tried to stomp on it. Pretending to be the girlfriend of this excitingly handsome man would be madness.

'I'm an only child,' he said. 'And the only grandchild, in fact.'

'There you have it.'

'You could be right,' he said slowly. 'Although I thought Granny had long given up trying to matchmake me with her friends' granddaughters.'

'Perhaps she's muddled me up with one of them.'

'I doubt it. None of them are as beautiful as you are,' he said dismissively. Had he really said that so casually?

'Oh,' she said, unable to meet his eye. He certainly hadn't found her beautiful when he'd first met her. Still, it was hard not to feel flattered.

He paused, tugged at the collar of his shirt. 'I know this is an off-the-wall plan. Not something I could ever have imagined I would propose. But I'm worried about Granny, and it seems nothing could make her happier than the belief that you and I are together.'

Marissa was still reeling at the thought of it. 'I suppose there's the chance that she might have forgotten about this girlfriend notion already?'

'Unlikely, with you around to remind her of it.'

'I could leave. It would be difficult to find you another event planner at this stage but I—'

'No,' he said with a dismissive gesture. 'You going could make her worse.'

'Or we could continue to deny it. Any relationship, I mean.'

'It would be more unsettling for her if we have to continuously deny it. Pretend to be together and we can all get on with the job of making this a memorable Christmas.'

She frowned. 'You're serious about this?'

'I am.'

'I… I don't know what to say.'

'*Yes* would be a start.' A hint of a smile lurked around the grim set of his mouth.

Slowly, she shook her head. 'I really don't know that this would be a good idea.'

'Name your price.'

'Excuse me? I'm not for sale!' He seemed different. But it appeared he hadn't changed at all since he was sixteen. He was still arrogant and overbearing. No. He was worse.

'Aargh,' he said, pushing his fingers through his hair. 'That came out wrong. Of course I don't think you're for sale. I meant we could make the pretence an extension of your role as our event planner. Pretend to be my girlfriend and I could add a substantial bonus to your fee.'

'Not interested,' she said, shaking her head.

Exchanging personal services for money? Not happening. Never happening. And she had vowed never, ever again to get involved with a client. That was how she'd met the Christmas mistletoe disaster boyfriend.

'In fact, I think I should leave,' she said. 'Now. Your grandmother has a good handle on what to do for Christmas, as our meeting showed, and that will solve the girlfriend problem.'

'I fear it wouldn't.' He looked up to the ornately patterned ceiling and back to her. His black hair stuck up in ruffles, which had the effect of making him look more vulnerable. Vulnerable? Oliver Pierce? *Huh*.

She frowned. 'Why is that?'

'I'm worried how she might react to you leaving so abruptly. What if she blamed herself? I couldn't bear it if she reacted badly.' He looked somewhere over her shoulder, not meeting her eyes. 'It's difficult for me to talk about personal stuff. Especially to a stranger. But given you've suffered your own loss, you might understand.' He swallowed hard. 'Granny is all I've got. She and Grandpa pretty much raised me. My parents... Well, they weren't that interested in their son.'

Marissa thought about the gossip pages she'd read. The supermodel mother. The rock-musician father. The way Oliver had felt the need to change his surname. His upbringing had been so different from her happy, secure childhood.

'Your parents. Where are they now?'

'My mother lives in New Zealand. I haven't seen her for years. My father took off a long time ago. He has another family now, somewhere in Cornwall.'

'I'm sorry,' she said. They felt like such inadequate words in the face of his loss, but she couldn't think of anything better to say.

'Don't be,' he said with a bitter twist to his mouth. 'They're no great loss. It's my grandparents who suffered when their daughter left. And now that Grandpa is gone—'

'You're all she has,' she said softly. 'In terms of family, I mean.'

He nodded. 'She's eighty-two and I want to hold on to her for as long as I can. I want to keep her happy. I want to do whatever I can to help her stave off possible dementia. And if that means pretending a woman I've only just met is my girlfriend—how did she put it?'

'Your *life-partner* girlfriend.'

'Yes. That. If I have to pretend to be in a relationship that doesn't exist with a beautiful stranger to make Granny happy for her first Christmas without Grandpa, then I will. If that stranger is willing.'

Not quite a stranger, but he didn't know that. Should she tell him? What would be the point? Their first meeting was so long ago, it wasn't surprising that he didn't remember her. She didn't remember other boys she'd met at that time. Only Oliver had lodged himself in her memory.

'I'm here for seven days,' she said. 'What would happen after that?'

He shrugged. 'I'd tell her we'd broken up. That wouldn't surprise her. I don't have long relationships.' His mouth twisted. 'Much as Granny would like to see me married, I'm not interested in being tied down.'

Why did that not surprise her? He had ranked high in a gossip page's list of elusive, eligible bachelors.

But he'd made her think. She empathised only too well with his fierce love for his grandmother. She'd lost her parents she'd adored in the accident. The only grandmother she'd known, her mother's mother, had died of a stroke just weeks afterwards brought on, the doctors said, by shock. Of her immediate family, her brother Kevin was all she had left. But Kevin hadn't been able to bear the thought of a Christmas without his mother and father and had escaped to Australia for the Christmas after the accident. He'd met a wonderful girl while in Sydney and had settled there. He and his lovely wife, Danni, meant everything to her but distance made things difficult.

She turned away from him, took a few paces forward and then turned back. 'If—and I said *if*—I were to agree to be your pretend girlfriend, how would it work?'

'I don't know. We'd have to work it out together. Figure out something you were comfortable with, but that seemed genuine. Does that seem reasonable to you?'

Oliver waited for her reply. He was so tall, so powerful, so very handsome, but she sensed again that surprising vulnerability. Awareness of him as a man shot through her like a sizzling electric current. He had been a teenage crush, but her attraction had been intense and no less real because of her age. Although long dormant, it might not take much to revive that attraction. She might want to be of help, that was her nature, but her own emotional safety needed to be considered, too.

*Be careful, Marissa.*

'I suppose so,' she said slowly. 'It's a lot to take on.'

'Understood,' he said.

But she saw hope flicker in his eyes and it chipped away at her resolve to walk away and drive her van back to London. He'd shown her a different side to him, one she hadn't imagined he possessed. He loved his grandmother, and she would be doing a good turn for a woman who had lost not only her soulmate husband but also, it seemed, her daughter. And acting as this man's pretend girlfriend could be, she had to admit, a fun distraction at a time of year she found distinctly depressing.

Fun, yes, but dangerous too, her common sense warned her. It was dangerous that she found this man just as hot as she had when she'd been a teenager. But she was thirty years old now, and no stranger to heartbreak and disillusion when it came to men. As long as she stayed aware of that danger, kept her guard up, there should be no risk to her emotions.

'Reasonable would not mean sharing your bedroom,' she said firmly. 'Let's get that straight up front.'

'Of course not. I'd tell Granny we…uh…weren't ready to be that public about our relationship.' The lie slipped out so easily it gave her a shiver of concern.

'And there would be no payment, no bonus, required,' she added. 'It would be purely an act of compassion on my part to help a lonely, bereaved old lady over the Christmas period.' That would ensure she kept the upper hand. She would be doing him a favour rather than being beholden to him.

'If that's the way you want it.'

She sighed. 'I have to say up front that I don't like lies and dishonesty—and the fake-girlfriend thing would be one big fat lie.'

His face tightened. 'I don't like lies, either. If there's one way to get on my wrong side, it's to lie to me. But for Granny's sake, I'd think of it as a kind of charade.'

'An extension of the Christmas celebration?'

'Something like that, I guess.' He raked his fingers through his hair again. 'Hell, Marissa. I've never done anything like this before. I don't know how it might work. But when I saw how happy she was at the idea of us together…'

He seemed so genuine. So committed. She wanted to help. 'I'll do it,' Marissa said. 'I'll pretend to be your girlfriend for seven days.'

# CHAPTER FOUR

OLIVER LOOKED DOWN at Marissa, searching her lovely face. Had she really accepted his proposition without requiring financial recompense? Or any other reward? Purely from the goodness of her heart?

For his grandmother's sake he wanted to believe that. Needed to believe that. Yet, his parents' treatment of him had made him cynical and distrustful, even as a child. Had he made a huge mistake in trusting this stranger with his off-the-wall idea? What was in it for her?

His life in London as a successful hotelier had only deepened that early cynicism. In business, but also when it came to dating. He'd become used to dealing with women with ulterior motives. For some people, money seemed to be the most attractive thing about another person. The wealthier he'd got, the more appealing he—or his bank balance—seemed to become to women.

But he wasn't looking for long-term relationships—a short-term affair with a negotiated use-by date was more his style. An affair where both partners knew the score, and nobody got hurt. Pleasure, fun and a pain-free good-bye. Not that he had a rotating list of lovers—in fact, he lived a large part of his life alone and celibate. Relationships were difficult. Love was a goal that had always remained out of his reach.

There'd been one woman who had tempted him to break his self-imposed rules on commitment. Sonya was a journalist, covering the opening of the Pierce Haymarket. She'd been vibrant, clever, gorgeous. He'd been enthralled by her, let himself dream of a future with her. Then had been shocked to the core when she'd told him she was polyamorous, he was one of several lovers and that was how she wanted it to stay. Oliver had respected her life choice—but he'd wanted a one-on-one exclusive relationship. The breakup had left him lonely, miserable and plagued by feelings he hadn't been enough for her. As he hadn't been enough for his parents to want to keep him.

Marissa looked up at him, a challenge in her clear blue eyes, a slight smile curving her lips. For a moment he felt mesmerised by that unexpected smile, and the way it brought into play a very cute dimple in her right cheek. 'Now that I've accepted, please don't tell me you're having second thoughts?' she said. 'Because I'm looking forward to starting the charade.'

How did she guess the doubt that had slithered its way into his certainty?

'Of course I haven't changed my mind,' he said firmly, to convince himself as well as her. 'Making sure my grandmother enjoys this first Christmas without Grandpa is important to me. I appreciate you agreeing to help. I can't thank you enough.' He couldn't say to anyone that it might be the last Christmas at Longfield Manor if selling became the most realistic option.

'So we're really going to do this?' she said.

'Yes,' he said. 'Yes, and yes.'

On reflection, he couldn't see why she would have an ulterior motive, or where it could lead. Caity had stressed her friend's honesty and integrity. Perhaps Marissa was exactly what she seemed to be—a kind person who had let herself get talked into his scheme because it would make an old woman happy for the holidays. 'And the timing is good,' he said.

'Why so?' she asked, again with that appealing tilt of her head.

'You're not known to anyone here and I'll need to introduce you to the hotel staff anyway as the person who is here to help us with Christmas.'

'And at the same time, you can introduce me as your girlfriend?'

'Who happens to be a professional event planner.'

'Who also knows Caity, and so it seemed logical I would come to help you.'

'On both a personal and professional basis.'

She raised her dark eyebrows on the word *personal* and he wondered if she was wavering. But she nodded.

'And if anyone asks why you hired Caity instead of me in the first place?' she queried.

'I'll say we didn't want to mix business and pleasure but with Caity out of commission it seemed only natural for you to step in, as you were going to be coming here to celebrate Christmas with me anyway,' he offered.

'That makes a lot of sense,' she said approvingly. 'Straight away, we need to formulate a strategy and get it clear in our heads.' Caity had said her friend was formidably efficient. Why would she be any different when formulating a plan for a mock-relationship?

'Understood,' he said. 'But we'll have to create that strategy on the fly. There are no rules to follow. No precedent to guide us.'

'If there are, I don't know of them. I guess The Complete Book of Faking a Relationship doesn't exist.'

She laughed, a warm, delightful laugh at their complicity. For a flash of a moment he thought the way she laughed sounded familiar. But that couldn't be. He met so many people in the hospitality business, and he had no specific memory of ever having met her. Perhaps she'd momentarily reminded him of some passing acquaintance.

'That book certainly isn't in our library here,' he said, taking his turn to laugh, a laugh that felt a little rusty. There hadn't been much opportunity for jollity since his grandfather's death. Besides, he wasn't known as a jovial, laugh-out-loud kind of guy. 'Serious with a tendency to brood,' was how his old friend Toby often described him. Oliver didn't mind the serious label, but that didn't mean he was humourless.

'Strategy one, we don't tell any other person about what we're doing,' he said. 'Not even Caity.'

Marissa nodded. 'I was about to suggest the very same thing. Safer that way.'

'We don't want leaks.'

'We also need to get our stories straight about how we met. It could be disastrous if we contradicted each other.'

'True. Shall we say we met at an event at the Pierce Soho hotel that Caity had organised?' he said.

'Inspired idea,' she said. 'When did we meet? Why not first week of November?'

'We're a relatively new couple?' he said. That would be believable. He wasn't known for lengthy relationships.

'Yes, that could be a good cover if we make any errors in our knowledge of each other.'

'Quick quiz,' he said. He tried to think of the things people got to know about each other in the first weeks of a new relationship. 'Your birthday?'

'Twenty-seventh of February. Yours?'

'August twentieth.'

'Favourite food?'

'Chocolate,' she said with a wicked grin. 'Okay, maybe not. I'll go for Italian.'

'You?'

'I'll go with Italian, too.'

She laughed. 'One thing at least we have in common.'

'Where did you grow up?' he asked.

'Putney, mostly. You?'

'Between London and Dorset. Whatever best suited my parents' peripatetic lifestyle. My grandparents used to have a London townhouse until they had to sell it.'

'Oh?' she said, the one word a question.

He turned to look at a painting of Longfield's famous walled garden that his grandfather had commissioned not long before he passed. 'They were very wealthy until they lost most of their money in an unwise investment of a big insurance company. That's why they turned Longfield Manor into a hotel.'

'I didn't know that.'

'But you would be expected to if you were my girl-friend.'

'Agreed,' she said, but he could see she was shocked. 'How awful for them.'

'Grandpa and Granny are canny with money. They managed to claw back much of their fortune.'

'Good to know,' she said. He wouldn't mention that his grandparents had been early investors in The Pierce Group and had done very well out of that investment.

'Where do you live now?' she said.

'In the penthouse apartment at the top of Pierce Soho.'

'Nice,' she said. 'I live in a mansion block apartment in West Kensington.'

'A good part of London. That must be very nice, too,' he said.

'I inherited it from my godmother,' she said. 'She was my mother's best friend.' He could hear the sadness that tinged her voice. If she'd inherited, that meant her godmother must have passed. Another loss.

'I'm sorry,' he said. 'For the loss of your godmother.'

'She was very special,' was all she said. She paused. 'Back to the get fake agenda.'

He laughed again. 'That's one way of putting it,' he said.

'We have to take it seriously, but not too seriously. If you know what I mean.'

'I think I do,' he said slowly. 'Otherwise, the relationship might not seem believable. Granny is quite astute. When she's not inventing girlfriends for me, that is.'

'I can see that,' Marissa said with another smile. 'With that in mind, we should try to be discreet. A private couple. No exaggerated public displays of affection, for example, to try and signal we're together. I'm not that kind of person and I suspect—judging by the very short time we've known each other—you're not, either.'

'Quite right,' he said, again amazed at her perception.

He did not like his private life exposed to the world. His very beautiful mother had been a magnet for the press and unfortunately, it had not been uncommon for drunken incidents outside nightclubs to be splashed across the tabloid newspapers. Too often, there had been a finger-wagging mention that she was the mother of a young son. His father, as handsome as his mother was beautiful, had got off more lightly. It seemed to be an expectation that a rock musician would be hedonistic, a suspected consumer of illegal drugs, a bad father.

'That said, to be convincing, there will have to be some outward signs of a supposed inner...uh...passion,' she said, not meeting his gaze. She flushed high on her cheekbones, which served to make her blue eyes even bluer and emphasise the creaminess of her skin. 'But again, not too exaggerated.'

Passion. Marissa. He had to force his mind away from such arousing thoughts.

*She was out of bounds.*

He cleared his throat. 'What would be on the list of approved hinting-at-passion behaviour? Holding hands?'

She nodded. 'Definitely. But not while we're in a business situation. If we were really boyfriend and girlfriend, we wouldn't be flaunting our relationship in front of the staff. Especially when I'm working for the hotel on behalf of Caity.'

'Flaunting only allowed in front of my grandmother.'

'Quite right. But again, a discreet flaunting. Nothing that would embarrass her.'

'After what Granny has said today, I doubt that we could embarrass her. It might be more the other way around.'

Marissa laughed again. Her laughter seemed to lighten the atmosphere of this traditional room, to invite mischief into a place that might never have witnessed it.

'I know exactly what you mean,' she said. 'I really didn't know what to say or where to look when she told us that our generation didn't invent sex.'

'Me, too. All the while fighting off any images from entering my brain of my ancient grandparents indulging in what we didn't invent.'

'Please,' she said, her eyes dancing. 'I'm going to try and forget you ever said that.'

He found himself laughing, too. 'So we're agreed, just enough flaunting to make us seem believable.'

'Yes. Perhaps a discreet brushing of a hand across an arm. A low-voiced exchange of what could be perceived to be private talk between lovers. Enough to make it believable.'

She paused, looking thoughtful. 'Actually, I think that might be the secret of making this work. We try to behave as though we really are in a relationship. When we're not sure what's appropriate behaviour, we conjure up thoughts of what we would do if we really were together and act on that.'

He looked down at her. Her dark hair was pulled back in a high ponytail, which drew attention to the perfect oval of her face. Her eyes were the deep, rich blue of the delphiniums his grandfather had so prized in his spring garden. He could not keep his eyes from her lush mouth with its Cupid's bow top lip, defined with glossy pink lipstick.

He cleared his throat. 'What would we do if I—behaving as though us being a couple were real—felt the urge to kiss you?'

'*What?*'

'If we were in a relationship, I would want to kiss you.'

He wanted to kiss her now. And the urge had nothing to do with pretending. She was so beautiful, and every minute he spent with her his attraction to her grew. Had it only been a few hours? Lust at first sight? But he couldn't let himself think this way, couldn't let her know how appealing he found her. The endgame was to help Granny. And finish the charade after seven days. 'And you might want to kiss me. If we were for real, I mean.'

Her dark eyelashes fluttered and she looked away from him and back. 'I...er... I guess. A light, affectionate kiss in front of others when appropriate would be on the cards.'

'We probably wouldn't want our first kiss in front of others to look like our first kiss ever. That might give the game away.'

'What do you mean?'

'I mean a practice kiss might be in order.'

Her eyes widened. 'Here? Now?'

'Now is as good a time as any.' He glanced down at his watch. 'Time is marching on. I need to introduce you to the staff. They'll soon be arriving to help decorate the Christmas trees and whatever else you want them to do.'

'The five fully decorated Christmas trees, each of which would normally take me an entire day to complete and which we need to get up ASAP? I'll try not to panic at the prospect of that.' She nodded thoughtfully as if kissing him was something to be checked off the list of pretend intimacies. 'Seriously. Yes. If we need to practise a kiss, now might be the time to do it.'

She took a step closer. Her eyes were wide with more than a hint of nervousness—a feeling he reciprocated. She bit her lower lip with her top teeth, which drew his eyes again to her mouth—so eminently kissable. She lifted her chin to bring her face closer to his. An atmosphere that had been amicable and warmed by laughter suddenly seemed fraught with tension. Her shoulders hunched up around her neck. She didn't seem to want him to kiss her. He wouldn't touch her without consent. He froze. What had he started?

Then she laughed, her delightful laugh that seemed already familiar. 'This is seriously weird, isn't it? Both of us holding back. I've been kissed before and I'm sure as heck you have been, too. If we need to practise, let's go for it.'

Before he could formulate his strategy for the kiss, she kissed him. She put her hands on his shoulders and planted a kiss on his mouth. Her mouth was firm and warm and fit his as if it was meant to be. But before he could relax into the kiss, it was over. She laughed again, but this time her laughter was high-pitched and tremulous. She flushed high on her cheeks. 'So, ice broken, we've kissed. Okay?'

'That's not much of a kiss,' he said, his voice husky. 'I think we could do better.'

Her eyes widened and her mouth parted. 'Er, okay,' she murmured.

He dipped his head to kiss her gently at first then, questing, exploring, her kiss in return tentative. When she responded, he deepened the kiss. She gave a little moan, which sent his arousal levels soaring. When she wound her arms around his neck to bring him closer, his arms circled her waist to pull her tighter. '*This* is a kiss,' she murmured against his mouth before returning to the kiss with increasing enthusiasm.

For practise purposes that was probably as far as they needed to go. But she felt so good in his arms. He didn't want to stop. Her scent was intoxicating, roses and vanilla and something indefinably hers. He traced the seam of her lips with the tip of his tongue, and she responded with her tongue. The kiss deepened into something hungry and passionate and totally unexpected. He wanted this kiss to be for real.

*He wanted more than this kiss.*

He scarcely registered the knock on the door when it came. He just wanted to keep on kissing Marissa. Then there was another knock. And his grandmother's familiar voice. 'Oliver, I wanted to ask—'

Marissa sprung back from his embrace. He caught a glimpse of flushed cheeks, her mouth swollen from his kisses, a flash of panic in her eyes, before he turned to face his grandmother.

'Granny,' he managed to choke out from a constricted voice. He tried not to make it obvious that his breath was coming in short gasps. He probably had Marissa's lipstick on his face and he swiped his mouth with the back of his hand.

'Edith,' Marissa said, smoothing down her top where it had come untucked from her trousers, pushing back her hair from her face. He noticed her hands weren't steady.

'You two,' said Granny with a fond smile, as she looked from him to Marissa and back again. 'I don't know why you tried to hide it from me. I knew you were together the second I saw you. And I couldn't be happier about it.'

Their first test. And they'd passed.

'We realised it was pointless to deny our relationship any longer,' Oliver said. 'Especially when you're so perceptive.'

His grandmother beamed in response. The plan was already working if she could look that happy from simply observing their kiss. Still, he found it difficult to look at Marissa—so delightfully sensuous in his arms just seconds before. Could she tell that kiss had been suddenly, urgently *real*?

'We're happy to have your blessing,' said Marissa.

Was she overdoing it? *Blessing?* But it seemed she knew exactly the right thing to say.

'You have my blessing indeed,' Granny said with another big smile. 'I'm looking forward to being a grandmother-in-law.'

Marissa was unable to stifle her shocked gasp.

But Oliver knew they had a plan, and he was going to work within the constraints. He wasn't exactly sure whether his grandmother was serious or teasing them.

'Granny, that's going too far. Marissa and I only started dating last month. Our relationship is still new. I don't want you to scare her off by getting ahead of yourself.'

Granny looked contrite. Again, he wasn't sure if she was playing them. 'Of course, darling. I won't say a word about marriage or even great-grandchildren.' Oliver protested but she put up her hand to stop him. 'I'll leave you two alone.'

'Wasn't there something you wanted to ask me?' Oliver said.

Granny gave a dismissive wave of her hand and a smug smile. 'That can wait,' she said as she closed the study door behind her.

Oliver turned to Marissa. She was shaking with the effort of suppressing a fit of the giggles. 'Flaunting it to Granny went well,' she choked out. 'Maybe too well.'

Oliver groaned and put his hand to his forehead. 'Sorry about the great-grandchildren thing.'

'I hope I hid my shock.'

'You hid it well, better than I did. In fact, you performed perfectly. Especially when we were caught by surprise. Thank you.'

'Edith's reaction proved we're believable in our roles,' she said. 'It's a good start.'

That kiss had been only too believable—and only too enjoyable. He had not intended for the kiss to go that far. He couldn't let it happen again. That surge of passion had been a lapse of judgement.

*But she had seemed to enjoy the kiss as much as he did.*

And that would make it difficult for him to hold back on kissing her again.

# CHAPTER FIVE

*WHAT HAD SHE DONE?*

Marissa turned away from Oliver, desperately trying to conceal how shaken she'd been by his kiss. Not a practice kiss. Not a pretend kiss. A passionate kiss that teased and aroused. She had responded as if she hadn't been kissed for a year. Which, in truth, she hadn't. But it had been more than banked-up carnal hunger. Not just any kiss but a kiss with *him*. She was reeling with the realisation of how much she'd liked it, how his kiss had made her dizzy with desire.

*How she wanted more kisses.*

If the kiss had been with anyone else but Oliver Pierce, who knows where she might have wanted to take it?

That wasn't how it was meant to be. This game of pretend couldn't work if real feelings and real desires entered into it. That could lead to disaster.

She made a further fuss of tidying her hair. Then turned back to pick up her folder and tablet. 'The practice kiss served its purpose. But I don't think we need to...to go that far again.'

'You're right,' he said, his voice gruff.

'We know we can be convincing and that's all that was required.'

'Yes,' he said. He was looking somewhere over his shoulder. Did he feel, like she did, that the kiss had got out of hand? She didn't know him well enough to ask.

'We're agreed on that, then?'

He nodded.

She looked down at her watch, staged a gasp of surprise. 'Look at the time. There's so much to do today.'

He looked back at her. To her relief, his glance said *business as usual*. 'First step, introduce you to the staff, as we agreed.'

'Then I'll need to get my van unloaded and be directed to the storeroom where all the rest of the Christmas decorations are kept.'

'Granny can help with that,' he said.

'About that.' She looked directly up at him. 'Oliver, I can't do my best work if Edith is interrogating me about our *relationship*. Would you mind if I politely say to her that it's all still too new and…er…precious for me to be discussing it? Pretty much what you said to her just then?'

'I'll back you up by saying the same thing when she inevitably starts to grill me.'

'Good. That's what we'd do if it was a real relationship.'

He frowned. 'There's something I didn't think to ask you. Is there a *real relationship* waiting for you back in London?'

'No. I broke up with someone about this time last year.'

She'd caught awful Aaron kissing his work colleague under the mistletoe at his company Christmas party— a serious kiss that made her instantly aware he must be sleeping with her. He hadn't even tried to deny it, and the woman concerned had sent her a glance of gloating triumph. It had been a sickening, heartbreaking moment as she had really liked Aaron and thought they were exclusive.

'There hasn't been anyone serious since. To be honest, I haven't wanted there to be. What about you?' she said.

'No one serious. I can't afford to let anything get in the way of growing my business. A new London hotel is in the planning stage. That's confidential, of course.'

She noted he said *anything* not *anyone*, which was telling.

'So, no one is going to come barging down here to Dorset to protest if anything slips out about us. As a *couple* I mean.'

'Not from my side. No.'

'Okay, then, it seems like two resolutely single people have found each other,' she said, forcing a light-hearted tone. 'Or that's our story, anyway.'

'You're good at improvising,' he said. 'Very good.'

'A lot of marketing is about selling a story, so I suppose you could say that. What I have to be careful of is that I don't overembellish our story. I have a tendency to do that.'

He smiled. 'Just stick to the facts, ma'am.'

She smiled back. 'You mean our made-up facts?'

'If in doubt, leave it out.'

'A suggestion that I'll try to stick to.' She paused. 'Nothing like a cliché or two to sort things out.'

He laughed. 'Clichés developed for a reason. They might be overused but we know exactly what they mean.'

Oliver was transformed when he laughed; his green eyes, warmed, the somewhat grim set of his mouth curved upwards, even his rigid posture seemed to relax. Caity had been right. He was hot. And he had never looked hotter than at this moment.

And her reaction to that kiss warned her not to give in to the attraction that time had not dimmed.

Even more of a problem was that, contrary to anything she could have imagined, she was beginning to like him. And that was seriously disconcerting, considering for how long she had nurtured her dislike.

Oliver introduced her to the hotel manager, Cecil Bates, a grey-haired man whom Oliver told her was on the point of retirement. He seemed warm and kind, but she could also see him being tough when necessary, and she began to see why this hotel had such a five-star reputation for comfort and good service.

'Cecil truly was Grandpa's right-hand man and will be sorely missed. Granny doesn't know that he's handed in his resignation,' Oliver explained in an undertone, after they'd left Cecil's office. 'Grandpa's death and the changes that brought with it are enough for her to deal with right now.'

She frowned. 'Edith will have to know soon, though, won't she? It seems a bit unfair to keep her in the shadows simply because she's elderly.'

He shook his head. 'It's not that at all. There might be other changes happening next year. I just want her to enjoy her Christmas without unnecessary worry.'

Marissa shrugged. She had the distinct impression Edith might not appreciate being kept out of the loop. Was Oliver being thoughtful or controlling? But it was none of her business. Nor were those mysteriously hinted at *changes*. On Christmas Day she'd be out of here and heading back to London, free of Christmas and Oliver

Pierce and his family. In the meantime, she had to make sure everything between her and Oliver stayed on an even keel.

*No more passionate kissing.*

And certainly no more thinking about how exciting and arousing that kissing had been.

She immediately liked the assistant manager, Priya Singh. Priya was the lovely woman who had greeted her when she'd arrived at the hotel. Priya seemed around her age, and Marissa straight away knew she would enjoy working with her. Priya's smile was warm when Oliver introduced her as his girlfriend and explained she was stepping in for Caity.

'I liked Caity so much. Fingers crossed all goes well for her. If you need help with anything, just let me know,' she said to Marissa. 'Christmas at Longfield Manor is so special. The extra work involved is worth it to make it the best ever Christmas this year.'

Oliver thanked Priya before he steered Marissa away. 'Granny just texted me. She's waiting for you in the store-room where all the existing Christmas stuff is, as well as the boxes you brought down with you. She's keen to get started.'

'So am I.' Anything to keep her mind off her growing awareness of Oliver.

But a room full of Christmas? How would she cope without giving away the game that she was in fact a bah-humbug Scrooge? *Stick to the script*, she reminded herself. *And step into the role of someone who loves everything about Christmas.* She needed to pretend to be the person she'd been before the night of that fatal car crash.

She took a step nearer to Oliver. It brought her whispering-distance close. She was again dizzyingly aware of his warm, spicy and very male scent. It was a mix of some undoubtedly expensive aftershave with a hint of something uniquely him.

'Wish me luck with Edith,' she murmured. 'I'll make very sure I don't say anything controversial about my beloved boyfriend.' She knew there were people in the foyer watching them, some of them most likely guests. She turned up the volume. 'Shall I see you later?' she said as she leaned up to press a kiss on his cheek, then trailed a finger down it in a proprietorially girlfriend manner.

'Of course,' he said. He caught her hand in his and pressed a kiss on it, playing his role to perfection. 'I won't be there for lunch. We'll meet for dinner.' Even that light kiss on her hand felt good.

*Too good.*

Dinner? Of course it would be expected that they'd have dinner together. Would that happen every night? If she was really his girlfriend, of course it would. Breakfast, too. She'd be seeking any moment to be alone with her hot, gorgeous boyfriend, whose very closeness sent tremors of awareness coursing through her.

'Text me if anything untoward comes up I should know about,' he said. 'We may need script amendments as we go along.'

A script. It was a good reminder of this crazy scheme she'd got caught up in. Both she and Oliver were essentially playing roles in a Christmas play. That kiss, however, had not felt like play-acting. Unless Oliver was a *very* good actor. She realised how very little she knew about him apart from the personal memory of a boy from sixteen years ago. A boy she'd never been able to forget. And she realised she wanted to know a lot more.

He took her to meet Edith in a storeroom behind the kitchens in the back end of the hotel, in the staff-only areas where guests were not permitted, so she could seriously start work. He had things to do, places to go, Oliver said with a grin before making his escape. Marissa watched his retreating back and felt suddenly alone and unprepared to deal with his grandmother.

The room smelled faintly of Christmas: the lingering scent of pine leaves and pine cones, a hint of dusty potpourri, the leftover waxy trace of perfumed candles. Marissa had to swallow against a sudden rush of nausea at the thought of the terrors of Christmas past and her fear for Christmas future. She took a deep, steadying breath and pasted on a smile for Edith's benefit.

Again, she wondered what on earth she'd got herself into. Yet, to be able to help Caity at a time of great need for her friend made it worth it. And, she could not deny it, there was a bonus in the totally unexpected chance to see again that man she'd had such a huge crush on when she'd been a teenager.

Edith greeted Marissa with delight but, thank heaven, no risqué references to her love life with Oliver. She asked after Caity and was pleased with Marissa's report on her friend's continued good health while on hospital bed rest.

'Caity didn't mention to me that Oliver was dating a friend of hers,' Edith said with narrowed eyes.

When it came to clichés, 'thinking on her feet' now came to mind. 'That's because we didn't tell her,' Marissa said. 'The Pierce Group is her client. We didn't want to make things awkward for her. Besides, you know how private Oliver is. I'm the same. Our relationship is too new and too precious for us to want to go public with it.' The words tripped quite happily off her tongue, much as she'd rehearsed them with Oliver.

'I guessed as soon as I saw you. Your chemistry is so obvious,' Edith said.

Chemistry? Is that what had fuelled that incredible kiss? Was it chemistry that had fired the intensity of her teenage crush on the same man? Marissa was too taken aback to reply to the woman who fancied herself as her future grandmother-in-law. 'Er...yes,' was all she could manage in reply. This conversation was suddenly heading way off script.

The older woman continued. 'You know how pleased I am about you being together and I respect your need for privacy. It's just that Oliver hasn't had an easy life and I do want him to be happy. As happy with the right person as I was with Charles. We had our ups and downs, of course we did, but we were always there for each other. That's a great comfort through life.'

All Marissa could manage to choke out was, 'That's lovely.'

*She couldn't do this.*

How could she possibly do her job properly when all Oliver's grandmother seemed to want to talk about was Marissa's *relationship* with her grandson?

Edith chuckled. 'That's *lovely*, you say. But you've already told me you don't want to talk about you and Oliver. And as I want to keep on your right side, I'll butt out.'

*Please do!*

But Edith was relentless. 'I just want to be sure, my dear, that you know where I stand.'

'I most certainly do,' said Marissa, stifling the urge to laugh.

It was clear that Edith loved her grandson just as much as he loved her, and each was working in their own way to make the other happy. Marissa appreciated that. If she wasn't stuck in the middle of it, she would appreciate it even more. Still, she could do this job standing on her head, and the intrigue of the fake dating made it entertaining and edgy.

Edith showed her where the containers of heirloom tree ornaments, lights, staircase swags, buntings and Christmas linens had been placed, all brought down from the attics from where they spent the rest of the year.

'Some of the glass tree decorations go right back to when Charles was a little boy, living here with his parents, long before we turned the house into a hotel. We don't always put them up and, when we do, they're on a small tree in our private residence.' She sighed. 'I don't think I'll bother this year. Not on my own. The five hotel trees in the guest areas will be enough.'

'Are you sure?' Marissa said. 'I'm here to help with everything Christmas.'

Edith patted her on the hand. 'Thank you for your kind offer, my dear. But I'll pass. For this year anyway.'

Marissa thought about where she herself would be next Christmas. On that Balinese island, for sure. On her own and loving it.

The Christmas trees were to be placed in the guest areas, including the foyer, the living room, dining room, reading room and in the living room of the converted barn.

Edith pointed out that the decorations for each room

had been packed together and put in clearly marked boxes and wooden packing crates. Marissa knew that from Caity's detailed handover document, but she had to check for herself to be sure. Attention to detail was all important.

Some of the ornaments and decorations were packed in very old suitcases that harked back to the golden age of sea travel to Europe, America and far-flung destinations of the Commonwealth before air travel took over. The suitcases were plastered with overlapping labels emblazoned with the names of grand ocean liners and stamped 'First Class.' Port labels told of voyages to destinations such as Marseille, Naples and Athens; transatlantic crossings to New York; further afield to exotic destinations like Bombay and Sydney, and back home to Dover.

She found the labels fascinating, telling a story of a glamorous era long gone for Oliver's wealthy family. She'd love to know more about their history. But now wasn't the time to delve into that. Perhaps it might be a good conversation starter over dinner with Oliver.

There were also the boxes of new product she'd brought with her in the van—including custom-made Christmas crackers. She cut open the box closest to her, using a utility knife with a retractable blade from the table nearby. She had, of course, inspected all the products at the designer's London headquarters to ensure the quality was up to scratch for her discerning clients. But she'd inspect them again for any possible damage sustained in transit.

She referred to her tablet. 'Soon, the team of contract staff will arrive,' she said. 'And the trees are due to be delivered from the Christmas tree farm later today. We have five trees of varying sizes for each of the five main public rooms. The trees will be stored outside in the barn and then brought inside when required.'

'We have the same helpers most years, so they know what to do,' Edith said.

Marissa had also engaged a professional interior designer with expertise in Christmas trees. Andy Gable had made a lucrative career out of decorating Christmas trees for private homes and hotels, department stores in both London and New York, along with many different magazines and catalogues. Marissa marvelled at how he made each tree so unique to that job. His job—his vocation, he called it—allowed him to take summers off to travel the world. Marissa had called him to ask for tree-decorating advice. To her delight, an unexpected cancellation had given him a free four days to help her out at Longfield Manor. He'd be arriving first thing the next day.

Caity had recruited fresh blood, too—a team of local university students on their Christmas break.

*Strong young people who will be safe on ladders, unlike some of the regular elderly helpers.*

That was what Caity had written in her notes.

Marissa smiled to herself as she read the notes but didn't read them out loud. She wasn't in any way ageist; in fact, she respected the knowledge and wisdom older people brought with them. But the fact remained that decorating a hotel of this size, with massive rooms and high ceilings, would be hard, physical work. Especially within this tight time frame.

She turned to Edith. 'I'm going to say goodbye and pop up to my room and change into jeans.' She'd dressed in business clothes for her first meeting with the clients, but now she needed to dress for hard work.

There was a guest lift, but she enjoyed climbing that magnificent staircase. For a moment, she imagined how it would be to be holding up voluminous long skirts of a bygone age as she manoeuvred the steps. Once in her room, she changed into jeans, a long-sleeved T-shirt and sturdy sneakers. Nothing scruffy, all designer, in keeping with the high-end hotel. Her role as event planner was a supervisory one. However, she had never been one to stand back if hands-on help was needed.

She pulled her hair back tighter into the ponytail; she hadn't realised stray wisps had come free during her enthusiastic kiss with Oliver. It was a battle to keep the luxuriant waves sleek. She looked in the mirror to check her make-up and touched up her lipstick where it had been kissed off. A shiver of pleasure ran through her as she remembered how good his kiss had felt. How was that possible when it had been with the man who had been so awful to her as a teenager?

Today Oliver Pierce had called her lovely. He had called her beautiful. And he'd sounded like he'd meant it. A stark departure from what had happened in the past. Back when he was sixteen and named Oliver Hughes, her friend Samantha's brother Toby had asked Oliver what he thought about his sister's friend. The boys were sitting on a sofa in Samantha's family's living room, where they'd been playing games on their consoles. They didn't know she could overhear them from the other side of the open door into the room.

*Eavesdroppers rarely hear good things about them-*

*selves*, her mother had told her. How true that had been back then.

Oliver certainly hadn't had anything flattering to say about her infatuated, self-conscious fourteen-year-old self. Neither had Toby, whom she had always liked up until then.

That day Toby had kicked off the critique by pointing out how flat-chested she was—true, she hadn't developed significant curves for another two years—how gawky— she hadn't grown into her long limbs yet then, either— and how she giggled too much—also unfortunately true, especially in the company of boys other than her brother.

It was such a cruel summing-up for a girl who was just beginning to find her place in a world where she had believed she might have something to offer. Where boys had become interesting rather than nuisances. Her heart had shattered when Oliver had agreed with Toby's assessments. Before that, she had never thought she was ugly, but when she'd seen herself through his eyes…she'd felt it.

Then Oliver had asked Toby, 'What's with those caterpillars crawling across the top of her face?'

Toby had sniggered. 'Marissa's monobrow, you mean.'

Toby had laughed and Oliver had joined in, too. Laughing at *her.*

She had been super-self-conscious about her eyebrows. Hearing the boys' laughter, she'd thought she would die of shame and embarrassment. But she couldn't crawl away, or they would have known she'd been there listening to them on the other side of the door. And for them to know she'd heard their mocking laughter would have made her feel even worse.

Thankfully, the boys had then headed off to the kitchen

in search of food, and she'd crept away and gone home, even though she'd been expected to stay for lunch with the family and Toby's friend. There had still been two days left of their half-term break but she'd made excuses not to go back to Samantha's house again. Not until obnoxious Toby and his equally obnoxious friend had gone back to their boarding school. Oliver had thankfully never visited again, and she had avoided Toby every holiday he'd been home.

After the pain and rejection she'd felt from that overheard conversation, that cruel laughter, she'd been determined to do something about her bothersome eyebrows.

Back then, her eyebrows had been bushy and black, and stray hairs had met in the middle above her nose. She'd hated those eyebrows but her mother had forbidden her to do anything about them, apart from the most gentle plucking. 'You can ruin your eyebrows for life if you pluck too much,' she'd warned.

So she'd saved up her pocket money and her babysitting money. Then she'd defied her mother by taking the bus to Knightsbridge to visit an eyebrow clinic reputed to be the best in London. Those errant eyebrows had been plucked, threaded and waxed into the elegant arches that today framed her eyes. She was still absolutely vigilant about keeping them that way.

Was that why Oliver hadn't recognised her? There was a curious satisfaction in knowing that he now found that skinny, gawky, monobrowed girl beautiful. That his kiss indicated he was attracted to her. But now her relationship with the client had veered into the personal, should she remind him that they'd met before? She still wasn't sure there would be any point to such a revelation.

# CHAPTER SIX

BUSINESS HAD KEPT Oliver confined to his office for most of the day. It was Christmas in his London hotels, with no vacancies across the three properties, which meant there were a lot of calls on staff. There were guests who'd come to London for shopping, London people who wanted to spend Christmas being pampered at a hotel, travellers from other countries wanting to enjoy a legendary English Christmas. He should really be in London himself, but he had excellent managers and for the moment he was putting Granny and Longfield Manor first. Thankfully, much of what he needed to do could be done remotely.

However, busy as he was, he found his thoughts straying often to Marissa. He was looking forward to having dinner with her. Not in his private residence—to be alone with her would be a test of his endurance as he definitely wanted to kiss her again—but rather at the hotel dining room. He wanted to get to know her better.

He'd had time to think about the fake-girlfriend scenario he had proposed. Where had that idea come from? Making quick decisions and taking risks in business had certainly paid off for him. But when it came to his personal life, he didn't do rash, impulsive things like asking a stranger to pretend to be his girlfriend. Or to suggest they practise kissing because all he'd been able to think about since meeting her was kissing her.

Yet, the scene in his office that morning had seemed so right. He recalled his fears for his grandmother, so caught up in her delusion. Marissa, an acquaintance of—what had it been then? An hour?—unwittingly caught up in it, unaware of the sad backstory of his family, so willing to be kind and thoughtful about Granny. This empathic woman seemed aware of his pain at his loss because she had suffered loss, too.

And it was working. Granny had a definite spring to her step that had been missing for a long time, even before Grandpa had died. Simply because she believed he had a girlfriend. No. Not just any girlfriend. Marissa. A girl she thought he must be in love with if he'd brought her home for Christmas.

He was so grateful to Marissa. He would find some acceptable way to reward her when this was all over. After he had gracefully 'broken up' with her. For the first time since coming up with his scheme, he felt a twinge of concern. If Granny was so obsessed with Marissa, how would she feel about having to say goodbye to her? Yet, no one would be surprised. Oliver did not do long-term relationships, and everyone knew that.

There wasn't much daylight left given that at this time of year sunset was at 4 p.m. and, as Oliver liked to take a walk around the gardens while it was still light, he decided to take a break. He pulled on his coat, hat and gloves as he headed outside. The sky was clear and blue and the air distinctly chilly. A heavy frost was predicted. But it was so good to be outside. He headed past the walled garden, enclosed within high walls of the same stone as the main buildings, a suntrap where spring came earlier than for the rest of the garden.

As he walked past, heading for the wild garden area, he saw that the iron gate was pushed open. For a moment he didn't recognise Marissa, in jeans, a puffer coat and scarf wrapped high to her chin. 'You startled me,' she said. 'I was taking the chance to get some fresh air.' She indicated the garden behind her. 'What a wonderful private garden.'

'Granny's pride and joy,' he said. 'It was originally the kitchen garden to supply vegetables and fruit to the house. In the old days, they also grew herbs for medicinal purposes. We still grow herbs there for the restaurant. And although it's now mainly a flower garden, you might have noticed fruit trees espaliered onto the walls.'

She laughed. 'I don't know much at all about gardening. Or what *espaliered* means. But I sensed a feeling of peace and fulfilment in there. In winter it has a certain bare beauty. It must be awesome covered in snow. But in summer, it must be delightful to sit on one of those stone benches and contemplate.'

'Granny grows lavender and roses and other scented plants there, because she thinks that way, too. She chooses plants with texture and others that attract butterflies. There's a fountain, too, emptied now so it doesn't freeze. She calls it her sensory garden.'

'Not that you get much time for sitting in there contemplating, I should imagine. Not with your hotel empire.'

'You're right. I don't.' But as a young boy he'd liked to hide in there behind the walls at the end of the school holidays, hoping they wouldn't be able to find him to take him back to boarding school. 'I'm walking down through the lawns to the wild garden if you'd like to join me.'

'Wild garden?' she said as she fell into step beside him. He didn't feel he had to hold her hand as there wasn't anyone to see them. Strangely enough, though, an inner compulsion made him want to reach out for her hand. Instead, he kept his hands firmly shoved into his coat pockets.

'An area that's been sown as a natural meadow. It attracts butterflies and wildlife like hedgehogs. It was my grandfather's idea. The Manor gardens are…were…his passion. He told me it was difficult for him to deal with strangers living in his home when they first opened it as a hotel. So the gardens became his domain.'

'How did you feel?'

'I don't remember it any other way,' he said. 'Guests tended to be nice to a little boy, so I was fine with it. Sometimes I got to play with children staying here and I liked that.'

'Liked it enough to become a hotel tycoon yourself when you grew up?'

'There's that,' he said, not wishing to be drawn in to further conversation about his childhood. Or the years spent relentlessly proving himself as a success in his own right.

'It must have been an amazing place to grow up in,' she said, looking around her at the formal gardens and the lawn that ran down to a rise from where the sea was visible.

'It was,' Oliver said. Which was why he would do everything in his power to keep Longfield Manor in the family. 'I hear you're doing brilliantly with the Christmas decorations.'

Marissa smiled. 'A report from Edith, no doubt? She's been great. No interrogation about possible birth dates of the great-grandchildren.'

Oliver laughed. 'I'm glad to hear that.'

'Seriously, she's just letting me get on with my job supervising the crew while she does her own thing with the family heirlooms.'

'I love Christmas at Longfield Manor,' Oliver said, looking around him. 'The happiest memories of my life are here and the happiest of all are from Christmas. I hope you're enjoying taking part in it.'

'About that.' Marissa came to a halt next to him. 'Before you go any further, there's something you need to know about me.'

Oliver frowned. What could possibly have brought that serious expression to her face? 'Fire away,' he said.

'I don't celebrate Christmas,' she said bluntly. 'In answer to your question, while I'm enjoying the job and liking the people I'm working with, Christmas itself leaves me cold.'

Oliver was so taken aback, he struggled for the right words. 'Is it your religion?'

She shook her head. 'Nothing to do with that. You spoke about memories… Well, my memories of Christmas aren't that great. My most recent ones, anyway.'

'But…but everyone loves Christmas,' he said.

'Many people don't celebrate Christmas,' she said. 'And there are people who find it stressful, or feel lonely and left out at this time of year.'

'Point taken. But you…?' Did she have an unhappy childhood? Abusive parents? He realised how very little he knew about her.

'I have my reasons, and I don't want to talk about them,' she said, looking at the ground. 'But I thought you needed to know why I don't wax enthusiastic about

Christmas. That doesn't stop me appreciating the beauty of the decorations we're putting up or the deliciousness of the menu. This Scrooge will do as good a job for you as any Christmas fan, I promise.'

'I appreciate that,' he said. 'But why did a self-professed Scrooge take on the job?'

'To help out Caity. She's my best friend.'

'Does she know how you feel about Christmas?'

'Yes.'

'So why did she choose you to replace her?'

'Because she trusts me to do every bit as good a job as she would to make this Christmas special for Longfield Manor.'

'Did you resent coming here and immersing yourself in Christmas?' He didn't like that thought at all.

'Not for a minute,' she said. 'And I'm enjoying being here.' She looked up at him and her eyes danced. 'Including pretending to be your girlfriend. That adds an edge to the job to make it even more enjoyable. Everyone is very interested in us, by the way. I've had to field lots of questions.' She put up her hand. 'Don't worry, I've stuck to the script.'

'I've been in my office for most of the day and have managed to avoid any questioning. Although both Cecil and Priya made a few less than subtle hints that they were interested in our story.'

'I think the staff might feel it would be out of place to question you about your personal life. You can seem… forbidding.'

He bristled. 'I'm the boss. It comes with the role.'

'Of course. But remember you're meant to be madly

in love. At the mention of your lover's name, you might want to soften a tad. Maybe show a hint of a goofy grin.'

He drew himself up to his full height. 'Me? A goofy grin? I don't do goofy.'

'You could try.' A mischievous smile tilted her lips and exposed that delightful dimple.

Oliver gave an exaggerated grin and he rolled his eyes at the ridiculousness of it.

She laughed. 'That's terrible and you know it. If you can't do goofy you need to try at least a gentling of your expression. You have resting stern face.'

She took a step closer to him and walked the fingers of her right hand up his arm to his shoulder. He was hyperaware of her touch, of her rose-and-vanilla scent.

'Now, look down at me with the dazed and besotted expression of a man in love. A man so in love he has brought a woman to his childhood home for the very first time.'

Oliver tried. And tried again. But he knew he was only achieving a grimace. He shrugged.

'Okay, call that a fail,' said Marissa. 'Why not try to picture someone who you were in love with and recall how you felt when you looked into her face.'

Oliver swallowed hard. 'I... I can't do that,' he said. He shook his head. 'I just can't do it.'

'Because you're not good at imagining?' Marissa paused. 'Or...or because you've never been in love?'

'Right the second time,' he managed to choke out. He saw from her expression that perhaps this wasn't an answer that reflected well on a thirty-two-year-old man.

'You've never been in love?' She sounded incredulous.

'Never. Attracted. Infatuated. Interested. But no, not in love.'

'Oh,' she said with a frown. 'But you're handsome, rich, nice. Women must be falling over themselves to date you.'

She called him *nice*? That wasn't a word often used to describe him. Oddly enough, he liked it. 'True,' he said without arrogance. After all, it was the truth. 'But that doesn't mean I've fallen in love with any of them.'

'I see,' she said. 'I wasn't expecting that. No wonder you can't fake it, then.'

'What about you?'

'Have I ever been in love?' Her perfectly shaped eyebrows rose.

'Yes.' He found himself holding his breath for her answer.

'Well, yes. A couple of times. But it didn't work out either time. Then there was—' She stopped.

'There was…' he prompted.

She didn't meet his eyes. 'Another time. When I was a young teenager I fell wildly, irrationally in love with a boy who…who didn't even notice me. I…guess I could put that down to infatuation. Kid stuff.' Her mouth set into a tight line at what seemed to be a painful memory. She opened her mouth as if to say something else but evidently decided against it.

'Infatuation can come easily,' he said, for want of saying anything more meaningful.

Had he consciously resisted love? He'd been so rejected by his parents he could see how that could have put a lock on his feelings. Or had his determination to succeed as a hotelier blocked anything and anyone that could get in the way? Could he have grown to love Sonya if given the chance? Or had what he'd felt for her been classified as infatuation?

He started to walk again and Marissa walked beside him. It was getting colder by the minute and her breath fogged in the sharp, late-afternoon air.

'What about someone else you loved?' she asked. 'We've got quite an audience back at the Manor. Can you manage to conjure up feelings to give authenticity to our mock-relationship?'

He realised the only people who had loved him unconditionally and whom he had loved in return were his grandparents. But that was a very different kind of love. And it was that love for them that was behind his determination to ensure the happiest of Christmases for his grandmother. Marissa was talking about romantic love, something entirely foreign and unfamiliar to him.

She stopped walking and he came to a halt near her. 'What about a pet? A dog or cat or horse? I adored my cat. She was old when I inherited her along with my flat from my godmother, so I didn't have her for long. But I loved her so much. If I think about her, I think love would show in my eyes.'

He stared at her. 'What? You think it would work if I called up the love I had for my dog?' He laughed. 'Seriously? You want me to fake a goofy grin with memories of my dog? Who I did love a lot, by the way. He was actually Grandpa's dog, but he was mine when I was here.'

'Er, it's a thought,' she said.

He turned her around to face him. 'So to evoke the required emotion, I look into your face and imagine you're Rufus, my black Labrador?'

Her eyes widened, she bit her lip and she laughed—an awkward, half-speed kind of laugh. 'Not one of my best ideas. Sorry. Scratch that one.'

She was obviously embarrassed, and he didn't want her to feel worse by saying anything else. Although the memory of the best-ever dog Rufus, who'd lived a good long life before succumbing to old age, did warm his heart. Grandpa had been feeling his years at the time, and they'd decided as a family not to get another puppy. But one day, if he ever settled down, he knew he'd want a black Labrador.

He and Marissa turned and walked back to the house. He was disconcerted to find that when he looked into her face, he couldn't conjure up images of past infatuations or even women he'd liked. Because the only face he was remotely interested in seeing was Marissa's own.

He also realised that with her talk of goofy grins and love and infatuation and dogs, she had diverted the conversation quite away from herself and her loathing of Christmas. What had happened there?

# CHAPTER SEVEN

OLIVER SAT AT his personal table in the hotel dining room. The staff knew it was his exclusively for the times he chose not to dine in his private quarters. Some of the guests gave him discreet nods, but most of them would have no idea he was the grandson of the owners of Longfield Manor and owner of the most fashionable hotels in London.

That gave him the opportunity to check on service. Every night he'd sat here, he'd seen exemplary service and high levels of guest satisfaction. His table, laid with the same fine but not fussy linen and china as the other tables, was in a secluded corner of the large, welcoming room. A fire blazed in the massive medieval fireplace at one end, emanating warmth and cosiness.

Oliver was dining here tonight with Marissa. He was early and she was spot on time. As she stepped tentatively into the room, looking around her—looking for *him*—he caught his breath. She looked sensational in a black dress that hugged her curves and ended above her knees. Her jeans and trousers had hinted at long, shapely legs, and his guess was now confirmed by the dress and sky-high black stilettos. Yet, her look was subtle, in keeping with her role as a consultant. If she hadn't been pretending to be his girlfriend, might she have kept her hair tied back from her face? Instead, she'd let it tumble below her shoulders, thick and luxuriant, glinting with highlights from the chandeliers. How would it feel to run his hands through it?

She spoke a few words to the maître d' who, with a flourish, led her towards Oliver's table. As she approached, Oliver got up to greet her. The maître d' made a fuss of her, pushing in her chair, making sure she was comfortable, shaking out her table napkin onto her lap. The older man had been with the hotel for years, and Oliver recognised the gleam of speculation as he sat his *girlfriend* opposite him.

Her blue eyes looked even bluer, outlined with dark make-up, and her lips were defined with deep red lipstick. He was often in proximity to beautiful, glamorous and famous women as The Pierce Group hotels were the current cool places to be seen in London. But not one of those women could hold a candle to Marissa. His heart started to thud. He couldn't let her know how attracted he was to her. That wasn't part of the charade.

'You look very beautiful,' he said slowly, his gaze taking in every detail of her appearance. The neckline of her dress revealed the swell of her breasts, an amethyst pendant nestling between them.

*Lucky necklace.*

As her boyfriend it would be *expected* of him to compliment her. But just being him, Oliver Pierce single guy, he found he *wanted* to tell her how beautiful she was.

'Thank you.' She smiled. That cute dimple was a well-placed punctuation mark to her lovely face. 'I thought

I'd better up my game if I'm to pass muster as your girl-friend.'

'You have no cause for concern in that regard,' he said hoarsely.

*She was super-hot.*

'As long as you approve.'

'I approve,' he said wholeheartedly.

Her eyes widened. 'Well done!'

He frowned. 'Well done?'

'That look. I see emotion. I see affection. I see every-thing we discussed earlier. You've got it.' Her eyes nar-rowed. 'Are you channelling your feelings towards your dog Rufus? Is it because I'm wearing black?'

Oliver laughed. 'Of course not. I'm just acting. Play-ing a role.' What had she seen in his eyes? What had he revealed about how he felt seeing her so sexy and viva-cious?

'Well, Academy award for you,' she said. 'There should be no trouble convincing people we're in a real relationship.'

He didn't like to say that his reaction to her had noth-ing to do with love but everything to do with lust. There could be no doubt he liked her more with every minute he spent with her. But liking someone plus being at-tracted to her did not equate to love—even the stirrings of love. Not that he and love and Marissa had anything to do with it. Would ever have anything to do with it. This was all pretend.

He indicated the menus on the table. 'Shall we start with a cocktail?'

'A mocktail for me, please. I never drink alcohol while I'm working.'

'You're not working now.'

'Aren't I?' She leaned across the table close to him and lowered her voice to a murmur. 'I'm on girlfriend duty, remember.'

'Point taken.'

She was doing the extra job for which she'd refused payment. And so far, she was doing it brilliantly. But even though he'd devised the whole scheme, something started to rankle with him. This gorgeous woman—more than one head in the restaurant had turned to admire her as she'd made her way across the room to his table—equated spending time with him as a chore. Perhaps he was the one who needed to lift his game.

He ordered mocktails for them both.

Marissa held the folder in her hand without looking at the carefully curated menu, which highlighted local produce. 'What a treat,' she said. 'This room is amazing. And the food sounds fabulous. I'm going to have a hard time deciding what to eat.'

'The food is excellent, even if I say so myself,' he said. 'But you haven't read the menu yet.'

'I don't need to. I had a quick meeting with the head chef today about the Christmas menus. He ran me through the menu choices for tonight. My mouth was watering by the time he'd got through the appetisers.'

The good-looking French chef was a notorious flirt, and Oliver was surprised at the sudden flare of jealousy that seared through him at the thought of Jean Paul turning on the charm for Marissa. He dismissed it immediately as foolishness. Besides, he knew Jean Paul was devoted to his wife and two young sons.

'Jean Paul is an excellent chef. We are fortunate to have him with us.'

'He told me how much he loves the lifestyle here for his family.'

Good. No flirting with Oliver's *girlfriend*, then. Jean Paul's job was safe. Oliver gritted his teeth. He couldn't believe he'd entertained that thought for even a second. He wasn't a jealous guy. And Marissa wasn't really his girlfriend. As a hotelier, if he had to choose between a highly regarded and sought-after chef and a woman, the woman wouldn't even get a look-in.

*But if that woman was Marissa?*

He couldn't go there, and was shocked at the direction his thoughts had taken him.

Marissa looked across to Oliver, darkly handsome in a charcoal-grey shirt. He'd obviously shaved to keep the stubble on his chin at bay. He must be a twice-a-day shave man. She'd read somewhere that meant high levels of testosterone. A shiver of awareness ran through her at the thought.

Why did he have to be so darn handsome? And such good company. Keeping up the fake-girlfriend thing in front of other people was stressful; there was no doubt about that. She had to be on the alert not to let the mask slip with an inadvertent comment or response that would reveal they were lying—there was no other word for it— about their relationship. Yet, when she was alone with him, she felt relaxed and enjoyed their conversations. Not to mention she was still wildly attracted to him. Good looks aside, he seemed so different from when he'd been six- teen. Did her concept of him, forged in teenage angst, no longer fit the man he was now? Twice today she'd started to tell him about their past acquaintanceship but twice couldn't find the courage to continue. But did it matter?

They ordered from the menu. For a starter, she chose the wild mushroom tart followed by the trout with almond butter. Oliver ordered the lime-cured salmon and the herbed fillet of beef. She'd been very impressed with Jean Paul, the chef, and wanted to see if the meals tasted as good as they sounded. Caity had, of course, already done a tasting of the proposed Christmas menus along with Edith, so that was one less thing to worry about.

Oliver sat back in his chair. 'I have to keep reminding myself that I only met you for the first time this morning.'

*Not quite the first time.*

'I feel as though I've known you for longer. As if we've put a week's worth of getting to know you into one day.'

'Funny, I was thinking the same thing. I guess it's because we had to accelerate the process to make it believable that we're a couple.'

'That must be it,' he said, not sounding totally convinced.

'It makes our relationship seem more authentic and that's all that counts, isn't it?'

She wondered if there was any chance of a continuing friendship or acquaintanceship of any kind between her and Oliver, or even with Edith whom, despite her outrageous comments, she had already become quite fond of. But that was unlikely, she thought. Although if she did a good job of this—of Christmas, of faking it—she could at least ensure Caity's ongoing business with The Pierce Group. And that was the sole reason she was here, wasn't it?

No, after pretend kissing that had seemed only too real, it would be impossible to see Oliver again after this was over and act normally. She would probably never see him again. And she wasn't sure how she felt about that.

'You have very good online reviews for Longfield Manor,' she said.

'You looked them up?'

'Before I got here.'

'There are many other letters and testimonials, too, from guests who aren't into the internet,' he said.

'That must be very gratifying.'

'It is, especially for Granny. A lot of guests feel a personal connection to this place.'

'My favourite review was one that said the hotel was like a home away from home, only a very posh home.'

Oliver laughed. 'I like that. It's just what we want them to think. The home-away-from-home bit, I mean.'

'Posh without being intimidating,' she said.

Again, she thought about what it must be like to grow up in surroundings like this. And how clever his grandparents had been to turn around their fortunes by transforming their home into a hotel.

'Of course it's posh but I don't think of it that way. It's home.'

An exceedingly posh home. 'How long have your family lived here?'

'Since the early nineteenth century. Going back to then, my ancestors were industrialists who cashed in on the railway boom. No blue blood but plenty of money and quick to seize an opportunity. They had good taste in real estate. I don't remember it but, by all accounts, the London townhouse was also very grand. I know my mother was devastated when it was sold.'

'And now there are your hotels in London. It must be in the blood.'

'Perhaps,' he said with a slight smile.

'Talking of posh, I loved the old suitcases that store some of the decorations. Your ancestors were very well travelled.'

'They're amazing relics, aren't they? From an era where travel was leisurely, not just trying to get from A to B as quickly as possible.'

'In those days it would have taken weeks to get to India or Australia.'

'I would be too impatient for that,' he said.

'Me, too,' she said. 'Have you travelled much?'

'Not as much as I'd have liked to. Establishing my business has always been my priority. Travel has mostly involved staying in other company's hotels to see how they worked and to size up the competition.'

'So you're a workaholic?'

'And proud of it.'

She would be proud, too, looking at what he had achieved. She wondered what motivated him to be so driven. His childhood, perhaps? She didn't dare ask.

Their meals arrived and the food lived up to its descriptions and more. It was so delicious she wanted to savour the taste, rather than chat. Jean Paul was a genius. Living at Longfield Manor for another six days was not going to be a hardship.

'Pudding?' asked Oliver.

'Not tonight, thank you, tempting as that menu is,' she said. 'I had an early start followed by a big day. And my Christmas tree designer will be arriving early in the morning tomorrow so I should turn in soon.'

'A Christmas tree designer. Is that a thing?'

'It is for Andy. He's made a career of it and he's in great demand. I was only able to book him as he had a last-minute cancellation because of a fire on the site where he was scheduled to be working.'

'Lucky us,' said Oliver.

'Do I detect a note of sarcasm there?'

'Certainly not. I respect any designer. My hotels wouldn't be the successes they are without the talented designers who work with me. They excel at Christmas trees and make sure everything they do fits with the over-all design vision for the interiors.'

'Whereas here there's a wonderful mishmash of old and new, family heirlooms and the new decorations Caity commissioned to be unique to Longfield Manor.'

'You're okay working with them? The Christmas dec-orations, I mean.'

She felt her expression shut down as it did when Christ-mas was mentioned. 'Of course,' she said.

Oliver paused before speaking as if he was carefully choosing his words. 'Is there a reason you don't celebrate Christmas?'

'Not one I care to discuss,' she said, aware of the chill that had crept into her voice.

Why had he ruined such a thoroughly pleasant eve-ning by bringing up her aversion to Christmas? Did he expect that she'd happily spill some answers? She could predict what would come next if she did so. Inevitably, the person she'd confided in would try to change her mind. Why would Oliver be any different? This whole place, him included, was happy-clappy about Christmas.

She got up from the table. 'Thank you for a marvellous dinner. But I really need to be getting up to my room.'

Oliver rose from his chair. 'Let me escort you.'

'I can manage on my own, thank you,' she said.

He came around to her side of the table. 'I'm your boyfriend, remember?' he said in a low voice.

'Sorry. How could I forget?' she murmured as she put her hand mock-possessively on his arm.

*Just don't forget even for a second that this—he—isn't real.*

Marissa wasn't sure what to say as Oliver walked beside her up that magnificent staircase to her room on the first floor. There was a small guest elevator, but she was determined not to ever take it and miss out on an opportunity to take the stairs and think about the grand past of the manor house.

In silence he walked down the corridor beside her, until they reached her room. Marissa pulled the old-fashioned brass key to the room out of her purse. 'Here I am,' she said, her voice coming out as an awkward croak. Why had he asked her about Christmas? They'd been getting on so well.

'Room eight,' Oliver said. 'That sounds so mundane, doesn't it? When my grandparents started the hotel, Granny had the idea she'd name each room after a Dorset wildflower.'

'A lovely idea.'

'She thought so, too. She started off with Honeysuckle, Snowdrop and Primrose. But when it came to Butterwort and Bogbean she decided to pass on the idea.'

'Seriously?'

'That's how she tells it.'

'The Bogbean Room wouldn't have quite the same cachet, would it?' Marissa laughed. But Oliver just smiled.

'You have a delightful laugh,' he said.

'Do I?' she said.

'Your face lights up. And your eyes, well, they dance. I never knew what that expression meant until I saw you laugh.'

'Oh,' she said, flushing, not sure what else to say.

She looked up to him—even in her high heels he was taller—seeking words for an answer that never came. His expression was serious; his green eyes darkened. She was conscious of her own breathing, the accelerated beat of her heart, his stillness. 'Marissa,' he finally said, her name hanging in the air of the silent, empty corridor. 'I appreciate so much what you're doing for me, for my family. Especially since you don't celebrate Christmas. If I get it right, you don't actually *like* Christmas.'

She put up her hand to stop him. 'Oliver, I—'

'The whys and wherefores of that are totally your own business. I'm sorry I brought it up over dinner and I won't ask you again.'

She didn't drop her gaze from his face, sensed his genuine remorse.

'Thank you,' she said.

She couldn't stop looking up at him, drawn to him as if mesmerised. Her breath came faster at the intensity of his gaze. He traced a finger down the side of her face, a simple gesture that felt like an intimate caress. She reached up to take his hand, not sure whether she meant to run her tongue along his finger or push it away. Instead, she laid her own fingers across his, keeping him close.

Then his mouth was on hers and he was kissing her. There was no need for him to kiss her, no witnesses in that corridor who could attest that their relationship was genuine. There was nothing pretend or fake about this kiss and she should push him away. But she didn't want to stop. She wanted to kiss him, to kiss him hard.

*To kiss him for real.*

She returned the pressure of his mouth with hers and wound her arms around his neck. He pulled her closer and deepened the kiss. Desire pulsed through her. She wanted him. He wanted her, too, she could tell.

She wanted more than kisses. When she thought of it, she'd always wanted him—right back to when she'd been fourteen years old. Back then her longing for him had gone no further than the hope of exciting, sweet kisses and cuddles. Her virginal imagination had taken her no further. Now her thoughts so easily took her to what would happen if she pushed her door open and they stumbled, kissing and caressing, into her room with the door slammed shut behind them.

There would be no going back.

Everything would change.

The game would be for real—and she would not come out the winner.

She broke away from the kiss, pushed him away, took a deep, steadying breath, felt her cheeks flushed. 'If we continue kissing like this we both know where it will lead us. And I don't want to go there. That's not part of the deal. To work with you after that would be so awkward.' She wanted him too much to play with the flickering flames of intense desire.

'We could make it work,' he said hoarsely.

'No,' she said, and he immediately let her go. 'I'm attracted to you. I think you know that. But I don't do one-night stands or casual flings.'

'Understood,' he said as he took a step back. She noted he didn't say he didn't do casual, either. But then that didn't surprise her. He'd made his stance on relationships very clear.

She wrapped her arms around her middle as if barricading herself. 'So far, we're doing well with the fake relationship for the sake of your grandmother. I'm happy to continue that. But now I want to say good-night, and when I see you tomorrow it should be as if this had never happened. Please.'

# CHAPTER EIGHT

AFTER A RESTLESS NIGHT, when sleep had proved elusive, Marissa was glad of the distraction provided by her friend Andy, the Christmas tree designer, and his visit to Longfield Manor. She and Andy had first worked together years ago when they were on staff at the same company.

Andy's full-on personality wouldn't allow time for regretful thoughts about Oliver. She was so drawn to him, the attraction so magnetic. Should she have invited him to her bed and taken the chance on something wonderful but ephemeral? Was she being overprotective of her feelings? On balance, she decided she'd made the right decision last night. It was hard enough to keep on an even keel surrounded by Christmas let alone being immersed in emotional angst if she went too far with Oliver. He had an immense power to hurt her. Even his thoughtless insults as a teenager had caused long-lasting pain.

She stood patiently by while Andy chastised her for not letting him go out to the Christmas tree farm to choose and cut the trees himself.

'I know you're Mr Perfectionist, and like total control over the tree,' she said. 'But this has all been a bit last-minute. I'm standing in for Caity,' she explained.

'I get it, you had to help Caity out,' Andy replied. 'And the bonus is the hot boss.' He made a lascivious face. 'How does he identify?'

'He. Him. Heterosexual.'

'You go, girl,' Andy said.

Marissa was about to totally deny any interest in the CEO of The Pierce Group. But she quickly pulled herself up. *No slips.* She was meant to be Oliver's girlfriend.

She smiled the fakest of smiles. 'We're together, actually.'

'Together as in *together*?'

'Yes. I'm dating him. Have been since early November. We met at—' There she went, overembellishing. 'Never mind where we met.'

'Congratulations.'

Marissa couldn't resist adding something vaguely truthful. 'I'm keeping quiet about it as Oliver isn't…isn't into long-term relationships.'

'And you are?'

'One day, yes,' she said, surprising herself. She hadn't thought she was ready.

'And you don't want to put pressure on him?'

'No. It's not like that. I don't want to be embarrassed when it ends.'

'You pessimist! Is it good to anticipate the end when you've barely started?'

'Less painful that way when it doesn't work out,' she said.

It would end and end soon. *Because it wasn't real.* And already she knew she would be sad when she had to say goodbye to her fake boyfriend. In spite of her longtime grudge, she liked him.

'If you say so,' he said, not seeming convinced. 'Now, take me to the Christmas trees.'

Marissa was on her own in the reading room, a drawing room also called the quiet room. It was one of the smaller public rooms where guests were encouraged to take time out to read, listen to music through headphones, or even nap in the comfortable sofas and easy chairs. The beautifully proportioned room was decorated, as everywhere in Longfield Manor, with impeccable taste in traditional English country house style with Edith's unique twist on it.

Marissa stood on the jewel-toned Persian carpet, just her and a Christmas tree, the smallest of the five trees to be placed around the hotel. Andy had started the decoration and had left strict instructions on the precise order in which to place each bauble, bead and star in exact colour combinations, a measured distance from the end of the branch.

It wasn't she who was meant to be actually dressing the tree with such precision. She wouldn't volunteer for the task in a million years. In fact, she'd only been in this room to introduce two of the temporary student staff to Andy and leave them to it. However, Andy had been so impressed with the students' design skills and willingness to learn, he'd spirited them away to assist him in dressing the tallest of the trees. That giant fir would tower in festive grandeur over the living room and be the star of the Christmas celebrations. He'd asked Marissa to watch the room and keep guests out until he returned with another team.

She was wearing black jeans and a smart textured

jacket and she began to feel uncomfortable. The room
was very warm, stuffy even, with a wood fire burning
in the fireplace. Marissa hated the smell of pine needles.
The scent from the tree pervaded the room, no matter
how far she stood away from it. There was no escape
from it. She put her hands to her head as it began to
overwhelm her.

The sharp acrid smell of pine permeated her lungs,
making her feel dizzy and disoriented. Her breath came
in short gasps. She clutched on to the back of a high-
backed chair. Nausea rose in her throat and she swallowed against it.

On Christmas Eve her parents had been transporting
the Christmas tree home on the top of the car when the
accident had happened. The pine needles had scattered
all over the car, all over them. Afterwards, she and her
brother, stricken by grief and disbelief, had wanted to see
where it had happened. Pine needles and broken glass
had been all over the ground where the car had left the
road and smashed into a fence. When she collected her
parents' possessions from the hospital, her mother's handbag had been full of the needles and they'd been scattered
over her father's favourite tweed jacket.

Marissa started to tremble and shake. She had to get
out of this room. As she pushed herself away from the
chair she stumbled and tripped. But strong arms were
there to stop her from falling, to hold her tight.

'Marissa, what happened? Are you okay?'

*Oliver.*

Oliver had thought Marissa was about to faint and hurt
herself on the way down. Thank heaven he had come into

the room, looking for her, when he did. As he held her tight in the circle of his arms, he felt a powerful urge to protect and comfort her. In this moment, she seemed so vulnerable, she who presented as formidably efficient and self-contained. She clung to him not just, he thought, for physical balance, but also for emotional support. What had happened here?

'Let it out,' he said. 'If you need to cry, do so.'

'I'm not crying,' she said, her voice muffled against his shoulder. 'I'm really not.'

He held her in silence, aware of her softness, her rose-and-vanilla scent, how much he liked having her there so close to him. He resisted the urge to drop a kiss on the top of her head. That would be too intimate, too personal, for a woman who had set very clear boundaries.

Finally, her breathing became more even. Marissa pulled away and looked up at him. She was very pale, in spite of the warmth of the room. There was no evidence of tears, but her make-up was smudged around her eyes and, without thinking, he reached down to tenderly wipe away the mascara smear with his finger.

'Thank you,' she said. 'And...and I'm sorry.'

He frowned. 'Sorry? Sorry for what?'

'For having you see my panic attack.'

'Panic attack? Is that what was happening? There's no need to apologise. I thought you were going to faint and fall, possibly get injured. I'm so glad I came into the room at the right time.'

'Thank you,' she said. Those unshed tears made her eyes seem even bluer. 'I'm glad you were here, too.'

'Are you feeling okay now?' he said, reluctant to step back from her. They were still close. At the same time, he was wary of treading where she didn't want him to be. 'Did you get bad news?'

'Not really. Not…not new bad news. It…it's the smell of the Christmas tree. The pine needles. They bother me.'

'An allergy?'

'In a way.'

'It's stuffy in here and the smell of the pine needles is very strong. We could open a window, but it would quickly get icy cold. It's bitter out there. They're predicting snow for Christmas. Besides, you wouldn't want wind coming through the window when you're decorating a tree in here.'

'It's not me dressing the tree, it's Andy.'

'So why are you in here by yourself?'

'Long story. But Andy asked me to keep the room free of guests and to keep an eye on these fragile, valuable decorations. I can't leave here until he gets back.'

'Why don't I ask Priya to send someone in here to take over guard duty, while I take you off for a cool drink or a coffee?'

'I don't want anyone to see me like this,' she said shakily.

'Let me take you to my apartment, where you can have all the privacy you want. If you feel like telling me why the scent of pine needles bothers you so much, you can. If not, you can take some time to get yourself back together and get on with your day.'

Her shoulders went back, and she stiffened. 'Are you worried this…this incident might affect the quality of my work? I assure you it won't. I'm on call twenty-four hours while I'm here.'

'I know how committed you are. I'm certainly not concerned about that. But I am worried about you.'

'Like a good fake boyfriend should,' she said with a curve of her lips that wasn't quite a smile, her dimple the merest indentation.

'I wouldn't be much of a fake boyfriend if I didn't look after you, would I? But just as one human being to another, you're distressed and in need of a break and perhaps something to eat.'

'Ugh, I couldn't eat a thing,' she said, shaking her head. 'But I like the idea of going somewhere out of sight. And, to be honest, I'm curious to see the private areas of the building. I feel I owe you an explanation for why I collapsed all over you. And I'm very grateful to you for catching me.'

Within minutes of Oliver's calling Priya, she was there. Priya looked curiously at the somewhat dishevelled Marissa but, being a perfectly trained hotel manager, she didn't say anything except to reassure them that the room would be guarded until Andy returned with a new team of decorators.

Oliver kept his arm around her as he escorted Marissa to the private wing of the Manor at the east end. His grandmother still lived in the large house-sized residence fitted out for her and Grandpa when they'd converted their country house into a hotel. They'd sold off the farmland that had still been part of the estate to fund the conversion. As a child, he had lived there with them on his frequent extended visits, then permanently when his mother had left the country. When he'd turned twenty-one, his grandparents had given him his own spacious apartment in their private wing. They'd been so good to him. Paid for the law degree studies he'd dropped out of, as he'd found hotels to be so much more interesting.

Helped bankroll the startup of his business. He could never repay them for what they'd done for him. Everything he'd ever been able to do for them had been worth it. Even pretending that Marissa was his girlfriend.

He showed Marissa to the oversized, squashy sofa—big enough for a tall man to stretch out on. Marissa sat tentatively on the edge, obviously ill at ease.

'Granny will be delighted I've dragged you to my lair so we can be on our own,' he said, sitting down next to her.

'Do you really believe Edith thinks that?'

'Of course she does. She'll be disappointed when you return to Room eight.'

'Which I now can't help thinking of as the Bogbean Room.' He was pleased to see her tentative smile—more of the dimple this time.

'Don't let Granny hear you say that. She would be horrified.'

'You think so?'

'I know so.'

Marissa looked around her. 'Your apartment is amazing. I could fit three of my apartment into it. Impeccably created by Edith, I suppose?'

'I was twenty-one when I moved in. I had no say in how it looked. Granny kept in mind what she thought I'd like when she chose the furnishing and decoration. It was done in a simpler style than the rest of the private wing, more contemporary but still with a nod to the building's ancient bones. Fortunately, it turned out she was right. In fact, I incorporated some of her design ideas into my penthouse at Pierce Soho they suited me so well.'

'What if you hadn't liked what she did here?'

'I wouldn't have told her. No way would I have wanted to hurt her feelings.'

'You would have pretended to like it?'

'Yes.'

She paused for a beat. 'You're good at pretending.'

'So are you. We wouldn't be getting away with the fake-relationship thing if we weren't equally good at pretending.'

'True,' she said.

But he wasn't pretending about how attractive he found her, how compelling. He couldn't remember feeling like this about a woman, certainly not over the space of a few days. It surprised him.

'Coffee? Or something stronger?' he asked, getting up from the sofa.

'A big glass of water, please.'

As Oliver poured the water in the kitchen, he remembered their discussion on favourite foods. He took a block of dark Belgian chocolate from the pantry, broke it into pieces and presented it to her on a plate. 'This might also help,' he added.

'How can I resist a man who gives me chocolate?' she said, but her voice was still shaky, and her smile didn't light her eyes.

'You did tell me it was your favourite food,' he said.

Oliver watched as she nibbled on the chocolate. She savoured every bite with exaggerated pleasure. It made him wonder if there was anyone back in London to look after her when she needed a boost to low spirits. Not to look after her in a patriarchal male way; he suspected she'd run a mile from that. Not in a warm, family way, either, as he knew her parents were dead and so was her godmother. But in the way of someone who cared about her and had her best interests at heart. Someone to be her wingman—or wingwoman. Perhaps that was Caity, but her friend ran a thriving business and would soon be mothering twins. Not that it was likely Marissa would ask for her friend's help. He got the impression she was so fiercely independent, she would tell him she didn't need anyone to look after her, thank you very much. Not a commitment-phobe like him, that was for sure.

But as he thought about Marissa, he realised he didn't have anyone, either. He had staff at his beck and call at his own hotels and here at Longfield Manor. Call room service from his penthouse and anything he wanted would be delivered within minutes. And his grandmother jumped at any opportunity to dote on him. He still saw his schoolfriend Toby on occasion, but Toby was married with young children and his family was his focus. Marissa had an air of aloofness about her that might very well be, he thought, loneliness. Was he lonely? He was surrounded by people and his business took up every second of every day. He didn't have time to be lonely.

Marissa downed the water as if she hadn't drunk for a week, then put her glass down on the coffee table. 'Do you mind if I sit back on your sofa?' she said. 'It seems too perfect to use with all those cushions so precisely arranged. I don't dare disturb them.'

'Toss the cushions on the floor if you want to. I do. But, again, don't tell Granny. She's a cushion fanatic. Wait until you see my bedroom. There are a million cushions on the bed.'

*What had he said?*

An awkward silence hung between them at the impact of his words. Inwardly, he cursed himself. 'I didn't mean—'

'I don't think—'

'You're not interested in seeing my bedroom? Point taken. But I won't pretend I don't want to see you in my bedroom.' He paused. 'In my bed.'

She flushed high on her cheekbones. 'And I won't pretend that I wouldn't like to be there. In your bed.' She met his gaze directly. 'With you.'

His breath seemed to stop, and his heart hammered at the sensual thoughts she conjured. Knowing she could match him made him want her even more.

She shifted away from him on the sofa as she continued. 'But I don't do flings and you told me you don't have long relationships. I've decided I want commitment and everything that comes with that. What you might find boring. Security. Marriage. Even kids. Not now. Maybe not for a long time. But it's what I ultimately want. Whereas you're not interested in being tied down. We're looking for different things.'

'That's true,' he said, thinking how crass his words sounded being quoted back at him. Had he really said that to her? Yes, he had. Because he always made it clear to a woman that short-term was all he wanted and that he would pull the plug if awkward emotions developed or demands were made.

'Truth is, I want you, but I also like you,' she said. 'Having a fling with you would most likely not end well. And I don't want that. Besides, I don't want to jeopardise this good thing we're doing for Edith by making things awkward and uncomfortable between us. So can we not mention your bedroom again?'

Oliver nodded. He would be respectful and not try to argue. Even as at the same time he regretted the lost opportunity to see where that mutual attraction might take them.

'And I'll take you at your word that there are lots of cushions in there,' she added.

# CHAPTER NINE

IN TRUTH, Marissa ached to count the cushions on Oliver's bed. To throw them one by one onto the floor followed by every stitch of Oliver's clothing—and then her own.

What had Caity said about Oliver? *Movie-star handsome.*

With his black hair and green eyes he was that all right—but he was so much more than his good looks. She was drawn to him like she'd never been drawn to a man—except, that is, his sixteen-year-old self. Who could have predicted that arrogant boy would grow up to be so thoughtful? But she'd meant every word about keeping her distance from him.

She was so attracted to this man it would be easy to let her senses take over. To share glorious sex—and she was convinced it would be glorious—with him with no thought of tomorrow. And then where would she be? Exactly what she would appear to be at the end of this seven days—another discarded girlfriend. Only she wouldn't have been a real girlfriend, rather a pretend girlfriend with benefits.

*Aargh!* She felt her head was spinning, not from the pine needles but by the realisation that she could fall for Oliver in a big way. Actually fall in love with him—and that would be disastrous. All those danger signs that had been beeping at her from the moment she'd realised who he was and what he'd been to her as a teenager were now urgently flashing a warning.

*Protect your heart.*

He was keeping a respectable distance from her on the sofa. How ironic. If there was anyone there to see them, they would have to keep up the pretence of their fake relationship and he would quite probably have his arm around her. But when there was no one there, they could be what they really were to each other—he the boss, she the contract employee. A possibility of something else he could be crept into her mind—*a friend*. They were half-way there; she enjoyed his company so much. If they kept out of that bed with its multiple cushions, could she and Oliver end up friends? Before the thought had a chance to lodge in her brain she dismissed it. For her, it would have to be all or nothing with Oliver. Because of the reasons she'd give him, *all* was never going to happen. Just these remaining five days.

'Thank you for the chocolate, for looking after me,' she said. 'I feel so much better now. In fact, I feel a little foolish. I probably would have been fine without—'

'Me catching you when you fell? I don't think so.'

He moved closer to her on the sofa. She was acutely aware of his warmth, his strength, the spicy scent of him, how grateful she was that he was there.

'You'd had a shock of some kind. Are you ready to tell me about it?'

Marissa angled her knees so it was easier to face him and took a deep, steadying breath. His expression invited confidence; his eyes were kind and non-judgemental. No matter, she still hated sharing her story—it never got easier. 'You deserve an explanation,' she said. 'You were right about it being linked to why I don't like Christmas. Why I'm reputed to be a Scrooge and a Grinch.'

He frowned. 'Surely not? Do people really call you that?'

'Sadly, yes. And it's true. Though only a very few people know why.'

She gripped her hands tightly together in front of her and looked ahead, rather than at Oliver. She couldn't, after all, face the pity she knew she would see in his eyes. He had a stark, black modern clock on the wall opposite that suited the room perfectly as its metallic hand ticked relentlessly around the clock face. She was shocked to note the time—there was so much to be done—but this needed to be said.

'Christmas used to be a big deal in our family. There were just my parents and me, my brother Kevin and my grandmother. Nana used to join us for Christmas, too. But my parents being the warm, hospitable people they were, our house was also open to waifs and strays who didn't have family to go to or were away from home. The house would be decorated to the max, and my parents cooked for days to have the full-on traditional feast with all the trimmings. If you'd asked me then, you would have heard me say I adored Christmas.'

She turned back to look at Oliver. Noticed that he swallowed hard. She'd told him her parents had died, but not how they'd died. He must have guessed she was about to recount something awful. She forced herself to continue. It was always difficult for her to tell someone what had happened. 'Five years ago on Christmas Eve, my mother and father were returning home with the Christmas tree when they were killed in a car crash. My mother went instantly, my father died later in hospital, early on Christmas Day.'

Oliver gasped. He moved closer, reached out, untwisted her hands and enfolded them in his much larger ones. 'I'm sorry, Marissa.'

She felt comforted by his touch, understood how difficult it was to utter more than platitudes at times like these. 'It was an accident, a horrible accident.' She would never, ever forget the shock, disbelief and deep, wrenching pain she'd felt when she'd been notified.

'The police couldn't be sure exactly what happened, as my parents were on a back road with no cameras. It was raining. The narrow road was slippery. They were running late with their decorating because of work commitments. Did they swerve to avoid an animal on the road? Did the tree slip free of its moorings and slide off the car? Perhaps they were rushing, driving too fast, but whatever the reason, the car went off the road and crashed head-on into a very solid fence.'

Oliver's grip on her hands tightened. 'I have no words. I can't imagine how you must have felt.'

'Because it happened at Christmastime, I can never forget it. Christmas is the anniversary of my parents' deaths. There were pine needles everywhere. All through the wreckage of the car, through…through my parents' clothes. My dad still had a few pine needles in his hair when he was in hospital. The smell… I hate it. It brings back so many bad memories. Back there, in the reading room, the scent was so strong I felt overwhelmed.'

'No wonder. There are pine Christmas trees everywhere you look at this time of year.'

'Which is why I try to avoid them. I wish more people used artificial trees, although nothing looks as good as a real pine. But even a fake tree symbolises everything I lost that Christmas.' She paused. 'You know, both Kevin and I had offered to pick up a tree for them, but Mum and Dad insisted it was something they liked to do themselves. They'd made collecting the tree a ritual since their first year of marriage.'

'So you and Kevin tormented yourselves with endless *if-onlys*. If only you'd gone instead…if only—'

'We tormented ourselves with many regrets and re-criminations. As you can imagine, Christmas that year was hell. Organising funerals instead of festivities. The paperwork, the legalities, the pleasantries while accepting condolences, when all I wanted to do was crawl into a dark hole and howl.'

He squeezed her hand. 'My grandpa's death wasn't a tragic one like your parents'—'

'Every death is tragic when you lose someone you love.'

'But at least it was expected. Grandpa was eighty-seven with inoperable cancer. We knew we were going to lose him but that didn't make his loss any easier.' He paused. 'Granny was too distraught to handle the formalities, so I had to do it. Who knew how much time and effort was involved?'

'Every time I had to write down their details it was another blow, another reminder they were gone and I would never see them again. I was never that sure of the year of my father's birth when I was younger. I sure knew it after filling out all those forms. Then, just weeks after the accident, our grandmother died of a stroke brought on, the doctors said, by the shock of her daughter's death. My mother was her only child. As next of kin, I had to go through it all again for Nana.'

'Loss upon loss,' Oliver said hoarsely, his grip tightening over her hands. 'How did you bear it?'

'We didn't cope well. When it was all over, we were left with nothing—no family except distant cousins in Norfolk we barely know, and friends who didn't know what to say so stayed away. My brother is two years younger than me. He took it very hard. The next year he couldn't deal with the prospect of Christmas without Mum and Dad. He took off on a trip to Australia and never came back.'

'What do you mean, *never came back*?'

'He met a wonderful girl, Danni, and they got married. He lives in Sydney permanently now.'

'That seems like a happy ending, though.'

'For them, not for me. It meant I lost my brother, too. I know that makes me sound selfish, and I don't mean it to. I'm really happy for them, and she's awesome. But they're just so far away.'

'Have you been to see them in Australia?'

She felt like she should get up and walk around the room, instead of sitting there, static. But she didn't want to lose the comfort of Oliver's hands cradling hers.

'The second Christmas after my parents' deaths, I flew down to Australia, glad to get away from London and the memories. Sydney is an amazing city. We celebrated Christmas with Danni's family. Although everyone was very kind and welcoming, I felt like an outsider, an interloper. As well, a traditional northern hemisphere Christmas celebration in a hot Australian summer just didn't seem right. And it wasn't different enough for me to forget my memories of that terrible Christmas.'

'I thought Aussies had barbecues on the beach for Christmas?'

'Some might. But I was told many prefer the traditional turkey, plum pudding, brandy custard, mince pies, Brussels sprouts, the lot. I felt so sorry for Danni and her family slaving away in a hot kitchen. I might not like Christmas but to me it means winter, fires roaring in the fireplace, frost and the possibility of snow. Like here, in this beautiful place. No wonder guests flock here at this time of year.'

'Sydney gave you another bad Christmas experience? I hope that was the end of it.'

'There's more to come. Are you sure you want to hear?'

'I do,' he said. 'I want to understand you, Marissa. I'm beginning to appreciate what an effort it must have been for you to come here as a Christmas event planner.'

'I did it for Caity. I'd do anything to help her.' She didn't go into detail; that was Caity's business.

'I see that now. I appreciate your help even more.'

'And I...well... I'm really glad I came.'

*And got the chance to meet you.*

'Dare I ask what happened the next Christmas?'

'The next year I decided to lock myself away in my flat for Christmas and come out when it was all over. Then out of the blue, I got fired from my job on Christmas Eve. The marketing company I worked for decided to close its event planning division. My position was made redundant.'

'That sounds grim. Can they do that on Christmas Eve?'

'It's heartless but legal, apparently. My Grinchiness really set in then.'

He slowly shook his head. 'A series of awful things that just happened to occur at Christmas. I mean, it's not really the fault of Christmas, is it? More like coincidence.'

'It's jinxed. Christmas is jinxed for me.'

'You can't seriously mean that.'

'Then how do you explain that the next year—last Christmas—I caught my boyfriend kissing another woman under the mistletoe at his office party. Passionate kissing. Complete with spiteful triumph from his so-called *just a friend* colleague.'

'Awful. Was the boyfriend a serious relationship?'

'I was gutted. I really liked him. He was a client and initially I knocked him back when he started asking me out. But he persevered. When he was no longer my client, I finally said yes. I fell hard for him. We were talking about moving in together.'

'That's serious.'

'As serious as I've ever got. And another regret. Up until then I had a strict *no dating a client* policy. That's been put in place again, I can assure you.' Not that anyone had tempted her with thoughts of breaking it again. Until now.

'Me being the exception,' he said with a smile.

'My policy didn't cover fake dating.' There it was, under all the angst, an easiness between them she felt very comfortable with.

He let go of her hands and got up. 'Would you like that coffee now?'

'Yes, please,' she said, also getting up to follow him to his kitchen, which was at the end of the open-plan living room.

'Where would you have spent Christmas if you hadn't

come here?' he asked, as his impressive espresso machine steamed and hissed.

'I had flights booked to Nusa Lembongan, a small island off the east coast of Bali. Christmas isn't part of the culture there, so I figured I wouldn't be immersed in festive cheer like I would be in London. The tourist hotels cater for Christmas, but I don't think it would have been difficult for me to avoid any festivities.'

'Instead, you're here, working for me, immersed in our Christmas events.'

'And loving every minute of it.' She looked up at him. 'I mean that. Working here has been a revelation.'

'Except for incidents when you're confined to a stuffy room with a Christmas tree.'

'There's that,' she agreed. 'But look how chivalrously I was rescued.'

He laughed. 'And not just because I'm your fake boyfriend. Let's get that clear.'

She smiled. 'That's another problem with this job.'

'And what's that?'

'I can't include my stint as pretend girlfriend to the CEO on my résumé.'

'We might have to keep that one to ourselves.'

'I wholeheartedly agree,' she said. 'Also, I'd appreciate it if you didn't share what I've just told you with anyone else. You know, my history regarding Christmas and why I'm a Christmas-phobe.' It was a relief to have told him, but she didn't want other people to hear her story, including his grandmother, Edith.

'That's understood. It's entirely your business. But thank you for opening up to me about the tragedy in your past. You've suffered quite the litany of grief, too much for one person. Tell me about your godmother. Did she pass at Christmas, too?'

'No, she died before my parents did. My mother took her loss badly. They'd been friends since primary school. And, before you ask, my cat didn't die at Christmas, either.'

'That's something,' he said cautiously.

She couldn't help but laugh at his comment, which lightened the atmosphere.

Oliver opened his pantry to pull out a packet of Italian almond biscotti. 'I keep stocked up on snacks. Needless to say, this kitchen isn't used much. Not when I live in a hotel.'

'Lucky you. I'd never use my kitchen if I could eat Jean Paul's food rather than cooking it myself.' What a difference her meal last night had been to her rotation of ready meals warmed up in the microwave, or hastily constructed salads.

'One night we could have dinner sent up here rather than eat in the restaurant,' he suggested.

'Do you think that's wise?' she asked, thinking how very unwise it would be for her to be alone with him— particularly near his bed or the inviting sofa.

'Probably not if you want to continue resisting my attempts to seduce you,' he said with a wry twist to his mouth.

Marissa's heart skipped a beat at the thought of a full-on seduction by Oliver, but she managed an appropriate response. 'Restaurant it is, then.'

She sat on a high stool at the kitchen counter to drink her coffee and he stood opposite her. 'Oliver, now that I've done so much soul baring, can you tell me some more about yourself? If it's not too painful, that is.'

He bridled and that easy moment of repartee evaporated immediately. 'Why would it be painful?' He shrugged. 'My parents weren't around a lot of the time, but I didn't lack for anything.'

She didn't reply, just let a silence fall between them, and waited for him to speak.

'Okay, except for parental love,' he said finally in a self-mocking tone.

Heartbreaking, she thought. 'A lack of love from your parents is kind of serious,' she said.

'Fact is, my parents weren't ready to have a kid. They hadn't known each other for long when my mother fell pregnant. I believe my father had doubts I was his, until I turned out looking very like him. A baby hardly fitted with their lifestyle—a model and a rock musician. They'd go away for months at a time and leave me with my grandparents. My schooling could only be described as erratic.'

She hadn't expected that, not when he came from wealth, his mother a well-known model and socialite—this place their ancestral home.

What was that old saying? *It's better to be born lucky than rich.*

'That doesn't sound great,' she said, not sure what else she could say. How grateful she was for her stable upbringing with parents who loved each other and their children, whereas Oliver seemed to have had terrible luck in that area.

'When I was eight, they put me in boarding school.' She knew he'd been in boarding school when he was sixteen but not as young as that. He'd put down his coffee and she noticed his fists were tightly clenched by his sides.

'Eight? You were a baby. How was that?'

'By being sent away, I felt I was being punished, I didn't know what for. There was no actual abuse, but my years at boarding school didn't rate highly on the scale of my youthful experience,' he said.

The tight set of his jaw, the shadow that darkened his green eyes, told her not to probe any further. But she couldn't help shuddering. 'I can't imagine it would,' she said. She'd heard some traumatic stories about boys' private boarding schools; bullying, cruelty.

'The marriage was on and off with screaming fights then dramatic reconciliations. They finally divorced when I was thirteen. When I was fifteen my mother chased after a man to New Zealand and settled there.'

'She didn't take you with her?'

'I wasn't wanted,' he said baldly. 'Her excuse was that it was a bad time to interrupt my private schooling by moving to a different system.'

'I'm sorry, but that's out and out cruelty,' Marissa said fiercely.

'I suspect my mother lied about her age, and it didn't suit her to have people know she had a child my age. I was…inconvenient.'

'Of course you weren't inconvenient. Don't say that. It couldn't possibly be true.'

He sighed a weary sigh. 'Marissa, you weren't there.' His voice dripped with cynicism. 'All I can say is thank heaven for my wonderful grandparents.'

'No wonder you want to do everything you can to help Edith.'

'They were my real family. The reason I love Christmas at Longfield Manor was that my grandparents always made it special for me when I was a child, and even my self-centred parents made an effort to be here. Although one year neither of them showed up, without explanation. I waited all day for them.'

She wondered, as she had several times, about their conversation at dinner the night before. Oliver's confession that he had never been in love had surprised her. But if he hadn't received love from the people who were supposed to love him most, was he capable of giving love?

She slid off her stool and walked around to where he stood. 'You need a hug. For that sweet little boy. For that betrayed teenager. For the wonderful man you are now.'

She put her arms around him in a big hug. He hugged her back, powerful arms circling her. They stood there, close together for a long moment. Body to body. Arms wrapped around each other. He pulled back from the hug, their arms still around each other to look down into her face. 'Thank you,' he said.

'I'm sorry I made you dredge up uncomfortable memories,' she said.

'All in the past,' he said brusquely, with a *conversation over* stamp to his voice.

He looked down into her face, and she met his gaze unblinkingly. Her heart started to beat faster at his closeness. His face was already so familiar, those green eyes, his nose slightly crooked, his smooth olive skin, already at 11 a.m. darkly shadowed, his beautifully sculpted mouth. A mouth she knew felt so good against hers. A mouth she wanted to feel again for a dizzyingly pleasurable kiss. As she swayed towards him, her lips parted in anticipation. Nothing had ever felt better than being with this man.

* * *

Oliver's arms tightened around Marissa as he bent his head to kiss her. Her mouth yielded to his as she pressed herself close to him and kissed him back with passion and enthusiasm that matched his.

This wasn't pretend. It was as real as a kiss could be. Her kiss was as exciting, as arousing, as their other kisses, but this also soared to a somehow different level. He knew it was because of the emotional connection he now felt for her. He understood her so much better after her confessions of heartbreak and loss. And she seemed to understand him, too. After revisiting his painful memories of abandonment, her spontaneous hug had been just what he'd needed but he would never be able to ask for. Somehow, she had known that.

*He didn't want to let her go.*

Yet, he would have to. He didn't have what it took to make a woman like Marissa happy. And her happiness now seemed somehow his concern. There should be no further kisses, no talk of seduction. She'd been honest about what she wanted for her future. He couldn't even commit to having a dog in his life, let alone a wife and a child. His focus was on a relentless drive to succeed. Riding the wave of the popularity of The Pierce Group hotels made him strive for more. He was looking for sites to expand into New York. Romantic relationships had never been part of his life plan.

One former girlfriend had accused him of being damaged. Not that she'd known of the tumultuous on-and-off relationship with his parents, particularly his mother. The way Mummy would arrive laden with presents, swoop down on him and cover him with kisses. Until boredom—with motherhood, with him?—had set in. Then she'd depart on a modelling shoot or on an extended holiday to heaven knew where, and he wouldn't know when he'd next see her. It was the same story with his father, although truth be told his father had never been effusive with affection. If it hadn't been for the love and stability given by his grandparents, maybe he would indeed be damaged. Although it was true that he didn't trust easily and was wary of commitment. And that sometimes he felt an emptiness that no amount of work and casual dating could make go away. But was that so uncommon in men of his age?

Marissa broke the kiss. Reluctantly, he let her go. She stepped back. 'I…er…have to get back to work,' she said, her voice not quite steady.

He looked down into her face. She was flushed and breathless and so beautiful his heart contracted. Not only was she the most gorgeous, sexy woman he'd ever had the privilege of kissing, she was also a thoroughly lovely person. Kind. Fun. Loyal. He really liked her. He'd only known her for two days, yet his gut instinct was telling him—screaming at him—that this woman was different from any other woman he had met, that she could be special. His gut instinct had never let him down. He'd made good business decisions about people on less acquaintance than two days, by listening to it. Yet, this wasn't just about him, and the last thing he wanted to do was hurt her.

'Are you sure you're feeling okay now?' he asked.

'Quite sure,' she said. 'Again, thank you for getting me out of that room and looking after me. How did you know I was there?'

'Granny said you might be in the reading room. I needed to talk to you.'

That wasn't strictly why he had sought her out in the reading room. Truth was, he'd missed her. He had simply wanted to see her and reassure himself that this amazing woman was still there under the same roof as him. He'd spent a restless night thinking about her. Wondering why he'd become so obsessed with her so quickly. She'd made her position clear that she wanted something more from a man than a fling with a short use-by date.

*But what if he wanted more than that with her, too?*

'I was looking for you to tell you I have to go to London for a few days.'

'Oh,' she said. 'That's a shame.' Disappointment flashed in her eyes before she blinked hard to dispel it.

'Something urgent has come up that requires me to be at my hotel in person.'

He'd been putting the visit off, but the way things were developing between him and Marissa meant now might be a good time for him to get away to London for a bit. The way that kiss, still warm on his lips, had made him feel was disconcerting. He needed to think through this mad attraction, these unsettling feelings, away from her. He didn't want sexual attraction to be mistaken for something deeper. He caught his breath. Was he really thinking about something deeper? He didn't like uncertainty. He needed to deal with this—and he could only do so away from the distraction of her beautiful face and body.

*Out of sight, out of mind.* Yet another useful cliché.

'I'll have to leave now,' he said.

'I understand,' she said. 'What will this mean for our

fake relationship? How will I explain your absence to Edith?'

'She'll probably suggest I take you with me.'

'I couldn't do that,' she said hastily.

*Why not?* he immediately thought. But wasn't her not being with him what he wanted, so he could think things through without distraction?

'I'm needed here,' she said. 'I'm here to organise your Christmas and there are things to do, teams to coordinate.'

'Tell Granny that's why you can't go with me. She won't be surprised I have to go. A hotel is a twenty-four-hour business. After all her years here, she'll be aware that emergencies arise. And it's not always something a manager can sort, no matter how good they might be. There are so many variables, not the least of which is the people—including staff and guests.'

'I bet you have some interesting stories to tell,' she said.

The smile, that enchanting dimple, was back and suddenly he wished he wasn't going to London at all. This was confusing. And Oliver did not allow himself to get confused.

'There might be a few tales I could tell—with names blacked out of course.'

'I'll look forward to that,' she said. 'But…in the meantime, I…er… I'll miss you.' She was obviously having difficulty in meeting his gaze, her eyes cast down to her feet.

He tilted her chin back up with a finger, so he looked right into her eyes. 'Me, too. Miss you, I mean. It doesn't seem like we've only known each other for such a short time, does it?'

'Sometimes friendships work like that,' she said with a slow smile.

*Friendship?* Did she only see him as a friend? He wasn't sure he liked that idea. But surely she wouldn't kiss someone who was just a friend the way she'd just kissed him?

'Reassure Granny that we'll be in touch the entire time I'm away,' he said.

'I've got so much to do,' she said. 'We'll make Christmas super-special for you and Edith this year, I promise.'

'While you'll loathe every minute of it?'

'I won't lie and say I love Christmas, and now you know why. But it's so very different here from any other place I've experienced Christmas. I'll be okay. I can deal with it.'

'Will you be all right in the evenings?' Without him, he meant, but didn't like to say.

'Of course,' she said. 'Andy and I might go to the pub in the village for dinner tonight. It's been ages since we caught up.'

Jealousy sparked through him. Maybe it wasn't such a good idea to leave her. 'You're old friends?'

'We used to work together. I went to his wedding last year. It was such fun.'

'He's married?' he said, hoping the relief he felt didn't sound in his voice.

'His husband, Craig, is a wonderful guy. They're very happy. They travel the world together when Andy isn't working on Christmas trees.'

'That's good to hear,' he said.

'And I expect I'll have dinner with Edith tomorrow night. I think she'd like that,' she said. 'If I let her do most of the talking and am very careful with my responses, I should be okay.'

'Nice idea,' he said. He couldn't possibly be jealous of his grandmother enjoying Marissa's company for an evening, could he? He wasn't used to feeling this possessive about a woman. He wanted her with him.

*He didn't know how to deal with these unfamiliar feelings.*

'I think so,' she said. 'I really like Edith, despite her odd vehemence that you and I are a couple.'

'Right. Back to the fray, then,' he said, turning towards the door.

'Onwards and upwards,' she said. She looked sideways at him with a mischievous smile. 'You do realise everyone will think we sneaked up to your apartment for a quickie?'

He could only wish they had.

# CHAPTER TEN

TWO NIGHTS OF Oliver being away from Longfield Manor turned to three, then four. Marissa missed him. She might pretend to herself that she didn't care—after all, how could she ache so badly for a man she'd known for such a short time? But she knew she was kidding herself.

*She cared.*

As he'd promised, although he seemed as flat out as she was, he kept in regular touch with brief businesslike texts and calls, even a video call. It was more contact than she might have normally expected between hotelier and contract event planner. And his cute emojis that accompanied the texts made her believe they were friends. Friends with the potential for more? Who knew?

When he returned in the morning of the day before Christmas Eve, she planned to be friendly but not over the top. Cool. Businesslike. A kiss on the cheek in greeting, as befit a pretend girlfriend who'd decided with him against public displays of affection.

That plan disintegrated the second she saw him. He'd asked her to meet him in the foyer of the hotel, near the recently placed, superbly decorated Christmas tree. She dressed carefully in a body-conscious deep purple knit dress and heels. She had her hair up in a messy bun and subtle make-up. She planned to be there before him and walked calmly down the staircase. Only to see him already there. Oliver. Tall and imposing in black trousers and cashmere sweater, and a very stylish charcoal-grey coat that spoke of Italian tailoring. He was talking to Priya behind the desk.

Movie-star handsome? *Oh, yes!* He was so handsome her heart accelerated into a flurry of excitement, her breath came short and she felt her cheeks flush.

For a moment she froze before she stepped down to the bottom step. Did he sense her closeness? He turned. For a very long moment they stared at each other across the distance of the foyer. Time seemed to stand still. There was just him and her and the ticking of the large antique clock. Then he smiled and she smiled back at what she saw in his expression. She broke into a run towards him, to be swung up into his arms.

'I missed you,' she said, her voice breaking with a sudden swell of emotion, breathing in his heady, familiar scent. She almost didn't even notice the pungent smell of pine from the Christmas tree.

'I missed you,' he said at the same time.

'It's been awful without you,' she said. She'd counted every minute he'd been away.

'I cursed the problems that kept me in London longer than I wanted to be.'

'Video calls were not the same.'

'You can't hug a screen,' he said.

He kissed her, briefly but passionately. Oh, the joy of being back in his arms! She felt like she belonged there.

*How could something pretend seem so real?*

At the sound of clapping, Marissa broke away from

Oliver's kiss to find Priya and one of the young admin staff smiling and applauding their reunion. All Marissa could do was smile back. It was impossible not to keep on smiling. Oliver was here.

'Thank you,' said Oliver with a slight bow and a grin to the hotel staff.

'We'll take this to my office,' he said to her. 'You can fill me in with what's been happening with the Christmas plans.'

He kept his arm around her, holding her close to him, as they walked the short distance to his office. Again, she had that feeling that she belonged there with him. That no other man would ever do.

Once they were inside the room, he closed the door behind them. Marissa looked up to him. It killed her to say the words, but they had to be said. 'You did that very well. The fake-girlfriend greeting, I mean.'

His face clouded over and he frowned. 'You think I was faking it?'

'I...assumed you were. That...that was our dating deal.' It was difficult to find the right tone. She hadn't realised just how badly she'd missed him until she'd seen him again, so familiar but still very much a stranger. Yet, he'd given her no indication that he felt anywhere near the same.

He put his hands on her shoulders. 'Marissa, not a word of what I said was fake. I genuinely missed you. In fact, I couldn't stop thinking about you and resented the time I spent away from you. Usually business occupies my every thought when I'm in London. Not so this time. Thoughts of you kept intruding.'

'Really?' she said, happiness and relief flooding her.

'What about you?' he said. 'Fake or real?'

She didn't have to think about her answer. 'Real all the way.' Her gaze took in every detail of his handsome, handsome face. 'I missed you and thought about you all the time.'

'Good,' he said, pulling her closer for a brief kiss before releasing her.

'I mustn't have done a good job of hiding how I was feeling, because I was constantly teased by Andy that I was pining for you, my boyfriend, the boss.'

'In reality, Granny is the boss.'

'Everyone here thinks of you as the boss, the new boss. They like and respect you. And some of them fear for the future of Longfield Manor. They're worried about Cecil retiring soon.' She paused a beat. 'Of course you probably know that.'

'Yes. He's worked for the family since my grandparents started the hotel. He'll be sorely missed and difficult to replace. Granny relies on Cecil so much and I'm worried about how she's going to take the news.'

Marissa laughed, but it came out as a kind of snort. 'You still think Edith doesn't know? Of course she knows Cecil is retiring. I sometimes wonder if you underestimate your granny, with her business acumen and people skills. Cecil and his wife are moving to Portugal. As he won't be on hand to advise his replacement, your grandmother is hoping you'll be here to keep your hand on the wheel as the hotel transitions to a new era, but she knows your Pierce Group hotels are your passion. I think she worries about the future of the hotel as she gets older.'

He nodded. 'You kept your ears to the ground while I was away.'

'Who else would the staff confide in than the boss's girlfriend?'

'And the fact that they all like you.'

'Perhaps. I like them, that's for sure.'

'They sing your praises. Anyone I spoke to while I was in London mentioned what a good job you were doing.'

'That's gratifying to hear,' she said. 'I don't know what you intend Longfield Manor's future to be. But you don't have to look far for someone to step into Cecil's shoes. Priya is excellent. A real gem. She knows everything about this place, how it ticks, peoples' strengths and weaknesses. She has some interesting thoughts about how certain things that have been done one way forever, could be done another, better way. She knows how to graciously interact with your grandmother, too.'

Oliver slowly nodded. 'I like Priya. I'll have to get to know her better. Perhaps put her through an interview process.'

'She'd be more than willing. And Cecil would approve of her taking over from him. I think he's been pretty much training her for the role.'

'I learn so much about what's been happening in my own home in my absence,' he said, but he smiled, and his words were in no way a reprimand.

'My priority is Christmas, of course, but it's been interesting to learn more about Longfield Manor.' She dreaded the prospect of saying goodbye to the hotel—and to Oliver—on Christmas Day evening.

'Back to our game of pretend,' he said. 'I was most certainly not pretending. My reactions were very real. In fact, when I saw you on the staircase, your hand on the railing, in that dress, not only did I think you looked hot, I thought you looked like you belonged there.'

'At Longfield Manor? I have come to love the place. Are you thinking of offering me a job?'

'Not at all. But come to think of it...'

She turned her head away, unable to meet his gaze. 'I don't want a job here. I... I would find it hard to work with you, after our charade ends.'

Not when she ached to be his girlfriend for real. Anything else would be untenable. Imagine having to smile and be pleasant when he brought other women here, maybe even a wife. The thought of him with someone else was like the sharpest of stilettos stabbing into her heart.

However, practically, she could see a real role for her here, taking over some of the duties that had always been Edith's but were obviously becoming too much for her. A job as an in-house event planner. The hotel already hosted weddings and other functions but she could see further scope to capitalise on the location. A paid role for something Edith had always done for love and pride in her hotel. Such a job could be an answer to Marissa's dissatisfaction with her current freelance career. But it couldn't be. Not when she was on the edge of falling in love with the boss.

'Which brings us back to where we started,' he said. 'The line between real and pretend has totally blurred for me.'

Marissa stared at him, stunned speechless. 'Me...me, too,' she said breathlessly. 'I can no longer think about you in a pretend kind of way.'

He cradled her face in his hands and looked down into

her face. 'I really like you, Marissa. I can't believe we've known each other for such a short time.'

'I… I really like you, too. So much.'

'I missed you so badly yesterday I nearly got in the car and headed down here to Dorset, leaving my business unfinished.'

'A trip to London to knock on your door entered my mind after the first two nights without you. Only…only I wasn't sure I'd be welcome and—'

He stopped her words with a swift, hard kiss. His voice when he spoke was hoarse. 'Can you, will you, stop looking at your role as pretend girlfriend as something irksome and—?'

'I never saw it as irksome.' It had started as fun, a game, a distraction from the reality of impending Christmas. A quiet poke back at that mean sixteen-year-old boy whom she now rarely gave a thought to.

'What I mean is could you see yourself transitioning into the role for real?' he said. 'As in…a real relationship?'

'To actually date you? To…to be your girlfriend?' She held her breath for his answer.

'Yes,' he said. 'That's exactly what I mean. What I want.'

This was so much more than she'd hoped for in those long nights he'd been away, and she'd realised how much she'd grown to care for him.

She let out her breath on a sigh. 'I would like that,' she said, a tremble in her voice.

He took her in his arms for a long, deep kiss, a kiss of affirmation of those unbelievable words.

*She was Oliver Pierce's girlfriend.*

'That felt more like a proper girlfriend kiss,' she murmured against his mouth, her entire body tingling with pleasure.

'I'm sorry, I should warn you that I can't promise you anything. I'm not good at making relationships last.'

'When you think about it, neither am I,' she said. 'Perhaps we should just take it day by day.' She couldn't worry about how long this thing with Oliver might last, if there was any future to it. She just wanted to be with him. Here. Now.

'I've never felt this way before,' he said, sounding bemused. 'So sudden. So quick.'

'Me neither. Your grandmother calls it a *coup de foudre.*'

His brow furrowed. 'A bolt of lightning?'

'Sudden, fast, powerful, from out of nowhere.'

*Love at first sight.*

That was what Edith said the French phrase meant. But Marissa wasn't going to share that particular translation with Oliver. Moving from fake to real girlfriend was enough for her to absorb, without progressing to contemplating actual *love.*

'That works,' he said.

'She said it was like that for her and Charles. That the power of that initial attraction kept their marriage strong through all those years—especially when things got tough.'

Oliver smiled. 'Grandpa used to look at her like he still couldn't believe she was his.' He paused. 'How come you were talking to Granny about *coup de foudre*?'

'She wanted to talk about us, of course. I had to tread carefully with her, as you know, so I didn't trip myself up. But I told her we liked each other straight away when we met.'

'Which was true.'

'It was, wasn't it?' She'd fought it because of a brief shared past he didn't even remember, but the attraction was too powerful.

He drew her to him for another, deeper kiss. She wound her arms around his neck to pull him closer as she kissed him back. There was a substantial vintage leather Chesterfield sofa in front of the fireplace. She started to edge him towards it.

As she neared her goal, she heard a sharp knock then the door open. She stilled. Oliver had told her his granny never waited to be invited in, a leftover from when this had been his grandfather's study. Oliver pulled away from the kiss.

'Good morning, you two.' Edith practically trilled the words. By now, Marissa knew just how very much Edith wanted her grandson to be happy in a committed relationship.

'So glad you're back, grandson of mine. You were missed. Your lovely girlfriend missed you the most. She was moping around the place, quite lovesick, wishing you were here.'

'Edith!' said Marissa, laughing. She was getting quite used to Oliver's grandmother's outrageous assumptions and exaggerations. And yet…had the older woman been on to something, seen a spark of real attraction between her grandson and the event planner?

Oliver smiled. 'I missed Marissa, too.' He looked down at her. 'I've got used to having her nearby.'

Edith nodded approvingly. 'It was true Marissa did do some moping, but she was very, very busy, too. I've never seen the Christmas preparations carried out so efficiently. The decorations are superb. The heirloom accessories have been used in different ways and the new ones are stunning. And I think you'll really like the creative new ideas for the Christmas table settings.'

'We're ahead of schedule,' Marissa said. 'All the trees are up, and Andy will put the final touches on them today. Edith tells me that Christmas Eve is a big day and, as that's tomorrow, everything is on track for Christmas to start at Longfield Manor.'

'The trees look the best they've ever looked, thanks to your charming friend Andy,' said Edith. 'What a find he is. I've already booked him for next year's Christmas trees.'

'Smart move,' said Marissa. 'He gets booked up very quickly.'

'As it's Andy's last day with us, I've invited him to have dinner with me tonight,' Edith said. 'It would be great fun if you could both join us.'

Marissa looked up at Oliver. They shared raised eyebrows and a glance that told her he was looking forward to having dinner with just the two of them. But that it would be churlish not to accept Edith's invitation.

'Thank you, Granny, we'd like that,' Oliver said.

Marissa was disappointed not to be with Oliver, just the two of them, in his apartment for dinner. But she knew she would enjoy the meal with Edith and Andy and be able to relax now she and Oliver were officially dating. There'd be no need to be on edge guarding against slip-ups in a fake-relationship performance in front of her perceptive friend Andy—not to mention Edith's eagle eye.

Marissa had enjoyed her dinner alone with Edith on

the second night Oliver had been away. Back on that night, she hadn't intended to pry into Oliver's past, but everything about him had become intensely interesting to her and she couldn't resist encouraging Edith's reminiscences. Edith had been only too happy to talk about her beloved grandson. She had told Marissa that, while she would never stop loving the daughter she rarely saw, she would also never forgive her for neglecting her child the way she had neglected Oliver.

'Little Olly was the dearest, brightest, most energetic little boy,' she'd said. 'We adored him, but grandparents can't fully make up for absent parents. Our daughter disappointed him so many times. Now he has no interest in her whatsoever, and I don't blame him—it's self-protection. He's done so well with his hotels and has big plans for expansion. But my husband and I were always concerned about the barriers he put up against letting people get close to him. Emotional barriers, that is. He always puts work before relationships. I mean, look at him now. He's up in London and you're here. That isn't right, especially just before Christmas.'

Marissa had reassured Edith that she totally understood why he'd had to go to London, because she was somewhat of a workaholic herself. Edith had seemed satisfied. Marissa's heart had swelled with compassion towards Oliver for what he had gone through as a child. All that wealth and yet he'd been starved of love from the people who should have loved him the most. But she had been left wondering if he would ever let her get closer.

She didn't see much of Oliver for the rest of the day, but Marissa didn't mind too much. It was like starting over with him, after the fake relationship had morphed into something genuine. Affectionate gestures that had been staged for maximum effect on an observer, now naturally sprung from genuine feeling and a desire to be together. The hunger for him was still there. But it was as if they'd given each other permission to take it slowly, to get to know each other better before they started tossing cushions off his bed.

Marissa felt energised by the shift in her relationship with Oliver. Reassured. *Happy.* There was still work to be done, the finishing touches put to the trees and decorations on this, the final day with the team of temporary staff. But they were nearing the finish line. As was customary, Edith hosted a lunch in one of the function rooms to thank the temporary crew for their work. Marissa was delighted to see that Edith's established people and the new crew recruited by Caity got on so well, working as a team. New friendships had been made. They hoped Edith and Oliver would have them back the next year. 'All in the spirit of Christmas,' Edith said.

Oliver disappeared for the afternoon with some of the crew, saying he had business in the village he needed to attend to. As he kissed Marissa goodbye, he said he'd see her at dinner. He didn't say what that business was, and she didn't ask him. She now knew him well enough to believe he was a man of his word. Still, she was intrigued. Curiously, Edith could not be drawn on his whereabouts.

That evening, as she made her way up the staircase to her room to get changed for dinner, she looked out the ancient mullion windows on the landing to the garden below. Andy had strung the large fir trees with the tiniest of twinkling lights. As she admired the spectacle, a lone deer made its way across the frost-rimed grass, stood in front of one of the sparkling firs and looked up at the building. For a long moment it was as if its gaze met Marissa's and she held her breath. At such a sight, even the most entrenched of Scrooges could not help feeling just a touch of Christmas magic.

# CHAPTER ELEVEN

LONGFIELD MANOR WAS completely booked out for the Christmas period and on Christmas Eve a high level of festive excitement thrummed through the high-ceilinged old rooms. It was that time of year when people didn't say hello to people they encountered, but rather, Merry Christmas. Oliver was kept busy with his grandmother greeting guests, many of whom were regulars returning for Christmas like they did every year. His grandfather's loss was felt, with guests offering condolences as well as greetings. Oliver was very aware that people saw him as stepping into his grandfather's shoes—but his grandfather's shoes didn't fit him, as Grandpa had known only too well.

The future of Longfield Manor was beginning to look very clear to him.

'Is all this making you too sad?' he quietly asked his grandmother. 'Are you sure you're okay with it? You don't have to greet everyone.'

'Absolutely I'm okay,' she said. 'Charles would expect it of me. Of course I miss him terribly. But you were wise to make changes to the way we celebrated Christmas this year. Things aren't quite the same, are they? Changes here and there, some more subtle than others? In a good way, I mean, an updated way, which shows we're moving forward. That makes it somehow easier to cope with. Thank heaven for Marissa.' She looked up at him. 'In many ways, thank heaven for Marissa.'

'I'll second that,' he said, not even trying to disguise the longing in his voice. 'She's wonderful in every way and I'm so grateful she's here with us.'

'She is special,' Granny said. 'And if I were you, I would think about getting a ring on her finger.'

'Granny,' he protested half-heartedly.

'Think about it,' Granny said. 'There is some magnificent heirloom jewellery in the safe, just waiting to be worn by a new generation.'

Oliver was getting used to having Marissa by his side. Where was she now? He was concerned that this immersive Christmas might be upsetting her, bringing back her painful memories of this time of year. Again, he marvelled at her loyalty to her friend Caity that had brought her down here, knowing she would be facing so much of what she hated and feared. He'd been calling her for the last half hour, but she must have her phone turned to silent. Had she locked herself away in her room?

'Granny, I've got to go find Marissa. Do you know where she is?'

'She's been flitting around checking everything she's organised is perfect for our guests. Right now, she's in the dining room with the head waiter, checking on the place settings with the new Christmas table linen. We're launching it tonight for the Christmas Eve carols dinner.'

'Thanks.' He turned to go.

'Wait,' said Edith. 'I said I'm okay. But I don't think I can deal with being Mrs Claus tomorrow.'

'I understand that might be difficult for you. Don't worry. I'll be Santa on my own.' He wasn't listening as hard as he should, keen to get back to Marissa. If he could, he would spend every minute of the day and night with her. Yet, he was taking it slow in their new, official relationship. They had time. He was thinking of taking her away somewhere after Christmas where they could be alone and private, away from interested observers.

'That won't work,' Granny said firmly. 'There must be a Mrs Claus. This tradition goes back a very long way, too long to break it.'

'I'll ask Priya if she can step in for you. Maybe next year you'll be feeling up to being Mrs Claus again.'

'Priya is a fine manager, but Mrs Claus has to be family. How do you feel about Marissa taking my place as Mrs Claus?'

He looked at Granny, aghast. 'Marissa isn't family, Granny.'

*Not yet, anyway.*

'Are you sure about that?' his grandmother said with narrowed, speculative eyes.

'I can't ask her to be Mrs Claus.'

He had honoured his promise to Marissa and not told anyone about her feelings about Christmas. So he couldn't tell Granny just why he couldn't ask this of Marissa. How it could traumatise her. She'd done enough for his family. Acting as Mrs Claus would be torture for a Christmas-phobe. And he didn't want anything to hurt or upset his lovely girlfriend. Not after what she'd been through. Not when she was beginning to mean so much to him.

'I couldn't ask that of her, Granny. And please don't *you* ask her. Promise me?'

He didn't quite trust Granny not to seek Marissa out and ask her herself. He had to find Marissa first. He looked around. 'There are Mr and Mrs Lee. They look like they want to speak with you.'

He headed to the dining room to find Marissa heading out. How she could walk around in those sky-high heels he didn't know, but he liked the sexy sway they gave her. Her face lit up as she saw him, and his heart turned over. How had this woman become so special so quickly? He kissed her in greeting. 'I've come to find you before Granny does.'

Her brow furrowed. 'Why? Is there something she wants to ask me to do?'

'Yes. Well, I've told her not to ask you, but you know what she can be like.'

'I'm intrigued. You'll have to tell me now.'

He led her away to a quiet end of the corridor. 'Granny has decided she can't face being Mrs Claus this year. It would be too hard for her without Grandpa as her Santa Claus.'

Her face softened. 'That's a pity. Poor Edith. I can see it would be very difficult for her. You told me they started being Santa and Mrs Claus long ago when your mother was a baby. Of course she wouldn't want to do it without her soulmate.'

'That's right,' he said. 'It's just too sad.'

'Perhaps you should put the idea in mothballs for this year?'

'Or I could play Santa Claus by myself.'

'Bachelor Santa,' she said. 'That could work.' She reached for his hands and pulled him towards her. 'Handsome Bachelor Santa.' She kissed him. 'You'll drive the lady guests crazy. Better steer clear of the mistletoe.'

He snorted. 'In the red Santa suit with a pillow down my front and a fake beard? I don't think so.'

'You could still be cute.'

'I could and I would. But Granny wants a Mrs Claus and she wants it to be you.'

Marissa dropped his hands and took a step back. *'What?'*

He put his hands out to placate her. 'I know. I told her I would not ask you. Of course I didn't tell her why.'

'To dress up as Mrs Claus and hand out presents, what torture that would be for a Scrooge like me?'

'You don't need to make light of it,' he said. 'I know Christmas holds painful memories for you and I totally understand.'

'And don't forget Christmas is jinxed, too.'

He wasn't so sure about that. 'It will have to just be me as Bachelor Santa, whether Granny likes it or not. I'll tell her that.'

'Wait. Not so fast. Perhaps I... I should try it.' She bit down on her bottom lip. 'Being Mrs Claus, I mean.'

'You don't have to do that. Really.'

'I know I don't have to, but what if I want to? A Long-field Manor Christmas is somehow different. Quite out of my experience. It's like a different world. Also, despite my Christmas phobia, I've helped to create these celebrations.'

'You have. Everyone is delighted with the way things have turned out.'

She looked up at him. 'Maybe I need to face up to my fears. Being Mrs Claus wouldn't be desperately difficult.

It's only for an hour or so, isn't it? Handing out gifts to the guests. Could it be any worse than helping to decorate a tree?'

'Perhaps not.'

'Does Mrs Claus go *ho-ho-ho*, too?'

'I don't think Granny ever did. It was Grandpa that liked to ham it up.'

'Was Edith a quiet, submissive type of Mrs Claus?'

'You could say that. She put talcum powder in her hair to be old Mrs Claus even when she was much younger.'

'So, a Mrs Claus with traditional values of what a wife should be? Defer to Santa?'

'I wouldn't like you to be like that,' he said. 'I want my Mrs Claus to be right up there with me sharing the spotlight.' Was he actually talking about Mrs Claus here or something altogether deeper? He just might be getting carried away.

'Equal rights for Mrs Claus?' she said.

'Something like that,' he said. 'But seriously, Marissa, you don't have to do it.'

'I know…'

'You really want to do it?'

She took a deep breath. 'Perhaps I need to challenge myself,' she said thoughtfully. 'Seeing everyone so happy and excited makes me remember what it was like before my parents died. What I'm missing out on. Do I want to run away from Christmas forever?'

'Only you can answer that,' he said. He hoped not. Christmas was important to him and he was beginning to hope that Marissa would be part of his life for Christmases to come.

Her brow furrowed. 'Only problem is the Christmas

couple costumes. We brought them out of the attic to air. They're definitely old-style Claus family. Not to mention they wouldn't fit either of us. But it's Christmas Eve, there's no time to get new costumes or even alter the old ones.'

'Granny has thought of that, of course,' he said. 'Which makes me wonder for how long she's been planning the Mrs Claus switch.'

'I have long stopped wondering about your granny's motives,' she said. 'What do you mean?'

'She had a parcel delivered to me in London and asked me to bring it with me when I came back down here. When I asked, she said it was new Santa and Mrs Claus costumes. I put the box in the storeroom.'

'Let's go get it,' she said.

Marissa tore at the wrapping in her haste to get at the costumes. She pulled out the Santa one. 'Much nicer than the old one,' she said. She held the red outfit up against him. 'More streamlined, and the white beard is not so outrageous, either.' Her eyes narrowed and she pouted suggestively.

*Did she have any idea of what that did to him?*

'You'll look quite the sexy Santa in this.'

'If there weren't so many people around, I might have to try it on and show you what a sexy Santa can do.'

To his surprise she blushed. 'I'd like that,' she said. She looked up at him, eyes wide and doing the dancing thing. 'Can I take a rain check on that?'

'There's a chimney in your room. Perhaps Sexy Santa can pay you a visit tonight?'

She laughed. 'I'll keep an eye on that chimney. Now,

let's see what Mrs Santa's costume looks like.' She pulled a red garment out of the box and held it up. 'This is cute. I've said it before and I'll say it again, your granny has excellent taste.'

The outfit comprised a long-sleeved red velvet dress with a short, flared skater skirt, all trimmed with white fake fur. Marissa burrowed further in the box and pulled out red-and-white-striped tights, black ankle boots and a black belt with a big buckle that matched the belt for the Santa suit. Plus, the requisite Santa hat with a white pompom at the end that also matched Santa's.

'There are even Christmas earrings in the shape of reindeer.'

'I don't know about the earrings, but you'll look hot in that dress, Mrs Claus.' He waggled his eyebrows and attempted to leer.

'As hot as a woman could look in red-and-white-striped tights,' she said with a delightful little giggle. Had she giggled like that before? He wasn't sure, yet it seemed familiar and very much her.

'What makes me think this outfit was purchased by Granny with precisely Marissa Gracey in mind?' he said drily.

'Everything about it,' she said. 'And it's the right size, too.' She looked up at him. 'I can't not wear it, can I?' Delight and mischief shone in her eyes and it made him smile to see her like that. Again, he felt that urge to protect her and care for her, to want her life to be secure and happy after all the loss she had endured. Like his grandfather had cared for his grandmother. Maybe he was more old-fashioned than he considered himself to be.

'So you'll be my Mrs Claus?' he said.

'I will,' she said.

He helped her pack the outfits back into the box. 'I'll take the box up to my apartment to keep it safe. We'll make our appearances after Christmas lunch tomorrow.'

'It will be a big day tomorrow.'

'Are you sure you'll be okay about it all? No panic attacks?'

'I'll try very hard not to have a panic attack but it's not something over which I have much control. But really, I'm determined not to let any jinx master ruin my time here with you in this truly wondrous place.'

'We're going to find ourselves without a second to spare tomorrow. Anything that's going to go wrong invariably goes wrong on Christmas Day. But after Boxing Day, things will settle down. There'll be more time for us to spend together then.'

She cleared her throat. 'You realise I'm meant to finish up tomorrow afternoon and head back up to London?'

Fear gripped him with icy claws. 'You wouldn't do that, would you?' He couldn't be without her.

'Not if you don't want me to.'

He put his hand on her arm. 'Marissa, I want you to stay.' If she went, he would follow her. Even if it meant leaving Longfield Manor in the middle of its busiest season.

'I'd like to stay here with you. I don't have any other work on, as I was meant to be on holiday in Indonesia.'

'Do you regret cancelling that trip and coming down to Dorset?'

'Not one bit. If I hadn't, I would never have met you. What a shame that would have been.' She paused. 'That didn't come out quite right, did it? I mean, we wouldn't have known we'd like each other if I hadn't agreed to the job and met you.' She smiled. 'Never mind, I think you know what I mean.'

'I know exactly what you mean,' he said, thinking how adorable she was.

There were so many things he badly wanted to say to her, but he'd never said them before and the words didn't come easily. It was too soon, anyway. After all he'd only known her for a week.

Marissa knew the Christmas Eve dinner at Longfield Manor was a very special occasion—the prelude to Christmas Day, which would be the pinnacle of Christmas excitement. For some of the European guests, Christmas Eve was the more important of the two days. The highlights of the evening were to be a special menu from Jean Paul and carols performed by the village choir. It comprised all ages and apparently was no ordinary choir—but a prize winner at national choral competitions. The choir was very much part of the community and led the door-to-door carolling in the village, too. That afternoon, Oliver had invited her to go to the village with him for the carolling, but she'd decided that might be a Christmas overload. Making a good show of being Mrs Claus the next day was more important.

Now she was at dinner with Edith and Oliver—back from the carols—at his private table in the dining room. She looked around her, quietly pleased at how fabulous the festive decorations looked, right down to the table settings. Thanks to Andy, the Longfield Christmas trees had become gasp-worthy in their splendour. People had got up from their tables to admire the dining room tree.

Fortunately, it was set up some distance from Oliver's private table so she wasn't bothered by the scent.

The string quartet played background classical music as she, Oliver and Edith enjoyed the first two courses together. But then Oliver excused himself. 'I need to help out with the choir,' he said.

'If they need help, surely that's my job,' Marissa protested.

'You're off duty now,' he said. 'Stay and enjoy the music.'

Edith put her hand on Marissa's arm. 'Oliver has friends in the choir,' she said. 'You'll see.'

Marissa couldn't help but feel a little left out. Crazy really, when Oliver had done so much to make her part of Longfield Manor and Edith had made her so welcome. But everything between her and Oliver had happened so quickly, she still felt she was on shaky ground.

The string quartet started to play a medley of Christmas carols as the choir of twenty-five people trooped into the room, wearing the traditional chorister's white surplice over a red cassock and red Santa hats with a pompom on the end. The look was perfect for the occasion and the room. Marissa was stunned to see the last chorister to take his place was Oliver. He looked over to her and smiled, obviously aware she would be shocked. She smiled back, shaking her head in wonder.

'I had no idea Oliver was in the choir,' she whispered to Edith.

'He wanted to surprise you,' Edith whispered back. 'He used to sing with this choir and asked if he could join them again for tonight.'

'That's amazing. I never would have guessed,' Marissa whispered back. She couldn't keep her eyes off him.

The choir launched into 'The Twelve Days of Christmas' and continued with a medley of favourite carols.

Marissa realised straight away that the singers were superb—as indeed was Oliver, who sang in a deep baritone voice. When he sang solo in 'The First Noel' she was spellbound. She couldn't sing in tune herself, and deeply admired those who could. He was so talented and she was so proud of him.

'Wow…just wow,' she whispered to Edith.

She saw the same pride and love shining from his granny's eyes as she must see in hers.

She pulled herself up. *Love?*

Marissa could deny it to herself no longer. Of course she was in love with Oliver. But that didn't seem as disastrous a realisation as it might have been just a few days ago—because, with a secret fluttering thrill to her heart, she was beginning to sense he might be feeling the same way towards her.

That thought was confirmed when the choir moved to singing contemporary Christmas songs. As they started on 'All I Want For Christmas Is You,' Oliver broke away from the choir and danced towards her table. She caught her breath.

*The man could dance, too.*

He serenaded her with the song before lifting her out of her chair to swing her around in his arms. Laughing, she blushed bright red with embarrassment, enchanted by his gesture. His romantic move was met with clapping and applause and good-natured catcalls. When he dropped a quick kiss on her mouth the other diners cheered. After he guided her back to the table, she dropped back into her seat feeling bemused, elated and very happy. She had never met a man like Oliver Pierce—and she wanted him so much it hurt.

He had introduced her to a Christmas like she had never before experienced. She realised that listening to the Christmas carols hadn't left her feeling nauseated or panic stricken. When the choir sang 'Silent Night' she thought about her mother, who had loved that carol and although her eyes pricked with tears, all she felt was peace.

'When did Oliver start singing with a choir?' she asked Edith, keeping her voice low.

'When he was a young child living here with us, he sang in the church choir. Then he sang in choirs at his boarding school—I think it made the place more bearable for him. His father is a musician. He obviously inherited his musicality and voice from him.'

When the choir finished, to rapturous applause, Oliver joined Marissa and his grandmother at the table. She stood up to greet him.

'I can't believe you did that,' she said, smiling.

'You didn't like it?' he said with a grin.

'I loved it. You're a man of many surprises,' she said. Marissa couldn't stop looking at him, wondering what other hidden talents he might have. She realised how little she really knew about him.

*She knew enough to allow herself to fall in love.*

'I don't want you to think I'm predictable,' he said.

'You were amazing. Such a talent. I'm in awe.'

'With that beautiful voice, he could have made a career of his singing, if he'd wanted to,' Edith said, ever the proud granny.

'I never wanted to make a career of it. No way would I ever follow in my father's footsteps. Singing for me is about relaxation and fun. So is playing my guitar.'

Oliver played guitar? He just got better and better. Not just movie-star good looks, but rock-star good looks, not to mention wealthy-tycoon good looks—and the talent and business savvy that took his appeal beyond his handsome face. She had a feeling that life would never get a chance to be boring around Oliver. And she longed to be part of his life. She realised with a painful jolt to her heart how empty her life would be if, her job here over, she went back to London and never saw him again.

'Is that where you went yesterday, when you disappeared?' she asked.

He nodded. 'Choir practice.'

'I'm glad you didn't tell me. Seeing you in the choir was a real surprise.'

'I was surprised at how much I enjoyed singing with them again. Unfortunately, my life in London doesn't allow time for a choir. So I'm making the most of being in this one. Part of the deal that the choir took me back was that I sang with them for the midnight church service in the village tonight. Would you like to come with me?'

One part of her wanted to go, another feared that might be too much Christmas overload. 'Thank you, but no. Mrs Claus needs her beauty sleep.'

'Mrs Claus is beautiful just the way she is.'

'But her looks are not enhanced by dark circles under her eyes.'

'I could debate that.' He paused. 'Do you have surprises in store for me?'

His question surprised her. She shrugged. 'Me? You'd

roll around laughing if you heard me sing. What you see is what you get.'

'Sounds good to me,' he said.

'Can I tell you something?'

'Any time.'

She looked up at him, hoping he would understand that her words weren't spoken in jest. 'I can't sing it, but I can say it. All I want for Christmas is you. And I'm very glad you want me for Christmas, too.' When she kissed him, it was to gentle applause from the tables nearby.

# CHAPTER TWELVE

IT WAS CHRISTMAS MORNING, her clock had ticked over past midnight more than an hour ago, but Marissa was still restlessly awake in what she took delight in calling The Bogbean Room rather than the somewhat pedestrian Room eight. She'd looked up the Dorset wildflower to find it was a plant that grew in damp soil with clusters of white star-shaped flowers. Not such a bad name for a room after all. That was if the mundane name was accompanied by an image of the pretty flowers. On the door.

*Aaargh!* Why was she letting irrelevant thoughts like that churn around her mind and keep her awake?

Then there was the song the choir had sung that urged 'Santa baby' to hurry down the chimney. It was going relentlessly around and around in her head. Oliver had teased her by saying he was going to do just that.

*There's a chimney in your room. Perhaps Sexy Santa can pay you a visit tonight?*

Would he? Could he? *Did he really want to?*

A quiet knock sounded at her door. She smiled a slow, secret smile to herself as she got out of bed to answer it. Through the security peephole, she confirmed it was Oliver.

'You came by the door,' she said, pouting, pretending

to be disappointed as she let him into the room and shut the door behind him.

'I didn't dare risk the chimney tonight. It's started to snow, so not such a good move to be clambering over an ancient, slippery roof in an effort to find the correct chimney.'

'Wise move,' she said. She wound her arms around his neck to pull him close. 'If you were covered in black chimney soot, I might not want to do this.' She pressed a kiss to the curve of his jaw, loving the roughness of his stubble against her skin.

'I don't think I'd care if you were covered in soot, I want you so much,' he said hoarsely, his hands around her waist.

'I want you, too, so much,' she said with a hitch to her voice. 'But if soot was a concern, I might have to strip off your clothes and take you into the shower with me.'

'Forget the soot, feel free to strip me anyway and drag me into the shower. If you strip, too, I'd go willingly.'

'I'd prefer it if you strip me first,' she said. 'And the bed might be more comfortable than the cold tiles of the shower cubicle.'

She reached up to claim his mouth in an urgent, hungry kiss that went on and on.

*The man could kiss.*

The time was way past for saying no to more than kisses. She wanted to make it clear she was saying yes to wherever he wanted to lead her.

She pressed her body against his, intoxicated by his now familiar scent, instantly aware of his desire for her and she shuddered with the answering desire that flooded her. She was wearing boxer shorts and a tank top. When he slid his hands up inside the top to caress her breasts, she gasped her arousal. 'Take it off,' she said. 'Now.'

'With pleasure,' he said hoarsely, sliding her top over her head and tossing it on the floor.

When his hand moved lower under the boxers, she moaned her pleasure and arousal. He knew just what to do to ignite her pleasure zones.

'My turn,' she said, pulling his cashmere sweater up over his head, followed by his T-shirt. That left him in only his black jeans. 'Oh my...' Marissa breathed, feeling light-headed as she feasted her eyes on his powerful chest, his six-pack.

She caressed his chest with the flat of her hands, revelling in the feel of smooth skin over hard muscle, the right amount of dark body hair. She fumbled with his belt, but her fingers were awkward with nerves and the more impatient she was, the less luck she had in undoing it.

'Let me,' he said. Soon, she was sliding his jeans down his thighs, her excitement levels soaring.

'Darn!' He was still wearing his boots and the jeans were going nowhere. He laughed. 'Again, let me,' he said, as he kicked off his boots and socks.

Then he was there in just his boxers. He kissed her again and she pressed herself close, warm bare skin against bare skin. There was a mirror behind him, and she looked up to see his back view reflected in it. Broad shoulders tapered down to the best butt a man could ever have. She almost swooned at the erotic vision of their nearly nude bodies entwined, her pale skin against his olive. She kept in shape, and clearly so did he, and she thought they looked beautiful together. It was another level of turn-on.

'Bed or bathroom?' he said.

'Bed,' she choked out. They could shower together some other time.

He picked her up and effortlessly carried her to the bed, an experience she found thrilling. He laid her on the mattress and lay down beside her, resting on his elbow as he looked down at her with those amazing green eyes. He traced her mouth with one finger. 'You are so beautiful.' His gaze roamed over her body and she felt it like a caress. 'Perfect, in fact.'

'I'm glad you think so,' she said huskily. 'You're utterly wonderful and perfect and I'm so very glad you're here, even if you didn't come via the chimney.'

'I couldn't have stayed away. I didn't want you to wake up alone on Christmas morning.' He paused. 'And I couldn't stop thinking about how much I wanted to make love to you.'

'What a magnificent man you are.'

'Says she, in the first flush of attraction,' he said, laughing.

*Not quite the first.*

She knew she should remind him of their first meeting but again, it didn't feel like the right time.

His hands slid below her waist and divested her of her boxer shorts. She did the same to him, taking time to explore and caress him while she did so.

He kissed his way down her bare skin to take her nipples in his mouth, one after the other, teasing them with his tongue until she ached for release. Then he explored her body with his hands and mouth until she bucked against him. 'Please, I want you inside me. Now.'

He took a condom from the thoughtfully provided

amenity pack in the bedside drawer, and she helped him put it on. Then he entered her and she welcomed him into her body. He fell into just the right rhythm for her and she orgasmed before he did and then again after, melting in ecstasy. The man sure knew how to please her. 'I have to say again how wonderful you are,' she murmured sleepily. 'When I said all I wanted for Christmas was you, I knew what I was talking about.'

She fell asleep in his arms, feeling happier than she could remember feeling for a very long time.

They awoke early in the morning, to the sound of church bells pealing out a joyous Christmas message and made love again. This time their lovemaking was tender and unhurried, building to a powerful, mutual climax before they sank back into sleep.

Marissa woke later to find Oliver sleeping beside her, his arm slung across her. She admired him for a long minute, his face even more handsome in repose, his body strong and sleekly muscled. How lucky she was to have found him. She slid out from under his arm, so as not to disturb him. The room seemed oddly quiet, with no noises coming from outside, just the steady sound of his breathing from inside.

She shrugged on the ink-coloured velour hotel robe she'd left on the chair and padded barefoot over the lush carpet to the window. She drew back the heavy curtains. Snow. She watched, entranced, as a flurry of fluffy snowflakes drifted past the windowpanes. The gardens below had been transformed by a heavy coverage of snow. The lights Andy had strung up on the fir trees struggled valiantly to twinkle through the layer of white that now frosted their branches. She might have to get some help to shake some—but not all—of the snow off.

Oliver came up from behind her and slipped his arms around her. She leaned back against him, rejoicing in their closeness, the warmth and strength of his body clad in the matching robe to hers he'd taken from the closet.

'It's unbelievably beautiful, isn't it?' he said softly. 'All the familiar landmarks transformed into something magical. Form becomes more important than colour or scent or anything else but this purity. A white Christmas. We'll have some very happy guests, especially those from Australia and South Africa.'

'It's utter magic,' she murmured. But the real magic was being here with Oliver, in the security of his arms around her, her body aching pleasantly from the sensual aftermath of intensely satisfying lovemaking.

'Thank you for letting me stay with you,' he said. 'As I said, I didn't want you to wake up alone on Christmas Day.'

'I'm so glad you stayed.'

'Now I don't know whether to wish you a Merry Christmas or not.'

'Please do. I think being here with you, becoming so involved with the Longfield Manor festivities have helped me. Perhaps, just perhaps, the jinx has been lifted. Maybe I can allow myself to enjoy Christmas this year without the fear that something terrible will happen.'

'I sincerely hope so. Do you think you'll ever be able to remember your parents without connecting their loss to Christmas?'

'I'm beginning to believe I will. Maybe one Christmas I'll even be able to eat a mince pie again without breaking down. They were my dad's favourite, you see.'

'Grandpa loved them, too. Can't say I care for them myself. Jean Paul's fruit pastries are far superior in my opinion.'

'I'll try them and I'm sure I'll enjoy them.'

'Maybe that's what Christmas will mean to you this year. Laying down new memories. Not banishing the old ones, but letting happy new memories override them.'

'What a lovely idea,' she said, hoping fervently that it could be so, thinking how perceptive he was.

Oliver turned her to face him, searched her face. 'Perhaps some of those happy new memories could be made with me, Marissa?'

Her heart leapt. This was something she hadn't dared to let herself imagine. 'Perhaps...'

'I know we haven't known each other for long but, as I've said before, it seems like you're meant to be part of my life. Not just for Christmas but into the New Year, too, and beyond. Maybe next year we could be enjoying Christmas together again at Longfield Manor?'

Exultation at his words fought with caution. 'That's a beautiful thought.' Could she trust this man who'd made it so clear he didn't want commitment? How she wanted to believe in a future together. But it was a big step forward.

'You're thinking that's perhaps too great a leap?' he said, obviously sensing her doubt. 'Maybe we could go away by ourselves in the New Year to talk about how we could make our relationship work? Paris maybe? Or anywhere you would like.'

'Paris would be perfect.' She could think of nothing better. Just him and her.

He cradled her chin in his hands, in the way she had come to love. It made her feel cherished, special, safe. 'I really like you, Marissa,' he said. He could not seem more sincere.

'I like you a lot, too. Being here with you means so much. I... I would like to look into the future with you.'

'So, I can wish you Merry Christmas?'

This Christmas was so different. 'Please do. Although I'll wish you a Happy Christmas.'

'Is there a difference?'

'You wouldn't think so, would you? My father had this eccentric old aunt who used to spend Christmas with us. She was a sweetie, but she very primly used to say that *merry* meant drunken, and that to wish someone a Merry Christmas meant you were wishing them a Drunken Christmas and that was simply not on. You can imagine the fun my brother and I had with that one. We thought it hilarious and, for a while there in our lives, it was probably true.'

'But you say Happy Christmas now?'

'I just got to like happy better than merry. Happy is the best thing you could wish a person to be, isn't it?'

He laughed. 'I think it's kinda cute that you do.'

He let her go and headed over to pick up his jeans from where Marissa had tossed them the night before. She was disappointed that he was going to cover up his gorgeous body that had given her so much pleasure. But no. He didn't put on the jeans but rather dug into a pocket and pulled out a small, professionally wrapped parcel. 'Merry Christmas, Marissa,' he said, handing it to her.

'A gift for me? Really?'

'It's Christmas morning, Marissa. Gift-giving time.'

Of course it was.

She tore off the wrapping—she was never very good at decorously opening a present or reading the card first—to find a small box embossed with the name of a famous London jeweller. With trembling fingers, she opened it to find a bracelet of finely linked platinum studded with diamonds. She looked up at him. 'Oh, this is lovely,' she said. 'But it's too much, I—'

'I wanted to get you something special,' he said.

'This is special, all right,' she said. 'But—'

'Let me help you put it on,' he said. He fastened it to her right wrist. 'It fits perfectly. I bought it when I was in London and had to guess the size.'

She held up her hand to admire it. 'It's a lovely brace-let,' she said. 'But it's very extravagant of you.'

'You deserve something lovely,' he said. 'If this is pre-varication because you don't like it—'

'No, I love it, I really do,' she said. 'It's just I wasn't expecting...' She kissed him on the cheek. 'Thank you very much. I shall treasure it.'

She went to the drawer under the desk and, in turn, pulled out a parcel of her own.

'Happy Christmas, Oliver,' she said, handing it to him.

'Me? You bought me a gift?'

'Why would you be surprised?' At the time she'd been unsure whether or not it would be appropriate, but she'd gone ahead anyway. She'd bought his gift from a shop in the village, and something for Edith, too, the afternoon she'd gone in with Andy. Then wrapped it in some ex-quisite paper she'd found in the same shop.

Would he like it? Oliver pulled out the soft, charcoal-grey Italian designer cashmere scarf in a muted windowpane check with an exclamation of pleasure. 'Thank you,' he said, holding it up. 'It's my favourite colour and perfect for this weather. How very thoughtful of you.'

'Are you sure? I wanted to buy you a book, but I felt I didn't know you well enough to know what you like to read.'

'The scarf is better. I confess, I don't get much time to read.'

'Let me,' she said, taking the scarf from him to put around his neck. She stood back to admire how it looked, somewhat incongruous in the neck of a hotel dressing gown. 'Yes, the colour is great on you.'

Truth be told, he would look good in any colour. Oliver dressed with a natural flair and style that befit a man of his position as CEO of London's most fashionable hotels, and heir to this awesome ancestral home.

But she liked him best wearing nothing at all.

# CHAPTER THIRTEEN

OLIVER HAD NEVER imagined the day would come when his grandparents wouldn't be playing Santa Claus and Mrs Claus on Christmas Day. The fond memories stretched right back to when he was a toddler.

And now he was Santa Claus and Marissa had stepped in as Mrs Claus. He wasn't sure Mrs Claus was meant to be so beautiful and sexy. Maybe Granny's interpretation of Santa's wife with a lacy white cap on grey hair pulled back into a bun, and wire-framed spectacles was more customary. But then he was only a thirty-two-year-old Santa, despite the white curly wig and ill-fitting beard. He wouldn't fool a kid that he was the real deal for a minute, that was for sure.

Marissa looked sensational in the new Mrs Claus outfit, her luxuriant dark hair waving from under her Santa hat to around her shoulders, her lipstick a rich, kissable red, the short skirt and striped tights showing off slender legs that went on forever. She'd replaced the plastic boots that came with the outfit with her own high-heeled black boots, which also added to the hot new Mrs Claus look. He didn't want her to take that outfit off after the gift-giving ceremony. He'd like to slowly strip it from her and make love to her. If he'd thought he'd been obsessed with Marissa before they'd spent the night together, it was nothing on how he felt about her now.

The Christmas feast was over. The guests who chose to take part in the gift-giving had gathered around the spectacular towering Christmas tree in the spacious guest living room. It was time for Santa and Mrs Claus to give out the presents, one for each adult guest. There were also age-appropriate gifts for the few children who accompanied their parents.

Christmas here was more an occasion for well-heeled adults than lots of kids tearing around the place. But Oliver liked their presence—Christmas didn't seem like Christmas without children. For the first time, he let himself imagine what it might be like to have *his* children spending Christmas at Longfield Manor. Little dark-haired children, because surely he and Marissa would have dark-haired babies—

*Stop!* He couldn't let his thoughts stray in that direction. Not now. Not yet. Maybe never, depending on what she thought of the idea.

This year the adult's gift was a handblown glass frosted bauble tree decoration with a resin miniature of the hotel inside it and the words *Longfield Manor* and the year hand-painted in silver script on the outside. It was an exquisite keepsake, the brainchild of Caity. He had a lot to thank Caity for—not the least of which was bringing Marissa into his home and his heart. Marissa reported her friend was doing very well in hospital, which pleased him.

Granny introduced the new Claus family, with a heartfelt homage to Grandpa, announced her retirement as Mrs Claus and then the ceremony commenced.

Who knew this could be so much fun?

Marissa was a brilliant sidekick and they traded banter and laughter with each other as they handed out gifts and well wishes to the guests. She was lovely with the children, squatting down to their level, giving hugs where appropriate. You would never guess Marissa was a Christmas-hating Scrooge. But might that be because she was that no longer? Thanks in part, he liked to think, to him?

When the gift-giving was over, one of the guests pointed out that Mr and Mrs Claus were standing right under a strategically placed bunch of mistletoe. Wasn't it time for Santa to give his wife her Christmas kiss? He looked to Marissa and she smiled back. Santa obliged with a passionate kiss and a backwards swoop of Mrs Claus. By now everyone knew they were a real-life couple.

'Are you two going to be naughty or nice tonight, Santa?' a longtime guest, who had known Oliver as a child, called out.

Marissa looked up at Oliver with wide eyes and a lascivious smile. Then she looked back to her audience and gave an exaggerated wink. 'Both naughty *and* nice,' she said in a slow and sexy voice.

To the guests' laughter and applause, Granny took the spotlight to thank everyone for choosing Longfield Manor to spend Christmas. She reminded them to book now if they planned to return next year, as returning guests had priority.

'I'll finish by thanking Marissa and Oliver for being such a brilliant Mr and Mrs Santa Claus.' She made a dramatic pause. 'And to express my opinion that they'd make a brilliant Mr and Mrs Pierce, too.'

'Granny,' groaned Oliver. 'That's going too far.'

But people were laughing and applauding, and Marissa didn't look embarrassed or upset; in fact, she was laughing, too.

And, really, was the Mr and Mrs Pierce thing completely out of the ballpark? He had never, ever felt for a woman what he felt for Marissa. He might need to think about securing her.

'Sorry about Granny,' he whispered to Marissa. 'She really got carried away this time.'

'Water off a duck's back,' she said. 'Nothing Edith says shocks me anymore. She means well. Remember, everything she says is motivated by love for you and her desire for you to be happy.'

Marissa was beautiful both inside and out. He hugged her, so grateful for the way she was unfailingly good to Granny. And the fact was, that since Marissa had been here, Granny had had very few forgetful or disoriented episodes. She was her old self more often than not.

The gift-giving over, waiters brought around trays with flutes of champagne and plates of exquisitely decorated festive cookies. 'These beat a mince pie, hands down,' Oliver said to Marissa.

She took a cookie shaped like a Christmas bell off the tray and nibbled. 'You're right. It's delicious. In fact, I might have to have another one. A Christmas stocking one.'

Oliver stepped away to call the waiter back with the tray, when Granny came over. She took his arm. 'Look who just got here. Such a lovely surprise. Toby and Annabel.'

Oliver was pleased to see his old friend. He greeted him with a hug. Then unhooked his Santa beard to better kiss his wife, Annabel, on the cheek—an awkward procedure with the Santa beard. 'Where are the kids?'

'Annabel's parents have a house down here so we're spending Christmas with them,' said Toby. 'They're minding the children to give us some grown-up time. You've always said I've got a standing invitation to visit, so here we are.'

'Great to see you. I must introduce you to my girl-friend.'

Toby's eyebrows rose. 'You? A girlfriend? One that lasts more than a week?'

Marissa had her back turned to them, chatting anima-tedly to a guest. Oliver tapped her on the shoulder and excused himself to the guest. 'May I borrow Mrs Claus? There's someone I really want her to meet.'

'Who?' Marissa said, turning to face him.

With a hand on her elbow, he guided her towards his friends.

'My old friend Toby,' he said. 'We go back a long time.'

He felt her stiffen. Perhaps it was too soon to be intro-ducing her as his girlfriend.

'Toby and Annabel, let me introduce—'

'Marissa,' said Toby. 'So you two finally got together after all.'

The colour drained from Marissa's face.

*This couldn't be happening.*

Marissa was so shocked she couldn't speak, just looked from Toby to Oliver and back again. She barely regis-tered Toby's blonde wife, who was looking curiously on.

'Do you remember me?' Toby said.

'Samantha's brother,' she said. 'How is she? We lost touch a long time ago.'

Toby wouldn't be diverted. 'Sam's fine. But how about

you two? This is a surprise. Olly, you sly dog. I thought you didn't see Marissa again after that summer we first met her. So long ago. How old were we? Sixteen?'

Marissa could see recognition slowly dawn on Oliver's face. Recognition and a tight, contained anger. 'Yes,' he said, tight-lipped, not looking at Marissa.

'And you were fourteen, right, Marissa?' Toby said. He looked her up and down. 'You sure have changed.'

'One tends to in sixteen years,' Marissa said through gritted teeth.

'You wanted to ask her out then, didn't you, Olly? But Sam told us her parents wouldn't allow it. She was too young to date.'

'I don't remember that,' Marissa said, trying to force a smile.

'Nah. I reckon Samantha only said that because she fancied Olly for herself,' Toby said. 'She was right peed off that he only had eyes for sweet Marissa.'

*Sweet Marissa?*

How about Monobrow Marissa? Gawky and giggly? Now she remembered she hadn't liked Toby very much back then, though she'd been forced into his company in the school holidays. And after that overheard conversation, she'd completely avoided him.

'Sounds like something Samantha would do,' Annabel said, shooting a sympathetic glance to Marissa.

'So when did you and Marissa hook up again?'

*Hook up?* Was Toby being purposely offensive?

'Quite recently,' said Oliver, still not looking at Marissa. 'We met at a function at The Pierce Soho.'

'Did you recognise her straight away? Bet you didn't.' He ran his fingers across his eyebrows. 'The eyebrows, right?'

'I think you've said enough, Toby,' his wife interjected.

'She was just as lovely,' Oliver said, without actually answering Toby's question.

'I didn't recognise him,' Marissa said, not daring to look at him. 'He was Oliver Hughes then, if you remember. I had no idea he was the same person.'

*For a while, that is.*

It wasn't excuse enough for not reminding Oliver they'd met before, and Marissa knew it. She'd had several chances to tell him. Now she'd blown it.

She tried to change the subject by asking Annabel about the children, but their conversation was stilted.

'I'm sorry, it's been lovely to meet you, but I'm helping Edith with something, and have to go find her,' she said after one too many awkward silences. 'Catch up later?' she said, knowing full well she wouldn't.

'I look forward to seeing you again,' said Annabel.

'Me, too,' said Toby, homing in for a kiss that Marissa adroitly avoided. He reeked of alcohol.

'*Merry* Christmas,' she said.

'I'll be back,' Oliver said to his friends. 'Grab some champagne.'

He followed Marissa out of the room and into a deserted part of the corridor, not giving her a chance to gather her thoughts, let alone to plan any kind of strategy. A grim-faced Pierce male ancestor with mutton-chop whiskers from the Victorian era peered down at her from the wood-panelled wall.

His equally grim-faced descendent took her by the arm, forcing her to look up at him. 'Why did you lie to me?' he said, his eyes cold and accusing.

'I didn't actually lie. It was more of a…a…lie of omission.'

'A lie is a lie. I don't tolerate liars, Marissa. In any shape or form.'

'Understood,' she said. She wanted to say she didn't, either, but that might seem more than a tad hypocritical.

'Did you recognise me straight away?' he said.

'You looked like Oliver Hughes, but you were Oliver Pierce. I had no idea there was a connection when I agreed to work here. Oliver isn't an uncommon name.'

'A misconception easily cleared up, I should imagine.' He let go of her arm.

'Yes, the first morning I was here. All it took was an internet search.'

'Why didn't you remind me straight away that we'd met?'

'Because you had no idea who I was, and I decided to leave it that way. I was only going to be working here a week. I didn't know you were going to ask me to be your fake girlfriend.'

'And you still didn't tell me.' His eyes narrowed. 'You know, I thought there was something about you that was familiar, an expression, a giggle, but I meet so many people.'

'What you don't realise is that I loathed you.'

*'What?'*

'Back then, I actually had a huge crush on you. Huge. Then I overheard you talking to Toby. Shredding my appearance to pieces. There wasn't anything about me that you both didn't snigger and sneer over. I was gawky, flat-chested, giggled too much and boy, did my eyebrows come in for ridicule. I was devastated. I slunk off to lick my wounds. Avoided you for the rest of your visit. My fragile teenage confidence was shattered. Can you imagine my shock when it turned out I was going to have to work with you for a week? Worse, stay under the same roof.'

'Did I really say all that about you?'

'You absolutely did. You were not a pleasant young man. And Toby was even worse.' She wanted to say that she'd forgiven him. That he'd grown into a wonderful man. That we all said stupid things when we were teenagers. But she doubted he was in a mood to be receptive.

'So you were looking for revenge?'

'The thought crossed my mind. But then...'

'Then what?'

'I very quicky got to like you.'

'But you still didn't tell me. You slept with me, and you still didn't tell me.'

'That's right, because by then I didn't think it mattered,' she said, which was a fib in itself. She knew she should have told him. She didn't actually have a leg to stand on.

'This changes everything, Marissa. You're not who I thought you were.'

Her chin rose. 'Perhaps I'm not,' she said.

'I've never felt more humiliated than when Toby outed you back there.'

'I actually don't think Toby saw it that way. He bought our story that we'd recently connected.'

'He's drunk. When he sobers up he'll realise I didn't recognise you as that girl we'd met sixteen years ago. He'll also realise you'd recognised me and wonder about that.'

'Does it matter what Toby thinks?'

'It matters that you made a fool out of me.'

'I think you're wrong, but if that's what you want to think, feel free.' She glared at him. He was right. Everything had changed. She'd been kidding herself there was something special between them. Besides, did she want to be with a man so rigid and judgemental?

'If you'll excuse me, I need to go up to my room.' She indicated what she was wearing. 'I need to get rid of Mrs Claus.'

'Go,' he said.

For a moment she almost laughed, a hysterical, non-funny kind of laugh, at the thought of them in this corridor, arguing in their Santa costumes. Thank heaven no one had seen them. It must have looked ludicrous.

As she headed for the stairs, she encountered Priya.

'That went so well,' Priya said. 'You were brilliant as Mrs Claus.'

'Thank you,' she said, barely able to string the words together.

Priya frowned. 'Are you okay?'

'Fine. But I finish up here today. I need to pack up my room and head back to London.'

'Haven't you heard? The roads are closed. We're snowed in.'

'You're joking.'

'We had some very heavy falls.'

'So I'll have to hope I can get out tomorrow.'

'Oh,' said Priya. 'We'd rather hoped you'd be staying.'

Marissa forced her voice to sound calm, businesslike. 'I'm sure I'll be back. It's been marvellous working with you. I have all fingers and toes crossed for you that you'll be taking over from Cecil when he retires.'

'I think I've got a chance,' Priya said with a smile.

'Look, I'm going to head up to my room to change.

Then I need to get outside for some fresh air, before it gets dark.'

'Be quick,' Priya said.

Marissa couldn't bear to linger in Room eight for any longer than she had to. Too many memories of her and Oliver making love. She had never been happier than she had been twelve hours ago. Now she couldn't look at the bed for fear of a heart-wrenching vision of their sensuously entwined limbs.

How stupid she'd been to think she could escape the Christmas jinx—that it could have turned out any other way. What had Oliver said?

*Anything that's going to go wrong invariably goes wrong on Christmas Day.*

Another horrid thing had happened to her at Christmas. What could be worse than breaking up with him when they'd only just begun? He'd appeared so kind, so understanding. But it seemed that underneath that gentlemanly facade beat the heart of that mean-spirited, arrogant teenage boy. She'd look on this in years to come as a lucky escape. But it didn't feel like that now and she was desperately fighting tears.

She cringed at her remembered jollity. At the way she had dressed up as Mrs Claus, for heaven's sake, when she should have been Scrooge. Flirting with Oliver's Santa as Mrs Claus, letting her feelings for him show in her eyes, making no secret of where her heart lay. How could she have let her barriers down like that?

She put on jeans, a sweater, her warm puffer jacket, boots and headed back down the stairs, carrying her hat, scarf and gloves. If she didn't get outside soon, away from the central heating and the ever-present scent of pine needles, she feared another panic attack.

Thankfully, there was no wind, but it was bitterly cold outside and light snow was drifting down. Long afternoon shadows were falling across the snow-blanketed garden. It was beautiful and peaceful and being out in nature should be good for her battered soul. She stepped out onto the snow that covered the driveway and onto the grass. The snow was deep but not impossible and she set out towards the walled garden, the occasional snowflake landing lightly on her eyelashes. She would miss Longfield Manor, she would miss Edith, but most of all she'd miss Oliver.

She refused to let her thoughts go there. She'd only really known him for a week—she would as easily forget him; of course she would. Truth was, she'd first met him a lot longer than a week ago, and that teenage attraction had been like smouldering coals ready to ignite into fierce flames when she'd seen him again. She wondered if the reason she'd never had much luck with men was because she'd compared them unfavourably with her teenage heartthrob. But what about now? Would she compare every new man she met in the future to Oliver Pierce and find them lacking?

As she neared the iron gate to the walled garden, the snow started falling more heavily, until suddenly she could hardly see ahead of her. When she got to the gate, she turned back to see her footsteps had already been covered. She didn't have the world's best sense of direction, and she wasn't quite sure which was the way to turn back to the Manor. She hadn't thought to bring her phone to use the compass app, either. Don't be silly, she told herself. The walled garden is in a direct line to the house; it's still light, you'll be fine. She pushed the gate open and gasped at the beauty of the garden covered in snow. She'd just take a few moments here to contemplate her future and then go back.

How could he have spoken to Marissa the way he had? Oliver berated himself. It had been such a shock to discover that they'd met before. That this Marissa was *that* Marissa. Why on earth hadn't she reminded him? Was it because she was too nervous to, because he'd been so critical of her then? He shouldn't have called her a liar.

He'd gone back to Toby to ask him what exactly had happened when they were sixteen, only for his old friend to confirm that they had indeed picked Marissa's appearance apart and had a good laugh. When Annabel had gone off to the bathroom, Toby had confessed he'd liked Marissa for himself and had wanted to put Oliver off her by enumerating her 'faults.' It had backfired on him, though, as Marissa had never again come around to her friend Samantha's house when her brother was in residence. Toby reminded him that they'd been private schoolboys at an all-boys school, desperate for female company and ignorant of what to do when they found a girl they liked. That was no excuse, Oliver knew. He had been keeping up with Toby, saying what he felt he was meant to say, as good friends had been few and far between in the hierarchical structure of his boarding school.

He had hurt Marissa, back then and just now. He had to apologise, grovel if required. Because he knew if he didn't, he wouldn't get her back. And he desperately wanted her back.

Priya told him that Marissa had gone outside.

'In the snow?' he said. 'When it will be dark soon?'

'She insisted,' Priya said. 'I'm sure she's okay.'

*But what if she wasn't?*

Fear sliced through him. What if she got lost in the snow?

*What if he'd lost her?*

Not because of the snow, but because of the way he'd treated her?

He couldn't bear it if, having found her again, he was once more without her. Because he had liked her back then, really liked her. He remembered now he'd told Granny he'd met a beautiful, friendly girl named Marissa in the midterm break when he'd visited Toby. But he'd been too shy and uncertain around girls to follow up with her. Had that name *Marissa* lodged in Granny's mind and that was why she'd made those extraordinary statements about her when Marissa had arrived at Longfield Manor. Who knew? But he did know he had to find her now, before she had time to hate him again.

There had been a light fall of snow since Marissa had set out, but not enough to completely obliterate her footsteps. He wasn't surprised to see she'd headed for the walled garden; she loved that place, felt a special bond to it.

But her footsteps were more obscured by snow when he got closer. 'Marissa!' he called. The word was loud in the silent garden blanketed by snow. He called her name again.

Then she was there at the open gate of the garden. 'Oliver. I'm here.'

He ran in the snow to the gate where she waited, all bundled up against the cold. 'Are you okay? I was worried.'

'Of course I'm okay,' she said. 'I just needed some

fresh air, to clear my head after…after what happened back there.' There was a distinct chill to her voice that had nothing to do with the snow.

'Marissa, I'm sorry, so sorry for speaking to you like that. I was wrong. I was so shocked by the fact you remembered me and didn't say. But that's no excuse.'

'I was in the wrong, too,' she said. 'I should have let you vent. I had so many chances to remind you we'd met sixteen years ago but I didn't.'

'I was awful back then. Toby confirmed that we did say those horrible things you overheard. I have no excuse. I really liked you but was too shy and ignorant to know what to do about it. I wanted to keep up with Toby because he was one of the few friends I had at boarding school. My life was pretty awful in the aftermath of my parents' divorce. So even though I was uncomfortable with what he was saying, I let him egg me on. And he's stayed a good friend. Obnoxious when he's drunk, but still a loyal friend. And Annabel is a darling. He's lucky to have her.'

'You liked me then? Really?' Her eyes were huge.

'I had a funny way of showing it, didn't I?'

He explained then his theory of why the name Marissa might have triggered Granny's odd behaviour.

'It's an interesting thought,' Marissa said. 'She was right, though, wasn't she? About us being together.'

'Are we together still?'

'If you want us to be,' she said tentatively.

'Will you forgive me for my crass sixteen-year-old behaviour? Teenagers can say such stupid things, behave so badly.'

'I already have forgiven you.'

'That wasn't us back then. Fourteen-year-old you and sixteen-year-old me. They were immature, semi-formed versions of ourselves.'

'And yet, I think that's when I was struck by the *coup de foudre*. Not a week ago. Sixteen years ago.'

'You think so?'

'I know so. I have a strong feeling you have always been the man for me. We just had to find each other again.'

'And will I always be the man for you?' he said hoarsely. He held his breath for her answer.

'You always will be,' she said.

'I love you, Marissa,' he said. He had never told a woman he loved her and he was struck by how...*wonderful* it felt. 'I really love you.'

She smiled a slow, sensual smile. 'And I love you, darling Oliver.'

He kissed her and their kiss told them everything they needed to know.

'I've had a thought,' he said. 'I liked having you as my Mrs Claus and calling you my wife. How would you feel about becoming Mrs Pierce?'

'Are you proposing to me, Oliver?'

'You mean sixteen years after I first met you, I still can't find the right words to say to you?'

'Think about it. I think the right words are probably on the tip of your tongue.'

He laughed. 'Marissa Gracey, will you marry me?'

She smiled. 'I would love to marry you, Oliver Pierce, so the answer is yes.'

They kissed again, long and sweet and full of hope for their shared future.

'There are things we need to talk about,' he said. 'The future of Longfield Manor being one.'

'Is it in doubt?'

'Grandpa wanted me to sell it.'

'No! You couldn't.'

'That's the conclusion I've come to as well.'

'Good,' she said vehemently.

'I'd want you to be involved with The Pierce Group. You bring something to the table when it comes to the Manor's future as a hotel.'

'I could be the events manager. And help Edith. She'd like Priya to take over from Cecil, by the way.'

'Can we schedule in us having a family here, too?' he asked.

She smiled her delight. 'Absolutely. It'll be our top priority.'

'The women have it sorted.'

'We're good at that,' she said.

'You're good at lots of things,' he said. 'Including making me the happiest man in the world.'

'You're very good at making me the happiest woman.'

She looked up at him, her beautiful face glowing with love. 'You know you said you wanted to help me make new, happy memories of Christmas?'

'I remember.'

'I think we've just made the most wonderful memories of Christmas, of Longfield Manor and of you. Something tells me my Grinch days are over.'

He kissed her again.

# EPILOGUE

*April the following year*

COULD THERE BE a more beautiful place for her wedding
to Oliver than the Longfield Manor walled garden? Marissa didn't think so. The day was perfect, a blue sky
with just a few wisps of white cloud trailing across the
horizon. She stood outside the iron gate to the garden,
looking in to the scene so perfectly set for the ceremony.

The fruit trees espaliered on the stone walls were blos-
soming in frothy bunches of white and pink, and tulips
and other spring flowering bulbs lined the stone path-
ways. A heady, sweet scent from lily of the valley wafted
through the air. Water trickled from a central fountain,
at the base of which, Marissa was tickled to discover,
bloomed the starry white flowers of the bogbean. The
string quartet—the same one as they'd had for Christmas—played romantic, classical music.

They both wanted a simple wedding, with a celebrant
from the village and an elegant lunch in one of the private
rooms in the hotel. The celebrant stood at the far end of
the garden, with Oliver and his best man Toby waiting
for her to walk down the central pathway so they could
start the ceremony. There were thirty guests, a mix of

friends and family, including her brother Kevin and his wife, Danni, who had flown in from Sydney, standing and sitting around the garden. Kevin kept a firm hold on Oliver and Marissa's black Labrador puppy, Rufus Two, who was being a very good boy.

Marissa took a deep breath. She would walk down that pathway in her lovely, long white dress, her dark hair up under an exquisite veil, as Marissa Gracey, and walk back up it married to the man she adored. She could hardly wait to be his wife.

She held on tight to her bouquet and got ready to walk—she'd been told she should glide—up the pathway to where Oliver waited. First up the pathway ahead of her, in an elegant violet lace dress, was her special attendant, Edith, beaming her joy that her dream for her grandson was about to come true. Marissa had a quiet, reflective moment that her parents couldn't be here. Her mother had always wanted to see her as a bride.

Her bridesmaid Caity stepped close to her long enough to whisper with a smirk, 'I thought you were immune to gorgeous men,' before making her own way down the pathway in her slinky orchid-coloured silk satin dress. Caity's healthy, perfect twin girls were with her husband, Tom.

The quartet struck up Mendelssohn's 'Wedding March.' Then Marissa stepped onto the pathway, seeing only Oliver waiting for her, his love shining from his eyes, as she walked towards her husband-to-be and her new life with him.

*To love, honour and cherish.*

\* \* \* \* \*

# SWIPE RIGHT
# FOR MR PERFECT

JUSTINE LEWIS

**MILLS & BOON**

For Eleanor and Melinda.

To cocktails, chats about dating and Catfish Princesses.

# CHAPTER ONE

LAURA HIT SEND on the condition report she had just prepared for a client on one of their paintings and stretched her
arms high into the air. Outside, the London air was warm
and the sky still bright as the city shook off winter and the
evenings stretched on a little longer. Laura loved that she'd
be walking home in daylight; the prospect buoyed her. It
had been a long winter, one that had felt particularly dark
given the pain she'd been in, and being bedridden following her last laparoscopy, which had taken her longer to re-
cover from than usual.

The offices of the art conservation firm where she
worked were not too far from her flat. Laura was glad to
be up and moving again and, for the moment at least, able
to enjoy the beautiful weather. Before packing and leaving
for the day she checked her phone and smiled. There was
already a message.

@FarmerDan: How was your lunch?

Laura replied as the online alias she used on the dating app.

@SohoJane: Lunch was delicious, my mother on the other
hand…

@FarmerDan: Not so tasty?

@SohoJane: Ha-ha. You'd like her. You'd both have at least one thing in common. You both want me to meet you.

Laura stopped before she hit Reply on the last message, deleted most of the words and simply replied with:

@SohoJane: Ha-ha.

@FarmerDan: How was *her* date?

@SohoJane: Which one? She goes on more dates than either of us.

@FarmerDan: The one with the guy you think did time?

@SohoJane: Oh, him. Yes, he wasn't an ex-crim just an ex-local councillor.

@FarmerDan: Fair enough. Is she seeing him again?

@SohoJane: No, there are too many better prospects apparently. The sixty-plus dating pool is where all the action is at.

Was it normal to talk so much about your mother with a guy you'd never even met? Laura shut down her computer, bid good evening to her colleagues, a close group of like-minded people who shared her passion for art and conservation and who had been amazingly supportive through the last few years of her life. Outside, the air was even warmer than she imagined. The temperature in their offices was kept constant to ensure the pieces they worked on were not further damaged. They did a lot of their work in their London studio, but also travelled frequently to their clients. As she walked across Hyde Park, marvelling at the number of people who had come out to enjoy the evening, she kept messaging Dan. It had become an early evening ritual for both of them to check in with one another at this time of day. Sometimes it was just a brief chat, other times their conversation would stretch on into the night.

@FarmerDan: Your mum could write the book on online dating. There's definitely a market for Fiona's dating wisdom.

Laura grimaced. He was probably right. Laura's father passed away nearly a decade ago. Fiona had struggled for many years after losing her husband, but the passage of time had eased her grief and Fiona had launched herself into her sixties and recent retirement with gusto. She called it her 'Fi-naissance' and had thrown herself back into the world: dating, learning photography, volunteering and travelling. Her mother's activities exhausted Laura but fascinated Dan.

@SohoJane: Yes, but you're not her daughter.

Fiona had a lot to say on the topic of online dating, and dating in general, though Laura was not in the right space to be receiving her mother's particular brand of advice at this point in time.

Laura had been messaging Dan casually on a dating app for a few weeks when she'd had a particularly devastating discussion with her doctor about her fertility status and future treatment options. She had told Dan she was stepping away from dating for a bit, but Dan had written back wishing her the best. Somehow they hadn't stopped messaging. Their conversations had been much more honest from that point on, as well. Once a relationship was taken off the table they both seemed to speak more openly, about life and in particular, dating. Dan would tell her about his dates and online dating disasters and she shared her mother's escapades.

Since then, Laura had had further surgery in an attempt to relieve her symptoms. After a terrible start, she was beginning to feel well. She was cautiously hopeful. She had to be. If this didn't work there were few other options left, apart from the most radical of all. A hysterectomy.

Dr Healy, who had been treating Laura for endometriosis for a decade, since her early twenties, said she almost never resorted to those steps in women who had not had children.

'Almost never?' Laura had questioned. 'What does that mean?'

'I mean, it's not a decision you make until we've tried everything else.'

Laura wasn't even sure if she wanted children; it was something she'd never really allowed herself to contemplate, knowing as she always had that it would likely be more difficult for her. Her main priority over the years had been trying to be pain free enough to live a full life.

Over the past few months, chatting with a farmer from Gloucestershire, a man she should have nothing in common with but appeared to have everything in common with, was a kind of solace. Most of her friends and colleagues knew about her condition—they had to. Her frequent absences from work, her need to cancel dates when her symptoms were too bad, made concealing her condition from people close to her impossible.

But Dan didn't know anything and that was freeing.

While she was laid up at home his messages were the

bright point of her day. All her friends and workmates wrote to her with sympathetic questions about how she was doing, but Dan was oblivious to everything else going on in her life and she liked that. She liked having someone who was not part of her world.

He didn't constantly ask her how she was. How she'd been. Didn't ask for a pain status update. He just chatted. About everything and sometimes nothing.

*Would you rather drink coffee or tea for the rest of your life?*

*Tea, though just writing that makes me long for my morning latte. You?*

*It would be an impossible choice, but I'd say coffee.*

*Would you rather be attacked by a shark or a crocodile?*

*Is neither an option?*

Apart from silly quizzes, she told him about her job as an art conservator. Usually once a new acquaintance had asked what her job involved the questions ended, but Dan had plenty more: What do you love about it? What era do you specialise in? Who are your favourite artists? She couldn't resist talking about her work. What did she love about it? Everything! She loved the science, the problem solving, the history and most of all making sure that beautiful and important works of art survived for generations to come.

In turn, she asked about his work. Why had he become a farmer?

@FarmerDan: Family business, I'm afraid.

@SohoJane: You're afraid? Did you not want to be a farmer?

@FarmerDan: No, I did. I do. I'm happy to do it. I love it.

Something about his choice of words indicated a level of hesitancy, but Laura let it go.

@SohoJane: What do you like about it?

@FarmerDan: Many things! The animals. Being outside. And it probably sounds corny, but I like the satisfaction you get by helping things grow.

She didn't think that was corny at all. It made her smile. Dan often made her smile. He seemed like a lovely, down-to-earth man. So different from many of the other men she met in London. Maybe she should listen to her mother's advice and meet him already.

No. She stopped that thought there. She and Dan worked well as friends. And she wasn't going to date anyone until she had a better idea about her condition and her next steps.

But they kept chatting. About life in general. They both had mothers who were very keen to see them settled. Dan's mother was a greater meddler even than Fiona, going so far as to invite single women along to occasions when Dan was expecting a lunch or dinner alone with his mother.

Laura knew their friendship had moved on from potential partners to friends when Dan started mentioning some dates he'd been on. At first Laura had a pang of sadness, but then quickly reminded herself that not only was she the one to say she didn't want a relationship, but that she actually *didn't* want a relationship. Not at this point in her life anyway.

At home, Laura sat on the couch in her small apartment, eating a sandwich she had been too distracted to eat at lunchtime and messages bounced between them.

A Deux was an exclusive app. Exclusive and expensive. The cost had given her pause, but she paid the money to

have her identity protected and to know that the users of
the app had been vetted first. By an actual person, not an
algorithm.

Many of the users revealed everything about themselves—there were some celebrities who were very keen for
everyone to know who they were—but just as many users
remained anonymous, or partially anonymous, like Laura.
The app had allowed her not to worry that the person she
was chatting with was a scammer. Or a stalker. Laura had
been burnt before by a man who had created fake profiles
to keep chatting with her once their brief relationship had
ended. Despite reporting him to the managers of the app,
he kept finding ways to reach her. She had almost given
up online dating entirely at that point, until her mother had
told her about A Deux.

Laura didn't use her real name, and while her profile picture showed her face, it was in black-and-white and didn't
expose every pore. She wasn't unrecognisable to someone
who knew her well but was anonymous enough she wouldn't
be spotted by an acquaintance. She hadn't had nearly as
many matches as she did on other apps, but A Deux promised to keep its clients safe and kicked off anyone about
whom a complaint had been made.

As an unexpected bonus, Laura wasn't on the same site
as her mother. She loved her mother, but dating alongside
her was strange. Fiona knew about Laura's friendship with
Dan and had gently been encouraging her to meet him, even
just as friends. '*A trip out of London would do you good*,'
Fiona had suggested.

Meanwhile, Dan had let it slip that he did spend some
time in London to visit his mother and 'do business.' Laura
wasn't exactly sure what visiting London entailed for a
farmer.

A farmer. She'd never known any farmers and couldn't

quite get her head around what he did each day, but she was curious to know. And dating stockbrokers and lawyers hadn't exactly worked out for her so she was open to anything.

*But you aren't dating Dan. You're just chatting.*

The next morning broke bright and clear again. Each day that was pain free filled Laura with hope. It was wonderful to be able to go so long without spending a day at home, curled up in bed. She was planning on continuing an assessment of a John Everett Millais painting. Working on a painting she'd known and loved for years was exhilarating, but also an honour.

'Laura, good news. They signed off on your trip to Abney Castle.'

Laura took off the magnifying glasses and torch with which she was assessing the canvas and refocused her gaze on her supervisor, Brett.

'You're going to Gloucestershire next week.'

Laura's mentor, Archibald Peterson, had been the conservator requested by Abney Castle for years, even when he was meant to be retired. He loved the collection so much and the family was so fond of him, he visited them biannually, as long as his health permitted. Before he'd passed away he'd recommended Laura take over for him and, much to Laura's delight, the family had taken his recommendation. It included an important and thoughtfully assembled collection of eighteenth-and nineteenth-century British art, including many by Laura's favourite artist, J. M. W. Turner.

It was a wonderful opportunity, and further evidence that something was turning around in her life.

'Great! I'll book my accommodation.'

'No need. They've said you can stay there.'

'At the castle?'

'Well, in the servants' quarters anyway. There's a cottage you can use.'

'Really?'

'Yes, really. You'll have all the privacy you need. But if you'd rather stay at a B & B in the village, you can.'

'I'm sure the cottage will be fine.' ·

Archibald had visited Abney Castle regularly for as long as she'd known him and come back with stories about how welcoming the elderly Duke and Duchess of Brighton were, even inviting him to join them for meals on occasion. While she doubted she'd obtain the same degree of intimacy Archibald had, she hoped she wouldn't let them, or Archibald, down.

Back at her desk, Laura googled Abney Castle and gasped. She was familiar with the paintings in the Duke of Brighton's collection, but not his seat of Abney Castle. England being England, the Duke of Brighton was based in Gloucestershire, nowhere near Brighton.

The website showed that Abney Castle was still privately owned, but opened to tourists six days a week. The castle was a Grade I–listed property and had been owned by the Dukes of Brighton for over four hundred years. It was also a functioning organic farm, with an animal nursery and cider distillery. The photos of the grounds made her breath catch. The place was gorgeous. And it would be her home for the next few weeks.

There was also a photo of the duke and his duchess. They were seated, straight backed, in an opulent room. He in particular looked frail, but both held friendly smiles. She hoped they were really as kind as they appeared in their photograph. While clients generally treated their conservators well, everyone had at least one bad story about a client who had unrealistic expectations. Laura's job was primarily to protect the art works from further degeneration—she

cleaned the paintings and suggested steps for further care—
but it was rare to recommend attempting to restore the art
to its original condition. As conservators, they did not do
anything to the artwork that was not reversible.

The job at Abney was significant. Several hundred paintings, some particularly large. The paintings would have
been well looked after under Archibald's care, and assessed
very regularly, which allayed most of her concerns. But it
was a big job. She'd be away for several weeks. What if she
became ill during her visit?

She closed the browser.

She was going to Abney Castle. For a few glorious weeks
she would escape her mother's interrogation, concentrate
on her work and have space to figure out her next steps.
And if she got sick, she'd manage. She always had before.

She might even meet a real-life duke.

That evening Laura met two girlfriends for a drink on the
way home. It was later than usual by the time she finally
connected with Dan.

@FarmerDan: How was your day? Best thing? Worst thing?

She loved that he took the time to ask this, it was like her
father had once done when she was a child. The memory
of her father was bittersweet; if she hadn't had a wonderful
childhood then his loss wouldn't hurt so much.

@SohoJane: Worst thing was the coffee. We tried a new
place and urgh. Won't be going back. But that probably
means I had a pretty good day.

@FarmerDan: So the best thing?

@SohoJane: A career highlight, I think.

@FarmerDan: Amazing, congratulations. Do tell!

Laura stared at her phone. Even if Dan was unlikely to say anything, she doubted the duke and duchess would be happy with her telling a stranger about her new assignment without their prior approval. She knew her firm would certainly not be. They had very strict policies around discussing their clients, which included royalty, celebrities and of course the aristocracy. Besides, if she told him what the assignment was and that she'd be staying close to where he lived for a few weeks then she'd feel extra pressure to finally meet him. He wouldn't press her, but it would feel strange to go to his part of the country and not suggest they meet.

@SohoJane: I can't say exactly, but I've been given a very prestigious collection to work on. It's very exciting.

@FarmerDan: Congratulations! I'm sure it's very well deserved because I'm sure you're fabulous at your job.

His absolute confidence in her made her entire chest warm with pride.

Should she tell him she was coming to Gloucestershire? It was hardly a small place, but she'd be closer than she was in London.

No. She'd wait a little.

At times she was overwhelmed with the urge to tell him everything about her, about her life. At times she wanted to call him, longed to hear the sound of his voice, but she had to keep those feelings in check. She had good reasons for holding back.

* * *

Henry took off his jacket and slung it over his shoulder as he walked down Piccadilly, towards Hyde Park. It was an unseasonably warm spring day and he was close to concluding the business on one of his monthly trips to London. He'd attended a board meeting of the children's charity of which he was a patron and met with the family accountant. He'd also managed to squeeze in a quick lunch with one of his university friends, but was now, thankfully, making his way back to his house in Mayfair.

His phone buzzed and he looked at it immediately. This was usually the time of day he'd start to expect a message from Jane. He had a self-imposed time of not messaging her before five in the afternoon. His impulse was to send her a brief message first thing in the morning, but he knew that not only would he be coming on too strong, but the rest of the day would be spent messaging with her. Chatting with her was like a compulsion for him; it seemed they had an endless number of things to talk about, especially for a couple who had never met in person.

Henry had almost given up on online dating when his friend suggested A Deux, an exclusive site with people who were vetted by the business owner. Women were attracted to the site because it was considered safer—Henry had been attracted by the idea that he could maintain his anonymity for longer than usual. He liked to get to know someone— and for them to get know him—before meeting in person.

Before they found out he was a duke.

He'd made the mistake of putting his full name, not even his title, on the dating sites before, but not this time. This time he was FarmerDan. He wanted to meet a person who liked him—not his name or his title.

He knew he had to marry, preferably within the next few years, because, and there was no way of getting around it, he needed an heir. In the absence of a direct heir—male or female—the Duchy of Brighton would cease to exist. A four-hundred-year-old title would end with him, the thirteenth duke.

Dukedoms and titles had become extinct in the past, probably not mourned by many people, except their own family. His own family—but particularly his own parents—had made too many sacrifices to preserve the title for Henry to lose it.

Besides, getting married? Having children? Those were both things that Henry longed to do—title or no title. He wanted a family and a woman to love and share his life with.

But so far, finding a woman who loved him, Henry Daniel Weston, not Henry, Duke of Brighton, hadn't happened. And he was beginning to doubt that it would.

Henry was in London for one more night. There wasn't an hour that went by that day, during his meetings, his lunch, his drinks that he hadn't started mentally composing a message to Jane.

*Hey, I've just popped down to London for business. Don't suppose you'd fancy catching up for a drink?*

But knowing her as he did, he didn't send that message.

She was not looking for a romantic relationship at that point; he didn't know why, but he respected it. Yet even though they both understood their relationship would remain platonic, they hadn't stopped messaging one another. He'd expected her to stop. But she hadn't, so neither had he. Knowing she didn't want a relationship hadn't made him less interested in maintaining a friendship. They understood one another, from nearly the outset, and talking to her was like talking to an old friend.

Back at Brighton House, a five-storey Georgian era townhouse near Grosvenor Square, he slipped off his tie and was just about to take off his shoes when he heard voices from the next room. The door to one of the reception rooms was wide open and he paused. Could he walk past and up the stairs without being noticed?

It was a decision he didn't have to make because his mother called out, 'Henry? Henry, darling? Is that you? Come and join us?'

His heart fell.

He didn't want to be speaking to strangers; he wanted to be messaging Jane.

But he was the thirteenth duke of Brighton and he had two jobs: first to keep the family estate largely intact without running up debt for the next generation. Secondly, produce that next generation.

Henry took a deep breath and made himself smile as he walked into the room. There were perhaps a dozen people mingling around, women of all ages, though he guessed that attractive women in the twenty-five to thirty-five age bracket were over-represented. He went over to his mother, Caroline, and kissed her cheek. 'Mum, good evening.'

'Henry, please join us.'

Even knowing he didn't have a choice, he said, 'Oh, no, I wouldn't want to intrude.'

'Nonsense. We don't mind. The more the merrier.'

'Really, I'm sure I could have nothing to add to your…' He looked around the room. Matchmaking party?

'Book club. I've just started a book club.'

Henry bit back a laugh. His mother was the last person on earth he'd imagine in a book club. A walking club, yes. Anything to do with horses, certainly. Art appreciation, maybe. His mother was cultured, but the type of reading matter by her beside was strictly magazines. In all his thirty years he'd never heard her discuss a book.

'Let me introduce you to everyone.'

Twelve sets of eyes looked up at him from where their

owners were perched on the various sofas in the room. There was a decent spread of ages, he had to give his mother that. But how on earth she'd managed to hand pick them all and bring them here under the guise of a book club, and tonight of all nights, he could only begin to guess. But Caroline Weston, the Dowager Duchess of Brighton, was known for her organisational skills and powers of persuasion.

Henry sighed, walked over to the sideboard and poured himself a Scotch. He wasn't going to get a moment to himself anytime soon.

'What book did you read?' he asked as he sat down on the nearest sofa and turned to the first candidate, surrendering himself to the evening.

At least, he thought, Jane is going to get a laugh out of this.

'You're angry,' Caroline said three hours later after she bid the last guest/prospective bride goodbye.

'No, I'm just tired.'

'Did you…that is…' Caroline fussed with the sofa cushions, though they both knew full well their housekeeper would come through in the morning to tidy.

'Did I like any of them?' he asked.

Her expression was so hopeful, so earnest.

'They were all lovely. Smart, attractive, good company.'

Her face fell. 'But?'

'But nothing.' He couldn't explain to his mother what the problem was because he didn't understand it himself.

He knew he had to marry and produce an heir. That was not in dispute, but why, when so many eligible, suitable women came across his path was it so hard to choose one? Probably because he used words such as 'eligible' or 'suitable' to describe his future wife. What he was looking for was 'amazing', 'heart-stopping' or 'soul lifting.'

'I just want you to be happy,' Caroline said.

'I know.'

Henry knew his mother wished for his happiness, but only because she believed marrying one of the suitable women she had invited tonight would lead to his happiness. Marrying a suitable woman and producing an heir was in fact the very reason for his existence. The very reason he'd been born in the first place.

His mother kissed him goodnight and Henry finally kicked off his shoes before flopping back onto the nearest sofa and taking out his phone.

There was a message from Jane waiting for him, asking him how his day was.

@FarmerDan: Send wine. And pity. You will not believe what I just walked into.

@SohoJane: A wall?

@FarmerDan: You're on the right track. My mother just ambushed me with a speed dating event disguised as a book club meeting.

@SohoJane: Wow! That's hard core. We must never introduce our mothers to one another.

@FarmerDan: It would probably cause a fissure in the space-time continuum, such would be their combined power.

@SohoJane: Absolutely and I don't know if we can trust them to use their power for good instead of evil.

He liked how he was with her. He felt funnier with her. Was that possible? Was she laughing at his joke? If he saw her in person, he'd be able to tell. He'd be able to watch her face as he spoke, hear her voice…

He was a fool. He should have continued talking to one of the eligible book clubbers, not be spending his time thinking about how to make a woman who wasn't interested in him laugh.

@SohoJane: You're in London?

His heart began to hammer against his ribs. Jane knew his mother lived here.

*Just ask her. It's still early.*

It was nine thirty. Late enough for anyone who had to work tomorrow.

@FarmerDan: Yes, I've popped down for a brief visit. I thought about letting you know, but I know how you feel so I didn't.

He sat back, waited.
But she didn't respond.

Two days later Henry still hadn't had a response from SohoJane to his message telling her he was in London. He was particularly glad he hadn't said more than that or asked her to meet, but two days was a long time for her to go without replying.

The damp morning gradually brightened into a warm, dry day. Henry spent the morning driving around the grounds and checking the progress of the calves and the lambs. It was spring and they expected two thousand lambs to be born and maybe three hundred calves. They employed a small team of farmers to oversee the farm, but he liked to help out where he could.

The duchy owned fifteen thousand acres of land, one thousand was farmland under his direct management. He had close to fifty tenants, over thirty tenants in the vicinity alone and the rest on the other ducal properties that were scattered across the country.

Then there was the castle.

Abney Castle, the seat of the Dukes of Brighton, was picturesque, but like anything that was several centuries old, it needed constant upkeep and regular health checks. Not to mention a significant budget to pay for them. Opening the castle to the public went some way to paying for its upkeep, but it brought other challenges as well—additional staff, operating costs and further maintenance.

He was fortunate that his father and grandfather had also been good managers and the bulk of their estates was in good order giving them a large buffer for the future, should disaster occur.

Later in the afternoon he had a teleconference with the conservation firm in London about the replacement conservator they were sending. Archibald, the man who had been visiting the estates for the past thirty years, had recently passed away, but they assured him they would send a highly experienced replacement to assess the art collection that his family had collected over the centuries.

The art collection at Abney Castle consisted of over five hundred paintings. From old masters to a significant collection of nineteenth-century British art, including Turner and the Pre-Raphaelites. The entire collection, some of which was lent to the National Gallery and the Tate, numbered in the thousands. The art collection was particularly special; his ancestors had had not only good taste and judgement but exceptional foresight.

Henry meant to see the buildings and the art collections housed inside them protected for generations to come. Other aristocratic families had sold off parts of their collections to fund maintenance of the rest of the estates, but Henry, like his father, saw this as a failure of his management. The estate needed to be maintained, protected and passed down to the next generation. He was only the temporary caretaker of his family's legacy. If anything, he wanted to be in the position of adding to the collection, rather than selling it off to pay for building repairs.

It was after four by the time he finally collapsed, famished, into a chair at his kitchen table. A plate of sandwiches that had been left on the table for him for whenever he finally wandered in sat in front of him. He realised he hadn't even stopped for lunch. Being a duke in the twenty-first century was much the same as being a CEO of a company. It was an exhausting role that needed every one of his skill sets and every ounce of his energy. It was then that his phone finally pinged.

@SohoJane: Hey there, sorry about the radio silence. I collapsed with exhaustion not long after your message. Are you back home?

He exhaled the breath he'd been holding for the past two days.

@FarmerDan: Yes, back home and back to the grind.

He pulled up one of the photos of the newborn lamb he'd taken that morning and sent it to her. She sent back half a dozen love hearts.

When it came to the farm he did what needed doing, but welcoming baby animals was one of his favourite parts.

# CHAPTER TWO

LAURA SLOWED HER car as she rounded the corner and the castle came into view.

The structure was built over several eras: the front part of the building looked as though it had been built in the eighteenth century, made primarily from the distinctive Cotswold stone, a honey-coloured limestone that glowed golden in the sunlight. It looked more like a grand Georgian manor than a castle, but either way it was stunning.

The driveway led to a deserted car park and a small building, with a sign proclaiming *Abney Castle—Entry.* Beyond that was a brick wall stretching off into the distance in both directions. In front of her was a wrought-iron gate, shut and labelled with a closed sign.

They were expecting her, but it still felt inauspicious to be met with a locked gate. She noticed a box that appeared to be an intercom and wound down her window. She pressed the button and a camera swirled in her direction. After a while she heard the line open. 'Good afternoon, how may I help?'

'I'm Laura Oliver. From…' The gate clicked and slowly parted. The voice at the other end of the line was gone.

Laura drove her small car slowly along the drive, taking in the lush green lawns, the magnificent vista sloping up to the front of the castle. The gravel drive led her directly to the front door where she stopped her car, but didn't turn off the engine. What next? Did she just park here and then knock on the door? She looked at the front door, if you could call it that. Double sided, painted a deep red with a knocker that might or might not be real gold. It was as wide and high as a double-decker bus.

Before she could decide, a single door to the side of the double entrance opened and a middle-aged woman with a friendly smile and a quick step came out and over to Laura's car.

'Laura! Welcome to Abney Castle. If you wouldn't mind driving around to the side of the building, I'll show you to the cottage.'

Laura nodded and drove as instructed to the side of the hall and turned the corner. There again was a further stretch of gravel drive, which she drove along slowly, following the woman.

Laura had been in amazing buildings before; she'd met nobility before. She'd been behind the scenes of the Louvre, the National Gallery and the Rijksmuseum. But this felt different. She was being invited into someone's home.

She felt the full honour of this assignment, and silently thanked her former mentor, Archibald, for recommending she take on this work on his behalf. Being given the responsibility of looking after a collection as important as this would be a highlight of her career.

The crunch of the gravel was crisp under her tyres. Along the driveway flower beds overflowed with spring colour. The woman led her to a wisteria-covered thatched cottage, half hidden in the grove of birch trees. It looked like it had been ripped from the pages of a Cotswold tourist catalogue.

This was her cottage.

'Laura, I'm Claudia, the family housekeeper at Abney

Castle and this is where you'll be staying. Come on, let me show you around.'

Claudia unlocked the wooden door to the cottage and then handed Laura the keys. 'Those keys also have the clicker to unlock the front gate, so you can feel free to come and go as you please. Of course, the village is actually a one-mile walk, that way.' She pointed in the opposite direction to the one Laura had come from. 'There is a key for that gate as well. Access is only by foot that way, but those are the two entrances you will most likely need.'

Claudia barely drew breath and Laura was still processing all the information, as well as her beautiful surroundings as Claudia led her into the cottage.

The ceiling was low, as to be expected in such a cottage. At least two or three hundred years old, maybe more, though it was fully renovated and modernised, while keeping the original charm.

'This is your sitting room.'

The room was furnished with two soft sofas covered in floral fabrics. There was a fireplace and a large television.

'Through there is the kitchen-diner. I've left some groceries in the fridge for you, but you'll need to do some shopping at some stage.'

'Thank you, you didn't have to.'

'Nonsense. Let me know if you want me to add anything to the order, but if you want to do your own, the village has a very good store. And down the back—' Claudia led the way down a narrow hall '—are the two bedrooms. They are both made up. I expect you would prefer the larger, but just in case the other is ready to go as well. And in case you want to have visitors.'

'I didn't…that is…' Flummoxed, it hadn't even occurred to Laura that she might be allowed to have guests.

'Of course, just let me know so I can tell security. And if you plan on having any wild parties—'

'I would never—'

'Then just make sure you invite me!' She laughed heartily and Laura wondered if she was joking or not. As if she'd throw a wild party in this gorgeous cottage. It didn't scream 'all-night raver'. Rather 'curl up with a book by the fire'.

'I will be sure to, but I expect I'll be too busy with the paintings to throw any wild parties.'

'Yes, about that. The duke is expected back later this afternoon. He'd like to show you the house and the paintings himself, if that's okay?'

The duke wanted to see her himself? She thought she'd be dealing with the estate manager or someone from the castle museum.

'Yes, of course.'

'So feel free to unpack, get yourself settled and even have an explore of the grounds. You're lucky to arrive on a Tuesday, when we're closed. The weekdays aren't too bad but on a weekend, the place swarms with day trippers. You'll have the whole place to yourself today. And the weather's splendid!'

After saying goodbye to Claudia, Laura collapsed into the nearest sofa and exhaled, her head spinning.

The duke would be here, showing her the castle personally. That was unexpected; as far as she could tell from the photographs online he was quite elderly, well into his eighties. Not that people that age couldn't be fit, but it did seem like unnecessary effort to go to show her around. He must be very proud of his collection. Or attached to it. She hoped she was equal to the task of looking after it.

After a phone call to her mother letting her know she'd arrived, Laura unpacked and explored the cottage.

Claudia had indeed stocked the pantry and the fridge.

There was a plate of sandwiches and two home-cooked meals with handwritten labels and cooking instructions. Shepherd's pie and vegetable curry. She salivated but took out the sandwiches.

The pantry was also generously stocked, tea bags in a variety of flavours, coffee pods also and two bottles of wine, a red and white. Laura made herself a cup of tea, opening several cupboards until she located everything. She ate the sandwiches as she checked in at work and read her emails.

When she'd finished, it was still only just after one and she wondered if she had a few hours to spare before the duke arrived. She didn't want to miss him and wasn't sure what 'late afternoon' meant, exactly, but figured she had time to explore the grounds and maybe even walk to the village. She gathered her phone and the keys, debated whether she'd need a jacket, but given the blue sky and gentle breeze, decided against it. At the last minute she dug through her bag for a sticky note.

'Gone for a walk, back soon, Laura' she wrote followed by her phone number. She affixed it to the front door in case the duke arrived while she was out. She didn't want to inconvenience any boss, let alone an elderly duke.

She made her way down the side of the castle and once she reached the corner, the full expanse of the building and its grounds came into view. The back of Abney Castle was every bit as impressive as the front. Unlike the front facade, which was all Georgian elegance, the back of the building showed more hints of the older history of the castle with smaller windows and some medieval-style pointed arches and turrets. Three generous stories high plus attics—the castle was beautiful.

The garden was equally impressive. Immediately before her lay a formal terraced garden, carefully designed in the French style with low hedges, innumerable flowers, fountains and statues. Beyond that, and stretching out to the horizon were the famous gardens designed in the English landscape style to look natural, but truly every blade of grass and every stone was meant to be exactly where it was. A stream gurgled off into the distance, forded by a pretty stone bridge. Laura hardly knew where to begin, but the bridge called to her. She wanted to walk along it.

The air smelt of roses and freshly cut grass and the oxygen filled her lungs like a balm. The sky was the bright blue of a spring day and she had the entire place to herself. She gave a quiet chuckle. Life was funny, a few months ago she'd been at one of her lowest moments ever and now, here she was, temporarily at home in some of the most beautiful gardens in the country.

The path to the bridge took her past ponds filled with fish, ducks and geese. Once she reached the bridge she crossed it, stopped halfway and looked back up to the castle. She couldn't believe she was getting paid to be here.

The grounds must have an army of gardeners looking after it, the castle too. But for the moment at least it was simply hers to enjoy.

She heard the sound of a barking dog behind a hedge and went to investigate. She didn't want one of the gardeners finding her and thinking she had no business being there. She rounded the corner of the hedge and saw two golden cocker spaniels barking and dancing around one another. And something else she couldn't quite make out at first.

As she approached the scene came into focus. It was a man. And an animal of some sort. A calf. Or a small cow. Both the man and the cow were on the other side of the wire fence from Laura. He was struggling and then she saw the problem. The calf appeared to be tangled in the wire.

Each time the man pulled the wire away, the calf inserted its head into the hole. He would steady the calf, but then the wire would pull tighter. He needed three or four hands for the task, yet he only had the usual allocation of two.

He was tall, well-built, and she paused and watched him for a while admiring the way the muscles in his shoulders flexed and rippled as he wrestled the calf.

The man was dressed in blue jeans, which nicely fit his strong thighs and bottom. His T-shirt looked as though it had once been white but was now a kaleidoscope of stains, mud, sweat and something else she didn't want to contemplate. Despite the mud and sweat, or maybe because of it, she wondered if the gardener was single and whether a country fling might just be the exact thing she needed.

*He's not a gardener, he's a farmer.*

FarmerDan?

No. It couldn't be. Dan would have told her if he worked for a duke, wouldn't he? The man had dark blond hair, just like Dan had. Could it be?

She heard the man curse and was jolted out of her thoughts.

Laura approached him and said. 'Here, let me help.'

His head spun and he regarded her with a mix of confusion and surprise. 'Do you know what you're doing?' he asked.

'Not in the slightest, but it looks like you don't either.'

Up close he was even more handsome; never mind his shoulders and thighs, the man had piercing blue eyes, framed by a strong brow and defined cheekbones. Resolutely handsome. If he looked good this filthy she really wanted to see how he'd look washed and clean.

No. This wasn't the time or the place.

'It does look like you could do with another set of hands,' she offered.

He sighed the sigh of a man who didn't want to accept help but knew he had no choice.

'I can't promise your clothes won't end up as another casualty.'

'I'm not precious and they wash.'

'If you're sure.'

She nodded.

'Then, if you step over here and hold up that part of the fence.'

She did as she was told, but pulling on one part of the wire only seemed to pull another tighter. The man had a hold of the calf with both hands now.

'And maybe, if you can reach, just there, above its ear.'

Laura stretched her arm, suddenly conscious that she was now very close to the man. Close enough that if she'd leant down just a little she could have pressed her lips to the back of his neck. It was a strong neck; veins protruded through the tan skin from the exertion and Laura's mouth went dry.

She wasn't really contemplating a fling with a gardener, was she? Or was she simply overcome by all the fresh country air?

The calf squealed and with a final grunt the man pulled the calf free.

It stood back, shook itself and then bolted away. The man stepped back, caught his breath and wiped his hands on his jeans. It did no good. His jeans were just as filthy as his hands.

Once he recovered his breath, he looked her up and down. Not in an appraising manner, just in an apparent effort to figure out who she was.

'Hello. May I ask who you are and what you're doing here?'

'I'm Laura Oliver. I've come to help the duke with the art collection. I was told I could have a look around the gardens while I waited for him to return. And you?'

His jaw dropped, and he nodded, his head bobbing up

and down for too many beats, like he was putting some puzzle pieces together.

'Laura, welcome to Abney Castle. I'd offer you my hand but I wouldn't recommend you take it.'

'Thank you?'

She could see him gathering his composure before saying, 'I'm the Duke of Brighton.'

No. The Duke of Brighton was eighty if he were a day.

'But you're...' Handsome? Hot? Strong? 'Younger than I was expecting.'

He coughed. 'Thank you?'

She realised her faux pas the second before he said, 'You may be thinking of my father.'

Suddenly she wished she were the one covered in animal excrement; it would've been less embarrassing than this. 'I'm so, so sorry, Your Grace. I saw the photo on the website and assumed...'

'It's fine, really. We really should get that thing updated. He did pass away nearly a year ago now.'

'I'm so sorry for your loss. My father passed away nearly ten years ago, but I remember at one year, it was still raw.'

She couldn't meet his eye. *Ground, swallow me up.* Her embarrassment was mixed with disappointment; he wasn't Dan. Of course he wasn't. And she was far too obsessed with Dan for her own good. She was meant to be having a break from dating until she figured out what she was going to do with her body.

She heard him say softly, 'Laura, it really is okay. Thank you again for your help with the calf.' His voice was kind and the last trace of frustration and awkwardness seem to melt away from him.

She looked up and met his eyes. They lifted slightly at the edges into a soft smile. Friendly. Familiar. And yet how could they be?

The Duke of Brighton. The owner of Abney Castle, was standing across a broken wire fence from her, dripping in sweat and goodness knew what else. Like a smellier, dirtier, version of Colin Firth after his dip in the lake.

Were modern-day dukes allowed to be this hot? Weren't they all old, stuffy and not at all capable of untangling a precocious calf from a fence?

Apparently not.

'I met Claudia. She said I was welcome to have a look around and that you would like to show me the inside of the house. I mean castle.'

He laughed, but she wasn't sure at what.

'We do just call it a house. And you should call me Henry.'

'Henry,' she said, in confirmation. It was far easier than saying 'Your Grace'.

'I apologise again, I didn't realise I'd be dealing directly with you.'

'That's all right. I was particularly interested to meet you.'

He was? How odd.

'Claudia's our housekeeper. She looks after my mother and me and our apartments, but also the cottage and your needs. If you need anything, please feel free to start with her. But the main house is managed by a different team in entirely. That's overseen by Louis, who manages the guides, the cleaning. You'll meet him tomorrow. And the chief groundskeeper is Harvey, who is also away today. Tuesday is usually everyone's weekend. Hence, this falls to me.'

He pointed to the hole in the fence. 'As does giving you a tour of the house, but I hope that's more pleasant than this.'

He gestured to himself. 'If you could excuse me for a

while, I think it's in everyone's interests if I shower before we do that.'

'Of course.'

He smiled at her and it was impossible not to smile back.

As if they knew it was their turn, the two dogs, golden spaniels who had been sitting patiently until now, began to bark again.

'And this pair are Buns and Honey.'

Laura laughed. 'Or Honey and Buns?'

'My mother named them. She thinks she's hilarious.'

'It's the kind of thing my mother would do too. May I pet them?'

He nodded. She loved dogs and this pair were beautiful.

'Good to meet you, Honey and Buns.'

At the sound of their names they stood and ran to her, putting their paws on the fence as if to reach for her.

She leant over the fence to pat them. She patted Buns, the boy, but Honey pushed her way in front so she settled for one hand on each, rubbing them behind their ears.

'You've made some friends. Do you have dogs?'

She shook her head. 'It's not practical in my apartment. But I do love them.'

'Once they know where you're staying they won't stay away.'

She couldn't help but smile. 'They're welcome anytime.'

She looked up and smiled, meeting the duke's gaze just as he was doing the same and his smile hit her with a force that almost made her breathless.

Uh-oh.

Wasn't her life complicated enough? She didn't need to add *Get a stomach-flipping crush on a duke* to the list.

# CHAPTER THREE

IT WAS HER. The feeling in his chest told him it was her, yet she had a different name.

*You didn't use your real name either.*

Could the conservator sent by the museum be *his* SohoJane?

No. That would too much of a coincidence.

And yet, how many art conservators who specialised in nineteenth-century British oil paintings were there?

*Probably more than you realise.*

She'd told him she had had a big career opportunity. Was coming to Abney Castle what she'd meant?

When Laura had walked away, Henry took out his phone and brought up the profile picture he'd studied many times in order to get a better idea of what Jane looked like. Her profile photo wasn't entirely clear. She had her back to the sun, her face mostly obscured in the shade. A second photo was sharper, but she stood at a great distance. When he zoomed in on her face all he saw were blurry pixels. He knew. He'd tried hundreds of times. But this woman, Laura, did look like the two photos he'd seen of SohoJane.

She wanted anonymity on the dating site and he could hardly complain because he did too.

He'd also used a real photo of him—he wasn't about to steal someone's identity—but his face too was half hidden in the shadows. He didn't want someone doing a reverse image search and discovering who he really was. Not until he was ready to tell them.

Could it really be her? He wasn't sure, but he didn't have a clue how to subtly find out.

After temporarily securing the fence with some pliers and some spare wire he had on the truck, he drove back to the house. He got out of his soiled clothes and had a shower that was as hot as he could bear. It was hardly the first time he'd found himself covered in mud and animal fluids but the first time he'd been caught like that by a beautiful woman.

A woman he wanted to make a good impression in front of.

That realisation made something shift uneasily inside him.

If she wasn't SohoJane, then what would it mean if he liked Laura too?

*Nothing, because you aren't currently dating either of them.*

Henry was a pure monogamist; he didn't have feelings for two women at one time, let alone relationships, but his attraction to Laura sat uncomfortably with him, even though what he had with Jane was purely platonic.

And Laura worked for him.

So he really shouldn't be thinking about *either* of them in that way.

*You could just ask her if she's SohoJane?*

He laughed aloud at the thought. He wasn't about to come right out and say, *Hey, are you SohoJane on the A Deux dating site?*

He shook his head. No. But he had to say something, didn't he?

He stood for a long while in front of his open closet, a walk-in arrangement that was full of clean, pressed outfits, suitable for a duke. And not one of them felt appropriate for this meeting. His father would have worn a suit and tie, but that was too much for Henry. Jeans and T-shirt felt too much like work wear. He settled on some brown trousers and a dark blue fitted shirt and studied himself in the mirror. Normally he didn't think twice about his outfits; his tailor always ensured his clothes fit perfectly and theoretically anything in this wardrobe should be suitable.

But what if Laura *was* SohoJane?

Should he have said something when he first saw her? If he'd had his wits about him, their first conversation might have played out differently.

'I'm the Duke of Brighton. But please call me Henry. Daniel is a family name, my middle name and the name I use in my dating profile. Ring any bells? And you look familiar, you aren't SohoJane by any chance?'

Of course he hadn't said that. Apart from anything else he'd been covered in cow manure, surprised by her presence and nearly knocked breathless by the sight of the beautiful woman in front of him. At the first sight of her blue eyes it had been a wonder he'd been able to say anything at all.

After changing the blue shirt for a green one, he made his way out of his apartments and across to the cottage.

Both Henry and his mother, the duchess, or dowager duchess as she officially was, had private apartments at one end of the castle. They were smaller and less extravagant than the main rooms that were open to the public. Yet they had undergone modern renovations and were far easier to heat, cool and maintain. His mother spent most of her time at their London residence, Brighton House in Mayfair, but she came and went from Abney with a pattern he'd never been able to ascertain. As long as she was still driving and independent he figured things were well with her and he had no need to worry. She'd spoken of moving out of Brighton

House and into her own place several times since Henry's father passed away, but Henry assured her there was no need. When he did marry, they might all reassess Caroline's living arrangements, but until then he was happy to share the castle and the London house with her. With over two hundred rooms between the two residences, they were hardly in one another's pockets.

Laura was waiting outside the cottage. As she walked towards him, excitement rose up inside him, but he pushed it quickly down. Laura was here in a professional capacity, for all intents and purposes as his employee. His family had an enduring relationship with the firm for which she worked and he couldn't ruin that.

He smiled, clasped his hands behind his back and tried to ignore how sweaty they had suddenly become as he watched her approach him across the lawn. She had changed out of her jeans into a long woollen green dress, and high black boots. Her dark hair was loose and flowed in silken waves around her shoulders.

She was beautiful.

He ignored that thought too.

*Even if she is SohoJane, nothing can happen between you. She's taking a break from dating. She's been clear about that from the beginning.*

'Your Grace.' Laura greeted him with an outstretched hand.

'Henry, I told you.'

'I know, I'm trying to pretend, for your sake as much as mine, that our first meeting didn't happen.'

He suppressed a smile. In this new outfit she looked professional and stylish.

And edible.

He was in trouble.

'Did you get very soiled? Please send your clothes up to the house and we can wash them properly for you. Sadly, we're not strangers to that sort of mess.'

She waved the suggestion away. 'I missed it all.'

'Yes, well.' The sooner they changed the subject from cow manure the better. 'Shall we?' He motioned to the house.

'Yes please. Can I just say first of all that it's an absolute honour to be here. Archibald was my mentor, he was a great conservator.'

'The honour's ours. And I'm sorry to hear that he passed away. Did you know he personally recommended you take over from him?'

She nodded, but looked sombre.

'Yes, as a matter of fact he'd written it in the file. It was…'

She had this habit of tucking her long hair behind her ears when she was nervous. Or affected. She did it now. 'I was very touched to read it. I miss him a lot.'

Henry had met the man a few times over the years. 'He was a character.'

'Indeed, but amazing at his job. Which is good for you. His notes of your collection are meticulous and go back decades.'

Henry nodded. He supposed this was a good thing but honestly did not have a great idea what art conservation actually entailed. Being a duke involved wearing a lot of hats, many of which he was only just learning.

'I'm so sorry again about not knowing about your father. I should've done more research.'

'It's all right, truly. We really should update the castle's website.'

Since his father died, he had, subconsciously, or otherwise, avoided any announcements or publicity that were not strictly necessary. It suited him for the wider world to not realise he was now the duke. It suited him that everyone else thought of his father as the duke. For crying out loud, most days, he struggled to think of himself as the duke.

*You should tell her now. That you're FarmerDan.*

No. He needed to make sure it was really her first. He had a strong suspicion, but there was no certainty that the gorgeous woman next to him now was the same woman he'd been chatting to for months.

Besides, SohoJane had made it clear, she didn't want to meet. Not him, not anyone. She had something personal going on was all she'd said and he hadn't pressed. Despite telling him she was stepping away from dating, she'd kept talking to him. That was a sign of their friendship and her trust in him. He couldn't come out now and spring this on her. Could he?

He'd wait to say anything. Apologise later, if necessary.

'Why is it called a castle? If you don't mind me saying, it looks more like a house. I mean, not that it's not amazing,' she said as he opened one of the front doors.

'I'll get to that part of the tour.'

'I can't wait.'

There was a twinkle in her eye that lit up the blue with a golden spark. Inside his chest hitched and his mouth went dry. Again.

It wasn't as though he wasn't meant to be dating: he was. He was the duke now; there was no heir, let alone a spare. He had to, as they said, get cracking and find a wife. It shouldn't have been an unpleasant task, or even a painful one. But somehow it was.

He'd been burnt too many times before. Women saw the title. They saw the castle and rarely looked past those two things to see him. Really see him. That was one reason why

SohoJane was so special. That was why he was persevering with the A Deux app to begin with.

Laura was attractive, and so far she seemed lovely. Trustworthy.

Though she was saying all the usual things women said about the castle—*It's beautiful, it's amazing...*

*Do you want her to tell you that it's ugly?*

Not at all. She was a conservator so actually knew about art and probably also architecture and history. She wasn't gushing because she had a tiara in her sights, but because she had a genuine interest.

Ever since Beatrice he'd never quite been able to trust anyone who was overly fascinated with Abney Castle. Beatrice had been his girlfriend at university, the first woman he'd ever loved. He'd thought they'd marry, he thought he was so lucky to have found the love of his life so young, so easily. He'd been mistaken all along.

'Would you like the quick tour or the long one?'

'Do you have anywhere to be?'

'I have a date with BBC One and the French Open at eight p.m., but apart from that, no.'

She laughed, but if she was SohoJane then she might piece it together? SohoJane knew about his love of tennis.

'I'll show you everywhere you need to know about, but you should still feel free to explore yourself. Please go wherever you need to. The family apartments have a separate entrance so you won't stumble in on me by accident.'

'And the rest of your family?'

Did he imagine the quaver in her voice when she asked this or was it wishful thinking? 'It's just me and my mother and she spends most of her time in London.'

'So, it's just you living here?' Her voice rose at the end of the sentence.

'Yes, Claudia and Louis both live in houses on that side

of the castle.' He motioned in the direction from which Laura had entered the grounds. 'And a few other staff live in the village, but generally it's just me in the house.'

She raised an eyebrow, but he couldn't interpret the look. Was it judgement? Or something else entirely?

She didn't say anything more.

Henry saw the treasures of Abney Castle with fresh eyes as he led Laura around. She would be examining the contents of most rooms in detail over the course of her visit. He simply wanted her to become acquainted with the house and show her the layout. Maybe the secret, private passages.

He delighted in her gasps and sighs at each new room, bursting with pride as if he'd built the place himself. Which was silly. He was going to have to check his emotions where Laura was concerned.

He showed her into one of the main bedrooms. Last slept in by his great-grandfather but decorated by his mother in a mid-Victorian style. The ornate four-poster bed was nearly as tall as the high ceiling and was covered in opulent velvet drapes that fell all the way to the intricate Persian carpet on the floor.

'Did you grow up here?' she asked, spying the bed. He didn't think it looked particularly comfortable and as a rule they avoided sitting on the old furniture, but suddenly the image of Laura sitting on the edge of the bed and beckoning him over to her popped into his head.

He was the duke. It was his furniture. He could do what he wanted with it...

But that was not a helpful thought.

'Partly. But not in these rooms. My grandfather's generation was the last to live in this part of the house. When he married my grandmother they adapted the apartments for the family to live in and began to restore and preserve these rooms.'

'Did it take a long time? It looks to be in good condition.'

'Thank you, and yes. It was a lifetime project for both of them. They started just after the Second World War and began opening up rooms to the public in the nineteen sixties.'

'They did an amazing job,' she said spinning slowly in the room. 'But it still must be a lot of work to maintain. Let alone clean.'

He smiled to himself. Beatrice had asked questions such as how much it had cost. Laura, clearly a conservator, was only interested in the cleaning.

'It is. But I have a great team who work with me and who love the castle as much as I do.'

Being a twenty-first-century duke wasn't about being waited upon, it was about mucking in with everyone else to clean, manage. And get calves unstuck from fences.

But it was a privilege. And his duty. He meant to see the estate, including the castle, passed on down just as it had been passed down to him. After all the hard work and good management of his forefathers, he didn't want to be the one to see the castle, or the estates, fall into ruin.

After taking her through all the rooms that were open to the public he took her to a door marked *Private—No Entry*.

'Now you've had the public tour, let me take you out the back.'

She smiled and his heart hit his throat. Regardless of who she was, he was going to have to learn to tame the physical reactions he was having around her.

The corridors and rooms behind the scenes were simply painted in whites and greys and mostly unfurnished. It was difficult enough keeping the main rooms in order—it was only family and staff that saw these rooms. They were mostly offices and storage rooms and corridors that connected the other rooms with passages that had once been used by the servants.

'Importantly, this is the staff room.' He pointed into a large room, furnished in a mismatch of periods but with a small kitchen and a large television.

Henry led her down the corridor and into the next room. 'This room was where Archibald set himself up. Hopefully there's enough room for you to work in here.'

'This is great.' She looked around the large, light-filled workshop, equipped with some easels, tables, chairs and another kitchenette. 'What was this room originally?'

'I've no idea. It was Archibald's for as long as I can remember. He insisted he needed it to be north facing.'

'That's right, we try to work as much as possible with the best light available.'

'If you need anything else, just let me or Louis know and we will take care of it. And if you need to move any of the larger paintings...'

'Ask first?'

'No, I trust you. I was going to say, ask someone to help you lift them.'

'Thank you.'

When she smiled at him, grateful, eyes sparkling, he wanted to spin her into his arms. Could he date Laura? She worked for him, but that didn't have to be an insurmountable barrier. He liked her; it would be foolish to deny it. But could she like him? Would she see past the title to the man behind it?

It was a question that was impossible to answer at the moment, seeing how he was currently engaged with showing her around his castle. And for the first time in years he wanted to show it off.

'Would you like to see why it's called a castle?'

'Yes please.'

He led the way down the nearest staircase and out a side door. At this side of the building the land sloped away sharply, down to the river. Unlike on the other side of the building, this land was now mostly wild, not cultivated or curated garden, but it still afforded a sweeping view of the valley below. 'There's been a fortification on this hill since Norman times. Some stones from the original keep still remain, but this part of the castle was built in the fourteenth century.'

Henry took out his keys and unlocked the gate that now blocked their path. It squeaked when he pushed it open. Laura entered first and pride welled up inside him. He could tell she saw it as he did, with appreciation of the history and a desire to look after it. Not with pound signs in her eyes.

What Beatrice, what many other women he met, didn't understand was that he didn't see the castle as his. It was his family's. His children's. He held it all in trust for the future. Far from being able to relax and enjoy his property, it was his job to maintain it.

Even though Henry wanted to find a woman he could trust would love him—Henry Daniel Weston—even he had a hard time separating himself from his title. It was the reason for his very existence, his very birth. Was he being foolish wanting someone to see him in a way he hardly did himself?

He felt Laura's soft sigh in his chest when the trees parted and the structure came into view. 'This was a working castle for over three hundred years. During the Wars of the Roses and Tudor times. Queen Elizabeth I even visited on one of her progresses. But this was the structure that suffered a direct hit during the Civil War and rather than repair it, they built the house next to it, but the name Abney Castle stuck.'

'Is it open to the public?' Laura asked as they made their

way around the ivy-covered ruins. The footprint of the four-teenth-century structure was mostly visible, though the roof had long gone and a few of the walls were missing. He took her to his favourite part, an intact wall where the Gothic-shaped window frames were still intact.

'It's not safe—for the public or the structure. We want to preserve it, but it's difficult. Some preservation attempts last century did more damage than good.'

'Yes, it's a trade-off I understand well. The first rule of conservation is do no harm.'

'Like Hippocrates?"

She laughed. 'I guess so.'

'It was open, a few years ago now, but we've closed it until we can get a proper survey done. Preserving medieval ruins is not a cheap business. Nor a common one.'

'I don't suppose it is.'

She knew all this stuff—why was he telling her all of this? As an art conservator she probably knew more about this than he did, but he couldn't seem to be able to stop talking.

'My father thought about handing it over to the National Trust. They may be able to do more than we can.'

'But he didn't?'

'No. They had some discussions, but my father decided that keeping the estate all together and in the family was the better option. He hoped to be able to raise enough money to come up with his own conservation plan.'

Laura brushed past him and he smelt roses. His stomach flipped.

'It's amazing,' she said. 'I can't believe this was in your backyard growing up.'

'It is something else.' And something to live up to.

'So much history. Your ancestors lived here. Your great-great-great...never mind. It would take too long.'

'There have been Westons here since the twelfth century, though Thomas Weston wasn't made duke until the reign of James the First.'

'I'm not even sure who my great-great-grandparents were. It's amazing that you know so much about your family.'

'It's a privilege.'

It wasn't just the title that he had to be proud of, it was this entire place. Even the moss-covered stones beneath his feet.

'It's been here for nine hundred years and hopefully another nine hundred. I'm just the caretaker.'

She scoffed. 'I think you're a little more than that.'

'Not really. It's my job to look after this whole place and leave it in a better condition than I found it.'

She gave him that look again, a flicker of her eyebrows. Doubting. Or surprise. He didn't know her well enough yet to be able to tell. All he knew was that when she looked into his eyes everything else in the world faded out.

'It was my father's philosophy, and my grandparents' as well. I intend to pass all of this onto my son. Or daughter.'

She coughed. 'We should get back. I've taken up enough of your time.'

As they walked back he asked, 'Do you have everything you need?'

'Yes, my equipment is all in my car. But if you have a spare ladder...'

'I'll see that you get one. But ask Louis tomorrow if you have any trouble.'

When they reached the front door to her cottage he wished, for the first time in his life, that the castle was bigger so that they could keep talking. Laura stopped and shifted her weight from one foot to the other. 'Thank you again.'

'It was a pleasure. I truly hope you don't get lost.'

She smiled and the sensation he felt in his chest when she did was starting to feel familiar. He smiled back and contemplated asking her out for a drink or dinner but her expression suddenly changed.

'First off, I will assess the paintings, check for damage, prepare a condition report on what needs to be done. You will look that over and then, depending on what needs doing, I can start work.' Her tone was businesslike.

He nodded.

'It's impossible to say how long it will take, but I understand that Archibald usually spent a few weeks or a month here. Is that okay?'

'Anything and everything you need. And don't feel like you need to rush. You're welcome to stay as long as you like.'

'I may need to go home for a week or so in the middle of my stay.'

The firm had said it could be a possibility that Laura would need to break up her visit but hadn't said anything more than that it was 'due to personal circumstances.'

'If we can play things by ear, that would be great.'

'Yes. The guides know you'll be working here. You can ask Louis for anything. Claudia as well. And me. I will be around tomorrow.' He took a business card from his pocket and handed it to her. 'Please call if there's anything you need, but go wherever you want to. The entire castle is at your disposal.'

'Thank you. I will. And I'll let you get on with your evening. I really appreciate you taking the time to give me a tour.'

She waved goodbye and left him standing at her front

door like an fool, regretting he hadn't just asked her out for a drink to welcome her to the area.

Regretting he hadn't figured out a way to find out if she really was SohoJane.

He walked back into the castle to check everything was locked up properly. The rooms and corridors were now dimly lit, the sun close to setting. He liked some rooms here more than others; each held memories—and not only his, but he could feel those of his ancestors in many of them. Most of all he could feel his father. Sometimes he even fancied he could feel his brother. His older brother, Daniel, who had died before Henry was born. Daniel who would have been the thirteenth duke if he hadn't fallen under his horse.

Daniel was a strange shadowy presence in Henry's life. When he was little he was kind of like an imaginary friend, and Henry didn't quite understand that they would never actually meet.

But as Henry got older, when he turned eighteen, he realised he was now the older brother. That he was older than Daniel ever would be. That he would go to university, travel…do things that Daniel would never do.

Including becoming a duke.

That was why he had been born in the first place. It was literally his reason for existing.

Henry sat on one of the visitor chairs in the great hall and took out his phone.

@FarmerDan: Hi there, how was your day?

@SohoJane: Wonderful!

Could this be her? The tour of the house might be described as 'wonderful' but the run-in with the cow?

@FarmerDan: I'm all ears.

@SohoJane: Work was great, my new assignment feels a bit like a fairytale.

@FarmerDan: With a handsome prince?

*Or a handsome duke?*

@SohoJane: Ha-ha. How was your day?

He looked at his phone and planned his next response carefully.

@FarmerDan: It was pretty good, apart from a run-in with a feisty cow.

He couldn't concentrate on anything while he waited for her response.

@SohoJane: You mean the four-legged type, right?

@FarmerDan: Of course!!!

@SohoJane: Ouch, sounds painful. Are you okay?

@FarmerDan: Fine, the only bruise was to my ego.

It didn't seem that she recognised the situation. If she did, wouldn't she have said, 'What a coincidence, me too'?
It wasn't her.
Laura wasn't SohoJane.

So where did that leave him? Attracted to two women at once? That felt all wrong.

*Jane doesn't want to date you. Or anyone.*

He should get to know Laura better. She was bright, gorgeous. Good company. They seemed to have a lot in common. She certainly seemed to fall into the 'eligible' category.

But he didn't want just anyone.

He wanted *Jane*.

He wouldn't be able to date anyone else seriously until he'd met her or knew what her secret was. What was keeping her from meeting him. What was keeping her from dating.

@FarmerDan: No pressure, but maybe the next time I'm in London we could have a drink. As friends. I know you're not looking for anything else.

@SohoJane: You're incorrigible.

Henry groaned. He'd gone too far. But a second later another message flashed up on his screen.

@SohoJane: But I'll think about it.

This was closer than she'd ever come before. Maybe it would happen soon.

But what if his feelings for Laura continued to grow in the meantime?

He looked up at the painting of the third Duke of Brighton staring down smugly at him. As well he might. 'You don't know how lucky you were, never having to date online,' Henry said to the painting.

# CHAPTER FOUR

BACK INSIDE THE COTTAGE, Laura's head spun. As Laura suspected, Henry looked only more handsome when he was showered and changed. He smelt good too. She'd caught faint traces of an understated aftershave when he'd held a door open for her or brushed past her. *He probably feels good as well*, she thought with a sigh.

He wasn't married. He lived alone.

What would it be like to be a duchess? She shook the thought away even before it was fully formed. It was his duty to have heirs. That fact alone would exclude her from the duchess contest. But another, more pressing, more urgent idea crept in. What would it be like to sleep with Henry?

She laughed. Probably great.

Probably so great there must be a queue of women waiting to bed him.

If Abney Castle wasn't a big enough turn-on, then surely Henry himself with his strong arms and tight glutes would be enough to make the women—or the men—line up.

Just as well. She wasn't interested in Henry. He was as good as her employer. And then there was Dan.

At the thought of him, her phone buzzed with a message.

@FarmerDan: Hi, there, how was your day?

Laura messaged him back, telling him as much as she could about her day without giving away anything about where she was. And it sounded like Dan had had an eventful day with a cow as well. What was it with the Cotswolds and cows?

*And FarmerDan likes tennis.*

*And he lives in Gloucestershire...*

No! That was ridiculous. Dan wasn't a duke. He was *Dan*.

Her thoughts leapt back to the first moment she'd seen him wrestling the cow, how she'd wondered if that farmer could be *her* farmer.

She immediately pulled up his profile photo.

Dan looked blond, at least with the sun behind him. And his hair was longer. And Dan was a farmer! Not a duke. And he had a different name. She could believe that a duke might want a degree of anonymity but why not just go with FarmerHenry?

No. It couldn't be him.

Lots of people had cows in Gloucestershire. Lots of people were following the French Open.

She squinted and zoomed in so far the image became unclear, but she still couldn't be sure.

Could she ask him?

No, she couldn't. Besides, it wasn't him. Dukes didn't need dating apps. They had an entire society of aristocrats trying to set them up with eligible misses.

Laura took off her boots, turned on the oven and put in the pie Claudia had kindly made her. Then she poured herself a glass of the white wine.

But if Henry was single...and she was here for a while. She shook the thought away as well. She already had enough on her plate. With the job. Her health. And Dan.

Besides, she wasn't the type to be interested in two men

at once. It made her uncomfortable. Not to mention exhausted.

She wasn't ready for one relationship at the moment, let alone two.

Laura woke five minutes before her alarm, fully rested and alert. The country air must agree with her. Either that or the fact that she had a magic key to a castle!

*'Go wherever you need. The entire castle is at your disposal.'*

She dressed professionally but practically in navy pants and a white shirt, and tied her long hair back away from her face. Today would likely involve a lot of walking and probably some heavy lifting as well. Thankfully, the small kitchen was equipped with a good coffee machine; Claudia was not one to skip an important detail like that.

Laura approached the castle and took in its loveliness, the famous Cotswold stone almost glowing in the morning light. She walked to the small entrance, the one Claudia had used and the one for which she had a key, but even as she turned it in the lock she half expected it not to turn. But it did, and with a satisfying click the door fell open.

The place was silent to begin with, but in less than an hour the first museum staff arrived and by midmorning a steady stream of visitors was wandering through the beautiful rooms.

Laura started out by assessing the size of the task and figuring out where everything was. Archibald had kept meticulous records of the collection over his years of involvement, which Laura had on her laptop. But despite his care, oil paintings needed to be regularly assessed. They could become acidic and brittle over time, leading to cracks developing. The timber frames could also degrade and distort, potentially damaging the canvas.

Her job was to check each item, consider whether it had deteriorated in the intervening years, and if and how it needed any cleaning or repair. Additionally, she had to check the position and manner in which each artwork was displayed or stored and recommend any environmental changes to help preserve the works.

There were over a hundred pieces on her initial review list. It was a big task, but the special surroundings meant it would be a pleasure.

The day passed so quickly Laura was surprised to notice that the visitors had disappeared and Louis was wishing her a good evening. She planned to work into the evening, but the sound of someone clearing their throat made her look up from her work on a Dante Gabriel Rossetti.

'Good day?'

It was Henry, but he was blurry, and she had to remove her magnifying glasses to see him properly.

She brushed herself off, despite not being covered in anything except a day's worth of hard work.

'Hey. How are you?'

He smiled broadly and she pushed her attraction down. She'd hoped that the belly flips of yesterday had been a blip, just caused by the whirlwind of being shown around a castle. But no. Her attraction to Henry was more than just that. It was physical and visceral and grabbed her right in the gut. He was wearing blue jeans, like yesterday, only clean, with a white shirt, loose with the top few buttons undone, giving her a tempting view of the tanned skin on his neck. Delicious. She had to swallow.

'What's the damage on this one?' he asked, leaning in and looking over her shoulder. Making her heart rate hitch up a few notches and her head light.

'It's not too bad, actually, but I'll have to clean it a little first to make sure. It is a truly beautiful collection. I mean,

I'm familiar with most of the works but to see them in person—it's very special.'

Henry smiled shyly. 'I wish I could take credit for it, but alas, my ancestors were the ones with the foresight. I'm always looking at ways to expand the collection, even with more modern works. I am conscious of passing down a collection better than the one I've inherited.'

'I can give you a little advice on that, but I can also put you in touch with people who know a lot more about that than I do.'

She was trying to keep their conversation professional, that way she wouldn't notice how the temperature in the room seemed to have increased a few degrees since Henry entered. Why had he come by? Just to check up on her or...?

*He looks edible.*

Her stomach growled loudly at the thought and her face burnt.

Henry grinned. 'Please don't feel you have to say yes, but I was wondering if you'd like to join me for a meal in the village? The pub's great and I can show you the shortcut through the garden.'

Even though a part of her thought that spending time with Henry was probably not great for her peace of mind, this was exactly how she wanted to spend her evening.

'What about Roland-Garros?' she asked, remembering he liked tennis.

'It'll wait.'

'Okay, that'd be great. Thanks.'

One hour later, fresh out of the shower, Laura looked at the contents of her suitcase. It was the second day in a row she was dressing for a date with a duke. Not that this was a date, date. It was an appointment, but she'd packed mostly plain working clothes and hadn't anticipated wanting to dress a little bit special. It had been months since she'd felt the need—or the desire—to dress up.

*It's a country pub! Your jeans will be fine!*

She slipped on her jeans and a white T-shirt and grabbed her blazer and scarf. The warm spring day was rapidly cooling to a fresh evening.

The sun was low in the sky as Henry led the way across the formal part of the garden, with its carefully designed garden beds planted with delphiniums and gardenias, to the less structured fields beyond.

She spotted the folly on a nearby hill. A stone building that looked like a small Hellenic temple. 'That's beautiful,' she remarked.

'Remind me to take you up there one day. It's not open to the public.'

'Why not?' It didn't seem as old or fragile as the castle ruins he had shown her yesterday.

'We have to maintain some mystery.' He winked at her and heat bloomed in her chest. Was he flirting with her? Surely not.

*Why not? Why wouldn't he flirt with you? Laura, you've just been out of the game for so long. Men do find you attractive.*

Once again, she was torn. She liked Henry, could almost contemplate a no strings attached fling. But she worked for him. And she wasn't meant to be getting entangled in anything at the moment. Even a fling.

He chatted to her as they walked along, pointing out things of interest, telling a few anecdotes about the place and before she knew it they had reached a high brick wall. She didn't notice it until they were upon it, as it was camouflaged by trees and shrubs.

'Wow.'

'I know. It's the way the ground dips here, it gives the

impression that the estate goes on for miles longer than it actually does.'

He unlocked a door in the middle of the wall and beyond it was a path leading to what she now saw was the nearby village of Abneyford. Like many Cotswold villages, Abneyford was picturesque.

'In summer this place is crawling with tourists, but tonight, it'll be mostly us locals.'

Henry led the way to a bustling pub, clearly the centre of the village. He was greeted by the barman and introduced her right away. 'Laura, this is Robert. He and his wife run the best pub in the county. Laura's our guest for the next few weeks, so look after her.'

'Of course we will.' Robert's smile was friendly. 'Are you after dinner?'

'Yes please.'

Henry took her through the menu at the bar like someone who had tried each dish multiple times. 'But the salmon is something to behold.'

'I'll have that then.'

They found a table for two in a quiet corner of the dining room. It was a typical traditional pub, with a low ceiling supported by dark beams, heavy furniture and years of laughter echoing in the walls.

'This place is probably as old as the castle,' Laura said.

'I'm not sure, but I can tell you the Weston family has been frequenting the pub since it opened.'

'Really? I would have thought they would have been waited on by all their servants.'

'The dukes had to meet their duchesses somewhere.'

She laughed. The thought was pretty preposterous. 'Surely your ancestors would have found their wives in London, at the marriage markets of the ton.'

'You'd be surprised. The eighth duke met his wife in the

village when they were children and the tenth, my great-grandfather, married the head gardener's daughter.'

'Really?'

'Really. We have a proud tradition of not marrying the women expected of us.'

Again, was he flirting with her?

And how did she feel about it if he was?

Maybe it was the wine, maybe it was being away from home, but Laura couldn't help but flirt back.

'And what about you? Have you dated any of the barmaids? Have your eye on a local governess?'

He laid his arms on the table and leant forward. His blue eyes darkened as he said, 'I haven't married—or even dated—any governesses or barmaids.'

'I meant…' Her face was flushed. What did she mean? The walls were closing in on the two of them and she was having trouble keeping her heart rate steady and her thoughts in check.

'I do have to marry though,' he said.

'I'd expect so.'

'If I don't have a legitimate heir, the title dies with me.'

'It dies?'

'Yes. My father didn't have any siblings. I don't have any siblings.'

'There are no cousins?' Surely he could find a long-lost cousin somewhere willing to move into a castle.

'Some distant, but the letters patent establishing the dukedom mean it must be a direct heir of the current duke or one immediately preceding. It can pass to a male or a female, so they at least allow that.'

A wave of disappointment rolled over her, which was so ridiculous. She already knew he planned to have children—he'd told her that the day before. She and Henry could never have anything more than a flirtation. She knew this—whether he was a duke or not. There was a good chance she'd be having a hysterectomy in the next year or so; this was why she wasn't getting herself into situations like this where she was so attracted to a man she struggled to think straight. *This* was precisely why she'd stepped away from dating.

Thankfully, someone was smiling down on her because at that point Robert delivered their fish to the table and Laura didn't have to respond to what Henry had just said.

The food was as good as Henry had promised, and the wine happily warmed her insides. Henry was leaning across from her, asking her about her career and her life in London, and listening carefully hanging on every answer.

'Where did you grow up?'

'London, born and bred.'

'Where abouts?'

'I lived out in Kew when I was younger, but now I'm in Soho.' She had a shoebox-sized flat but loved how central she was to everything. 'It's certainly a lot busier than it is here.'

'I suppose you find all this deadly dull?' He gestured around the pub.

'Not at all, I'm having a great time. I love the city, but this is great as well.'

He asked her all about her job, hanging on her answers, though Laura didn't read much into that, she was there to look after his paintings after all. He asked her what made her decide to become a conservator and she told him the story about how, when she was fifteen and her grandmother had died, Laura had been shocked to find out that there were no photos of her beloved grandmother as a child. Some had been taken, but many had been lost in the war. There were hundreds of Laura's mother and literally thousands of Laura on her parents' digital camera. So she'd set about preserving all the available letters and photos belonging to her grandmother.

'When my father passed away, I made sure we kept all the photos of him. And all the letters he'd written. At the time I was studying fine art, but it quickly became clear to me that what I love—what I really love—is looking after the past. Preserving it for the future. Not everyone thinks that's important, but I do.'

When she finally finished her speech she became aware that Henry was smiling directly at her, in a soft, dreamy sort of way. His jaw slightly slack, his eyes focused entirely on her. It was such an intense gaze Laura didn't know how to answer it. The skin on her arms prickled and her chest warmed. His blue eyes were light, as though lit from within. The only response she wanted to give to a look like that was to kiss him. But she couldn't, so she told herself to sit back in her chair and pretend she wasn't looking at one of the most handsome men she'd ever seen.

She sipped her water and coughed. 'So tell me about your work.' Getting distressed cows out of wire fences was decidedly unsexy and she needed the heat levels of this conversation to drop considerably. Potentially to freezing. 'It can't be much fun farming in winter. It must get cold.'

Henry gave one small shake of his head. It would have been imperceptible to anyone but someone who was now achingly alert to every single movement, every blink and every breath he was taking.

'I have a friend who's a farmer,' she said and instantly regretted it. It felt strange to mention Dan to someone else.

'Oh, yes? What does he farm?'

'Sheep, mostly. Cows, I think. And apples. It must be a Gloucestershire thing.' She almost blurted out Dan's name but stopped herself. How would she explain that she didn't even know his surname. She wished she'd kept Dan's existence to herself.

Thankfully, Henry didn't ask anything more.

She was more than a little tipsy when they walked back through the moonlight to the castle and the cottage. As he told her about the unlikely matches the former dukes had made she was aware of her phone sitting in her pocket. She was also aware of the fact that she hadn't heard from FarmerDan all evening, which was unusual.

*You haven't messaged him either.*

'Now I know why there's a secret gate at the back of the garden. So the dukes could sneak out to meet the barmaids.'

They passed the path to the castle and she stopped to say goodnight, but he kept walking.

'I'll walk you to your door.'

She was sure the castle gates had been locked and the chances of something happening to her between there and the cottage were slim to none, but she was touched by the gesture. The spring air smelt of gardenias and she made small talk about the garden as they walked along the gravel driveway to the cottage.

She unlocked the door and turned; he was still standing there, head bowed under the low entrance.

She pressed her lips together. He mirrored her action.

*Oh, no.*

First the possible flirting, and now this. She wanted to kiss him—there was no point lying to herself.

*He wants to kiss you too.*

And so what if he did?

Nothing. Absolutely nothing. Leaning into this moment would be a very bad decision indeed.

'Thanks again for a lovely evening and for showing me the village, and the pub.'

Henry reached out his right hand, but a look of confusion crossed his face and he dropped it again. He looked as conflicted as she felt and she wanted to laugh out loud, but held her giggle back.

He lifted his hand again and held it out for a shake. She took his hand. It should have been a perfectly formal gesture, but when his hand enclosed hers it was nothing of the sort. Warm, secure tingles shot up her arm and directly into her heart. His hand was rougher than hers but his grip was tender. She felt her insides melting.

Henry leant forward, just the merest of fractions, just enough to make her heart leap into her throat, but then he drew back.

'Goodnight, Laura.' His voice was rough and low and it rippled through her insides, reaching every long forgotten crevice.

Inside, fingers still shaking, she sat on the end of her bed and unzipped her boots. What was she going to do?

Last night Dan had suggested they meet. As friends. She was in his part of the country. It made sense that they should finally meet. But yesterday had thrown her a curveball. A handsome duke-shaped curveball.

FarmerDan was solid, caring and interested.

Henry was handsome in a get-your-pulse-racing-into-overdrive kind of way.

He was also as good as her employer. They had a business relationship.

Henry was a distraction.

Dan was a friend.

*But what if they are the same person?*

The idea still seemed impossible, the product of an overactive and clearly stressed imagination, but the coincidences were starting to stack up.

Tennis.

No, many people liked tennis.

Cows.

Ditto. There was more than one dairy farmer in the county.

It was yet another coincidence.

She wouldn't know until she finally met Dan once and for all.

She took out her phone and before she could think too closely about all the reasons why it was a bad idea she typed and hit Send.

@SohoJane: Hi, sorry about all the prevarication. I'd like to meet. I'm actually staying in your part of the country for a few weeks. Near the town of Epemere. Do you know it?

She contemplated suggesting Abneyford for a meeting, but if she was wrong she didn't fancy accidentally running into Henry and/or anyone she knew from the castle. She'd driven through Epemere on her way to Abney and it seemed lovely.

@FarmerDan: I know it well. There's a great little pub on the main street, near the park. Tomorrow?

Tomorrow? He was keen, but whether he'd remain so when she told him what she had to tell him was another thing altogether.

@SohoJane: Tomorrow would be great. Around seven?

@FarmerDan: I can't wait.

Laura was breathless as she put down her phone. This time tomorrow she would have met Dan. This time tomorrow she'd know.

She made herself a cup of tea and flicked through her phone for a while, trying, without success, to wind down after the evening, but she didn't seem to be able to. A warm shower made things worse and by the time she was ready for bed, a sense of dread had fallen over her. The feeling was difficult to explain, except that something inside her had shifted.

She knew what it might be, logically, objectively she knew exactly what it could be, but she refused to believe it. The laparoscopy should have given her a few more pain-free days per month, not decreased them.

So she refused to believe it. She climbed into bed pretending it wasn't happening. This was not happening. This was too soon.

# CHAPTER FIVE

THEY WERE GOING to meet. Tonight!

In Epemere, of all places. Near his village.

Laura was definitely Jane. During their conversation at the pub the night before he had been so sure they were the same person he had almost confronted her directly.

Laura lived in Soho. Jane lived in Soho!

*Lots of people live in Soho.*

He didn't receive a message from Jane the entire evening when they were together.

*That doesn't mean anything.*

A strong suspicion wasn't the same as being sure and he had to be sure so he held his tongue.

But then, not long after he'd arrived home, he received a message.

@SohoJane: Hi, sorry about all the prevarication. I'd like to meet. I'm actually staying in your part of the country for a few weeks. Near the town of Epemere. Do you know it?

It had to be her.

*You want it to be her.*

Henry knew other people quite happily dated a variety of people at once. But it was different with Laura and Jane— he could see himself with either of them. He had a solid friendship with Jane and loved sharing the little parts of his day and random thoughts with her. He got along well with Laura too, though he didn't know her nearly as well. Most telling of all, his pulse rocketed when he was around Laura, his hands became embarrassingly sticky and something else came over him. An urge to reach over and touch her. To lean in and discover how her skin felt against his lips...

Even though he would be meeting Jane tonight, Henry still longed to see Laura as soon as possible. He walked through the main house, anticipating seeing Laura at the threshold of each new door. But he went through room after room, and there was no sign of her. After he'd walked through the whole house twice he asked Louis if he knew where she was, but Louis hadn't seen her all day.

He asked a few of the guides, who shook their heads as well. His heart rate kicked up a notch. No one had seen her since yesterday.

It was a Thursday, a workday, and while Laura was free to come and go as she pleased and not be beholden to a timesheet, it was worrying. Her absence didn't fit with everything he knew about Laura and her passion for her work. He needed to check on her.

He passed the lines of visitors and walked briskly to the cottage. The small red brick house looked still and the curtains were all drawn. He knocked gently and waited. He knocked again, and this time counted to sixty. When there was no answer still he knocked harder. No response. He contemplated going back to the house for the master key, but before he had to decide whether that was a good idea he heard the lock turning.

'Laura, it's Henry. Are you all right?' he said before she opened the door fully. His throat closed over when he saw her. She was drawn, dishevelled, with a thin sheen of sweat on her forehead. But it was the absence of colour from her skin that worried him most.

'I'm sorry to barge in. I was worried—are you all right?'

'What time is it?' she asked.

'It's after midday.'

'Oh, no, I'm so sorry.' Laura grimaced and gripped the doorframe, clearly in pain.

'There's no need to be sorry. You aren't well and you need to get back into bed.'

Laura didn't respond but took the three or so steps required to the nearest sofa. She sat, her face still scrunched up with pain and then lay down. Henry's heart rate was now through the roof. She wasn't well. Not a bit.

He opened the drapes to let some light in the front rooms of the cottage. Laura wrapped herself into a ball.

'Do you need an ambulance?'

'No,' she said but it came out as a croaky whisper.

'Can I call your doctor or should I get mine?'

'There's no need,' she said, 'I know what this is, but I didn't get my latest prescription filled. This has taken me by surprise.'

'No problem—I can do that for you. Do you have a copy?'

'It's in my handbag.' She pointed a floppy arm to the coffee table. 'I thought I had another week to fill it, but obviously not. I'll be okay, at least I'll be able to stand when I've had some.'

He looked down at the script for a strong painkiller. Then he looked back at Laura.

'Are you sure you're all right?'

'Yes, well, I'm in a lot of pain so no, but it's not life-threatening. It's endometriosis.'

Period pain. Bad period pain, that's what he knew.

Alarmed as he was by how she looked, he was relieved it was nothing worse. Still, her appearance was worrying.

Henry looked around the cottage. It was dark and untouched. 'Have you eaten anything?'

'No, but I don't feel like it. I'm so sorry I didn't know what time it was. I was awake half the night and then I just must've slept through my alarm.'

'Please stop apologising. Will you be all right if I leave you for a minute to get a few things?'

'I'm not going anywhere,' she groaned.

Henry first called Claudia and explained the situation. Claudia said she would bring some food there shortly. Then he got into his car and took the script into the village. He worried for a moment the pharmacist wouldn't fill it for him, but he shouldn't have. He was the Duke of Brighton—the pharmacist barely blinked. While he waited for the script to be filled, Henry looked around the pharmacy. He saw the heat packs and hot water bottles and picked up some of each. As he wandered around the shop he picked up one of everything and everything that might have anything to do with periods, not knowing what she used or what she needed. None of the staff even gave a second glance at his basket, overflowing with pads and tampons of all shapes and sizes. He threw in some jelly beans and chocolate for good measure and returned to Laura.

Back at the cottage he took the medicine and a glass of water to Laura, who thanked him again. 'Give me ten or fifteen and this will start to work,' she said. 'I may not be high-functioning, but I'll be lucid briefly before I fall asleep.' She let out a sad, half laugh after she said that.

He passed her the bag of supplies. She looked inside and he could see that she was trying not to smile.

'There's ibuprofen and paracetamol underneath all of

that as well. The pharmacist said you know what you can take with your other medicine.'

She nodded, and he could see she was biting back a laugh. He didn't care if his lack of knowledge of endometriosis showed, he simply wanted her to have everything she needed.

Claudia kept the place in perfect order, but Henry thought about what he liked most when he was unwell. He put on the kettle and when the water had boiled, he filled the hot water bottle he'd just purchased. There was enough left over, so he brewed two cups of tea. Laura shuffled into the kitchen, wrapped in a cotton robe and he passed her the hot water bottle. 'How do you have your tea?'

'White with one,' she said.

'Sit down, please.'

She went back to the sofa and he brought her the tea.

Laura sat, her feet tucked under her and her body wrapped around the hot water bottle. She pulled a blanket around herself and sipped the tea gratefully.

'This is so embarrassing,' she muttered.

'Not at all.'

There was nothing to be embarrassed about, though this was one of those occasions he suspected the 'being a duke' thing got in the way of him just wanting to be a good person.

'Are you feeling better? You look better. There's a little colour in your cheeks.'

'Yes, thanks, the medicine is kicking in. Of course, shortly it'll make me dozy and I'll be out again.'

'Claudia will be here soon with the food, if you can hold out that long.'

'I'm so sorry, I didn't realise it would be so bad. I thought…' Her words lifted off. Whether it was from the pain medication or something else he couldn't tell.

'Is this worse than usual?'

'Not exactly, but it's unexpected. I had a procedure a month ago and it was expected to help avoid times like this. But I guess not.'

'Please excuse my absolute ignorance, I've never known anyone it affects.'

She looked down, looking both devastated and in pain. He knew that look. It was a look seen on his father's face in the weeks before he passed away.

*Laura isn't going to die.*

He knew that, logically, but the worry building up inside him felt a little familiar. And it was awful to watch someone you care about in so much pain.

'It isn't like a bad period. It's not *not* like that, but my friends get cramps that go away after some anti-inflammatories and a sleep. This is still there when I wake up and goes on for days. And it's more than just a cramp. Sometimes it feels like I'm being stabbed.'

Henry couldn't help but wince. 'And the procedure was meant to help?'

'Keyhole surgery, a laparoscopy, to remove some of the scar tissue.'

'I don't understand.'

'The lining of my uterus grows where it isn't meant to on the outside round my ovaries. My doctor has made several attempts to remove the material from where it isn't meant to be. But this can also create problems over time if adhesions grow over the scar tissue. Basically, my insides are a mess. I've also been taking hormones to simulate early menopause. It isn't great, but I'm running out of options.'

'What causes it?'

'No one knows.'

'Isn't there anything else they can do? Further surgery?'

Laura grimaced. 'There is. But it's radical.'

'Radical? How?'

'A hysterectomy.'

'Oh. That is…radical. Yes. But surely after you have children?'

She sighed. 'That's what my mother says, but the thing is that isn't very likely.'

'Why not?'

'Endo can affect fertility. And given the history of mine, it's severity and the number of operations I've already had, the chances of me conceiving and carrying a baby to term are close to nil.'

His heart broke for her. It was such a cruel, insidious disease. Not only did it leave her in excruciating pain, but to possibly cause infertility as well. It was so unfair.

Something else slowly dawned on him. If Laura couldn't have children then he couldn't marry her.

And if Laura was Jane…then neither of the two women he was hoping might become his wife could have children.

*It isn't about you*, he reminded himself. He stood, went to the window and looked out over the lawn. He took a deep, focusing breath.

'So then why not a hysterectomy?'

'That's what I've been saying, it does seem to be the best chance I have to be pain free.'

'Is it like this every month?' he asked, still disbelieving that in this day and age a woman had to go through something like this.

'More than not. I'd hoped that this most recent procedure would give me a few more years to decide, but now—' she looked down at her stomach '—it doesn't seem to have made any difference. If anything, this is sooner. And worse. The plan was to see how this went and then make up my mind about the next steps.'

'You're in the process of making this decision now?' The significance of what had been going on in Laura's head all this time was only now occurring to him. Sometimes you really had no idea of the burdens other people were carrying.

She nodded. 'They really don't like giving hysterectomies to women who haven't had children and who are still in their childbearing years, but I've been seeing my doctor for a long time. I have a good relationship with her and she knows my history. The plan was to have the laparoscopy, see how it went and then wait a few months before having another serious discussion about it.

'She's not going to refuse to do it as some doctors might, but she does want me to be sure.'

Henry ran his hand through his hair. 'Oh, Laura, that's a huge thing to have been on your mind.'

She nodded. 'Yes.'

He felt helplessly ill-equipped for this conversation and for something to say. Most of his male friends didn't closely consider fatherhood, or if they did, they didn't speak about it, but he understood both the need and the desire to have children and suspected it was a feeling that was even stronger in many women, with both biological instincts and societal expectations pushing them towards it.

'Do your friends, your family, do they know?'

'Yes. My mother's been supportive, but I know that she wants me to wait a bit longer. She's convinced I'm going to meet someone.'

'But it isn't about that,' he said. 'It's about asking you to live the next few years of your life in pain on the off chance you might conceive a child, which doesn't seem very fair.'

'Life isn't fair,' she mumbled sadly to herself.

'No it's not,' he agreed, feeling the unfairness intensely himself.

At that moment there was a knock on the door and Claudia came bearing hearty soup and fresh bread. Accepting

Laura's urging for him to leave and let her rest, he did, closing the door to her cottage quietly behind him.

The first thing Henry did when he got back to his apartment was take out his tablet and type 'endometriosis' into the search engine.

He was shocked to learn that it affected roughly ten percent of women globally, not to mention the life-impacting nature of its symptoms. It wasn't just painful periods, as he'd vaguely thought, but could involve chronic pelvic pain, bloating, irregular bleeding, nausea, fatigue and depression.

His heart broke for Laura. And all the other women affected, particularly those who could not access proper treatment or those whose symptoms were dismissed by their doctors.

Laura's endometriosis was found in the ovaries, but there were several types and several stages. The more he read the more he learnt and the sadder he became.

And angrier.

Women were expected to carry on through normal life while being in debilitating pain or being so fatigued they couldn't function. No wonder depression was a side effect, he thought as he read through more and more accounts.

Then he looked up 'endometriosis cure' and what Laura had said was essentially it. Pain management, keyhole surgery, hormone treatment and then more radical surgery. Looking up from his tablet he realised it was late afternoon. He put it down, knowing there were things he should get on and do but at a complete loss as to where to begin.

He sighed and his phone vibrated with a message.

@SohoJane: Hi, I'm really sorry but I'll need to take a rain check on tonight. Something has come up. I'll be in touch.

SohoJane was cancelling their date.

Henry buried his face in his palms.


'Is everything okay? You didn't answer yesterday,' Laura's mother asked the following afternoon.

Laura was out of bed and had managed to shower, dress and even eat a little. She was contemplating doing some work, though Henry had told her to keep resting and not rush back when he'd dropped around more meals Claudia had prepared that morning.

But Laura felt guilty about coming all the way to Abney Castle to work on this special assignment and then being unable to show up to work. She was also feeling vaguely guilty about the amount of food that was building up in her refrigerator and worried how on earth she was going to be able to get through it all.

Henry had been letting her rest but was checking in morning and evening and using food delivery as an excuse. She was touched by his caring and generosity.

But she still felt guilty.

'Not really,' Laura said.

'What's up?'

'I've been laid up for the last two days.'

'Not with…oh, no. Already?'

'Yes. It's like the laparoscopy didn't even happen.' Talking about it now brought the disappointment up to the surface and she felt something welling up inside her.

'Oh, darling, but that doesn't mean this is how it's going to be.' Her mother, the eternal optimist. Managing to stay positive in the face of all the evidence to the contrary.

'I wish you'd told me. I would've come.'

'It's okay, they're looking after me.'

'They?'

'Claudia, the housekeeper, has been cooking for me.'

'And the duke?'

Henry had definitely gone above and beyond. It was touching, but confusing as well. They both knew now that regardless of any attraction they might share or frisson they might enjoy, they would never be more than colleagues or friends. 'He's been very understanding as well.'

'Good. As he should be. How are you feeling now?'

'I'm slowly feeling like myself again. I'll try and do a few hours work this afternoon.'

'You shouldn't rush back.'

'But I feel guilty.'

'You're allowed to take leave,' Fiona said but Laura barely listened. Her mother didn't understand that given all the time Laura had to take off she had to work extra hard to make it up to everyone. No one understood this, not her mother, or even her friends.

Fiona filled her in on her own weekend and just as Laura was about to end the call Fiona said, 'And have you been in touch with FarmerDan?'

Laura wasn't about to tell her mother her suspicions—or delusions—that Henry and Dan could be the same person. She wasn't going to tell a soul anything until she met Dan and found out one way or another.

'I'm going to arrange to meet him,' she confessed.

'Fantastic! When?'

'Soon,' Laura said and ended the call.

Now that she told her mother she'd have to go through with it.

The town of Epemere was a fifteen-minute drive away from Abney. It was the first time in over a week that Laura had left the idyllic world of the castle and the village, though driving her hatchback along the hedgerows and lanes of the picturesque Cotswolds, as the sun lit the honey-coloured stone was hardly like re-entering the real world. The directions Dan gave her were good and she had no trouble finding the town or the pub.

It had taken her a few days to get through her recent attack. She had returned to work in the castle but Henry's initial attentiveness had appeared to cool. Which was fine, she told herself, he was her employer. He had already gone above and beyond to help her when she was unwell. It would be strange for his twice daily visits to continue once she was well again.

But her worries about whether they were the same person lingered and as soon as she was confident her pain had passed she rescheduled the meeting with Dan.

They had again agreed to meet in the nearby town of Epemere. The pub Dan had suggested looked as though it was cut from the pages of a tourist guide, complete with a set of loyal locals. It was the sort of place she'd love to have as her regular. She looked around the bar for someone likely to be Dan. Or someone in roughly the right age bracket, but saw no one. She was ten minutes early. It was always difficult to decide whether to order a drink first or wait for a date to arrive.

She wanted a drink—heavens, she needed something to quieten the nerves that were conducting a gymnastic competition in her stomach—but she didn't trust herself not to slam it down in one gulp.

*This is Dan*, she reminded herself. The man she'd been messaging for months, who had been nothing but kind and understanding. He would be just as lovely in real life as he was online. She shouldn't feel nervous—she *knew* him.

But then she thought, *This is Dan*. The man she'd been messaging for months. The man she felt a connection to. The man she really liked, but at the same time didn't want to like too much because she had enough going on in her life already.

She walked up to the bar and picked up the wine list. As she waited for the bartender to serve another customer a jingle at the door caught her attention and she spun.

It was him.

Of course it was him.

She wasn't attracted to two men at once, she was attracted to the same man. Twice.

Relief. Pleasure. Excitement.

Her instant feelings were short-lived when she saw the look on his face. His smile was soft, almost shy. But it held no hint of surprise. As he walked across the room to the bar his face darkened, became serious. Almost businesslike.

The reality of their situation washed over her and she felt every muscle in her body sag. FarmerDan was really Henry Weston, the thirteenth Duke of Brighton. And he needed an heir. He needed a wife who could give him something she could not.

Instead of embracing one another, as she'd once foolishly thought they might, he held back, aloof. Standing stiff and shifting his weight from one foot to the other.

'Can I get you a drink?' he asked.

'Yes, white wine, please.'

The business of ordering drinks gave her a moment to collect her thoughts and lower her heart rate.

What a mess. What should have been a wonderful meeting was now high on her list of all-time most awkward first dates ever. The only consolation, if you could call it that, was that she hadn't been paranoid or mistaken—her suspicions had been spot-on. But that gave her little comfort.

He wasn't overjoyed to see her. Surely even the coincidence should cause his lips to twitch upwards. But it hadn't.

'You knew, didn't you?' she asked.

He lowered his head. 'Didn't you?'

She looked down as well. 'I suspected. I wasn't sure. That's why I asked to meet.'

Without speaking, they took their drinks from the old wooden bar and found a table in a dark, unoccupied corner of the pub. Given the weather was so warm, most patrons had chosen tables outside, but the dark secluded corner suited them best.

'When?' she asked.

'Almost as soon as you arrived.'

She could no longer stay calm. Rightly or wrongly, she was annoyed. 'You knew all this time and you didn't say anything?'

'Yes, no. I wasn't entirely sure and I didn't know what to say without being sure. I didn't expect to feel…'

That sentence lay unfinished. Neither wanted to pick it up and analyse the meaning behind it.

'I knew you weren't ready to meet me,' he continued. 'I knew Jane wasn't ready to meet Dan and I didn't know what to do. Honestly. I didn't want to lie, but I didn't want to pressure you either.'

She sipped her wine. He made a fair point and yet everything inside her still felt wrong.

'Are you angry with me?' He pulled a face so dejected she felt his sadness in her gut.

'No, I'm…'

'You are.'

He held her gaze in his. She felt his blue eyes pierce into her mind, her chest, her heart. It was almost too much to keep looking at him. Familiar, strange. Wonderful. Impossible, all at once.

Henry's expression softened and the look between them broke. She couldn't be mad at him, no more than he should be mad at her.

'No, I'm not angry,' she said. 'It's a mess, that's all. I'm sorry I didn't say anything as well.'

'No, I'm sorry. I wanted to wait for you to suggest it. I didn't know if you would ever be ready.'

That was, she conceded slowly, the truth. She'd made it clear that she didn't want to meet him and that she wasn't in the market for a relationship. She'd also, more than once, rejected his gentle invitations for casual meetings.

'But...' she started to say.

*But when you met me, wasn't it too late?*

He answered her unspoken thought. 'Yes, when we met I should have said something, but I struggled and I'm sorry. I made a whole lot of excuses—you're working for me, you don't want to meet me, you have your reasons... I wasn't sure you liked me. I wasn't sure you wanted it to be me. All those excuses added up to me not telling you.'

Buried in that long list was a brief but heartbreaking reason and she didn't hear much of what he said after that.

*I wasn't sure you liked me.*

There was much insecurity buried beneath that comment. How could someone so handsome, charming, intelligent, impressive and downright lovely be so insecure?

'I do like you. Very much,' she said softly.

A touch of pink glowed on Henry's cheekbones.

If she didn't like him so much this wouldn't be hard. Or so confusing.

'I don't think I ever explained why I was on A Deux,' he said.

'You said it was because of bad experiences.'

'Yes, but you probably assumed I meant the same sort of bad experiences that you had. Catfish, scammers.'

She nodded.

'I had all that, but when I put my real name up, or even a proper photo, I'd get so many messages.'

'That should be a good thing, shouldn't it?'

'It should be. And I met some wonderful women. But…'

'What?'

He sipped his beer and looked around the room, even though they were on their own. 'It's hard to phrase it without sounding like a jerk.'

She reached over and touched his hand. Henry wasn't a jerk and she wanted him to know it.

'Usually around the second date they'd start to ask a lot of questions. About the estate.'

'I'm not following. I've asked you heaps of questions about the estate.'

'I don't mean the sort of questions you asked. You have a reason to ask questions. I mean mentioning things out of context. About how it's run, what sort of shape it's in. Financial questions.'

Now she was following. She nodded.

'Once or twice they asked about my family circumstances, about my father. His health.'

'Oh, no. I'm so sorry.'

'And even if they were subtle, I'd suspect that was why they'd matched with me. It got to the point where I'd simply just suspect every single woman of being out for my money and my title. And I'm sure they all weren't, but I could never feel sure.'

She was certain there were many great women out there who would instantly see Henry's wonderful qualities without caring whether he had a title. She was one of them.

'And I might be a little paranoid after…' Henry ran his hand through his hair with so much force she was surprised when he didn't come away with a fistful. He was so nervous he was practically vibrating. She reached across the table, picked up his hand and squeezed it. If he felt the gesture was overly intimate, he didn't say anything. Laura felt strangely anchored by gripping him; the rest of the world was swirling around them—secrets had been discovered, revelations were being made. They would not be the same two people walking out of this pub as they had been coming in, but holding on to him she felt she'd know which way was up.

'When I was at university, I was with a woman for over a year. Her name was Beatrice. She was a medical student and I thought we were happy. I thought she loved me.'

His voice cracked on the last words.

'What happened?'

'I found out she was considering dropping out of her studies because she decided she was going to be a duchess.'

'I don't understand.'

'It wasn't something we talked about—I hadn't even proposed, though I was seriously thinking about it.'

'You didn't want her to give up her career for you?'

'Of course I didn't. But it was more than that. When I asked her about it she didn't understand what the big deal was if we were serious about one another. I told her I didn't expect her to give up her career, but she told me it wasn't important to her. Basically, she let me know that I was her ambition. Being a duchess was more important than being a doctor. I asked her if she'd still love me if I wasn't heir to a dukedom and she couldn't answer me.'

'I'm so sorry.'

'That's why I don't tell prospective dates. I don't want to lie to anyone, but I don't want it to be everything. Do you understand?'

Laura nodded. She knew exactly what he meant, because she knew about dating with secrets. And deal-breakers.

She always struggled to find the right time to tell a man about her endometriosis and its likely impact on her health and fertility. When she mentioned it early on in a relationship, before even meeting, the men rarely suggested a date. Sometimes she'd waited, only to be accused of hiding things. Or in the case of one very unkind man, misleading him.

'You don't want it to be everything,' she said. 'But it isn't insignificant either. It is part of who you are.' She was talking to herself as much as to him.

Henry nodded and thankfully smiled.

Why was she surprised, the one thing about her and Dan—and her and Henry now she came to think about it—was that they did understand one another most of the time.

'I thought discretion was such a good plan, but it seemed to have backfired on me this time,' he said, thoughtfully tracing the rim of condensation his glass had left on the coaster.

Laura waited for him to finish. His shoulders were falling noticeably as he was getting all of this off his chest.

'There was one more reason I didn't want to tell you who I was. An important one.'

'Yes?' Even though Henry had just opened up to her about a great deal of painful matters, she had a feeling she knew exactly what he was going to say. There was still one more matter that was unspoken between them.

'You're unlikely to be able to have children.'

'And you must have them.'

'I wouldn't put it exactly like that,' he said.

'I would. You have a family legacy to uphold.'

And apart from anything else, he probably wanted to have children because most people did. It was a biological drive, people longed to carry a baby in their arms, or hold a toddler's hand. People even wanted to steer moody teenagers to adulthood.

As the light outside faded, his eyes became darker, but no less earnest. 'I like you, Laura.'

'I like you too and having a family is something I would never want to take away from you. Dukedom or not.'

'I suspect that's why you stepped away from dating? Why you first told me you wanted to keep things platonic?'

'Yes. But for some reason we kept chatting.'

They smiled sadly at one another across the wooden table, still holding hands. Her stomach, still annoyingly melting as his blue gaze held hers. His thick brown lashes shadowing his eyes, the corners crinkled, his soft pink lips twisted into a sad grin.

'What do we do from here?' she asked.

'I don't know. But I think to start with, would you like to join me for dinner?'

# CHAPTER SIX

THEY ORDERED A meal and another drink. Henry was worried the conversation might dry up, now that they had everything between them out in the open, but it was the opposite. He found they had more to talk about with one another than ever.

They both had two people to reconcile, two relationships to merge, and after the initial awkwardness, it was almost fun. They compared notes openly and honestly about their first connection, and then the first meeting at Abney. She still laughed about the calf and what a mess he'd been. By the time they had finished eating he could hardly believe he'd ever thought Laura and Jane were two different people.

He wasn't sure what made him open up so honestly with Laura, probably simply the fact that he had always talked so honestly with Jane. He hadn't expected all the stuff about Beatrice to come tumbling out, but, he realised they really were friends. After this conversation they could be nothing else and he didn't want to lose her from his life. They might not be able to marry or have a relationship, but that didn't mean they couldn't be friends. Nothing had to change, did it? They could keep messaging on another; the only thing that would change would be that they would use each other's real names.

* * *

When they left the pub, it was still twilight and Henry led Laura around the laneways of the town, of which he was familiar and she was not.

'Why is all the stone around here so beautiful?'

'It's the fossils. From the Jurassic age. The Cotswolds were over a hundred million years in the making.' His family only went back a fraction of that, but at times it felt as though it didn't make any difference. That they had lived here for ever.

'Tell me honestly,' he asked. 'Why did you keep messaging me after you said you were stepping away from dating?'

'I… I guess… I liked you. And you seemed to understand. Even though you didn't know what was wrong, you understood.'

'I had no idea what it was, I thought you might have a family member who was sick or dying. Or something like that.'

'Because of your father?'

'Probably. When he was dying, dating was the last thing on my mind. I stopped for over a year. I only got back onto A Deux after very sustained pressure from my mother. It's strange—once I inherited the dukedom the pressure on me to marry really kicked up—but it was, at that time, the absolute last thing I wanted to do.'

'And now?' she asked.

It was difficult to answer her.

'Dating is still the last thing I want to be doing.' But now the reason was different. Laura and Jane were the only women, or rather, the only woman, he'd felt any connection with in the past year, but she was not his future wife.

'But you have to.'

Did he? He supposed he did. But it would be nice, if just for this evening they could forget about the future and just concentrate on getting to know one another, face-to-face, with no secrets between them.

'Why did you choose SohoJane as your name?'

'Jane's my middle name and I live in Soho—no other mystery. And you?'

'I'm a farmer and my middle name is Daniel.'

'Henry Daniel,' she whispered.

'It's a family name, it was my father's name as well.'

He didn't mention his brother.

They drove back to Abney separately, as they had come. Henry insisted Laura follow him but made sure she was following close behind as she wasn't as familiar with the roads as he was. She parked at the cottage and he pulled up his car nearby and walked over to her.

What should have felt like a hello had the heavy weight of a goodbye. He'd anticipated this moment for so long, part of him had been hoping that whatever it was that was keeping SohoJane away from meeting him would resolve itself—hopefully in the happiest way possible—and that she could see a way through to meet him. To be with him.

And once he'd met Laura, yes, he had hoped they were the same person, not simply because the coincidences were so numerous, but because he wanted them to be the same person.

And they were.

And everything should have been perfect.

But of course it wasn't.

They met at her door. She turned to him and a small line creased her forehead between her eyes. She released a sigh that he felt in his gut. 'It's such a shame,' she said.

'I know.' Because they both knew a future together wasn't in the cards it felt safe to also admit, 'I really like you.'

'I really like you too.'

He wanted to step into her, let her embrace him, to feel her arms around him, to feel her body against his. To comfort one another. But sensibly she stepped back.

'Friends?'

'Of course.' Was that ever in doubt? Maybe it was. Maybe a friendship would complicate things; maybe she wasn't ready to label this thing platonic and carry on. Maybe he wasn't either. His heart still raced a little too fast when their eyes met; his palms sweated a little too much.

'Goodnight,' she said.

'Goodnight. And Laura, despite everything, I still am so glad we finally met.'

The smile she returned didn't reach her eyes.

Laura flopped on the soft sofa, spread her arms wide, and let out the groan she'd been holding in for the past few hours.

Far from being delighted that Henry and Dan were the same person, now everything between them was as tangled up and confused as peak hour traffic in London.

The only thing she knew for sure, the thing she had to keep reminding herself, was that no matter how rapidly her pulse raced when she was around him, she and Henry would only ever be good friends.

*Friends isn't nothing.*

But friends wasn't enough when all she could think about when she was with him was sliding her hand around his waist and her tongue into his mouth. Friends in circumstances like that would be nothing short of torture.

Her phone pinged. It was probably her mother and she should get breaking the news to her out of the way.

*Yes, Henry is Dan, but he's the last in a long line of dukes and the thing he needs most of all is the thing my messed-up womb can't give him.*

But it wasn't her mother. It was Dan.

*Henry. You need to remember that he's Henry Weston, the Duke of Brighton, and all the baggage that comes with that and he's not just your easygoing online friend.*

@FarmerDan: Hey, how you doing?

@SohoJane: I had a rough first date tonight.

@FarmerDan: Oh, no, me too. Wanna talk about it?

Talk or cry, she thought. But instead she wrote:

@SohoJane: I was really looking forward to meeting this guy, and he was as wonderful as I'd hoped.

@FarmerDan: Yeah, I know what you mean. Fate is fickle.

Exhausted but still knowing it would be a while before sleep claimed her, Laura found her limbs positively itching to do something. It was getting dark, but the grounds of the castle would be safe. If she could just work off some of the excess energy coursing through them she might be able to sleep.

She took off her boots and replaced them with her runners. Then she grabbed her phone and keys and set off quickly to catch the last of the light.

But when she opened the door, there he was. Looking at his phone, but still standing where she'd left him less than ten minutes ago.

Henry turned at the sound of the door and his eyes met hers, loaded with want. She knew what it was because she also felt it in her gut. She stepped towards him and before she could think twice she did what she'd been wanting to do for days; she slid her hands around his waist and lifted herself up onto her toes to meet his full pink lips.

Henry froze for perhaps half a beat, surprised no doubt at her lack of ceremony, but then she felt it—his arms, his hands, his strong hard body, and at the centre of it all, his lips, which met hers like they were made for one another. Relief and release wound through her in happy spirals, his tongue sliding against hers, cautiously at first, then deeper, wider, like his arms, that reached around her, holding her tight and close and matching her want, stroke for exquisite stroke.

It was illicit, dangerous and the most perfect kiss she'd ever had. She wanted to keep climbing into it, to lose herself in his arms for ever and never have to face what waited for her on the other side.

But eventually she felt his arms slacken and felt his breaths mix with hers. Panting, he pulled slowly back.

'Friends don't usually do that, do they?' he asked.

'Not all friends. We might need to come up with our own idea of friendship.'

His body was still pressed against hers, feeling quite unlike any other friendship she'd had in the past. She felt his inner turmoil each time his hard chest rose and fell against hers. She wanted him. She needed him like she needed air.

'Maybe,' he said and with that, the spell was broken, the mood shattered. Laura pulled away, extricated herself from his uncertainty.

She'd overstepped, badly. Embarrassment, desire rose up inside her, threatening to break over her face.

'Anyway, goodnight!' she said as cheerily as she could.

'Laura, wait. I don't know what's going on between us—I don't know if kissing you is a good idea.'

She nodded. 'You're right. We talked about this. I'm sorry.'

'No, we didn't, not really. Not properly. Laura, I don't think kissing you is a good idea because I don't know if I can stop.'

Ah, her thoughts exactly.

Did they have to stop?

Laura imagined five minutes into the future, taking his hand in hers, pulling him wordlessly into her cottage and closing the door behind them. Maybe she'd lead him down the hall to the bedroom. Maybe they wouldn't even make it that far. Maybe their knees would buckle on the living room floor as their need and want consumed every breath they had. One thing was certain, that if he came inside with her now she also would not be able to stop. Not tonight. Maybe never.

He wanted her as much as she wanted him, so one of them had to stay strong, because Henry Weston must not fall in love with her.

And most importantly of all, she must not fall in love with him.

'You're right.' She nodded slowly, taking a further, safer step back, out of his warmth, out of his reach.

'I want to,' he began.

She waved her hand up to indicate that she understood, her throat suddenly constricted, her mouth now incapable of making a sound.

'Goodnight, Laura Jane.'

'Goodnight, Henry Daniel,' she managed before fleeing inside, with the door safely between them.

By the time Henry was up, dressed and about the next morning he still hadn't figured out what had happened last night. The facts were clear enough: his suspicion was correct and Laura was Jane. It was so obvious he could hardly believe he'd doubted himself. The relationship he had with Laura was so similar to the one he'd had with Jane: an easy, happy understanding and a conversation he never wanted to end.

But, instead of being glad that the two women with which he had this amazing connection were one and the same, instead he knew they didn't have a long-term future and their relationship must remain a friendship.

Except that once they had spoken about all of this and agreed, she'd kissed him.

He'd been waiting outside her cottage, his feet unwilling or unable to take him home, and then there she was, coming outside and kissing him and he'd kissed her back like his life depended on it, because for those few stolen minutes it had. His lips still throbbed, and other places besides, at the memory of her body in his arms and her mouth on his.

Where did that leave them? The same place as it had before the kiss—absolutely nowhere, but twisted up in it.

There was some small chance Laura could conceive, but not only might it take a long time and a lot of assistance, while she waited to conceive she'd be in pain. He couldn't ask her not to get any treatment she needed; he couldn't watch her be in as much pain as she had been last week— that was out of the question.

They had to remain as friends only and that was better than nothing. They didn't belong together and this evening he'd take her up the hill and show her why.

At around 5:00 p.m., the time FarmerDan would usually message SohoJane, Henry made his way through the house where he found a few staff members helping Laura lift a painting back onto the wall. There was much laughing and a lighthearted banter between Laura and the others and Henry held back for a moment watching her. Her long hair was tied back, but loose strands had escaped their bindings and fell into her face. She wore overalls over a white

T-shirt, her usual work attire. But she didn't look usual to him today. She was SohoJane. And Laura. She was impossible, but no less lovely, he realised with a pang.

He had to take her up the hill because then she'd understand. And when she understood she'd realise why he couldn't keep kissing her, as much as he wanted to.

Henry cleared his throat to gently let the others know he was there. The mood shifted slightly, as it often did when he made his presence known. There were nods and 'Good days,' but then everyone left him alone with Laura.

'How are you feeling?' The question was loaded with too many implications and he quickly added, 'Physically.'

She smiled. 'I'm okay. Physically.'

'You're taking it easy though, aren't you?'

'I'm fine, really. I bounce back quickly.'

'But still, you should look after yourself.'

'Aye, aye, boss.' She was smiling.

He was stalling and they both knew it.

'I was thinking, I still owe you a tour of the monument. Up the hill.'

A long beat passed and he could see her thoughts ticking over. Weighing up the fact she wanted to go with the doubt as to whether it was a good idea.

'I'd like to show it to you.' This was the truth. So far he'd told her a little about his family, but once she went up there, she'd really know.

She nodded. 'Yes. That would be great.'

'This evening?'

'Yes, please.'

By the time he knocked on the door to her cottage, with Buns and Honey eagerly at his heels, he was excited to be seeing Laura but wondering at the same time if he was being a fool asking to spend more time with her. How could they just be friends if every time he anticipated seeing her his heart rate ran a little faster?

*Because when she sees what is at the top of the hill she'll get you.* The monument at the top of the hill, or rather what was inside it, could explain Henry Weston to Laura better than any words he could come up with ever could.

Laura was wearing jeans that fit her shapely body snugly and a soft white sweater. The spring evening had a slight chill to it, but it was clear and perfect for a walk around the castle. Her long hair cascaded down her back in dark, silky waves. As they made their way across the grounds and up the gentle hill, he couldn't stop thinking about running his fingers through it, but evidently Laura's mind was more safely occupied. 'Why isn't it open to the public?' she asked.

'A few reasons. It's special to our family. But we've also set it, and this entire area aside as a protected wildflower sanctuary.'

'Why is that?'

'Most of the wildflower meadows in the country have been lost over the past century, so to preserve and regrow them we, along with many others, have set aside land for the meadows to grow wild.'

The hill was dotted with blue and purple flowers. There were dogviolets, pasqueflower and cornflowers the colour of Laura's eyes. Butterflies danced over them. The dogs raced each other along the path.

He unlocked the gate and Laura entered first. As they climbed the hill to the monument, the wild, overgrown nature reminded him of the length of time his family had lived there and his responsibility to them. When they approached the summit the path gave way to stone steps. At the top, there was a three-hundred-and-sixty-degree view of the countryside, taking in the entirety of the castle's grounds, their village and several more besides.

'Wow. It's amazing,' she gushed as she caught her breath.

'And if you come over here, you can see all the way south down the valley, across three counties.'

Laura stood where he motioned and he watched her shoulders sag as she exhaled and took in the view. The sun was low in the west, bathing the whole place in a honey-coloured light. The ruins, the house and the villages glowed in the sunset.

'It's so beautiful. Thank you for showing me. It's a shame others don't get to see it.'

'Yes, but it's also important to have areas like this left as they are. Preserved for the future.'

She smiled softly and gently touched his forearm. 'Then I'm very thankful you showed me.'

The touch of her hand made something in himself melt. Resisting the urge to pull her to him he said, 'Would you like to see inside?'

'We can go in? I'd love that.'

He held up the keys and led her over to the double wooden doors.

The room was always lighter than he expected; apart from a few stained-glass panels, the circular building appeared to be windowless, however, once you were inside you realised that a circle of windows at the bottom of the dome gave the room all the light it needed. The three stained-glass panels cast the occasional rainbow.

Laura sucked in a breath and whispered, 'It's beautiful.'

He nodded. The architect who had designed this space over two hundred years ago had been inspired.

After admiring the ceiling and its dome, Laura made her way slowly around the room. 'Oh, Henry. There are graves.'

He stood back and watched her look, a lump rising in his throat. He'd only ever known one of the people lying here. The twelfth duke. His father. Yet he knew the names on all the plaques.

She turned back to him, eyes wide. 'I'm so sorry, I didn't realise it was a mausoleum. I assumed it was simply a folly.'

Henry nodded. Most people did—after all it looked like a small Greek temple, just as all the other eighteenth-century follies of the time did.

'It was a folly, at least once. The sixth duke built it in the eighteenth century for his wife, but she loved it so much she asked to be buried here. Ever since then, every duke and his wife have been interred here.'

Laura spun and stared at him, her jaw slack. 'And your father?'

He nodded.

Laura met his gaze and held it, wordlessly acknowledging his loss. 'Would you mind showing me?'

Henry walked over to the place, though as the newest, shiniest plaque it was easy to spot. It read:

*John Daniel Weston*
*Twelfth Duke of Brighton*
*Dearly loved, terribly missed*
*Son, husband and father*
*Honour, faith, love*

He heard her draw in a deep, serious breath. 'Tell me about him.'

'My father?'

She nodded.

Why did he struggle to describe him to Laura? The plaque said all the important things; he was a son, a husband and a father and he was loved. And missed. 'He was my father, and he was wonderful. He adored me and my mother, and he loved this place. He devoted his life to Abney Castle and the people of this region.' As he opened his mouth to say something else his throat closed over and from nowhere he felt something well behind his eyes and nose. He swallowed it back.

She smiled softly. 'I miss my dad too, and it's still hard to talk about him. Even after all these years.'

Henry wanted to step closer to her, pick up her hand and squeeze it, to comfort her as much as himself, but he remained rooted where he was, his chest tight, emotion unexpectedly threatening to break through the surface of the careful calm he was trying to maintain.

Laura didn't push her comment further and walked sombrely around the room. There was no rhyme or reason to where his ancestors were interred. Many were under the ground, some in the walls.

'The ninth duke. Tell me about him.' Laura pointed to a bust of a moustached man on a pedestal. One of the largest and most ostentatious monuments in the room.

'Well, his wife is over there.' Henry pointed across the room. 'As far away as she could be from him.'

Laura laughed. 'Yet they are both here.'

'He spent a lot of his time in India. She spent a lot of hers with one of the stablehands. And this was their son, the tenth duke.'

'The one who married the gardener's daughter?'

Henry paused, amazed at her memory. 'The very one. And the tenth duke had ten children, or rather, his poor wife did. Apparently he was very proud of the fact.'

Laura grimaced, as well she might.

'And this is the sixth duke and his duchess, Frances. Together.' He pointed to the marble slab that marked their resting place.

'It's a lovely stone.'

*Unable are the loved to die*
*For love is immortality*

Did love that strong really exist? If it did, it was so rare. He understood, maybe for the first time in his life how lucky two people were to find love like that. Until now he'd taken it for granted. His parents had loved one another deeply. As had his grandparents. But what if that was not going to be his fate? He was thirty years old and yet today he felt further away from it than ever.

Laura stopped in front of the next plaque, as he'd hoped she would.

'Daniel Weston,' she said and touched her fingers gently to the dates. Then she looked at him, her face creased with questions.

'Was he your brother?'

Henry nodded.

'But he…'

'Yes. He died before I was born.'

'Oh, Henry. How old was he?'

'He was seventeen. It was a riding accident.'

It was strange to tell this story because it wasn't exactly his story. Even though, were it not for the accident, he, Henry Weston, would not exist.

'Your poor parents. He was their only child?'

'Until then, yes. They…well.' Henry looked at the stone floor. 'After he was born they tried to conceive again, but they couldn't. They weren't overly worried. They had an heir after all. But then my brother died so they had to try again. But this time with assistance.'

'IVF?'

'Yes. It took a while, nearly two years, but they got me.'

'How old was your mother?'

'She was forty-three when I was born. It was a high-risk pregnancy, she was on bed rest for the last two months and she nearly died giving birth to me, but…' He didn't want to speak for either of his parents; he knew the sacrifices they had made for him. His mother had been forty-three when he was born but his father had been fifty. Henry knew he'd had a different upbringing to his older brother.

'It would have been so hard for both of them. So hard for her,' he finally said.

Laura turned her back and stepped away from Daniel's plaque. 'Is that how the Weston women are meant to be? To go to all those lengths to provide an heir?'

'No, that's not it at all. I would not expect my wife to go through what my mother went through just so there could be another duke.'

'Then what do you mean?'

He scraped his fingers over his scalp. 'My parents went to a great many lengths to have me. The entire reason I exist is so I can be the duke. It is my sole destiny. I can't just ignore that.'

'I'd never ask you to give that up. I do understand.'

'Do you?' His voice cracked across his throat.

'I do. I do understand…really, I do. And honestly, it wouldn't have mattered to me if you were a duke with a title to bequeath or just a man who wanted to be a father—I'd never ask anyone to give up something like that.'

He believed her—she was Jane. And Laura. Laura Jane. There were few people in the world he'd ever trusted more.

'That's why I stepped back from dating in the first place. But you…'

'I didn't listen.'

'No, that wasn't what I was going to say,' she said with a grin. 'I didn't follow my own advice either.'

They faced one another, just a few feet apart. Their bodies pulling together, but the weight of the history in the room pushing them apart.

'Let's go, that is if you're ready?' she said.

He nodded. He'd had enough of the Weston family crypt for one day.

'Graveyards always make me philosophical,' she said.

'Not sad?'

'Not exactly. They remind me that life is finite and that makes me remember to treasure every day and strangely that makes me happy.'

'I don't think that's strange. It means you're remembering to be grateful for the life you lead and that's always a good thing.'

She was amazing... She held so much goodness within her. But the more he found to like and admire about her, the harder things became.

His mind leapt back to how she'd been last week when he'd found her unwell, ashen, sweaty, her face creased with pain. She'd been enduring that sort of physical misery regularly for years.

'How do you manage to stay so upbeat, so grateful after everything you have to go through?'

Laura regarded him, temporarily lost for words, and then looked at the ceiling. 'I guess when I'm in pain, I remember that it will pass.'

'And when you're not?'

'I try to focus on the here and now. I try my best not to think too much about the future.'

He led the way outside, surprised by the light; the countryside still glowed like golden honey.

Laura waited a few steps away while he relocked the door.

*Be grateful for the life you have.* If he could just keep remembering that then it might be easier to keep Laura at a safely platonic distance.

They didn't speak on the walk down and Henry's thoughts kept coming back to his father, his brother. All the dukes resting at the top of the hill. With their devoted duchesses. And the not so devoted ones.

Would that be his lot? To be buried across the room from his wife like the ninth duke?

Or would she be like the wife of duke number six and lie for eternity with her husband? Would he be like duke number ten and sire ten children. He shuddered. That did seem unlikely.

Had any of them worried about the things that he worried about? His father had, certainly, but the others? Had they worried about the future in the same way that Henry did? Constantly and fearfully?

Laura waited for him at the gate at the foot of the hill. It was unlocked, but he held it open for her. When she walked past him their arms brushed against one another's and his entire body flooded with warmth and sparks and every muscle in his body waited, as though they all knew that being next to Laura, touching Laura was their one true purpose. Laura paused as well; the warmth from her body spread into his, the gentle friction between their bodies only exciting him more. A brush wasn't enough. He needed all of her.

He leant in. When he was this close to her the rest of the world dropped away. Became an insignificant afterthought. Laura let out a half sigh, half groan and his insides flipped. Pleasure laced with desperation. Was that how she'd sound if he was holding her, properly and forgetting the rest of the world existed? Should he live for the future? Or should he live for the here and now? No one knew what the future held.

*'They remind me that life is finite and that makes me remember to treasure every day.'*

'I don't know what to do,' she whispered. 'I don't know why it's so hard.'

'Because we like one another. It was always going to be hard.'

'I don't want to lose you from my life, but I don't know how to do this. I don't know how to be near you without wanting to do this.' Laura lifted herself and her lips found his. He could taste her wanting because he felt it too. She was there in his arms but would never be his. He stepped back before he tasted too much more and was lost for ever.

The trip to the folly was meant to help, it was meant to put something between them, but instead it had only seemed to bring them closer than ever.

*'I try to focus on the here and now.'*

Maybe his problem was that he was focusing too much on for ever when he should just be focusing on here and now?

# CHAPTER SEVEN

'CAN I BUY you dinner?' Henry said as he stepped away from another almost kiss, leaving Laura struggling for breath and composure.

The entire evening had been moments of 'almosts'. Almost hugging him when he spoke about his father, almost pulling him to her when he read her the inscription on the plaque marking the spot the duke and his wife were buried together.

Now at the gate an 'almost kiss'. She'd brushed her lips against his but instead of doing either of the two things she'd expected, kissing her back or pushing her away for good, he'd asked her out to dinner.

'Is that a good idea?'

'You've been to the village pub, it's pretty good.'

He knew what she meant, and he'd dodged her question neatly, but she took his point. He was offering her dinner, not a night of passionate lovemaking. Dinner and probably a drink. That was all. He was being the sensible, rational one, whereas she was in turmoil.

Why was it so hard? She'd had male friends before, even ones she'd been attracted to, but it had never been like this. Her body had never felt so torn in two.

The dogs came with them to the village. The four of them sat at a wooden table outside, Honey and Buns sitting at Henry's feet as though they were accustomed to the routine. They ate and drank in the setting sun. He insisted she try the local cider, fermented in his distillery, which was pleasantly dry and refreshing. Henry waved and nodded to the locals, some of whom stopped for a quick chat, careful to acknowledge Laura without appearing too curious. Henry's explanation that she was an art conservator working for him a few weeks elicited warm smiles. Henry was easy with the locals and they were with him. The brief conversations ranged from wool prices to the upcoming village fair. He was less lord of the manor and more respected colleague, neighbour and friend.

This only made her ache further. Couldn't he have at least one downside? A single red flag? Some flaw, however minor, upon which to hang some hesitation.

But no.

Henry was lovely.

Quite possibly perfect.

But he wasn't perfect because he wasn't perfect for *her*. How was she meant to carry on a platonic friendship with him when every cell in her body wanted to throw itself at him?

It was dark by the time they left the pub though and as they made their way back, she lost track of the path, veering into the grass. Henry was far more familiar with the route than she was and grabbed her arm to set her straight. But once she was back on the path he didn't let go of her arm. Instead he linked it through his and they continued to walk, arm in arm, warm body against warm body, along the path and through the castle gate.

She liked it. No, she adored it. Henry's body rubbing against hers was perfection, but it was also sending her thoughts into overdrive. This was how the almost kiss at the gate had started—they were veering into dangerous territory.

Yet she was helpless to remove her arm from his.

'Can you...' he began after a while. He cleared his throat,

his voice raw, he began again. 'That is… I've been doing some reading on endometriosis. I know it's more than simply bad period pain. I know it can have all sorts of other effects.'

'Yes, but pain is one of my main ones. Bloating sometimes and nausea, but it's the pain that's the biggest problem.'

'Does it affect any other activities?'

'Like work?'

'Yes, that but other physical activities.'

It took her a moment to gather his meaning and when she did, her heart missed a beat. 'Are you asking if I can have sex?'

'I wasn't going to put it so unromantically.'

'It's not unromantic to talk about it.'

'Then, yes, I guess, I was. I don't want to ask you to do anything that is painful. I don't want to hurt you. I want to understand how it affects you and what I can do for you.'

*'What I can do for you.'*

Laura's heart leapt into her throat, almost cutting off her airway. Her body rippled with sparks.

*You can carry me to my cottage, rip my clothes off and touch, stroke and kiss every single inch of me, quickly, then slowly, and then quickly all over again. You can do anything you want to me provided I can do the same to you.*

But, breathless and barely able to keep walking, let alone speak, she didn't say that out loud.

'And by answering that question, that doesn't mean I expect…'

This man.

She stopped walking and squeezed his arm. When she'd calmed her excited body and caught her breath she spoke, 'It doesn't hurt, not usually. I enjoy it, as long as I'm not in pain otherwise.'

When she was in the middle of an attack, intercourse was almost the last thing on her mind. But when she wasn't, sex

could be wonderful. Especially when she was with someone caring. And if she was with someone like Henry then
it might be amazing.

'We're clearly friends who like to kiss. We could see if
we could also be friends who like to have sex.'

'And…'

'And…do we need to know anything else? Can we not
think about next week, or even tomorrow?' he asked.

'Most relationships don't last…they burn themselves
out or end anyway. So we shouldn't be putting pressure
on ourselves,' she agreed and felt a weight lift from her
shoulders. She was overthinking all this, when really the
answer was simple: make the most of life. Live for the moment. At any time either one of them might end up in the
grave. Of course hers wouldn't be in a Grecian temple on
a hill overlooking three counties in the Cotswolds but the
end result was the same.

'We're making this more complicated than it needs to
be,' she went on.

'I agree—it feels like a lot of pressure not to give into
something we both want.'

'Oh, yes,' she said, exhaling.

They didn't say much more as they walked the rest of
the way back to the castle, but their pace picked up considerably. There was something exhilarating about knowing
what they were about to do.

Sex. They were going to have sex. The anticipation alone
raised the hairs on her skin, the fizz under it.

Her heart still beat in her throat and she stole glances at
him in the increasing darkness, could make out the silhou-
ette of his beautiful jaw, sometimes glimpsing a smile on
his lips which only made her chest burn more.

'My room or yours?' he said as they approached her
cottage.

'Yours. No mine.'

'There are twenty bedrooms here.' He grinned. 'Or any-where else you'd like.'

'Mine.' This time she was sure. She felt more comfort-able there and, more importantly, it was closer.

He stood a foot or so behind her as she unlocked the door, but she felt him anyway. She stepped back to let him and the dogs in first and then shook as she shut and locked the door behind them. Honey and Buns gave a cursory glance around the cottage, as though it wasn't their first time vis-iting, and then both sat obediently by the unlit fireplace.

'Will they be okay?' she asked.

Answering her question themselves, the dogs lay down and sighed, tired after their long walk.

Henry smiled at her, but the adrenaline or the nerves, she wasn't sure which, rose up inside her. She started to fuss around the room checking windows, closing curtains, which was entirely unnecessary, but the anticipation was so overwhelming she didn't trust herself not to fall apart.

She'd wanted this since the first time she saw him in real life, and probably before that as well, if she were being completely honest.

'Is everything okay?' he asked softly.

'It's great.'

'Exciting?'

'You have no idea.'

'Try me.' He smiled again and this time she noticed the muscles around his eyes quivering. He was struggling as much as she was. 'Show me where your room is.'

'You know where it is.'

'I want you to show me.'

She nodded and led the way down the short hall to the room she'd been sleeping in. He kept a few feet between them, both knowing that once they touched stopping would be next to impossible, engulfed by a passion that neither would be physically or emotionally able to quell.

Henry stood a foot away from her and a smile grew slowly across his lips. She shifted her weight from foot to foot, knowing she was teetering on the edge of a cliff, but also knowing that all she had to do was take a step forward and she would be caught.

By the time they finally came together she wanted everything at once. She pushed her body towards him, opened her mouth wide and started tugging at his shirt.

Henry was having none of it. He took her shoulders and held her at a short distance.

'Slow down, please.'

'Slow?'

'Please. I want to remember this. I want you to as well.'

'How on earth do you expect us to slow down?' she gasped. She wanted him yesterday. She wanted him last week already. Slow down? It would be easier to stop a runaway train.

'Lips only,' he whispered and lifted his hands from her shoulders. Their eyes met and she blinked in agreement, her entire body buzzing. He leant forward and touched his lips gently against hers. She opened her mouth as slowly as she could, savouring each movement, each breath, each stroke.

Slowly at first his tongue began to explore her mouth and she let hers wander. Every ounce of blood in her body flooded to her lips, every other cell screamed with jealousy.

Half opening her eyes she realised that Henry was tilting slightly; she wasn't the only one struggling to stay upright. She pulled back and grinned.

'Tops only,' he conceded.

She groaned but didn't need to be told twice. She pulled his shirt from under his belt, then, as she caught her breath she unbuttoned his shirt, carefully, deliberately.

'I'm not going anywhere.'

'No, because you're a giant tease, Henry Weston.'

She felt his gorgeous lips curl into a smile as he pressed them against hers again and her heart felt like it was melting. She was going to be a puddle on the floor at the rate they were going.

Moving back and catching her breath, she decided to give him a dose of his own medicine. She spread her fingertips over his chest as she pushed back his shirt, examining every inch of him, the lay of his muscles, the pattern of his veins his alert nipples, his firm chest covered in a smattering of hair.

Then she walked behind him and did the same to his bare back—slowly traced the lines between a few random freckles, watched his shoulders rise and fall with each rough breath. She spread her hands over his bare back, feeling the muscles she'd been admiring for days, exploring his arms with her fingertips, his neck with her lips.

The air in the room was so charged she wouldn't have been surprised if she'd seen sparks flicker in the air.

'My turn.' His voice was hoarse as he turned and stilled her gently. He slipped the fingers of both hands in hers and time stopped as she watched both their hands entwine and dance together. Then he took the hem of her shirt between his fingers and lifted it over her head. He repeated her ritual, explored the sensitive bare skin of her shoulders, her chest and her back. His lips made a pilgrimage down her body, to the edge of her bra and traced the line between her breasts. Finally she felt his fingers push the annoying fabric of her bra down and as the clasp released he gave an audible sigh.

She looked into his bright blue eyes now darkened with desire. She stepped back towards him but he gave his head a quick shake and nodded to the bed.

Thank goodness. She was shaking so much her knees were about to give way.

He pulled her to the bed and she waited, stretching across it, every one of her pores crying out to be touched by him. He lay on top of her, warm torso to warm torso, and his lips made their way slowly over her neck and back home to her own mouth.

His groin pressed against hers, and any desire he might have had to keep their bodies apart was now abandoned. Hard and persistent, she reached for his belt, but just before she claimed it he shifted his weight, lowered his head and took one of her nipples into his mouth. The tension that had been coiling inside wound even higher and she saw stars. 'You do realise that will almost be enough to break me, don't you?' she said, panting.

'That's my aim,' he murmured as he licked her again, his lips making their way from one aroused breast to the other and then lower, to her waistband, where he paused and looked up at her. Laura was desperate to get out of her underpants but just as desperate to get him out of his. She shook her head. 'You first.'

Henry rolled over dutifully. She ran her hand over the front of his jeans, saw his eyelids lower and could tell, finally, that his resolve was breaking too. She unbuttoned his jeans and pulled them down slowly, so that every movement was a caress. She ran her hand over the front of his pants, feeling him hard and ready under the thin fabric.

He gave permission with a grunt and she grabbed his waistband, dipped her hand beneath it, grasping his long, full length, feeling him shiver.

'Damn.'

'What?'

'Do you have protection?'

She didn't. 'I'm healthy and we both know pregnancy isn't on the cards and the drugs I'm taking make it impossible.'

'I'm healthy too. But do you want to be sure?'

'I'm sure if you are.' She rubbed his length, which was hardly conducive to good decision-making, but she didn't care. If they only had this short time—if they only had this one time—she wanted them both to enjoy it as much as they could.

She kissed his cheeks, his neck, collarbone, breathing in the delicious smell of his skin, that was heightened by the warmth of their bodies against one another's. His lids lowered and he nodded, grabbing her again and pulling her close.

By the time he entered her she could hardly see straight from longing. His strokes were long and certain; her entire body ached and clenched for him. He reached parts of her that she'd only reached in her dreams.

She nearly lost her mind. The climax when it came was even shocking in its intensity. She felt every one of his sighs in her gut.

'Henry,' she cried and felt him shuddering. The world slipped away for a moment and slowly came back together. He held her close, both panting, gathering their breath.

When she opened her eyes the world looked different. Something had shifted. Months of tension had been released, but there was something else.

A new weight. A new reality.

Was it possible? Had she been this careless?

Not to sleep with him without protection, but to sleep with him at all? Could she simply sleep with a man like Henry and not start to fall for him?

Laura slid out of her bed and into the bathroom.

Henry rolled onto his back, spread out his arms and moaned softly.

He was in big trouble.

He was going to remember this night for the rest of his life. Nothing, or rather no one, would be able to come close to making him feel what Laura just had.

Laura was amazing, but he felt that he'd put on an exceptional performance too. He'd never been so motivated, so desperate, to please someone in his life. She made him a better lover. Thirty years old and he'd just had the best sex of his life. Except that…he looked at the closed bathroom door. What was she thinking behind that door?

He'd suspected that sleeping with Laura might not be the most sensible idea he'd ever had, but he hadn't expected it to be this problematic. He hadn't expected to see colours he'd never known existed. He hadn't expected everything to shift so significantly.

He had foolishly hoped that his desire for Laura might fade once he gave in to it. He hadn't even imagined that his desire could only grow. This evening, as they ate and talked, he thought he wanted her as much as it was possible to want a person. But almost as soon as they'd come together he realised that everything that had come before was only the beginning. Like an addict, now that he'd had a taste he only craved more. To the exclusion of everything and everyone else.

He breathed in deeply.

*Get a grip.*

This was simply the afterglow of an amazing lovemaking session talking. Once he left, went out into the rest of the world, he'd see sense.

Pain healed. Hurt faded. He knew that. He'd got over women before; he'd moved on, life had returned to normal. And after Laura left, things would return to normal again. But was he just supposed to turn this off now? Not spend time with her, simply because it might hurt when she left?

It was already too late for that. They might as well make

the most of things while she was here. Like she'd said, most relationships don't last, they burn themselves out.

The bathroom door clicked and Laura emerged wearing her robe and chewing absentmindedly on her thumbnail. He noticed the exact moment she realised what she was doing and she pulled her hand quickly from her mouth. 'You're welcome to stay, but I understand if you'd rather go back to your own bed,' she said.

Was she saying she didn't want him to stay in her cottage or was she as self-conscious about this moment as he was?

'Is it a problem if I stay?'

'No, not at all. Just in case you'd be more comfortable in your own bed.'

'The only way I'd be more comfortable in my bed is if you were with me.'

Her shoulders dropped and she sat on the edge of the bed, exhaling.

'You're wondering what now?' he guessed.

She nodded.

'Me too.'

He liked that they were so honest with one another and talked so openly about what was going on. It made things easier.

'That was…'

She nodded again. They were both there, it was clear to anyone in the room that something pretty wonderful had just happened.

'Pretty good,' she said after a moment.

'Pretty good? Do I need to try harder next time?'

She stifled a laugh. 'If you can do better, I'd like to be there.'

He picked up her hand. 'You're only here for a few more weeks. It'd be a shame not to live in the moment for a little while longer. To see if I can't do better than that.'

He held his breath while he waited for her to answer. If this was their one time, if he never got to hold her again, then he wasn't sure how he'd manage to be around her for as long as she was working and living here without wanting her.

'It would be a shame. I think I'm going to take my own advice and live in the moment. The future will take care of itself.' She leant down and kissed him gently, sealing their promise. 'You should stay,' she said. 'Do you want another drink?'

'Are you having something?'

She smiled. 'What I'd really like is a cup of tea.'

He laughed. 'That sounds perfect.'

She brought the cups back to bed where they sipped them and lay together, chatting just as Dan and Jane had each evening. About everything and nothing.

When their cups were drained she looked at him. He stared into her eyes, feeling as though he'd known her for ever. She grinned and moved towards him.

Pleasure tumbled through him again as he felt her weight press deliciously against his and as her lips sought out his. Her pressure soft at first, but the kiss opened and deepened quickly and naturally.

Her skin was like silk against his fingertips, her warm body pliant and soft in contrast to his own which was suddenly hard, alert and ready again. When they made love a second time it was no less earth-shattering than the first, maybe more so as he was finding the places she liked to be touched, learning the rhythm she needed.

He needed to please her, to pleasure her. He wanted to make her happier than she'd ever been before, but he didn't know why. And he didn't want to know.

*Live in the moment.*

*The future will take care of itself.*

# CHAPTER EIGHT

LAURA'S PHONE RANG just before she was about to get into
the shower after work. She glanced at the screen.

Mum.

Laura hadn't been actively avoiding her mother, but she
hadn't been rushing to return her calls either. If she didn't
speak to her mother soon she'd be bound to send out a
search party.

'Darling, you're a difficult girl to get a hold of.'

'I'm sorry, I've been busy.'

'Good, I was worried you were sick again.'

'No, I've been fine.'

Laura sat, untied her shoes and put her phone onto
speaker mode.

'What's been keeping you so busy then?' Fiona asked.

'This and that...'

*Spending every spare moment I have with a handsome
duke. Last night he picked me up in his light blue Aston
Martin convertible and we drove through the hills to Chel-
tenham for an amazing dinner. The night before that we
made love in his bedroom with the huge French windows
wide open and the smell of the spring garden floating. This
morning he mentioned taking me to Paris for the weekend
so we can visit the Musée d'Orsay. He says that it's work*

*related, but we both know it isn't and would probably be breaking all the rules we silently set for ourselves.*

But she didn't mention any of that.

'How's the work going?'

'Good. It's going well. The paintings are wonderful and thanks to the way Archibald and the family have looked after them, they're in very good condition.'

'So you'll be home soon?'

'We'll see.' Laura wasn't taking any more time with the work than she ordinarily would, though she wasn't rushing to finish it either.

She had to tell her mother. If she didn't and she somehow found out, Fiona would make it into a bigger thing than Laura wanted it to be.

'And, look, please don't get excited, because it isn't anything serious, but I've been going on a few dates.'

'With the duke?'

Despite Laura's warning, Fiona's excitement almost caused Laura's phone to vibrate.

'Yes, and Dan.'

'You've been dating both of them?'

'Sort of. They are the same person after all.'

Laura braced herself for more squeals over the phone line but none came, which was even more ominous.

'How? I mean...how?' Fiona asked finally.

Laura gave her a brief run-down of her suspicions, Henry's behaviour when she was unwell, her suggestion they meet and then the date at the pub in Epemere. By the time she'd finished, Fiona wasn't squealing any more, she was subdued.

'So, that's why I told you not to get so excited. It's just a temporary thing. Just a bit of fun while I'm here, that's all.'

'But, darling—'

'But nothing, Mum. I thought you'd be happy for me.'

'I want to see you getting out, having fun, but I don't want to see you heartbroken.'

'I won't be, Mum.' She would be sad when she and Henry parted, but she'd gone into this with her eyes wide open and she was keeping her heart locked safely away. She knew as well as anyone this was a temporary thing and they had both decided to simply enjoy the time they had together.

Fiona let the subject drop. 'What are you doing tonight?'

'A quiet night by myself.'

'Really?'

Fiona wasn't usually a judgemental mother and she probably wasn't being one now, but Laura was unsettled. She was reading things into her mother's remarks that were not there or at least unintended.

'I've a lot of television to catch up on.' And sleep too.

Henry was busy with the final arrangements for the village fair that was coming up in two weeks' time, on what would probably be Laura's last weekend at Abney. The Dukes of Brighton had been hosting an annual village fair for over two hundred years. There was a small but active organising committee, of which Henry was the chair. Each fortnight he attended a meeting with the committee, but now that the fair was nearly here, the frequency of the meetings had increased.

'You should come up and visit. I'll only be here for another fortnight or so and the Abney Fair is happening in two weeks.'

'You want me to meet him?'

That wasn't exactly the piece of information Laura wanted her mother to take away from the invitation, but it was out there, nonetheless.

'I want to see you. And I'd love for you to see where I've been living and the castle. And yes, you'll meet Henry too, but please, don't read anything more into it than that.'

'Of course. I'd love to come. I'll be there.'

After saying goodnight to her mother, Laura made herself a light dinner and flicked through the television several times, looking for something to watch, but nothing seemed to quite match her mood. Happy, but on edge. Content but anticipatory.

She couldn't help but think of Henry, meeting the committee at the village pub, finalising the last-minute details. There would be over a hundred stalls, many from local producers, food vendors, as well as animal displays and children's activities.

His work on the committee energised him. She could see how much he loved this part of his job. He wasn't annoyed by the minor frustrations and setbacks that occurred as a part of organising an event such as the fair, but rather revelled in helping others, finding the humour in everything.

She was just thinking about pulling up off the sofa and taking herself to bed when her phone buzzed with a message.

Henry: Are you still up?

Was this what she'd been anticipating all evening?

Henry arrived, barely five minutes later, with all the appearance of having walked very quickly back from the village.

It was impossible not to smile at the red-faced and slightly dishevelled man who walked across her threshold, his blond hair slightly askew. The brightness in his eyes lit the fire in her belly.

He slid his arms around her waist and she stood on her toes to reach his lips.

Their kiss was tender, adoring, but slowly moved deeper. His tongue explored her lips and mouth, searching, probing and she opened her mouth and her heart to him.

'Hey,' he said, pulling back after a while for air.

'Hey, there. I didn't think I'd see you tonight.'

His face clouded over. 'Is it all right that I'm here?'

'It's more than all right—it's a wonderful surprise.'

Henry exhaled.

They undressed one another carefully, taking their time to kiss and stroke each new inch of skin as it was revealed. Sometimes they rushed, as though they had only minutes left, sometimes, like tonight, they took their time, pretending, she thought, that they really did have for ever. Kissing every inch of one another's bodies, exciting every pore, and making sure no part remained unexplored, untouched or unloved.

After, as they lay together, he told her about his evening, making her laugh with stories about the organising committee, a diverse group of people of all ages and by the sounds of things the only thing they appeared to have in common was that they were as devoted to bringing the fair together as he was.

Her heart swelled at the love he had for his community, for the work they were doing, making people happy, supporting local businesses and making money for charity to boot.

Henry loved his village and his community.

*Be careful.*

It was one thing to live in the moment and ignore the future, but the more she got to know him the more her heart grew for him. She had to keep reminding herself to hold that part of herself back.

She yawned and rolled to the side, feigning exhaustion and hoping that sleep claimed her quickly before he said anything else. Not only did she have to keep her heart safe, but she couldn't let Henry risk his. She cared for him too much to let him jeopardise his future. Sleeping with one another might be harmless fun, but by spending time with her Henry wasn't spending time finding the mother of his children.

*The best way to keep your heart safe is to make sure his does not belong to you.*

It was exceptionally bad timing that the lead-up to the annual fair was in the same few weeks of Laura's visit. At other times of the year he had more free time, but this was one of the busiest times of year for him. The fair had several official organisers, but they had reached the pointy end where everyone had to pitch in. Dukes included. It was the biggest day of the year for the village and the castle—they spent all year planning it in one way or another. It was fun to organise—even with the inevitable setbacks—and he always felt an immense sense of achievement watching everyone enjoying themselves. He'd been taking on more organisational responsibility for the last few years, as he had gradually with many other tasks as his father's health declined. His mother was also expected back, but this was a slight source of worry. His mother, Caroline, would be bound to meet Laura.

What if his mother didn't like her?

No. The idea was preposterous. How could anyone not love Laura?

Not that he *loved* her as such. That would be foolish. They were enjoying her time at Abney for the next couple of weeks, but they both understood that their relationship had an end date. It was unspoken, but implicitly agreed, that once Laura had finished her work at Abney she would return to London and their relationship—at least their physical one—would end.

The physical distance between their homes had never struck either of them as a barrier; she travelled around the country for her work; he visited London regularly. Both had begun their time on A Deux looking for matches in a large geographical area. If they wanted to keep seeing one other after she left Abney they could make it work…

But he reminded himself, it didn't matter if they *wanted* to see one another after she finished her work at Abney, they had tacitly agreed *not* to. Their entire fling was predicated on an agreement that it must be temporary.

But it was now Saturday night, and he just wanted to put that all to one side to spend the rest of the weekend with Laura. She'd met him in the village for a drink and dinner and they were now strolling slowly back to the castle and what he hoped would be an evening of languid, luscious lovemaking.

'Are you still on the app?' Laura asked out of nowhere as they were walking through the back gate to the castle grounds. Her tone suggested she intended the question to be light, casual. Almost as though she was asking him what he thought of the weather, but it stopped him in his tracks.

'A Deux?'

She shrugged.

He spluttered. 'How can you ask that?'

'I was wondering. We're friends still, aren't we?'

'Yes, of course we're friends but…' They were so much more as well.

He had to get married if he wanted a legitimate heir to carry on the title—there was no other option. But now that he imagined himself opening up the app again, swiping through the photos for a prospective duchess, his gut clenched. And not in a good way. In an I-might-just-lose-my-dinner-in-the-nearest-bush kind of way. Dating someone else would be like cheating on Laura. Marrying someone else would be worse. How could he do that to Laura, let alone his poor wife, whoever she might be?

'I'm not on that app. Or any app. I haven't opened a dating app since you arrived here. And I have no immediate plans to do so.'

Laura nodded and pursed her lips together but he got the impression the conversation wasn't over, just put on ice.

Hours later, after shedding their clothes, their inhibitions and the awkwardness of their earlier conversation, Laura sat on his couch, wrapped only in one of his shirts, sipping a glass of cognac, an after-sex ritual they seemed to have adopted. They had a routine. They had rituals. They were a couple, whether she wanted to admit it or not.

'So, do you happen to have plans the weekend of the Wimbledon final?'

'Why?'

'I have tickets. I thought we could make a weekend of it.'

Laura's body stilled. The room seemed to go silent as if even the frogs croaking outside the open window were judging his comment. 'That's months away.'

'Yes, but they're difficult to get.'

It was difficult to get tickets unless you were a duke with a long connection with the All-England club. She didn't answer him, and he didn't press. Instead they talked about the fair, the dogs, the ordinary minutiae of his day that he'd become so used to sharing with Laura.

He was up, pouring himself another drink and telling Laura about Natalia, one of the castle guides who also helped with publicity for the fair. Natalia had managed to get a video of some newborn lambs playing with some eight-week-old puppies advertising the fair to blow up on social media with well over a million likes.

'It was great advertising, but I'm not sure we can handle thousands more people turning up next week.'

Laura laughed. 'Relax, the video of the lambs and the puppies was gorgeous—you might get a few extra visitors, but I don't think you'll be overwhelmed with people. Natalia is great.'

'Yes, and a good employee.'

'She's single,' Laura said looking into her cognac.

Henry's jaw locked and he could only mutter, 'What do you mean?'

'Only that there are lots of eligible women out there.'

'You're trying to set me up with Natalia?' His tone was furious, but he couldn't help it. He felt like she'd just pulled his heart out. And then looked at it with disdain.

Natalia was nice, but he'd only ever seen her as an employee. How could Laura even think he was looking at Natalia as a prospective future partner?

'I...um...' Worry creased Laura's beautiful brow.

'You're wearing nothing but one of my shirts and telling me to date other women?' Aware that every cell in his body was vibrating, Henry stepped toward the windows and took some deep calming breaths. The conversation was very close to running dangerously out of control.

*Are you angry at her, or are you angry at yourself? Are you upset because you know she's right? Because you know, deep down, that what you and Laura are doing right now is reckless and has been for some time?*

Laura pulled the shirt tighter around herself. 'It's what friends do, isn't it?'

He stopped himself just in time from saying, 'But we're not just friends,' because it was his silly idea to call this thing they had between them friendship.

He sat next to her, the anger dissipated. He only felt tired.

'Laura, tell me. What's going on?'

'I've been distracting you from doing what you need to do and I feel guilty about that.'

'Guilty? Why?'

'Because, for months now you've been messaging me when you should be meeting other women, and now we're spending all this time together when...'

'I'm with you because I want to be with you. I'm not waiting for something better to come along.'

'But that's the thing, you *should* be.'

'I'm confused.'

'You should be looking for someone else.'

'I don't think I've ever heard you so down on yourself. What's the matter?'

'I'm not down on myself. I'm really not. I've always accepted who I am and what my body is and isn't capable of and I've made my peace with it. Honestly.'

He nodded. She was one of the strongest, most self-possessed women he'd ever known.

'It's nothing like that, but exactly what I said. I've been distracting you from what you need to be doing.'

'You want to stop...this? I don't, but if you do...?'

She spoke softly. 'I don't want to stop. I just always assumed that when I finished work here that it would be over, but now you're talking about Wimbledon. That's months away.'

'Ah, I see. You don't want to see one another at all afterwards?'

'Afterwards.'

Afterwards had once seemed like a theoretical time, in the long distant future, and the rules of afterwards had never been clear.

He assumed it would mean their physical relationship would end, but everything else? Their friendship? The thought of losing that made him hollow. They had been friends for far longer than they had been lovers.

'Whether you want to talk about it or not, it's going to happen. You're going to date someone else. Marry someone else. And I'm okay with that. I understand that. I understand that our time together is finite.'

'But will we still be friends, afterwards?' He hated asking the question, but dreaded her answer more.

'Your wife may not like me. She may not like the idea of us remaining friends.'

'I'm not going to marry someone who doesn't like you, or who doesn't want me to be friends with you.'

Laura smiled, but the serenity of her smile broke his heart.

'That's sweet, but don't you think that expecting your wife to be happy with a past lover hanging around is a little bit insensitive?'

He was quiet.

'Who are you going to marry?' he finally asked.

'Oh, I don't know. But I'm not on a timetable. There's less at stake for me.'

'How can you say that? Your happiness is as important as mine.'

'Yes, but it's different and we both know it.'

He was helpless to show her she mattered; she was important. Just as important as he was.

*She can't give you the one thing she knows you need.*

He hadn't thought this through—it wasn't meant to be like this. He hated the way he was making her feel. But he couldn't change it; it was his birthright, the very reason for his existence. He couldn't change it because it was the one thing he had no control over whatsoever.

And he hated it. He hated his title, his inheritance, his duty in a way he never had, even for a moment, before. Because of the way it was hurting Laura. The way it was tearing them apart.

'You are enough.' It was all he could say, because what else could he say?

'I know that.'

'Do you?'

'I do.'

He brushed his lips against her, tasting her, smelling her, savouring every pore, every scent. It was Laura who deepened the kiss, pulling him towards her. He could feel the desire in her and was powerless to stop himself being pulled along with it.

She wrapped her legs around him, pulled him tighter and he was helpless to let go, even though the only thing settled between them was that their bodies fitted perfectly together. She branded him with her fingerprints, delicate horseshoe shapes from her nails imprinted all over his body. She kissed him with her lips, tattooing herself across his heart.

There was nowhere else in the world he'd rather be.

Sunday was like any other workday for him, but it wasn't for Laura. And given the number of days she had left in Abney were likely limited, he intended to do the absolute minimum required of him today and spend as much time with Laura as was physically possible.

Last night's discussion was now pushed to the far recesses of their consciousness, like a bad dream. They were both naked, their ideal state as far as he was concerned. His eyes could enjoy the sight of her soft curves and strong limbs and his skin could luxuriate in the feel of her against him. Her warm shape pressed against his, with nothing to constrain or limit his reaction to her.

Bliss.

He lay on his back, Laura rested her chin on his chest and they looked at one another, making lazy conversation, exchanging dreamy happy noises and just generally forgetting the rest of the world existed. He ran his fingers through her dark hair, like a thick comb, hypnotised by the way when it slipped through his fingers he could see strands of gold and silver reflected in the sunlight.

'What would you like to do today?'

'Do you have much work to do?'

'Nothing I can't delegate. There's another meeting, but that's just to check in later this evening. We could go for a walk or we could play tourist somewhere else. Castle Combe? Chedworth?'

'Oh, I'd love that.'

'We could have lunch. Come back for an afternoon nap?'

Her eyes twinkled. She knew he wasn't anticipating sleep.

Laura shifted off him. 'Tea?' she asked.

'I'll get it.'

'No. Don't you dare move. I need to get up anyway and I expect you to be right there when I get back.'

'Just like this?' His arms were spread, his body entirely exposed.

'Just like that.'

He was entirely at her mercy and he felt himself rouse again just in anticipation of what would happen when she returned.

She slipped one of his shirts over her shoulders but wore nothing under it and did not button it up. He watched her leave, appreciating the view of one bare shoulder and her long smooth legs as she walked out of the room.

He hoped they had moved on from her doubts the previous evening. Yes, they both knew their arrangement had a shelf life, but he couldn't believe she'd think he was considering dating other women. His head and his heart were full of Laura and he was not thinking about the future. He was doing what he'd promised himself he would do: Live in the moment. The future would take care of itself.

The next thing he heard was Laura scream.

# CHAPTER NINE

HENRY LEAPT OFF the bed and rushed to the living room, realising too late that he probably should have thought to dress. Or at least grab some fabric to cover himself. As it was, his mother saw more of him than she had since he'd been a child. Shocked, she covered her face with her hands at the same moment Henry covered himself with his.

'Mum! What…?'

Laura at least had his shirt to cover herself though their current state left Caroline Weston in no doubt as to what had been happening in the bedroom.

'I sent you a message that I was on my way, though I can see you've been—' she peeked a glance at Laura from behind her hands and added '—busy.'

'Mum, this is Laura.' Henry almost removed his hands from where they were hiding himself to motion in Laura's direction but returned them to his groin just in time.

'Your Grace,' Laura said. 'Lovely to meet you.'

'Why don't I make you that tea I believe this young lady was on her way to prepare?' his mother said. 'And why don't you two get dressed?'

Despite his protests, Laura slipped out and back to her cottage as soon as she was dressed. It wasn't necessary that she leave and it made their whole situation look more casual than it was, but she insisted. 'Catch up with her, call me later.'

Henry threw on some shorts and a T-shirt and joined his mother at his kitchen table minutes later, reeling from the sudden change in the direction of his morning. He took a sip of the tea, scalded himself and placed it back down.

'Careful, it's hot. She didn't want to stay?' Caroline said.

'No, um. She had to get on with her day.'

'Really? It looked as though you both had your day planned already. The next few hours at least.' His mother grinned.

'Yes, well.' Henry looked into his tea.

'Why so coy? Tell me about her.'

*Tell me that it's serious between you. Tell me that you're about to propose and that I can expect grandchildren within the year.*

'She's the new art conservator they sent to replace Archibald.'

Caroline's face widened with delight, as he knew it would.

'She's been staying here for the past few weeks, in the cottage, and we've been getting to know one another.'

'Getting to know one another well by the looks of things. You worked fast.'

'It's a funny story, we'd actually already connected on the dating app I'm on, though we'd never met. And she's doing an amazing job here, she's so passionate about her work and the paintings and the whole castle really.'

Caroline's expression melted from delight into utter dreaminess. 'You really like her, don't you?'

'I do, but...'

'But what? Why does there have to be a "but"?'

'Look, Mum. We're not serious about one another.'

'Is she not serious about you?'

'Why do you say that?'

'Because, darling, your affection for her is written all across your face. Your skin changed colour when you started speaking about her, your eyes literally brightened.'

It wasn't his place to tell his mother about Laura's condition, so he didn't. He couldn't.

'We both like one another.' A lot. 'But we've agreed that this is only temporary. For while she's staying here.'

Last night he'd made the mistake of mentioning seeing one another after Laura's return to London and it had backfired. The memory of that conversation still pressed painfully against his ribs.

'But why? Where does she live?'

'London. Soho.' His tongue stumbled over the second word.

'Then we're practically neighbours.'

'But I don't live in London—I live here.'

'The distance between London and Abney is hardly insurmountable.'

If only the length of their commute was their biggest problem.

'If you want to move into Brighton House for a while, let you have some more space in London, I'm happy for you to do that. I've been thinking of spending a stretch of time in France. Or maybe Italy...'

'No, Mum, that's not it and not necessary.' If he suggested to Laura that he was going to spend more time in London to be closer to her she'd pack her bags immediately.

'It wouldn't be a problem. It's your house.'

He hated when she spoke to him like that. As far as he was concerned, Brighton House belonged to his mother. The castle belonged to a vague entity he called 'his family.' None of it belonged to him. Not properly.

'Mum, you will stay there. I will stay here and the week after next Laura will go back to London and that will be it.'

Laura's phone rang as she was dressing after her shower. It was her mother.

Did mothers have a secret code?

'What are you doing today?' Fiona asked.

Until an hour ago Laura's single plan had been to spend as much time as possible horizontal with Henry.

'Not sure yet. Henry and I were going to spend the day together but...'

'But?'

'But his mother just arrived. Unexpectedly. And now I think I'll do some work.'

'Did you meet her?'

'Yes, but—'

'Wonderful! What's she like?'

Laura could picture her mother sitting at her kitchen table leaning closer over her phone, which would be in speaker mode, expectantly waiting for Laura's answer.

'She seems fine.'

'Fine?'

Fine was as much as Laura was going to commit to at this stage. Shocked, surprised, certainly. But not quite warm and welcoming. At some point Caroline was bound to become outright hostile at the idea of a woman who had no intention of marrying her son monopolising so much of his time.

'It wasn't an ideal meeting.'

'What happened?'

'Well, we were both as good as naked, so there was that.'

Fiona laughed and laughed. 'Oh, darling, she's seen it all before.'

That wasn't Laura's hesitation. It was that Henry's mother saw instantly how involved they were. Henry's mother *must* disapprove of her—Laura was the woman who was disrupting all of Caroline's attempts to set Henry up with a suitable duchess.

Laura was a lot of things: she was smart, capable, talented and kind. But she wasn't duchess material. Laura changed the subject.

'And how was your date?'

'Oh, lovely, but he's getting very serious.'

'That's good, isn't it?'

'No dear. He wants us to be exclusive.'

Laura pulled a face, not for the first time glad her mother didn't like to video call.

'And that's a problem because?'

'Because I have a date with Tony tomorrow night and I like him as well.'

Oh, to be this sanguine about relationships.

'Mum, were you this… I don't know…this relaxed about men when you met Dad?'

'Heavens, no. I was very caught up on everything.'

'What changed? How did you get to relax about it all?'

'Oh, I don't know. Time, I think, is the only thing. I'm not looking for someone to spend the next fifty years with so the stakes are different.'

'But you still want to find love?'

'Of course I do…but, Laura, what's going on?'

Laura felt her insides welling up. The temptation to blurt everything out to her mother was suddenly overwhelming.

'Are things not going well with Henry?'

'No, I mean, yes, they are going well. And that's the problem.'

'Ah, I see. Look, chances are it will burn itself out soon anyway. Burn bright and fast, don't they say?'

Laura murmured agreement, hoping her mother was

correct. They were certainly 'burning bright', but she and Henry so far showed no signs yet of burning out.

Laura passed Natalia in the corridor and her gut churned with regret. She'd suggested Henry go out with her. She'd practically suggested he marry her. Was she out of her mind? Henry seemed to think so, judging by his reaction to the suggestion he date anyone else. Or go back on A Deux. The conversation had become far more serious than Laura had intended, but when they'd made love everything had seemed so unimportant. It always did; when she was in his arms the rest of the world faded away.

Wasn't Henry the one who insisted they were just friends to begin with? He was the one who had told her it was temporary. *Wasn't he?* Laura was having trouble remembering what either of them had said, that day in the wildflower meadow. So this morning, after the argument, after making love and especially after his mother, she wasn't sure where they stood, only that something had changed. Had they grown closer? Or further apart?

Laura climbed on the stepladder to reach the top of the canvas, a two-metre-high painting of Venice by Turner that was one of the centrepieces of the collection. She hadn't yet moved it from its position in the main gallery, hoping that wouldn't be necessary. Two years ago, Archibald had taken it down and cleaned it extensively. So far its condition looked excellent, the frame, which was less than twenty years old, also showed no signs of damage. It was a magnificent painting and she was always relieved to find works such as this so well taken care of. That was one thing about the Duchy of Brighton; it took great care in preserving its legacy.

Behind her, Laura sensed the air in the room shift. She felt the people stop moving, silence fell.

Laura turned her head, and nearly overbalanced. Louis

was standing with Henry's mother. 'Your Grace, this is Laura Oliver. The conservator who has taken over from Archibald. Laura, this is the dowager duchess.'

Once she regained her balance, she made her way down the ladder. At least she was dressed this time, though her overalls were still not as chic as the stylish blue knee-length dress Henry's mother was wearing.

'Your Grace, hello.' Laura held out her hand, not acknowledging their earlier meeting, though the dowager duchess did not either.

'Call me Caroline.'

'Caroline, nice to see you. Would you like to see what I'm working on?' Laura said for the benefit of the small group of staff watching them.

'That would be lovely.'

'As you know, this is a Turner from the mid-eighteen thirties. It was reframed several years ago and cleaned extensively two years ago and you will be glad to know that it still appears to be in excellent condition. I will get some help to take it down shortly so that I can examine the back and be sure, but my first impressions are positive.'

'Lovely.'

'It's a beautiful piece, as you know. From his second visit to Italy.'

As Laura spoke she got the impression from the way Caroline kept diverting her gaze that she was only listening to be polite.

'And that's all,' Laura said, to wrap things up. She could talk about Turner for hours. 'Unless there's anything else you'd like to know?'

'Laura, you must need a break. You're already working on a Sunday. It really is above and beyond. Would you like to have afternoon tea with me? Maybe we can talk more about your work.'

Laura looked down at her outfit, stained overalls and a faded T-shirt.

'Don't worry about that. You must know by now we don't worry about such things here,' Caroline said.

Laura took a moment to tidy up her things then followed Caroline through the castle and back to the family rooms. Afternoon tea had been Caroline's object in seeking her out all along. Laura half hoped that Henry would be joining them, but she gathered by the way they walked in silence through the castle, Caroline just half a step ahead of Laura, that Laura was being led to the principal's office for a talking to and she was not at all surprised to see that Henry would not be joining them.

He had probably already had his talking to this morning.

*It's just afternoon tea with your employer. You can do this.*

She'd been through far worse interviews.

And besides, Laura had no intention of stealing Henry, of diverting him from his duty. Caroline had nothing to be angry about.

Caroline had a set of rooms close to Henry's but entirely separate. Claudia was waiting for them but after nodding to Caroline and smiling at Laura she disappeared, leaving behind an afternoon tea spread laid out like they were at high tea in an upmarket hotel.

*She's a duchess—did you really expect a packet of assorted creams?*

They made small talk about Laura's job, family and the weather before finally Caroline started to come to the point.

'I see you and Henry have hit it off.'

That was one way of describing it. 'Yes.'

'He says you both have a lot in common and he's glad you were chosen to replace Archibald. He says you're a very impressive woman.'

Laura couldn't be sure if Caroline was paraphrasing, but her chest warmed at the compliment, nonetheless.

'I'm glad Archibald chose me as well. I've enjoyed getting to work here. And getting to know Henry.'

Laura looked at the woman, in her seventies but made of steel. She'd lost a husband and a son and made goodness knew how many sacrifices to have another. Laura didn't want to upset her, but she didn't want to lie either. 'What else has Henry told you?'

'This and that. He seems quite serious about you.'

'Oh, I don't know about that.'

Carline raised an eyebrow. 'You're not serious?'

'No, I mean yes. I mean I care about him a lot.'

Caroline smiled, relaxed back into her chair.

'But neither of us are wanting to commit at this point.'

'I guess it's the fault of the internet.'

'What is?'

'Your generation.'

Laura's hackles were up at the mention of intergenerational divide.

'The apps you use, they give you so much choice you don't know what to do with it. Always waiting for something better to come along.'

'It isn't like that.'

If she met a thousand men none would be as wonderful as Henry. Laura began to suspect that Henry hadn't actually told his mother much about her at all.

'I know committing is hard, it takes a leap of faith, and heavens, being a duchess isn't about the jewels—it is hard work. But a strong friendship is the best basis for a marriage.'

Laura chewed on her sandwich far longer than necessary, allowing her thoughts a moment to recalibrate. Now that she thought about it, Caroline didn't seem as disapproving as Laura had expected. In fact her hesitant manner might also be interpreted as nervousness. Caroline was trying to persuade her into a relationship with Henry, not chase her away.

'It isn't that,' Laura said.

'Then what is it?'

'I'm not sure what he's told you about me, but I don't think he's told you everything.'

Caroline put down her tea.

Laura took a deep breath. 'I have endometriosis.'

'Oh, I'm sorry.'

'It's unlikely I'll ever be able to have children.'

Caroline shook her head. 'There are all sorts of treatments available now.'

'I know, but none are a guarantee. And it's more than just that. The treatments that I need now are the type that would make it difficult, if not impossible to conceive. But I want to reassure you, I know how important the title is to him, and he and I have no intention—' Laura didn't get to finish.

'I expect he's told you about Daniel.'

Laura nodded. 'I'm so sorry for your loss.'

Caroline's hand fluttered to her throat and she looked out the window into the distance. 'Do you know what's funny?' she said after a while.

What on earth could be funny about the situation?

'I never really had a chance to mourn Daniel. It was awful, of course it was, but it was so soon afterwards that I had my first specialist appointment. I made the appointment even before the funeral. You're probably horrified, but I had to. For the family's sake.'

Laura hadn't the faintest idea what to say, so she let Caroline speak.

'When we married, I promised my husband we would be partners in the whole enterprise. And yes, running a duchy is an enterprise, make no mistake. It's as though you are in charge of a company. You own it, but really you're just holding it on trust for the next generation. It has a life, an existence, that is separate from any person. It should out-live us all.'

Laura nodded, now fully understanding Caroline's point.

'Do you care about the past? About tradition?' she asked Laura.

'I care about it very much. My job is art conservation, but it isn't just paintings I want to see preserved, it's all kinds of things. I do value your family history, which is why Henry and I...well, we care about one another, but we both know it will be short-lived.'

Caroline smiled gently. 'The treatment wasn't fun, I'm not going to lie, but it's far better now than it was thirty years ago. But it can still be an emotional and physical roll-ercoaster and you should know that going in.'

'Henry and I...' She started to say, *Henry and I aren't about to get married*, but something made her stop. 'I'm not going down that path, it isn't an option for me. For ei-ther of us.'

'We did try for other babies after Daniel, we never re-ally stopped trying. It wasn't as though we gave up, so each month, although I'd be hopeful, I'd try not to get my hopes up. Sometimes I'd be so sure, I'd have a feeling that this was the month. It wasn't just about a spare, in fact it was hardly that at all. I wanted a sibling for Daniel, I wanted to feel the warm weight of another baby in my arms. I wanted a daughter.'

Laura's throat closed over.

When Caroline said that Laura also felt the sensation of holding a child, and the subsequent, inevitable, sense of loss.

'But then each month I'd get those familiar pains and I'd realise yet again that it wasn't to be. But then we lost Daniel and it wasn't enough simply to hope. I had to get assistance. And it took years—they were the worst two years of my life. First losing Daniel, then the treatment and so many disappointments. And once I was pregnant it wasn't over, then I worried about whether I'd be able to carry him to term, worried about all the things that could go wrong. The birth was difficult…and so on.'

Caroline's entire story was horrible—from feeling pressure to keep having children to provide a spare. The years of trying and failing. The worry. Then the unthinkable, losing their one son. Only to be thrown headlong into years of fertility treatment.

Why on earth would she share this story with Laura, if not to scare her away?

'What I'm trying to say is that the treatments are better now, the doctors are good. And the earlier you get started the better. If I can get pregnant at forty-two, you surely can.'

Oh, no. Caroline wasn't trying to scare Laura away, she was trying to get her to endure years of pain, treatment after treatment.

'The technology is so much better now.'

But was it really? In so many respects Laura would be in no better position than women from hundreds of years ago, expected to bear her husband an heir. If she stayed with Henry she'd feel the weight that had been on hundreds of royal and aristocratic women over the ages to make their body do something they had absolutely no control over. And while she might not be blamed these days for not conceiving, carrying and giving birth to an heir, she'd still feel something else.

Expectation.

Hope.

Pity.

She'd feel pressure.

It was bad enough her body didn't work, but to have everyone know and look and judge. Even their hope and pity would be too much.

'Caroline, I'm sorry, but I don't think the treatments today are even good enough to help me.'

'Nonsense.'

'I'm on drugs to simulate early menopause. The next step for me is probably a hysterectomy. But I want to reassure you I know how important your family is to you and I'd never ask Henry to do something to jeopardise that.'

As Laura spoke she realised the lie she'd been telling herself.

Because she was. By being with him, by distracting him, she was preventing him from finding the person he was meant to be with.

'Henry and I have an understanding,' Laura said.

'I'm sure you do. All I'm saying is don't close your mind to possibilities.'

Laura considered trying to convince Caroline that her mind was not for changing, or taking the approach she took with anyone who tried to interfere with her choices about her fertility and her body: telling them it was absolutely none of their business, but Caroline was Henry's mother and indirectly her employer, so Laura just nodded and crawled deeper within herself.

She wasn't the right person for Henry. He deserved someone who could give him what he needed. He deserved someone who could give him the world.

Laura made polite small talk with Caroline before she said she had to get back to work. Caroline promised the three of them would have dinner together at some point and Laura agreed at the same time thinking up ways she could avoid it.

She was relieved to get out of Caroline's apartments and

back to work, though instead of going back out to the public areas and the Turner she went to the privacy of her workshop, relieved to be able to put the conversation with Caroline out of her mind and be alone for a while.

What had Caroline told her that she didn't already know? Assisted fertility treatments were hard and very often heartbreaking. They messed with your body and they were emotional torture.

With no guarantees.

The one thing Henry's mother had let her know was how important it was to her that Henry settle down with someone. And soon. She should have felt honoured that Caroline thought that she, Laura, would make a good duchess, but another thought kept rising to the top of her consciousness like an annoying itch she couldn't scratch.

*You're not good enough for Henry.*
*You can't give him the one thing he needs.*

Ever since her endometriosis diagnosis Laura had been aware that her fertility was unlikely to be high. Or even in the normal range. Each time she'd had every one of her keyhole surgeries to remove the lesions, she'd been warned that there was always a risk of further damage. As her condition developed she knew, without even being told, that her chances of conceiving naturally decreased every year. Assisted treatments were unlikely to be an option, her ovaries were so scarred by previous lesions, she was unlikely to have viable eggs. But she refused to feel that there was something wrong with her.

She was not her condition.

It was something she had to manage, but it wasn't her. It didn't make her any less of a person. It didn't make her broken.

And she'd never thought anything else.

Until this afternoon.

Until a woman she hardly knew implied that she needed fixing.

Something inside Laura—the stubborn, determined side, the side that had pushed her to achieve in her life, the side that had propelled her through her studies, through work, through her father's illness and death, hardened and said, *No. You are not going to beat me or break me.*

But the other side of Laura—the tired, the aching, hurting part—just wanted to lie down, curl her body around a pillow and then cry a little before sleep claimed her.

For a while the determined part of Laura pressed on, slowly and carefully cleaning the canvas, brush stroke by careful brush stroke. But when she dropped the brush for no apparent reason, Laura knew she'd had enough.

She longed for her own bed. And not just in her cottage, but back in Soho. Where her room was never entirely dark and the hum on the streets helped to distract her from the even louder hum of her own thoughts.

She sent Henry a message:

I'm not feeling well and I'm going to have an early night.

It wasn't entirely a lie, she didn't feel well, but Henry would assume she was in physical pain, not the emotional pain she was actually experiencing.

He sent a message right back:

Henry: Do you need food? Painkillers?

Laura: No, thanks, just sleep. You should spend some time with your mother.

# CHAPTER TEN

WITH LAURA HAVING an early night, Henry had little choice but to spend it with his mother. If he cried off and took himself out she'd suspect he was trying to avoid her.

Which he probably was. Though he couldn't figure out exactly why.

He loved his mother, he enjoyed her company, but her unexpected arrival had punctured the bubble he and Laura had created in the castle over the past few weeks and he resented that.

As he showered before dinner his mind wandered. Was Laura actually unwell or did she also not want to have dinner with him and his mother?

No. Surely she knew she was more than welcome to join them. Surely Laura knew what an important part of his life she was.

*She might be important, but she's also temporary.*

Caroline hadn't disapproved of Laura; if anything she was overjoyed that he was dating someone. His mother's enthusiasm at finding someone in his bed that morning probably shouldn't have surprised him, but it had. Probably because he understood that his relationship with Laura would end soon but his mother did not.

Caroline had already poured herself a gin and tonic by the time he'd dressed and made his way to the living room.

'Claudia has prepared some dinner for us. It will be ready soon. Is Laura joining us?'

He shook his head. 'She's not feeling well.'

Caroline prepared him a drink as well, despite his protestations that he could fix it himself, making him feel very much the guest in the room. She handed it to him with a sigh.

'I ran into Laura this afternoon.'

Henry raised an eyebrow.

'Okay, I sought her out and asked her to join me for tea.'

Henry wanted to slap his own forehead. 'And? Do you not like her?'

'That's not it and you know it. She's lovely, but it doesn't matter what I think of her.'

His mother's opinion may not have been the most important factor in any future partner he had, but it did matter.

'She told me about her endometriosis.'

Henry's chest tightened and he took a generous mouthful of his drink.

'No one wants to see their children go through the pain of struggling to conceive, let alone to lose a child, at any age.'

'Mum, I know. And you don't have to worry, I'm trying to put this as delicately as I can, but Laura and I have an understanding.'

Caroline shook her head. 'You're not—and never have been—the casual type. You're loyal, dedicated, dependable. All the reasons why you are a wonderful duke.'

Henry didn't understand his mother's point. The fact that he was loyal and dedicated was the very reason why he and Laura would end their relationship when she returned to London.

'Laura knows that this is short-term thing. We've spoken about it. We've been very honest with one another.'

Caroline raised an eyebrow and he felt his expression from moments before mirrored back at him.

'You don't have to worry about us. Apart from anything else, I'm not sure Laura actually wants to have children. Even if she could.'

'Have you asked her?'

'Well, not…not outright.' It seemed like a highly insensitive question to confront her with.

Caroline nodded, but didn't press. They ate dinner and made perfunctory conversation about the farm, about the fair.

When he couldn't stand it any longer he asked, 'And what else did you talk about?'

'This and that. I told her that the treatments these days are so much better than they were thirty years ago.'

'You didn't!'

'It's true, they are.'

'But that's not the point.'

He shook his head, wanted to get out of there as quickly as possible to check in on Laura, even via message if she didn't want to see him.

He could understand her staying away now. Caroline wasn't trying to send Laura away—what she was trying to do was just as bad. If not worse.

They ate in silence for a while, Henry's annoyance gradually subsided as he realised his mother wasn't trying to be unkind, she was simply coming from a different place.

'How did you both stand it?' he finally asked.

'What?'

'The pressure to have an heir. And to deal with that when you'd already lost Daniel. Didn't you ever think it wasn't to be? Didn't you ever just accept it and give up?'

'We couldn't give up. It wasn't an option.'

Yes, not having an heir wasn't an option. Not for his parents. Not for him. Or for his own children.

'But Henry, darling, we had you. And we couldn't love you more or be more proud of you.'

\* \* \*

The week leading up to the fair was hectic. He and Laura had a few stolen moments together, though he still made his way to her cottage and her bed each evening. The pair of them had silently conceded the space of the castle to his mother while she was staying. While he was frustrated that the work on the fair took him away from the time he had left with Laura, he was downright glad of every excuse to avoid his mother. She'd never come out and said anything directly, but every look, every sigh she gave suggested she thought that if they were not planning a future together, continuing to spend time with Laura was a mistake.

But his mother was wrong. Or at least, partly wrong. Not spending time with Laura felt like the bigger mistake. Yes, it would end, yes, Laura would return to London and they would see less of one another, but cutting her out of his life completely? Impossible.

Besides, Laura knew the score. If anything, she was more focused than he was on finding him someone else to date, but even thinking about touching another woman was impossible.

Every time he walked past Natalia he wanted to wince.

Life would be simpler if he'd fallen for someone like her in the first place.

But he hadn't. How could he once SohoJane had come into his feed and Laura had walked into his life?

The morning of the fair was bright with a cool breeze that promised to subside during the day. He kissed Laura and slid out of her bed at 5:00 a.m. She groaned softly and went back to sleep.

When he saw her next, several hours later from across the main field, every breath left his body. She was at the jam and fresh strawberries stand with a woman who looked like an older version of Laura.

Laura was wearing a long floral dress; her loose hair swayed a little in the breeze. He watched as she tucked a strand behind her ear and laughed with her mother about something.

Everything else at the fair, the sounds of the cows moo-ing, the squeals of delighted children, the tractor roaring during a demonstration, all fell away and there was just her. Amongst the vintage cars, the skittle games and the chil-dren's rides, Laura turned and her eyes found his.

He crossed the field, taking in everything about her, an-ticipating the softness of her cheek against his, the bliss of holding her hand in his.

'Henry, this is amazing. I've never seen a fair like it.'

His heart expanded against his ribcage with pride. He loved being a part of this event, being a part of the com-munity. He loved the role he got to play in it.

'Thank you. And you must be Fiona. I am so happy to finally meet you,' he said and held out his hand. Fiona took it but also leant in to kiss him briefly on the cheek. When she pulled back she gave him a quick wink. Both her eyes sparkled.

As pleased as he genuinely was to finally meet the amaz-ing Fiona, there were now two meddling mothers too many here today and he hoped that chance and circumstance would keep them both apart.

Fiona introduced her companion, a man named Tony, who was looking eagerly at the cider tasting.

'Are you having a good time?' Henry asked them all.

'Wonderful,' gushed Fiona. 'The fair is lovely, but I'm mostly so glad to be seeing this one again.' She put her arm around Laura.

Henry couldn't argue with her. As proud as he was of the fair, it was Laura who was the brightest part of his day.

'Let me show you all around.'

'Oh, no, we can find our way and see you later on. You two enjoy yourselves,' Fiona said.

Taking in the smells of frying food, fairy floss and fresh grass, he led Laura around to all the best sights. She licked her ice cream made with the milk from the local cows. Admired the cleverly decorated cakes and the flower displays.

'What's your favourite thing?' he asked her.

'I don't know yet. I've heard a rumour there are puppies and kittens.'

'You heard correctly.'

'Well, I'm guessing, that will be my favourite thing.'

The barn was across the field, so he took her hand and they walked through the groups of smiling people. He couldn't help but beam at everyone he knew, noticing as they noticed Laura and smiled broadly at both of them. Walking across the fair holding Laura's hand made him almost as happy as seeing the entire fair come together again successfully for another year.

'What's your favourite attraction?' she asked.

*You*, he thought, but said, 'The pony rides.'

'Why?'

'It's one of my earliest memories. I went on them every year and as soon as I was old enough, I'd run them.'

'How old were you?

'I think I was about eight.'

She laughed.

'What's so funny?'

'I was imagining an older teenager, not an eight-year-old!'

'I may have had some help,' he conceded, but for as far

back as he could remember he'd helped in the running of the fair in some way.

'I love all of it—it's just about my favourite day of the year. I've never missed one.'

The smile on Laura's face faded, but he wasn't sure why. The many animals would be sure to cheer anyone up. They had chicks, piglets, lambs and of course the puppies and kittens. As usual, the barnyard was one of the biggest attractions, with a line-up of people young and old waiting to see the baby animals. Henry and Laura lined up with everyone else, but when they reached the pen with the eight-week-old sheepdog pups, Annabel, who was running the barnyard, gasped. 'You didn't have to line up, Your Grace.'

Henry's cheeks warmed as the heads of the tourists turned and looked at him with wide eyes.

'He's waiting with me,' Laura said, as though that explained it.

Introductions were made and then Annabel turned to Laura, 'Would you like to hold one?'

'Am I allowed?'

'Of course.'

Annabel let Laura into the pen, where the pups circled her ankles. Annabel scooped one up and handed her to Laura.

Laura beamed and started talking softly to the pup. Henry couldn't hear exactly, but it sounded as though Laura was reassuring the pup that she was both safe and gorgeous.

'Oh, she's so lovely. They are all lovely,' Laura gushed, and Henry couldn't agree more.

*She* was lovely.

Love. It had so many meanings, so many possible uses. He loved his mother. He loved the annual fair. He loved the castle. He loved the taste of the vanilla ice cream from the homemade ice cream stall.

Laura was lovely and he adored her.

But did he love her?

The word 'love' was so overloaded with implications. If it was love he felt for Laura, was it the type of love that would last a lifetime? Was it the type of love to overcome everything that he would have to sacrifice to be with her?

They left the barnyard and he took her to the cider-tasting tent, no more certain about his feelings. After tasting a few varieties and choosing their favourites they took their drinks out to the shade of a nearby tree.

Henry knew it was a question that was bound to cause pain and maybe he shouldn't even ask it. But his mother's question had got him thinking. He cared about Laura and wanted to know the full extent her condition really was having on her life.

'I have a question for you, but I'm not sure if I should ask it.'

She tilted her head. 'Why not? We've always been able to be open and honest with one another, haven't we?'

They had.

'Did you want to have kids? I don't mean now. I understand that's too complicated. I mean when you were younger did you want kids?'

As suspected the question did cause pain. She grimaced.

'I guess when I was I kid I did, in the way that you do when you don't really understand what something actually involves. And now I don't really let myself think about it. I want to live pain free and besides, I'm happy with my life the way it is—I love my job, my family, my friends. I don't feel as though anything is missing from my life.'

He nodded, glad of the answer.

'I'm sorry for bringing it up, I just want to know you and know what you're thinking and feeling.'

'It's okay,' she said, sipping her drink. 'Like you said, we've always been able to be honest with one another.'

The sun had dipped below the horizon and the crowds were dispersing. A hardcore group were still enjoying the cider but the pony rides and farmyard nursery had all packed up and gone home. She watched Henry, just out of earshot, talking to a group of people. He was smiling broadly and gesturing enthusiastically.

*'It's just about my favourite day of the year.'*

She could feel the passion and satisfaction emanating off him.

That was when she knew she was lost. A duke, who was at home in London's boardroom, but at heart was a farmer. An animal lover. A tireless supporter of his local community.

He wanted to pass on the pony rides to his children, and not even because he was a duke, but because he was a man who longed to be a father, whether he'd admit it to her or not.

And her lack of fertility had never hurt this way before. It had always been a theoretical idea that she'd accepted—before her maternal instincts had ever kicked in she'd shut them off.

But now, she wanted children for *him*.

She wanted him to take his own kids to the pony rides, to watch them grow and take over the running of the fair and the castle as he had done.

She watched him bid goodbye to Natalia. She would make a good partner for him. She loved the estate. She would give him a brood of cherubic blond children. Laura's stomach ached, but not with a cramp. She clutched her arms around herself but sat up straight when Henry approached.

He sat down next to her with a sigh, his hair mussed,

face red maybe from exertion or sun, it was hard to say. He looked tired but content.

A little like he looked after they'd made love.

'Are you all right? Do you want to go?'

'I'm fine,' Laura lied. 'It's not a cramp. Just too much ice cream.' And too much gorgeous duke. 'I want to find my mother though.'

They located Fiona sitting at one of the tables set up near the food vans. Tony had made some friends in the cider tent and was talking to them. He seemed kind and friendly and was taking the whole, 'Please meet my daughter's boyfriend the Duke of Brighton' thing as though he met dukes every day, for which Laura was glad.

'We'll make a move shortly,' Fiona said. They were staying at a B & B not far away in the village. Laura had suggested they stay with her, but Fiona had scoffed. 'Bring my boyfriend to stay the night under your roof? I'd sooner take him to my own mother's.'

It had been lovely to see her mother and to meet Tony. Laura began to slip back into her reverie about Henry as she watched him stand again and talk to some departing stall holders.

'He's quite a man,' Fiona said, softly.

'He is.'

Laura waited for the 'but', though Fiona seemed waiting for Laura to speak next. Finally Fiona said, 'You'll never guess who I ran into.'

Laura was sure she'd never guess. Her mother knew precisely no people in this part of the world and she couldn't begin to guess which of her mother's many friends would end up at the Abneyford village fair.

'Caroline.'

'Caroline?' There was only one Caroline here Laura knew.

'The duchess, silly. She told me to call her Caroline.'

'You met? How?' Laura spluttered. *And why are you only dropping this on me now?*

'She thinks you're very impressive.'

'Yes, she's happy with my work, not with my relationship with her son.'

'I didn't get that impression at all. She says Henry is very taken by you.'

'Yes, but…that's why…'

'You told her about your endo?'

'I had to. It didn't seem fair not to, and Henry hadn't. She needs to know that Henry and I aren't serious about one another.'

'Endometriosis isn't a reason not to be serious about one another. It's obvious to everyone here today that you like each other very much.'

'But it's the reason we can't be together.'

'You know, I've watched you struggle with the condition for the past fifteen years, half your life, and do you know what has impressed me? You never give up. It might stop you for a few days, but you get back up there—you have refused to let it stop you obtaining your dreams.'

'This is different, Mum, it's not a degree or a job. It's not something I can overcome by hard work and willpower.'

'I thought you'd accepted that you probably wouldn't have kids.'

'I have. But Henry hasn't and it's different for him.'

'How is it?'

'Because he's a duke—he needs an heir or the title dies.'

'Is this what he thinks? Have you let him make his own mind up?'

'Of course—but, Mum, I'm not letting Henry risk his family's future on me.'

'Isn't he a risk worth taking? Aren't you a risk worth taking?'

Oh, if only he was. Oh, if they could both forget everything else about their lives, if she was pain free, if he didn't have a title and responsibilities to his family...then it wouldn't be a risk at all.

But they did have those things. They did live in this world, not a fantasy one and they both had issues and burdens that made living a life together impossible.

Laura shook her head, trying to find the words. She was saved by Henry's arrival.

'We don't have the final figures, but it looks as though we raised over a hundred thousand pounds.'

'Amazing. Well done. And what will the money be used for? A local charity?'

'No, actually, we usually choose an international one. We are all so lucky to live somewhere like this. This year we're donating it to Doctors Without Borders.'

Henry's attention turned fully to Laura and her heart melted under the warmth of his smile.

'I won't be too much longer. I just need to check on things at the finance office and then we can head back, if you like?'

'Great.'

'Fiona, will you and Tony join us for a nightcap?'

Fiona laughed. 'Thank you, but we've both had enough of the cider for one day.'

Henry held out his hand to her again and Fiona stood and kissed his cheek. 'It's been so nice to finally meet you. Thank you for looking after my little girl.'

Laura watched her mother and Henry share a moment and had to look away. They would have got on well together, she thought, though this was likely the last time they would ever meet.

# CHAPTER ELEVEN

HENRY FOUND LAURA in her workshop. The room was un-renovated, stripped back to its original floorboards and with simple white paint on the walls, but with large windows and a view over the ruins.

The room was tidier than when he'd seen it last. Only one painting, the one she was examining, remained in the room. The significance of this was clear to him; he wished they'd had a little more time.

He half hoped she'd discovered several paintings with almost irreparable damage that would require her to stay for weeks.

'Hi there, can you give me a few more minutes?' she said when she realised he was there.

'I haven't come to hurry you. I'd just like to watch, if that's okay.'

'Of course.' She gave him one of her gentle, soft smiles. The one that did wild things to his insides and made him want to pull her into his arms and breathe her in for ever.

She was brushing the canvas with a small soft brush, soft enough to clean away dust but not damage the paint.

He watched her work, carefully, methodically. Lovingly.

He *had* to stop using that word.

It took so much effort to look after the collection of paintings, several weeks' work most years. And then there were the tapestries. The soft furnishings. And the marble statues, the ones in the garden and the ones inside. Not to mention the castle building itself. He didn't think about the effort and cost of keeping everything up too often, otherwise the scale of it would overwhelm him.

'Is everything worth preserving?' he asked after a while.

'What do you mean?'

'How do you decide what to look after and what to leave?'

'You're not just talking about the paintings, are you?'

'Paintings, tapestries, documents, historic houses.'

Dukedoms.

She took her magnifying glasses off and focused on him properly. Obviously confused by what she saw she looked away and took her gloves off as well.

Placing them down and stepping away from the canvas she said thoughtfully. 'I guess it depends on the significance of what it is. Its historical importance. How expensive it is. How much it's loved.'

Loved.

There was that unhelpful word again. 'Yes,' he replied.

'But most of all it depends on the cost.'

'The cost?'

'Yes. You're paying me. Not everyone who owns artwork has the resources or time to look after it. It depends on what it costs to preserve something for future generations.'

The estate could afford the cost of preserving the paintings; from an economic point of view, the cost of preserving them was less than the increase in their value each year.

But preserving the title of the Duke of Brighton? Preserving his family line? What was that worth? What would that cost him?

That wasn't a mathematical equation.

Or was it?

'So some things aren't worth what it'll cost to keep them?'

'You could say that. But I think I mean, at least in my line of work, sometimes the cost of looking after the thing is more than the owner can afford.'

'But if you have the money? If you can afford to protect the thing?' he asked. Who better to ask this question of than a conservator? Someone who cared as much about preserving history as he did, if not more.

'Then I think it should be fixed. And I'm not just talking about nineteenth-century artwork, I'm talking about the environment, the forests, the oceans. All of it.'

She was right. And he realised, it wasn't about him. The castle, the title, the estates—it was bigger than him. It was there before him and would be there after him. He'd been being selfish. Too focused on himself and his own desires.

'I don't have much more to do. I'd like to get a second opinion on the Rossetti and I'll need to go back to London for that. If it's okay with you I could always come back for a day or two in a month's time, when we have those results.'

'Of course that's okay. Are you saying you'll be finished soon?'

'Yes, probably tomorrow.'

Tomorrow! 'So soon?'

'It's been six weeks.'

Had it? It seemed shorter…but also long enough for his life to change. How slippery time was when you were falling in love.

Love? Why did he keep using that word? It wasn't helpful. Particularly when he wasn't sure it was even true.

Laura tidied her tools up and brushed her hands together. She lifted her arms up and stretched out her limbs and torso.

He took in every movement, tried to take a photo with his mind of her long limbs, the sublime look on her face as she closed her eyes as she extended her arms as high as they would go above her head, entirely unaware of how glorious she was.

She shook her body out, the signal she'd shifted her mind from work to play and gave him a different smile now, broad and sparkly. A definite gleam in her eyes. Wordlessly, they reached for one another's hands.

He led her through the quiet rooms of the castle, then through the back corridors to his rooms, the family apartments thankfully empty since his mother and her friends had departed. It was theirs again, for one more night.

He tried to push that thought from his mind as he placed a trail of kisses from her delicious lips, past her soft ear lobes and along the silky skin of her neck and collarbone. He tried not to think of it as she shivered under his touch, sighed against him or groaned when his lips finally reached her hard nipples.

He tried not to think of it when she took him in her hands and softly, expertly brought him just to the brink. But it was a hard balance to maintain, needing to forget that this was their last night together while also wanting to ensure he memorised every kiss, every shiver. They both held on and on, in silent but unanimous agreement that this was it. That this must be it. They both knew it and they were both keeping one another honest; if he started to waver, she'd remind him of what he really wanted.

They were lucky in a way, to know it was the last time. He'd never known before. Couples didn't usually, did they. They'd make love like it was any other time, not knowing or even thinking it would be the last time.

But they both knew.

They held on, they went over every inch of one another's bodies, committing each pore to memory. Each sigh. As she moved on top of him with her eyes closed he watched her, felt himself inside her, breathed her in, held on for as long as he could. When release came it wasn't a relief—ecstasy was mixed inevitably with heartbreak.

No. He must enjoy each moment. Make the most of it. They'd always known they had an expiry date. He could hardly complain now when this had been the deal he'd made with his heart all along.

'That was nice,' Laura murmured into his neck.

He could only give a hum in agreement, any other words would give his thoughts away and he didn't want her to know that his heart was breaking.

That would only complicate matters. He knew enough about Laura to know that he'd only make her feel worse if he confessed to all the feelings that were currently rolling through his body like an out-of-control wave. Not to mention he'd been the one to suggest the friends who have sex arrangement in the first place. He'd sound like he was reneging on their deal.

And he wasn't. He knew she would return to London. He knew this must be their last night together. But that still didn't stop his heart from slowly cracking and quietly disintegrating as he held her.

Henry knew it would be impossible to search for sleep when he wanted to spend every available minute looking at her, at the way her thick lashes rested against her cheek as she slept, at the creamy clear skin of her shoulders that tasted slightly different to the creamy white skin of her breasts, at how, feeling her skin against his own, breathing her in. Filling his lungs with as much of her as possible in the hope that something would be left to sustain him through the weeks, months and years that would follow.

Despite his resolution, when the sun started to make itself known above the horizon, the exhaustion from his all-night vigil caught up with him and he finally gave in to his body's demands for rest.

When he woke a few hours later, disoriented, the sun bright, Laura was sitting, dressed, on the edge of his bed.

'We need to talk, don't you think?' she said.

'What if...?' Laura started talking before she'd even managed to articulate the thought.

*What if I tried. What if I stopped taking the drugs? What if we gave it a year? What if we saw the best fertility experts in the country?*

Was that a crazy thought? Was she ready? Was he? Even though in some ways she felt as if she'd known him for ever, in reality they'd only met properly a little over a month ago.

She took a deep breath. She'd wonder for ever what might have happened if she stayed silent.

'What if...and I'm not saying we should, I'm just asking, what would it look like if we tried?'

Henry was silent for a long while before finally pulling himself up and rubbing his eyes. She regretted not letting him wake properly, at least give him some caffeine before dropping all of this on him. The thoughts had started after the talk with her mother, even, if she were honest, after the talk with Caroline.

Henry rubbed his eyes, still trying to focus. Or delaying.

She stood. This was probably a big mistake.

'Laura, wait. Please just give me a moment.'

'Yes.'

She went to the kitchen, put the kettle on for her, turned the coffee machine on for him. When he came out of his room a few minutes later he was wearing shorts and a T-shirt, but he'd accessorised with a grim look.

She placed two fresh mugs on the table and sat. He sat too.

'What would it look like if we tried to have a baby?'

'Now?'

The doubt crept back. 'Yes, I mean, I know it's soon. Forget I said anything.'

He reached for her hand, ignoring the coffee. 'For starters, we'd need to get married,' he said. 'Because any heir would need to be born in wedlock.'

She nodded. She'd kind of forgotten that part. Marrying Henry would be the easiest thing in the world.

'And we'd try to have a baby. You'd get advice from your doctor, we'd get all the best help we could.'

Laura was already lucky enough to have an excellent doctor. Her chances of conceiving in Dr Healy's care were as good as they could be.

'And if it doesn't work?' he whispered.

She looked down, tried not to cry. *This* was what they really needed to be considering. The possibility that after years of pain they'd have nothing to show for it. The pain and disappointment could rip them apart, but if it didn't, if it made them closer then what? He'd be childless.

*He'll leave you for someone else. He'll have time.* Laura would have spent years of her life possibly in pain, but she'd spend them with Henry. That wasn't nothing.

She projected forward five or ten years. She'd be disappointed because she'd allowed herself to get her hopes up; Henry would be disappointed and trying not to be bitter. They could be even more heartbroken than they both were now. Or worse, they'd be bitter and resentful.

Either way they'd mostly likely be in a worse position than they were now.

'You're right, I'm being silly. It's just the fact that I'm about to leave and I'm confused.'

'No, Laura. I like that we talk about this. I love that we can talk openly and honestly with one another. Don't ever stop doing that.'

They could both picture what might happen if she stayed, likely slightly different images of the projected mess, but the outcome was the same.

'Laura, this is important. I care about you too much to put you through that. I don't want you to go through what my mother went through. But most of all, I don't think I can stand to keep seeing you in pain, month after month. I don't want that for you.'

'There's no need to make excuses, I do understand.'

'What on earth do you mean?'

'I'm strong, Henry, I can make up my own mind about my body.'

'I'm not...' Henry's face reddened. 'I didn't mean you couldn't. I'm trying to tell you, maybe awkwardly, that I care about you. I care about you so much that I don't want to put you through the same pain.'

Laura's skull seemed to tighten and press on her brain. She closed her eyes, but the pain filled her head, impairing her thoughts.

'It's exactly what I said. I don't want to see you in pain. And I don't want to see you disappointed.'

And then she understood because it was the same for her. She wasn't going to stay and she wasn't going to put either of them through this because she cared for him as well. She cared for him too much to let him give up everything he'd been born to do.

It was silly of her to suggest it, but she wanted him to know that she would be prepared to make those sacrifices for him.

'I know what your mother went through after losing Daniel and then those years of treatment and I just want you to know that I'd be prepared to try. I'd be prepared to do that for you.'

'Oh, Laura. Is that what this is about? I know you care

about me. But it's different for you. Mum wasn't in the same kind of pain that you are.'

Embarrassingly, she started to taste salt. She took a gulp of tea but as soon as she looked back to Henry and deep into his blue eyes, so full of soul and worry, the taste came back. She spoke quickly to get the words out.

'I'd be prepared to do all that, but I'm not going to let you do it. We both know it has to be like this. Even if I don't have the operation, the chances of me conceiving are so low. Miracle level low. The chances of me carrying a baby to term are lower too.'

He passed her a tissue and she wiped her nose.

'I don't want to put you through any of it, Laura. It wouldn't be fair.'

He was right, but she added, 'Henry, it wouldn't be fair to either of us. And it's okay to say that. I won't do that to you or your family. It would not be fair to anyone.'

He nodded and she knew they were making the decision together, they were talking like rational adults. Then why was it so goddamn hard?

Because they were both calm, and rational. And because they both knew.

It wasn't a screaming match. Even her tears were calm. Soft, silent and so, so calm. The only outward sign that this was actually it, that it was actually over was the clump of wet tissues in her hand.

She held her stomach. Not because of the familiar pain that had wracked her every month for the past fifteen years, but a different pain. It was the pain of her heart tearing apart, not her ovaries.

Laura stood, but before Henry could as well, she touched his shoulder, leant down and kissed his cheek.

'Let's just remember last night. I don't think I could stand it if you hugged me now.'

Laura was using every ounce of bravery in her to walk out that door. If he held her again she knew she wouldn't be brave enough.

# CHAPTER TWELVE

'WHAT ARE YOU doing here?'

'I came to check on you.'

Henry had walked into his kitchen and found his mother sitting at the table flicking through a magazine.

Henry couldn't remember the last time his mother had called by to 'check on' him. She hadn't made such a gesture when his father had died, or when he'd broken up with Beatrice. It wasn't that she was uncaring, she just seemed to know that he was coping both those times.

Unlike now.

No. He was coping. He was getting up each day. Eating. Well, mostly. Showering. Every other day at least. Sleeping? Well, no one was perfect.

Not that his mother should have any idea about what he'd been up to. He'd been keeping to himself, keeping busy with work. He hadn't wanted to impose himself on anyone. And it had barely even been a week.

'Why? I'm fine.'

Caroline said nothing but glanced at his attire. His pyjamas. It was midday on a Monday.

'I worked late last night. I slept in.'

'I hear you've been keeping quite irregular hours.'

He had a traitor in his midst. Did Claudia work for him or his mother?

She worked for his mother. Who was he kidding.

'I got engrossed in some research about liver fluke in sheep and I just kept going. I'm keeping the place running. I'll get dressed soon enough.'

Caroline pulled a face, and shook her head before going to the coffee machine. Henry sat at the table while she brewed him a cup. The sun had been easing its way above the horizon by the time he fell asleep. Since Laura left he'd felt as though he was suffering some kind of bizarre jet lag that only seemed to get worse as the days wore on, rather than better.

But it would get better. It would. He'd been heartbroken before and survived.

But then he'd had a plan. And a future that stretched on for years.

Now what did he have?

It felt like he had an impossible to-do list.

*1. Get over Laura*
*2. Find someone else to fall madly in love with, preferably before I get too old to actually hold the child I can't even dream of having with someone else*

The thought of loving someone else turned his heart to stone.

Caroline passed him the coffee.

'I'm sorry, I didn't realise you loved her so much.'

'I…' He opened his mouth to deny it or to dismiss it but that was impossible. 'I'll get over her. I just need some time. But Mum, please, I'm not ready to start dating again. Please just give me some time.'

'Was it her decision?'

That was blunt. 'Is that relevant?'

'I'm not sure.'

'It was both of ours.' Was it? Their last conversation was now a jumble in his head, but he'd been utterly convinced they were doing the right thing. It was only now that he wasn't sure. 'But mostly me. I guess.'

She regarded him now. He knew he didn't look like a man who was happy with his decision.

'Because of her condition?'

He nodded. 'Yes.'

Caroline sighed.

'I thought you'd be happy,' he said.

'Why would you think that?'

'Because now I can find someone else who doesn't have fertility issues, because now I can produce an heir.'

Caroline looked at the ceiling and sighed deeply. Then she took his face in her hands. 'Never, never think that I want you to be unhappy. Never think that I want you to be heartbroken.'

Henry looked into his mother's face. The last time she'd held him like this had been years ago.

'Sweetheart, I'm so sorry. I wish there was something I could do.'

'There's no way around it, though is there? You know it—I know it.'

'How do I know it?'

'Losing Daniel.'

'It's not the same thing.'

He was filled with shame and spoke quickly, 'No, I didn't mean that it was like losing a child.'

'No, you misunderstand me. Losing Daniel was awful, as was losing your father. But I didn't have a choice. Those were things that happened that I had to live with. *You* have a choice.'

'I don't, not really. I don't want Laura to suffer. I don't want her to be in pain and I don't want to put her through years of procedures and attempts to have a child that we just may never be able to have.'

'But why do you have to do that?'

'Why do you think?' Had she forgotten the small detail of needing an heir? Had she forgotten all the sacrifices she'd made herself to secure the inheritance?

'Do you mean for the title?'

'Of course that's what I mean. What else?'

'Henry, darling, I didn't go through all that just to provide your father with an heir. We did it because we wanted a child. We did it because the pain of losing Daniel was so much, because I couldn't stand the thought of no longer being someone's mother. The title wasn't the only reason. It was about us still wanting to be parents. Do you understand?'

Henry shook his head. All he understood was that his mother appeared to be changing the story he'd been told all his life.

*You were born to inherit the title. You were born because your brother died.'*

That was what he'd been told for as long as he could remember. By his father. His mother. Everyone.

'I was born to inherit the title. I was born because Daniel died.'

'Yes, but that doesn't mean…' Caroline shook her head. 'You are more important than a tradition. You are more important than this.' She waved her hands around the room.

'No. I'm not. This *is* me. I am the dukedom, I am Abney Castle.'

She shook her head. 'No, dear, no. Those are a job and possessions—you are more than that.'

'You went through half a dozen rounds of IVF, you nearly died giving birth to me. You sacrificed so much.'

'But that was my choice. I'm not expecting you to do the same thing. I'm certainly not expecting Laura to.'

Not outright, he wanted to say. But Laura knew as well as he did, that the expectation to produce an heir would be on her. It would be on both of them.

'I'd never ask her to go through that.'

He'd never let her. Besides, once she had the hysterectomy, it was a moot point.

'We wouldn't be able to have our own children.'

'And that's okay. If you love her, be with her.'

Henry shook his head.

His entire life he'd been taught that the family title was the most important thing. More important than him.

'We did it for the title, yes, but most of all, we wanted you. Don't ever forget that. I don't regret having you for a moment and I'd do it all again in a heartbeat.'

Henry finished the dregs of his coffee and stood.

She couldn't change history with a few assertions. No one could. Neither of them could. He was born to be the duke. He was born because his brother died. They were facts, pure and simple, and no one could change that.


Fiona had been very gentle since Laura had arrived back in London. She'd left her alone to begin with but this evening had suggested they meet for an early dinner since the weather was so nice.

Laura was throwing herself into work, into London, into anything that wasn't Henry. Of course each time she looked at a painting one of the ones at Abney Castle came back into her mind. And then, so did he.

It was the right decision. She'd been brave. As brave as she could be. She hadn't been brave enough to message him. Or hug him goodbye. But she'd been brave enough to pack her car and drive back to London and to pick up her life again.

Fiona was already seated at a table outside at one of their favourite Italian restaurants. She stood when she saw Laura and hugged her as though they hadn't seen one another in months.

'How have you been feeling?'

'Sad.' Awful, distracted, tired.

'I know that. I meant pain wise.'

'Oh.' Laura had to think. It had been weeks since her last attack. It had been that time Henry had found her in her cottage. It had lasted a few days but after that she'd been fine. Maybe the operation had worked better then she'd first thought. She'd been so distracted with a different kind of pain, the one in her heart, she hadn't realised that remarkably, her pelvic pain had been manageable. She'd had twinges here and there but nothing to stop her from working.

Or from any other activities.

The irony of it made her laugh. If she hadn't been so well, she wouldn't have spent so much time with Henry, wouldn't have grown so close to him. Wouldn't be struggling to be parted from him.

'Are you going to stay in touch?'

'It's just too hard.'

'For you?'

'For everyone. For me, yes, but him too. And for the woman he does marry.'

Fiona frowned. 'What makes you think he's going to up and marry someone else?'

'Because he has to.'

'You think he will marry someone he doesn't love?'

'No. But he will find someone to love.'

'Not when he's in love with you.'

'He's not. He can't be.'

'Saying it isn't so doesn't make it not true.'

'He can't love me because that wasn't the plan.'

'And was you falling for him the plan?'

'No, but it doesn't matter if my heart is broken.'

Fiona took her daughter's hands and leant across the table. 'Now, you listen to me. Your heart is every bit as important as his. You have just as much right to happiness.'

Laura shook her head,

'I can't believe you're saying this, Laura.'

'I just mean that I always knew the outcome of this in a way he didn't. But I know I'm worthy of love and happiness, of course I do.'

'Do you?'

'I do.'

'Then let him love you.'

'That's not what this is about.'

'Isn't it? Have you given him the choice to love you or did you just rule it out for him?'

Had she? She didn't know. It was so hard to remember, when all that came to her mind was his touch, his smell, how she felt so good with him, how she was powerless to stop the attraction between them. How it seemed so inevitable.

*'I won't do that to you or your family. I'm not going to let you do it.'*

It didn't matter whose choice it had been, the decision had been made. Henry hadn't stopped her, hadn't contacted her. He knew it was for the best even if her heart was having a hard time accepting it.

Henry trudged up the hill, through the wildflowers. Often he strode up there, determined, focused. But today he could only be said to be dragging his feet. He was going up to the mausoleum, not because he wanted to, but because he *had* to. Because the answer would be up there. He had to go up there to remind himself why he was putting himself through this torture.

He was doing it for his family. For the twelve dukes who held the title before him, not to mention their wives. He was doing this for his family. For his father, his late brother.

And most of all for his mother.

*'We did it for the title, yes, but most of all, we wanted you. Don't ever forget that. I don't regret having you for a moment and I'd do it all again in a heartbeat.'*

Surely she didn't really mean for him to give up everything she and his father had done to have him, to raise him? Surely his ancestors didn't think he should be knowingly and willingly putting an end to the family line. To a four-hundred-year-old tradition?

He reached the classical-style building and unlocked the door. The last time he'd been in here was with Laura, all those weeks ago.

The night after he'd shared the story of Daniel they'd made love for the first time. He'd told her they were friends, but even then he knew that their relationship had changed for ever.

*I love her.*

He loved her then and he loved her now.

His knees buckled and he fell onto the marble bench in the middle of the room and held his face in his hands.

He loved Laura.

It was only because he'd been denying the truth to himself that it was actually a revelation. He'd loved her since that day. He'd probably loved her well before that, but admitting it had been impossible. Except now that he had uttered those words, now that he had to face the truth, what would he do?

He couldn't marry her. She wouldn't have him for starters—she'd made it clear that she wasn't going to let him give up everything for her, even if he'd wanted to.

So he had to love her and be apart from her. That wasn't the end of the world, he told himself. People did that all the time and they still got up every day and ate food and went to work.

They found other people.

But did they? Really?

How would it be fair to any women he might marry if he still loved Laura?

And what if, though it was unthinkable now, his pain faded enough for him to let someone else in and what if for some reason they didn't have children? Did that mean his life wasn't worthwhile? Far from it. Everything he had done and built would still exist. His life would still have meaning.

*'You are more important than a tradition. You are more important than this.'*

He looked up and over at the graves. First his father. His wonderful strong, devoted father who had lived a life of duty, dedicating himself to his family and the estate.

Daniel, the brother he'd never known but desperately wanted to, first as a child and especially now. Daniel could have given him advice. Except he couldn't. Because if Daniel had been here then Henry would not be. There was no version of reality where he and Daniel would both exist.

Henry looked to the bust of the ninth duke, who was buried across the room from his wife. Had he been honourable? Henry doubted it. Was it worth giving up Henry's own chance of happiness for that particular duke?

The fourth and fifth dukes? They'd dabbled in slavery and the tobacco trade. Not worthy of celebration, let alone emulation.

But there was the sixth duke, who had built this building

for his beloved wife, where they chose to spend eternity together. By all accounts they were honourable.

Henry pulled himself up and walked over to his father's and brother's graves.

*Honour, faith, love.*

Was it more honourable to lead a loveless life of duty? Was that really what honour was about? Was that really what his ancestors had lived for?

Was it honourable to turn your back on the person you really loved just because tradition demanded it? Required it?

*You were born to inherit the title.*

*You were born because your brother died.*

Maybe those two things were separate? And maybe they didn't have to define him. Yes, both those things were true, but that didn't mean he had to sacrifice everything. Maybe his mother was right—it had been her choice to have him. And maybe, just maybe, by focusing too much on the first word in the epitaph, he'd neglected to consider the other two.

Faith.

Love.

Was he free to make his own choices? Was Laura?

And if so, would she still have him?

# CHAPTER THIRTEEN

IT WAS FIVE o'clock in the evening, but the sun was still bright and high. Laura couldn't decide if she would work another hour or leave with her colleagues who were slowly pouring out the door for the day.

Since returning to London she'd been working late most nights, mostly because being alone in her apartment in the evening was excruciating. If she worked late and got home even later then it was like the evening didn't happen. Like she didn't miss having dinner with Henry, talking about their days.

Like she didn't miss messaging FarmerDan.

For the first time in months she had no Dan. And no Henry either.

At the thought of his names, her phone lit up with a notification.

@FarmerDan: How was your day?

Laura's heart rate went from resting to tachycardic in a second. They hadn't spoken about not contacting one another, but she'd assumed it was implied. Maybe in several years' time, when the shape of their lives had shaken out, then maybe they could catch up with one another, but not a week later. That was too soon. Her phone shook in her hands and another message appeared.

@FarmerDan: I know you probably weren't expecting to hear from me, but I'm in London and I'd like to see you. It's important.

*It's important.*
He wouldn't just ask to meet if it were not important. He wouldn't say it was important if it were not.

His mother? Had she damaged one of the paintings and not realised? What could it be? Every scenario she could think of was bad news.

@SohoJane: I'm just finishing work now.

@FarmerDan: I'm one block away.

While willing her heart rate to remain calm, she grabbed her bag and left her office as though she was evacuating the building. She saw him as soon as she exited the door. He was ten paces down the street, facing the opposite direction, giving her a moment to look at his back, his broad shoulders, his hair, neat for once. London hair, not farm hair. Her body felt like it was breaking in half.

Would it ever stop being this hard?

By the time he'd turned and noticed her she was wondering if it wouldn't be easier just to turn and flee. They walked towards one another, slowly, but inevitably.

Should they hug? Kiss?

Henry leant down and pressed one cheek briefly against hers, like an air kiss with a relative, not an old lover. Her heart sank.

'What happened? Is everything okay?' she asked.

'I hope so.'

'Is anything wrong?'

He looked around. 'Where can we talk? Is there a pub or a cafe nearby?'

Something was wrong. Yet, he didn't look devastated, tired and washed out to be sure, but there was something buoyant about his demeanour.

A thought hit her like a stab.

*He's met someone.*

Surely not, she told herself. It had barely been a week.

But if he did what she'd suggested and got back on the app then...

She didn't want to know. She wanted to turn and run home and never think of Henry Weston ever again.

*Henry wouldn't do that to you.*

She nodded to the park across the road. He found a bench and they sat.

'What's the matter? What's wrong?'

'Everything.'

'Everything?'

'Yes, everything. I've made a mistake. About us.'

Her foolish, hopeful heart started up its dance again.

'Oh.'

'I can't do it—I can't stop thinking about you.'

She wanted to fling herself into his arms, but sat on her hands instead.

'Do you just think you've made a mistake because we miss one another? That will happen—that's to be expected.'

Henry took her right forearm in his hand and she let him tug it from under her to hold her hand in his. Warm and earnest, his grip was pleading.

'No. It's more than that. I don't want to get over you. I

don't want anyone else. I only want you for the rest of my life and I'm so sorry I didn't say that last week.'

She looked down. 'I want to be with you too, but I'm not going to make you happy. I won't make you give it all up. I won't let you resent me.'

'I've been thinking a lot over the past few weeks. I've been thinking of nothing much else really. I've decided I hate it.'

'What?'

'My title, my inheritance. In a way I never have before. I hate that I'm powerless to change it. It's my identity…but then again, is it? I will always be the Duke of Brighton, for as long as I live. I'll run the estates, help the village. And when I die, the estates can be left to anyone or anything I choose. I can't take it with me. No matter what.'

'But the title? It'll be lost.'

'Not lost. Just no longer living. It doesn't mean that everything that happened before loses its meaning. It doesn't take away anything my father did, or my mother, or my great-grandfather. It also doesn't fix all the bad things some of my other ancestors did.'

'Are you saying you don't mind if we can't have children?'

'I'm saying, unless you want to, I don't think we should try. I think we should agree on that now. That way we both understand and agree what our life will be like now. No one will get their hopes up, or be resentful if it doesn't happen.'

She couldn't disagree, but was he sure? What if he changed his mind? What if…?

'I want to show you something else.'

He opened a window on his phone and showed her a calendar entry.

'We met with the National Trust this afternoon. My mother and me. We had an initial meeting, putting the process in train, for them to eventually take over the management of the castle. You need to understand—I'm not risking the chance to have an heir. I want to give it up. Now. Once and for all. I propose to bequeath the castle to the National Trust.'

'You're giving up your castle? For me?'

'I'm not looking at it like that. I'm making sure that it's preserved for ever by people who also want that. Besides, who's to say I wouldn't have irresponsible kids who'd run it into the ground anyway? It's too much responsibility for one person. Too much of a burden. And my mother agrees.'

'She does?'

'We had a good talk. It was her idea actually.'

'But what about Daniel? Everything she went through?'

'She says that was her decision, she never intended that I would feel obligated to carry on anything, unless I wanted to.'

'But don't you? Want to?'

'I thought I did, but I realise I hadn't thought about it properly at all. I took so many things for granted. I don't want to have an heir if it means I can't have you. You are more important. Happiness is more important.'

He was prepared to give it all up for her. Not just risk it, but give it up.

It was like a fog was lifting from her thoughts and suddenly everything she saw looked different.

'Your mother knows? She's really okay with it.'

He nodded. 'Yes. She… I was wrong about her. I was wrong about a few things.'

'What will you do?'

'I'm not giving it up just yet. I'll still have plenty to do.'

She almost believed him. Almost. Bequeathing the castle to a trust, she understood that. Letting the title die, she understood that too. But there was something else, something so many people wanted with all their very being.

'But you won't have kids. You won't be a father.' Then she added quietly, 'Will I be enough for you?'

'You are enough for me and always will be. You have to believe that.'

'I do. It was never about me not feeling good enough for you. It was about not wanting to disappoint you or your family.'

'You could never disappoint me. I love you, every part of you.'

Love.

That word.

She opened her mouth to say it back but the words caught. It was too much.

'That's why we met with the National Trust. I don't want you to be in pain and I don't want you to feel pressure. I want you to know that I've made the decision. I love you, Laura.'

That word again...

'I love you too, Henry.' This time when the words flowed it was like breathing.

And then it was real. He moved forward quickly, as though she would take it back, and kissed her.

*I love you... I love you...*

The words swam in her thoughts as he pulled her closer.

Henry drew back and screwed up his face. 'Will you still love me if I don't have a castle?'

She laughed. 'I didn't fall in love with a duke. I fell in love with a farmer wrestling a calf. I fell in love with a tennis tragic. I fell in love with a man who loves his family. And pony rides.'

'I fell in love with a woman on a dating app who said she was taking a break from dating.'

It was true, she'd fallen in love with the man who messaged her each evening just to ask about her day. Who always listened, who was always there.

'So, tell me, how was your day?' she said. 'Best thing? Worst thing?'

He smiled and kissed her.

# EPILOGUE

DR HEALY'S ROOMS were familiar, but the mood Laura took in with her today was not. She felt centred, determined, and for the first time in a very long time very, very sure.

The feeling of calmness might also have had something to do with the fact that Henry was with her. She always came alone to these appointments, but he'd insisted on coming today. Going to tell your gynaecologist that you were ready for your hysterectomy was a big deal, even if the decision had already been made.

She had made her peace with it, as had Henry. They were both looking forward to spending the rest of their lives together. He loved her as she was, and she did not feel any pressure to put her body through something to fulfil anyone's idea of what sort of wife she should be.

Laura had relocated to Gloucestershire but had been given a consulting role with her firm. She would still do occasional work in London, but most of her work would be around the country. She and Henry had nascent plans for their own business, helping the owners of other listed properties to preserve the properties and the paintings.

They had shifted their focus from Abney Castle to English Heritage as a whole and it was invigorating. They were embracing the idea of handing the property over to the National Trust when the time was right. They both felt that even though one door may have closed, many more other doors had opened.

They were also both looking forward to a long and languorous honeymoon in Italy once Laura had recovered from her surgery. The future was bright.

Laura's name was called, and Henry squeezed her hand.

Dr Healy smiled at Laura and Henry when they walked into the consulting room together. 'This is Henry, my fiancé,' Laura said.

'Congratulations, have a seat.'

They all sat, and the doctor began. 'How have your symptoms been lately?'

'It's been mixed, I suppose. The month immediately after the laparoscopy was one of the worst yet.'

'And after that?'

'I've had some respite actually, but I know it's only a matter of time.'

'When was your last period?'

Laura thought.

'It's been...'

'Ten weeks?' guessed Dr Healy.

'Er...gosh... Well, possibly, yes.' Her cycles were never regular, but ten weeks did seem unusually long. She must be mistaken. With everything that had gone on with Henry she'd been very distracted.

She'd been experiencing discomfort, though it had been different. Higher up. Not as severe.

She'd been tired too, but that wasn't unusual.

'I've got your recent blood results here. They are...interesting.'

'Interesting? How?'

'You prepared for a scan? You've drunk enough water?'

Laura had a full bladder; it was hardly her first pelvic ultrasound. She nodded and went behind the curtain, took off her pants and put on the gown. Dr Healy would see the extent of the adhesions.

'May I stay?' Henry asked.

'Of course,' Laura and the doctor said.

Dr Healy directed Henry to the best place to stand. He picked up Laura's hand and squeezed it again.

'By the way, I've had some spotting between periods for a while now. I assume that is because of the medication?'

'That could've been due to ovulation.'

'I thought the medication was meant to stop that?'

'It may have, but not necessarily. We've only started you on a low dose to begin with.'

'What does that mean?' Laura was suddenly concerned. Was there something else wrong with her as well?

'Let's just see what the ultrasound says.'

The gel was cold on her stomach, the pressing of the probe hurt her full bladder, but Laura took her mind elsewhere. To Henry. Waking up in his arms this morning in Brighton House, to the life they would have together.

'Ah, yes.' Dr Healy was smiling. 'It's as I thought. Now, I know this isn't what you wanted to hear, but you may want to rethink the hysterectomy.'

'I've made up my mind. I know there are many things I have to sign—'

'That's not why. There's something you need to know. Do you see this?'

Laura was familiar with what her ovaries and uterus looked like, but the picture in the screen was slightly different. She saw something pulsing and drew in a sharp breath.

Surely not.

'Do you know what you're looking at there?' the doctor asked.

'I'm new at this,' Henry said. 'I think I'm going to need you to explain it to me.'

'It's consistent with your blood results. I'd say you're about twelve weeks in and there's a heartbeat.'

'A heart what?'

'A heartbeat. Laura, you're pregnant.'

Henry dropped her hand but only to step over to the monitor to get a closer look.

'You're sure?' he asked. She was glad he'd asked that question. She didn't think she was capable of speaking.

Dr Healy laughed. 'As sure as I can ever be. Your dates match, the blood results are clear, but that heartbeat doesn't lie.'

'How?' Laura gushed.

'The usual way, I expect.' Dr Healy laughed. 'Were you using contraception?'

They looked at one another and shook their heads.

'There's always a chance. And the first few months after a laparoscopy can sometimes be the most fertile, as they appear to have been for you. I hope this is a good surprise?'

'It's certainly a surprise,' Henry said.

'Shall I leave you two a moment? I think this isn't what you both were prepared for.'

Prepared? She'd been preparing for a hysterectomy, a wedding and a honeymoon in Italy. Not a baby.

'I'm not prepared at all.' Then a horrible thought. 'But I drank alcohol and coffee. I didn't take vitamins.'

'Relax, it's still early days. It's very common for women not to realise. The baby will be fine. Though we should keep a reasonably close eye on you, given your history.'

They left the rooms in a daze, not knowing what to do first. Laura led Henry to the same bench she'd sat on back in the depths of winter just after she'd received a different type of news.

'How are you?'

'Shocked. I don't know what to think…it's not something I ever allowed myself to even dream of.' Her baby. Their baby. 'I'm going to have to get up to speed very quickly.'

Henry laughed. 'We have nine months.'

'Not even! Six, according to the doctor.'

'It is ages away.'

'But I don't know anything!'

He laughed again. 'You think both our mothers are not going to want to be closely involved?'

'Oh, my.' The thought of telling them both made her head swim. But she knew she'd have all the support and love she needed from their mothers. And Henry.

She glanced around the square; the grass was green and the trees heavy with leaves.

'Back in the winter, I sat here and told you I couldn't date. Dr Healy had just told me there was very little chance I'd ever have children.'

'Very little is still some.'

'Yes, but realistically. Oh, Henry, I said you didn't need a condom. I wouldn't have suggested we forget the condoms if I'd known.'

'And thank goodness you did.' Henry was as shocked as she was, but she could tell by the brightness in his blue eyes that he was overjoyed.

'But… I…' She wasn't yet sure how she felt. Or even if the news had sunk in.

'Laura, this is the best news I think I've ever had…but how do you feel about it, really?'

'I'm still shocked and scared. No, I'm terrified.'

Henry's face creased. 'But are you unhappy?'

'No, I don't think so. I'm amazed. But also terrified. Henry, I never even let myself dream about this.'

It was going to take some thinking about, some planning. But Henry was with her and would be all the way.

'How are *you* feeling?' she asked him.

'All of the above. Laura, like I told you, I love you no matter what. This is a wonderful surprise, but it also isn't what I was expecting either. We'll have to move the wedding date up. How do you feel about a small register office wedding?'

'I'd marry you anywhere. Anytime.'

'We could do a bigger thing, later, if you like?'

She smiled. She didn't need a big wedding. Just being with Henry was enough.

'I'll marry you as many times as you like,' he said.

'Oh, Henry,' she laughed. 'It's too ridiculous. I never even let myself imagine this.'

'Try now.'

She closed her eyes and in a flash she saw a child's face. It had dark hair, like hers, but Henry's eyes.

She wasn't just having a baby; she was having Henry's baby.

He squeezed her hand again. 'This child will be able to make its own mind up about what it does with its life. There's only one thing I want it to inherit.'

'What?' she asked.

'Your eyes.'

She laughed and shook her head. 'Absolutely not. No way. I think they should have yours.'

\* \* \* \* \*

# COMING SOON!

We really hope you enjoyed reading this book.
If you're looking for more romance
be sure to head to the shops when
new books are available on

## Thursday 21st November

To see which titles are coming soon, please visit
**millsandboon.co.uk/nextmonth**

MILLS & BOON

# MILLS & BOON®

## Coming next month

## CHRISTMAS BRIDE'S STAND-IN GROOM
### Sophie Pembroke

'Okay, so what are you suggesting?'

Giles's head was spinning with all the contradictions. She didn't love Charlie, but she loved the idea of marrying him. She *desired* Giles, it seemed, but not the life *he* wanted. So what *did* she want, really?

'A pre-wedding fling,' she said bluntly. 'No expectations, no *feelings*, even. Just…scratching an itch.'

'No, really, stop…you're embarrassing me with your flattery,' he replied in a monotone.

Millie rolled her eyes. 'You know what I mean. You don't love me. You don't *want* to love me. And nothing that happens between us is going to change your feelings about marriage, is it?'

'No.'

That much, at least, he was sure about. Everything else seemed to be shifting sands.

'And I want my future with Charlie too much to risk it by engaging in anything more than a fling with you,' she said simply. 'But…I can't ignore this feeling between us, either. I've tried—trust me, I've tried.'

'So have I,' he admitted.

'I know that passion…chemistry…doesn't equal love or for ever. It's just sex. It's far safer than love. So I figure the best thing to do is to get it out of our systems before the wedding,'

Millie explained. 'I mean, it would only be worse if we kept on feeling this way *after* I was married, wouldn't it?'

'That's true.'

He was certain there was a flaw in her logic somewhere, but he was struggling to see it right now. Was that because she was right or just because he was just hypnotised by her eyes.

'I haven't… Since I broke up with my last boyfriend—and that was a while ago—I haven't been with anyone. I might even have forgotten how, it's been so long. And it would be… useful to have a reminder before I get married.'

'So this is purely practical?'

He raised an eyebrow at her and she blushed, shaking her head a little.

'No. It's not. I just… I want this. I want to settle down and have the life I've planned with Charlie. But I also want *you*. I want to enjoy these last weeks before the wedding, and I want to see where this connection leads. Don't you?'

Her eyes shone with determination as she met his gaze, and he could see the fire behind them. The passion.

And, God, he wanted to taste it. Taste her.

Giles didn't have it in him to deny it any longer.

So, instead of answering, he leant forward and captured her lips with his own.

*Continue reading*
**CHRISTMAS BRIDE'S STAND-IN GROOM**
Sophie Pembroke

*Available next month*
millsandboon.co.uk